Praise for *The Auralia Thread*

"Overstreet's writing is precise and beautiful, and the story is masterfully told."

—PUBLISHERS WEEKLY

"The rich details, well-developed characters, and complex story will make this a new favorite among fantasy readers."

—LIBRARY JOURNAL

"With a skillful pen, Overstreet shows a world that exists in another dimension. A true treat to fantasy fans."

—AUTHOR'S CHOICE REVIEWS

"*The Ale Boy's Feast* is a great, sprawling poem. Its rich language moves and breathes and awakens every sense. Jeffrey Overstreet has made something beautiful here. His story reminds us that beauty is an agent of grace."

—JONATHAN ROGERS, author of *The Charlatan's Boy*

"Jeffrey Overstreet's imagination is peopled with mysteries and wonders. Reading *Raven's Ladder* is like staring at a richly imagined world through a kaleidoscope: complex, intriguing, and habit-forming."

—KATHY TYERS, author of *Shivering World* and the Firebird series

"Jeffrey Overstreet writes like Van Gogh painted. He is a literary impressionist, and his understated yet vivid narrative style overwhelms the imagination. *The Ale Boy's Feast* does more than just tell the end of a story; it invites the reader into the world of the Expanse with a cast of beautifully complex characters to join them in pursuit of the mystery that calls us all."

—LINDSAY STALLONES, evangelicaloutpost.com

"Through word, image, and color, Jeffrey Overstreet has crafted a work of art. From first to final page, this original fantasy is sure to draw readers in."

—JANET LEE CAREY, award-winning author of *The Dragons of Noor*

"It's entering a beautiful dream you don't want to leave, with exhilarating tension that takes you beyond story and into deep truths."

—SIGMUND BROUWER, author of *Broken Angel* and *Flight of Shadows*

"A darkly complex world populated by a rich and diverse cast of characters, in which glimpses of haunting beauty shine through. Sometimes perplexing but always thought-provoking, *Raven's Ladder* is the work of a fertile and striking creative imagination."

—R. J. ANDERSON, author of *Faery Rebels: Spell Hunter*

The Ale Boy's Feast

Also by Jeffrey Overstreet

Fiction:

Auralia's Colors

Cyndere's Midnight

Raven's Ladder

Nonfiction:

Through a Screen Darkly:

Looking Closer at Beauty, Truth, and Evil at the Movies

The Ale Boy's Feast

A Novel

Jeffrey
Overstreet

Author of Auralia's Colors

WaterBrook
Press

THE ALE BOY'S FEAST
PUBLISHED BY WATERBROOK PRESS
12265 Oracle Boulevard, Suite 200
Colorado Springs, Colorado 80921

The characters and events in this book are fictional, and any resemblance to actual persons or events is coincidental.

ISBN 978-1-4000-7468-6
ISBN 978-0-307-72938-5 (electronic)

Copyright © 2011 by Jeffrey Overstreet
Map copyright © 2011 by Rachel Beatty

Cover design by Kristopher K. Orr; illustration by Mike Heath, Magnus Creative

Published in association with the literary agency of Alive Communications Inc., 7680 Goddard Street, Suite 200, Colorado Springs, CO 80920, www.alivecommunications.com.

All rights reserved. No part of this book may be reproduced or transmitted in any form or by any means, electronic or mechanical, including photocopying and recording, or by any information storage and retrieval system, without permission in writing from the publisher.

Published in the United States by WaterBrook Multnomah, an imprint of the Crown Publishing Group, a division of Random House Inc., New York.

WATERBROOK and its deer colophon are registered trademarks of Random House Inc.

Library of Congress Cataloging-in-Publication Data
Overstreet, Jeffrey.
The ale boy's feast : the white strand in the Auralia thread / Jeffrey Overstreet. — 1st ed.
p. cm.
ISBN 978-1-4000-7468-6 (alk. paper) — ISBN 978-0-307-72938-5 (electronic)
I. Title.
PS3615.V474A78 2011
813'.6—dc22

2010051190

Printed in the United States of America
2011—First Edition

10 9 8 7 6 5 4 3 2 1

For Anne

Her imagination inspired the adventure,
her belief in these stories gave me confidence,
her listening ear helped me tune the instruments,
her hard work alongside me made the series possible,
and her presence was a blessing on the journey
from the grasses beside the River Throanscall
to the mists beyond the Forbidding Wall.

CONTENTS

THEY CALL THE BOY "RESCUE" FOR A REASON...

The ale boy was once an errand runner, almost invisible as he served House Abascar. As he grew up—an orphan raised by House Abascar's beer brewer and winemaker—his real name remained a secret, even from him.

But what he did know proved useful indeed. As he gathered the harvest fruits beyond Abascar's walls, worked with brewers below ground, delivered drinks across the city, and served the king his favorite liquor, the ale boy learned the shortcuts and secrets of that oppressed kingdom.

When the ale boy met Auralia, a mysterious and artistic young woman from the wilderness, they formed a friendship that would change the world. Auralia's artistry shone with colors no one had ever seen, and when she revealed her masterpiece within House Abascar, the kingdom erupted in turmoil that ended in a calamitous collapse. Auralia vanished, as did her enchanting colors. And hundreds of people died.

Brokenhearted but brave, the ale boy sought out survivors in Abascar's ruins and helped them find their way to a refuge in the Cliffs of Barnashum. There, led by their new king, Cal-raven, the people endured a harsh winter and an attack from the Cent Regus beastmen.

During those hard days, the ale boy became a legendary hero. The people called him "Rescue."

Afterward, King Cal-raven sought two things: the origins of Auralia's colors, and the Keeper—the mysterious dream-creature who had inspired Auralia in the first place.

Cal-raven trusted that the Keeper would lead his people out of their desperate circumstances and into a glorious future. And in that belief, he discovered an ancient, legendary city called Inius Throan standing in the shadow of the northern mountains.

But now his hopes of leading Abascar's remnant have all but collapsed.

His people have found protection and provision in the care of House Bel Amica on the western coast. They've settled in. Bel Amica's a dangerous place, even for its own rulers, who have exposed treachery among Queen Thesera's advisors, the Seers.

Heightening their peril, the Deathweed—a creature made of roots and branches—has spread across the Expanse, poisoning and killing everything within its reach.

Worst of all, Cal-raven has made a disastrous mistake. Taking the beastman called Jordam with him as a guide, he left House Bel Amica behind to make a risky journey into the heart of beastman territory. There he hoped to rescue some of his people who were imprisoned and enslaved.

But even though Jordam and the ale boy offered Cal-raven help, things have gone terribly wrong. Many are dead. The ale boy has fallen from a bridge into a dark abyss. And Cal-raven's faith in the Keeper has collapsed in the aftermath of a shocking discovery.

Now, Cal-raven too is lost in the chaos.

Captain Tabor Jan and the people of Abascar wait in desperate hope for their king to return. Their future seems uncertain.

Shall they go on alone toward Inius Throan without Cal-raven to guide them?

Was the promise of Auralia's colors just an illusion?

Is the Keeper in their dreams just a figment of their imaginations?

Did the ale boy perish in the darkness?

All these questions will be answered in this, the final strand of The Auralia Thread.

The Forbidding Wall
House
Bel Amica
Mawrnash
Tilianpurth
Baalke Hills
Ruins of
House Cent Regus
THE
EXPANSE
DURING THE SEARCH
FOR NEW ABASCAR

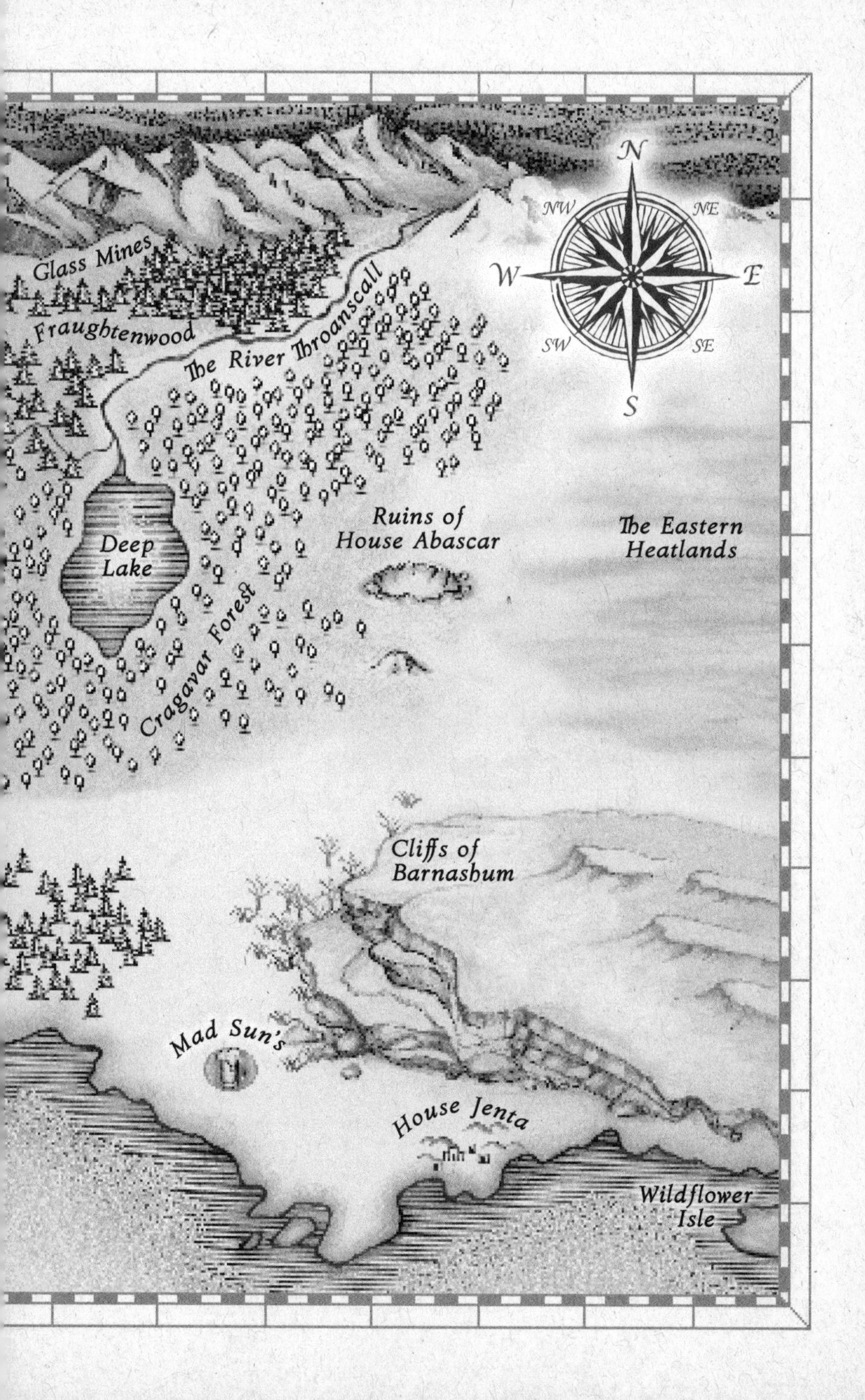
N
NW
NE
W
E
SW
SE
S
Glass Mines
Fraughtenwood
The River Throanscall
Ruins of
House Abascar
The Eastern
Heatlands
Deep
Lake
Cragavar Forest
Cliffs of
Barnashum
Mad Sun's
House Jenta
Wildflower
Isle

Prologue

A mystery led the old man from the shelter of the trees.

Krawg, raising his picker-staff like a spear, pursued the creature eastward into the open and watched it plunge down the slope toward the River Throanscall. A flash of green wings, an unfamiliar chirp, and the scampering prey was gone, vanishing into the riverbank grasses that stood shoulder high.

He paused, remembering Captain Tabor Jan's orders.

At the travelers' suppertime counting, the counters had come up short. Growling, the captain had handed out shrill-whistles and sent seekers to comb the surrounding forest for Milora, a young glassworker who had strayed. The seekers were not to move beyond the safe range of a shrill-whistle as they fanned out through the trees.

But this southwestern branch of the River Throanscall was an endless sigh as it coursed through the seed-heavy reeds, and that familiar music attracted him.

"Bird got away, lucky rascal. Must be rough, don't you think, Warney—havin' wings but never flyin'?"

The snarling reply came not from his friend but his stomach.

"Wish I was carryin' a gorreltrap," he sulked. "Whatever it was, I bet it'd crisp up good in a pan. I'm so krammin' sick of nuts and seeds." He stirred the dry husks of dead leaves with his harvesting rod and watched the river grasses waver. "Could be the start of a story, I s'pose. There once was a bird who couldn't fly, until one day when—"

That blur of glittering green burst from the grasses and bounded toward him. He dropped to the root-rumpled ground.

It was not a bird but a corpulent puffdragon, flinging itself about like a grasshopper in the autumn twilight.

Peering out from beneath his leaf-pasted cloak, Krawg watched while the wild wyrm played. It seemed to jump just for the crackle and crunch of it. But at times it paused mid-scamper, attentive, its gill-slit ears flaring and one scaly foot lifted like a hunting hound's paw.

Though it was small and lithe as a house cat, it seemed large and dangerous when it trotted to within an inch of Krawg's nose and spread the sails of those useless, translucent wings, which made a sound like shaken bedsheets. Hoping puffdragons were as day blind as common wisdom claimed, Krawg fought the urge to blink.

It blasted a sneeze, and the flare singed the rowdy ruckus of whiskers on Krawg's upper lip. Then the creature wandered off to snuffle through dead leaves for a many-legged meal.

"We'll be seein' more of their kind, won't we, Warney?" Krawg whispered. "Only fire-breathers can survive in a forest where Deathweed snakes through the ground."

He thought of the black branches. At any moment one might thrust up through the soil, impale his chest, and drag him into the ground. Twitchy, he rose and walked down the slope, stabbing the marsh with his picker-staff all the way to the river's edge. He did not want to think about Deathweed.

"Here's another story I might tell. There once was a puffdragon who leapt before he looked..."

Silverblue water breathed a blanket of mist that beaded on his eyelashes. He'd spent many a day strolling along the Throanscall's melodious strand north of Deep Lake. But if he listened to complaints from his neck, knees, and back, those days were coming to a close.

The river's rush could not drown out the forest's unnatural groan. Autumn was dawning, but these Cragavar trees were already skeletal, shaking off leaves and shedding their bark, exposing sickly flesh like plague-bearers begging for a cure. They clacked branches together as if to keep themselves awake.

He tightened his picker-staff grip, desire rotting into resentment. Most creatures of the ground and air had vanished from the Expanse, caught by the underground menace or fleeing its clutches. Krawg had pursued that rusty-hinge chirp, compelled by hunger and, even more, by a longing to see feathers lift a mystery into the air, to hear a song take to the sky.

So when a cry pierced the dusk and a solitary shadow winged low over the river—a stark and simple rune written on the sky's purple scroll—he held his breath.

Beauty.

He glanced about to make sure he was alone, then smeared his tears with his sleeve. It was a bird. A bird with tousled crestfeathers and a ribbon tail gliding northward. In Krawg's chest a pang rang like an alarm bell. He wanted to join the bird there, suspended.

"Ballyworms, Warney. What's wrong with me?"

The bird sailed away, tilting, a kite with a broken string.

"Milora's gone missing, Warney. But you know who I'm thinkin' about instead." He swiped at the reeds on either side, sending seed-heads sluicing into the river. "And, no, it isn't you."

Staring north, he watched the bird merge with the darkling boundary, the Forbidding Wall, which stretched from the western coast all the way into the impassable Heatlands of the east. Those mountains loomed as formidable as the front line of an army. In ancient tales that all four houses embraced, they were all that stood between the Expanse and a terrible curse.

"We're not forsaken in the wild anymore, Warney. We're the king's helpers now. So why do I fret as much as ever?"

Perhaps, he thought, *it's because we have no king to serve.*

Jordam the beastman had returned to Bel Amica with several prisoners he had helped rescue from the Cent Regus prisons. But the joy of their arrival was overshadowed by their dire tidings. During the escape many other Abascar prisoners had been caught and slain by the Cent Regus. In that violent frenzy, which also claimed the life of King Cal-raven's mother, Cal-raven had disappeared. Jordam, having delivered these few survivors, had gone back alone to search for him and any other survivors.

After several days of silence, Abascar's Captain Tabor Jan announced he'd take a small company and make the journey that the king had planned, following his map to find that mysterious place where Cal-raven hoped to establish New Abascar.

"So what happened to you, Warney?" grumbled Krawg. "Why'd you go missing on departure day? The captain wouldn't wait. And now here I am, on my way north toward Fraughtenwood, with nobody to try out my stories on."

He scribbled in the air with the picker-staff. "Once upon a Keeper's footprint, a naked child was found..."

The reeds upriver suddenly rustled. For a moment Krawg thought it might be a memory. They rustled again.

"Freakish teeth of Grandmother Sunny!" He turned his picker-staff so that the apple-hook end was behind him. He'd sharpened the blade end in case he ran into something fierce. But his three practice throws had fallen short of the targets. He didn't want to miss again. "Let it be something feastable," he muttered. "Not something nasty and green."

A cool line of sweat trickled down behind his ear as he took a step forward.

Nothing dove into the water. Nothing bolted back to the forest.

His feet began to sink into the sludge. *You're more scared to see a child than a monster.*

Reaching the riverbank, he carefully parted a curtain of grass.

At once he remembered his purpose. For there she lay, the missing woman, curled in sleep on a broad riverstone. She still wore the winding white glassmaker's wrap around her head, but her woolen cloak was dark and heavy—a gift from House Bel Amica's Queen Thesera. Milora, the glassmaker's daughter. Milora, mother of that rambunctious child Obrey.

Krawg drew out the shrill-whistle and put it to his lips.

That's when the puffdragon, which Krawg suddenly noticed lying in Milora's embrace, flicked out its forked tongue and drew back its lip from its flame-blackened teeth.

He screamed into the whistle.

The dragon burst from Milora's arms and was gone. The woman leapt to her feet. And Krawg stumbled and fell with a splash into the shallows.

Milora flailed like a puppet on unsteady strings.

"Beggin' your pardon, my lady," Krawg blurted. "Everybody's lookin' for you."

Milora's eyes narrowed. Then she lifted Krawg's picker-staff and offered him the apple-hook end. He took it, raising himself from the ground's dark glue. "I just meant to rest awhile," she said. "But there's something about the river. It makes me feel safe. Close to home."

"Safe? That was a dragon, not a puppy! You hurt?"

She ignored him, looking into the eerie evening colors above the mountains—the Northern Lumination. "Any news of the king?"

"Out here? How would it come to us?"

"He's alive," Milora insisted.

"I reckon you're right." Krawg tried to smile kindly, as if to reassure a troubled child. But then he remembered seeing his smile in a Bel Amican mirror and decided against it. "Come with me. Tomorrow we're takin' you and Obrey back where you came from."

"If you know where I came from, you know more than me."

He led her uphill toward the trees. "Thought that glass mine in the mountains was your home. And you went to House Bel Amica because you had a fever."

"I was poisoned. The Seers wanted to bring the glass miners to Bel Amica and control them. Frits refused. And suddenly I got sick."

"Cruel, them Seers."

She shrugged. "They said I had bad blood and that they'd cure me. Said they'd bring back my memories too."

"But they didn't, did they?"

Milora pulled something off the edge of her cloak—a scamperpinch. It scissored the air with curved, shiny claws, and its many legs flailed. "Look," she said, strangely unoffended by the ugly marsh-dweller, curious as a child. "He wants a hold on something."

"How many years you spent?" *Twenty-five,* he thought.

"What would you guess?"

"Nineteen," he said. He'd learned it was wise to subtract.

"Wish I knew." Milora touched a finger to her temple. "Crack in my head. Lots of years have spilled right out somewhere along the way."

They walked on in silence, back into the trees, where Krawg beat at the bracken in search of the path he'd made. Then he turned to offer the staff as a walking stick. "Surely your papa knows."

"Perhaps. I can't...I can't remember him."

Krawg began to chew at his lip. Wasn't Frits waiting for them just ahead in the camp?

"All I can tell you," she said, "is that Frits found me on a mountainside. That way." She pointed northeast. "He woke me and asked me questions. I reached for what any head should hold. But the shelves were bare. I could only tell him this: I'd been looking for somebody. But that, too, was gone."

"You still don't remember?"

She smiled on a secret. "I do remember. It came back."

He kicked at bracken. "Don't leave me strung up in the hangers, now! Who was it?"

Milora raised her fists up high, stretching, and the front of her dark woolen cloak parted to reveal her gown, which glittered as if it were made of dark scales. She had woven it from silky flakes brushed from the outer layers of brownstalks. She sighed, smiling softly, and whispered, "Cal-raven. King of House Abascar. I recognized him in the Bel Amican glassworks."

Krawg opened his mouth, silent as if a bristlefly blocked his throat.

"You're wondering why. Well, I felt a rush of heat when I saw him, like I had hold of something for a moment. But it slipped away. And what would it matter? Cal-raven's a king. To him, I'm just a homeless stranger whose memories were knocked from her head."

Krawg shrugged. "We're all homeless out here in these wicked woods."

"I certainly agree with you there," she replied.

Krawg wondered again where Warney had gone. He took a swipe at a hollow mudpod, an abandoned owl's nest that swung like a pendulum on a dead vine. "Everything's gone but those puffdragons, darting about and chewing up the peelin' bark."

"Kindling for their bellies," she said. "Aren't they marvelous?"

Krawg flinched.

Faint red flowered in the distance—torches circling the cluster of tents.

"Milora!" Obrey came hurtling through the bracken in mad excitement. "They all thought you'd gotten lost! But I knew you were—"

"What're you doing alone away from camp?" shouted Krawg. "It's too dangerous for little girls!"

Obrey, smug, folded her arms. "I escaped."

Milora laughed. "Who—or what—are you supposed to be?" Even in the dusk it was evident that the girl had been braiding coils of red bark into her hair.

"I'm House Abascar's queen," Obrey announced. "If King Cal-raven comes back, he'll need a queen to make him happy."

"Well, little queen of Abascar, I hope you'll pardon me for being late." Milora gave Obrey a playful shove. "Go on. Tell the others we're coming."

"It's straight to the dungeon for you!" Obrey shouted, striving unsuccessfully to look serious. "That's where crooks belong!" Then she burst into giggles and happily fought her way back through the winding weeds.

"Somebody's been dreaming," Milora sighed. "Comes so easily to her."

"A few more nights and you and your daughter'll be home in the glass mine." Krawg stepped up to the edge of the camp's broad clearing.

"It'll be good to see the workshops again," she said. "But you've got me all wrong. Frits's glassworks aren't my home. I wandered there. He calls me Milora because that was his daughter's name. She died."

"Milora's not your true name?" He scowled. "Somebody must've knocked you on the head with a rock."

"Well, maybe when I sleep, you'll hit me with another. Bring everything back." She took his arm and rested her head on his shoulder. "Thanks for rescuing me from that vicious dragon," she laughed, her voice warm with affection. "You're a good man, Krawg. You feel like. . .family."

Krawg was so startled he didn't know whether to laugh or cry.

Milora pulled away to chase after Obrey, but Krawg paused to examine his thorn-shredded leggings. As he dabbed at the crisscrossing scratches on his legs, a memory suddenly seized him. He didn't have his picker-staff. And Milora wasn't carrying it.

He turned around in dismay, afraid that he'd lost it. But, no, there it was.

He went back several strides, uprooted it from the ground, and then gasped, holding it out before him with two hands.

The picker-staff was no longer a dull, dark wood. It sparkled, glazed with some kind of glittering golden dust. Flourishes of red grass tassled the ends. And at its base. . .was it sprouting roots to become a tree?

He searched the shadows between the tents for another look at his new friend, and a surge of wild hope blazed up behind his ribs like a flame within a lantern.

1

The Wayward Mage

Like anxious road-sweepers, dust columns whirled between the purple dunes, brushing bones, branches, and snakeskins aside in their hurry.

The muskgrazers, shaggy as haystacks, ignored the whirlwinds. They hung their hairy heads and thrust curly, sinuous tongues into the grit, probing for burrow-birds and redthistle bulbs. After the dust phantoms passed, the cattle shook clouds of debris from their golden hair.

A large and featherless dust-owl raised a taloned foot, seeking to snatch flea-mice from a muskgrazer's matted hair. If the owl was quick, she could catch one as it scurried around a haunch or a knee. The muskgrazers, yearning to be free of the itchy, tickling pests, permitted the owl's attention.

Watching from beneath his black, wide-brimmed hat, the carriage driver lounged in the shade of a dead parch-tree at the herd's edge, waiting for his pursuer.

In this bleak and barren country, hunter and hunted could, using farglasses, track each other's movements more than a half-day's travel away. When the driver had noticed the stranger approaching, he determined to wait. No sane man would pursue a carriage across the desert on foot unless he was desperate.

A sleek red hiss-lizard perched anxiously on his shoulder, watching the top of the northernmost dune. When the stranger appeared, wrapped in a bright red tent of a cloak, stark against the curling wave of evening storm clouds, the reptile tasted the air with her forked tongue.

Few things amused the driver more than muskgrazers interrupted while grazing. This bright-robed newcomer bothered them. Or maybe it was the advancing storm. Whatever the trouble, they were suddenly eager to move off, skating on the long, bone-railed feet that kept them from sinking in sand. But their tongues were still deeply rooted in the ground. Stuck, the muskgrazers choked as they sought to retract those thick, purple lines.

Rain began to fall as the approaching stranger slid down the dune. "A ride!" he shouted. "I must drink at Mad Sun's."

The driver's voice was made of dust. "I'm bound for House Jenta." He raised a Bel Amican rain canopy as if to shield himself, but his mind was on the hidden blade in its rod.

"Take me to Mad Sun's, and I'll buy you all you can drink. Then take me to the Jentan harbor, and I'll give you more besides."

"Boating to Wildflower Isle? Is it true those lonely Jentan ladies are anxious to find good husbands?"

"Don't presume to know a mage's business." There was a growl behind the mesh of the stranger's dark, featureless mask. "I'm not asking you why you're off to bother with those Aerial tyrants."

Nervous, the driver's lizard wriggled down between his vest and his shirt. "You don't consider yourself one of the Jentan Aerial?" The driver laughed quietly. "Are you the infamous mage who turned against his brothers?"

The stranger brushed sand from the sleeves of his cloak. "You would have abandoned them too. Who could live among such villains? The Jentan mages tricked their own people into moving off the mainland, then stranded them on that island."

"You're off to join the island uprising?" The driver knelt and tugged the wooden wedges out from under the carriage wheels.

The stranger didn't answer. Instead, he pointed to the departing muskgrazers. "I've traveled for days without a glimpse of a creature. But down here, they're still moving in herds. Is the desert discouraging the spread of the Deathweed?"

The dust-owl remained, her head turned sideways, her gaze shifting from the stranger to the driver and back.

"That owl knows me," said the stranger.

The driver sensed a smug smile behind the mask. "Maybe." He shrugged. "Or maybe she's just hungry. But who am I to doubt you? You're just like the tales say. You travel alone. You commune with the animals. What an honor to meet you, Scharr ben Fray. And out here, on the hairless chest of nowhere."

The owl blinked her apple-sized eyes, opened her leathery wings, then rose awkwardly into a zephyr and was gone.

"An Abascar man, then?" said the stranger. "The accent says so. But I don't remember you from my years of counseling King Cal-marcus."

"I lived there. Once. Before the collapse." The driver stood and urged the stranger up the rope-ladder steps and into the carriage. "You must have been too busy to notice." He followed into the shelter.

As the canvas closed, muffling the sound of the rain, the stranger spoke softly as if casting a spell. "A hundred years I've been away from my homeland, counseling kings, questioning birds, digging up mysteries. I've missed Mad Sun's. My stories will buy my drinks. You'll see." He did not remove his mask.

"You talk like I should pay for the privilege of carryin' you." The driver could see the stranger's boastful smile now; the glowstone's light caught the glint of teeth behind the mask's dark mesh. "If you're the prodigal mage of House Jenta, you'd better be ready to prove it. At Mad Sun's they're rough on posers."

He climbed through the slit in the canvas at the carriage front to seat himself on the driving bench, then affixed his rain canopy to shelter him and seized the storm-slick reins.

"You're carrying a lot of bricks," the passenger mused. "Building something?"

The driver ignored the question. Soon he heard the stranger rustling around in the carriage, unstacking and restacking the bricks to see what might be concealed in the piles. He smiled and spurred the horses on.

The horses flinched at the lightning that smote the sand. The storm pummeled the desert until it ran out of rain. They pressed on for a day, which would have been silent but for the passenger's snoring, and then through another cool night, watching stars streak across the sky as if frightened by the moon. They passed between pillars of stone upon which desert monkeys danced and screeched, and sand-spiders scurried out of the horses' way.

By sunrise they were moving among mirages of ghostly green trees and deep blue pools. They steered around vast mirrors of new glass formed by lightning strikes. And they crossed the paths of two more carriages, whose drivers glared at them suspiciously.

At midday they paused in the lee of a massive stone tooth, and the horses slurped from the water stored in the heavy pouches of skin at their throats. The driver shared a packet of grains and seeds with the passenger but never glimpsed his face.

That afternoon they came alongside a swarm of writhing dust-vipers just beneath the sand's surface forming a turbulent line that wound between the dunes. The vipers were poisonous and violent; travelers did not dare cross a snake-stream without a bridge.

So they rode on until they sighted a simple stone arch—not a natural span, but a stonemaster's bridge—that offered safe passage. Beyond, they descended a slope toward a cluster of stone huts. Horses, vawns, and beasts of burden were bowed low by the heat outside a large pavilion of bricks and branches. A storm of voices, a clamor of dishes, and the heavy autumn scents of cider and beer wafted from the windows.

The hiss-lizard returned to the driver's shoulder to whisper in his ear. He stroked the creature's rugged back, dampening his finger with the cooling oils that oozed out between the scales, and then drew lines across his burning brow.

"Sharpen your stories," he called to the passenger. "We've come to Mad Sun's."

Jayda Weese, manager of Mad Sun's, rose from beneath the blankets spread in the shade of a flourishing parch-tree behind his bar. He rolled and lit a leafwrap, clenched it between his teeth, and muttered, "Yup. More customers."

"Someday the youngsters will do the work for us." The leisurely yawn under the covers belonged to Meladi, his wife. "And you'll get to kiss me all day long."

Weese shrugged himself into his leather vest and tied his curtain of yellow hair into a cord. "Yup," he said.

He opened the back door, went inside, and passed through the steamy kitchen with a nod to his workers—Hunch, the hulking custodian and carpenter who only ever asked him questions, and Rik-pool, his singing, fast-handed dishwasher.

"Two," he said, referring to the customers he'd heard approaching.

He thrust a heavy curtain aside and stepped into the narrow span behind the bar, inhaling the heavy haze of beer, sweat, dust, and hot grease from fried gorrel strips. The sensation always caused a few moments of blissful dizziness. Every afternoon the place became an oven, heated by the sun and the flaring tempers of the angry drinkers who circled the five round tables. So long as it was hot, so long as they were engrossed in debate, they'd keep on drinking, and Weese would be happy. He hummed an old Jentan soldiers' song as he gathered empty clay mugs from the bar.

Two travelers pushed through the swinging doors and crossed the sand-swept floor to the bar. They drew glances from all directions.

The one wrapped from head to toe in red—even his face concealed in a mask—paused and pondered the tables as the glances became gazes. The other newcomer, a carriage driver with a wide-brimmed hat, slumped against the bar and stared wearily down at its polished wood.

Weese sensed that the driver deserved pity for having drawn this garish passenger across the desert. He gave him a mug of dark, foamy ale. "First one's free for drivers," he said in his very best attempt to sound welcoming.

"You sound as bad as I feel," said the driver. "Hard times for soldiers out of work?"

Weese sighed.

It was, he supposed, obvious. He still wore his long yellow hair tied back in a tail in the tradition of Jentan Defenders. But his days of swords and shields were behind him. The word *freedom* tattooed down his arm declared that he had broken away from dependence on the Aerial—the society of mages who ruled the Jentan School.

House Jenta's Defenders had once fought beastmen and thieves. But three generations ago the mages had changed history. Promising their people that they would flourish if they separated themselves from the Expanse and its corruption, the Aerial led everyone out of the desert settlement and took them in ships to Wildflower Isle on the southern horizon.

Then, as Jenta's island settlement grew, the mages had combined their powers to contain their people there. Returning to the School to pursue their meditations and studies in solitude, they kept only a small company of servants.

In time, the mages' need for protectors dried up. They were powerful enough to defend themselves and too self-absorbed to care about sustaining any kind of society.

So the Defenders, men with no society to protect, became self-reliant, hiring themselves out to defend the scattered clans of herdsmen in the desert—cattlemen and shepherds who were similarly abandoned by the house they had once served.

In these days of independence, Weese had become known throughout the southern dustlands as a brewer, a cactus hog roaster, and a club-wielding punisher of reckless inebriates. (A collection of blunt instruments decorated the wall behind the bar.) He was the most beloved brewer in the region, for since the mages had lost any care for the art, he seemed to be the only brewer left. So he shipped generous amounts of his beer off to Wildflower Isle, hoping to cheer the angry, troubled settlers there.

Thus, Weese was the largest sponge for news and rumors in the Jentan territory. He earned as much for his information as he did for his unremarkable drink.

As the driver reached for the mug, Weese pulled it back. "Who's yer smug, prancing passenger, driver?"

The red-robed stranger had settled on a bench at a crowded round table where herdsmen were placing bets on a tabletop duel between two broad-shelled, grappling sandpinchers. The herdsmen regarded the masked visitor quietly, studying his sensational costume.

"He's not one of them Seers, is he?" Weese asked.

The driver scowled. "Says he's the prodigal mage."

Weese snorted. "The third Scharr ben Fray this season." He released the mug and reached backward, closing his hand over the handle of a polished stick the size of his forearm. Smacking it against his open palm, he said, "It's gonna get ugly."

"He's expecting a hero's welcome."

"He might have had one if they hadn't already bought drinks for the other Scharr ben Fray at that table." Weese nodded toward the elderly longbeard seated next to the newcomer.

The driver licked a line of foam from the side of the mug. "Why are herdsmen so eager to believe the prodigal mage will return?"

"Simple. They hate the other mages of the Aerial. Scharr ben Fray, he's different. He's the one mage who walked away in protest. He went off to serve kings and commoners alike. He made something of his life. He's the last living remnant of the ancient government that the Jentan Defenders were proud to protect. Some hope he'll return to restore the house to its past glories."

The driver looked over his shoulder. "Why do you let these impostors carry on?"

"The prodigal's myth is powerful. It draws crowds. And crowds buy drinks."

The driver smiled. "The prodigal's myth?"

Weese shrugged. "Think Scharr ben Fray's still alive out there?"

"I hear all kinds of stories," said the driver. "Killed by beastmen. Killed by the Seers. Killed by Deathweed. Killed in a cave collapse by his own stonemastery. Who knows? The sightings go on. Scharr's been seen helping House Abascar's survivors. He's been seen traveling with a young boy rumored to be the world's last firewalker. He's been seen in the shadow of the Forbidding Wall. Some say they've even seen him riding a dragon."

"A dragon? Haven't been any big ones in the Expanse since before our fathers were born." Weese took the driver's empty mug. "Enough about rumors. Give me real news, and I'll pour you another."

"How's this?" The driver drew an invisible map through beer puddles on the bar.

He spoke of House Bel Amica on the western coastline. Deathweed had invaded the harbor, forcing Queen Thesera to move her ships south of the Rushtide Inlet.

Then he described turmoil in the Cent Regus Core as beastmen fought for control after the death of their chieftain. "The beastmen are desperate and dying," he said. "They're cut off from the source of their strength. But Deathweed is spreading like the roots of some accursed tree. And if we don't find a way to fight back against it soon, we'll all have to find new homes across the sea."

Weese gave the driver a new mug twice the size of the first and full to the brim. "What about House Abascar's survivors? Rumors have them wandering Bel Amica's streets."

The driver confirmed it. The remnant of Abascar, he said, now lived under House Bel Amica's protection, while their king, Cal-raven, had gone missing during a venture to rescue slaves from beastmen. "Some say he's been seen haunting the ruins of House Abascar. Like a man who's lost his mind."

"I want news," said Weese, "not rumors."

The driver grinned, beer fizzing on his upper lip. "You think that story's strange? Try this one on. A sky-man's been seen over Deep Lake, soaring on bright golden wings."

"A sky-man?" Weese raised his eyebrows. "That nursery story's still around? It's tired as talk of the Keeper."

Hunch, the custodian, moved among the tables with his broom, bent low as if he were watching for some lost gemstone in the dust. As he passed behind the driver, he leaned in and murmured, "Shall I water your horses, son?"

The driver nodded, surprised. "They'll be grateful, I'm sure." Then he leaned across the bar. "Say, what'll you charge me for a bowl of Ribera stew?"

"Ribera stew?" Weese narrowed his eyes. "I haven't heard that name in years. I bought this place from Ribera Dan just before he died. Long time ago."

A mug smashed at the corner table. Uproarious laughter exploded from the drinkers there. Weese, teeth clenched, reached for the polished stick.

The bearded geezer stood and pointed an accusatory finger at the red-cloaked stranger. "Me? A liar? I'm the real Scharr ben Fray. Everybody here knows it!"

A small man with a Bel Amican glass over one eye squeaked in the longbeard's defense. "I'd walk out of here now if I was you. This is the prodigal mage. I'm travelin' with him to chronicle his past for posterity!"

The stranger calmly pulled up his mask from under his chin so he could take a swig of beer. Then he said, "We'll see if his stories can match mine."

"Shtories?" roared a drunkard. "Forget about shtories. We wanna shee tricks 'n' powers! Scharr ben Fray, he talksh to animalsh!"

The herdsmen agreed. It was time to expose the liar with a test. In a flourish that seemed rather magical itself, they produced two birdcages and planted them on the table before the rivals.

Both men stared at the nervous birds. Both offered interpretations of what the chirps meant. The intoxicated audience quickly concluded that they had no way of verifying these translations. The cages were removed and set aside on the windowsill just inside the door.

"Stonemastery," rasped the red rider, turning to shake his opponent's hand. "Which one of us can mold stone as if it were clay?"

The longbeard did not accept the handshake. "I'm not a performing monkey," he barked. "I'm leaving." Then he began to groan, his face reddening, his hands splayed on the table, pressing as he tried to stand.

The herdsmen gasped.

The longbeard's rump remained stuck to the bench.

"He's glued!" someone shouted. "His backside's been affixed by stonemastery!"

The newcomer stood and bowed.

Weese began to tap the club against the bar to remind his customers that he was watching.

"Well, then." The driver drained his glass. "My passenger said he'd prove it. Now he'll want to move on." He slid unsteadily from his barstool and staggered toward the door. "I'll prepare the horses." He chirped a friendly farewell to the twittering birds on the sill, and they fell silent, watching him go.

Meanwhile, the red-robed stranger made slow progress, his hands raised as if to deflect the praises of herdsmen who followed him to the door.

As Weese calmly dragged a towel down the length of the bar, he looked at the birds in their cages. They were staring out the window, watching the driver.

As the new hero and his admirers left the bar, Weese hurried to the table where the longbeard was furiously trying to free himself from the stone bench.

"He's no mage!" the impostor snarled, spitting a spray of beer. "That wasn't stonemastery! Can't you see? This here's just a plate of fast-drying clay. He slipped it beneath me while I was standing. I just didn't see him do it."

"Another impostor?" Weese sighed. "I thought we might really have Scharr ben Fray in our midst this time. Let me get my tools. We'll set you loose so you can run."

"Run? I'm not running anywhere."

In the distance Weese could hear carriage wheels and the horses' *trip-trap.* The departing carriage had reached the stone bridge over the snake-stream.

"That mob? They're coming back. And they're going to punish you for lying."

The old man's anger vanished on a sudden surge of fear. "I'm an actor," he stammered. "Sometimes I...I just like to practice. Why would they punish me?"

"They spent drink money on you." Weese jerked a blade from his belt and cut a square from the back of the old man's leather trousers. "And worse, you got their hopes up. They all wanted to meet the real Scharr ben Fray. He's independent. Untethered. Won't take orders from anybody. He is, to all of us betrayed by the Aerial, a hero."

Just then the cheers and laughter outside diminished. In the awkward hush, Weese sensed new troubles brewing.

"They're coming." The impostor leapt forward, dashing like a young athlete through the bar and out the back door, his hind parts plain to see.

Weese ran to the swinging front doors and stepped outside. The mob of herdsmen was not coming back. They were charging toward the bridge. The carriage was rumbling off crookedly into the distance as if it had no driver. And the red-robed stranger was on the bridge over the snake-stream, down on all fours.

"What happened?"

"The driver!" Rik-pool, the dishwasher, exclaimed. Wiping his soapy hands on a towel, he went on. "The driver kicked the mage out of his carriage. Then he gave the fellow a reprimand. And the mage...he sank up to his elbows in the stone of the bridge!"

Weese blinked. "Wait. You're telling me that the *driver's* a stonemaster?"

"See? That red fellow's stuck on the bridge. Hands and knees sealed in the stone." Raising an eyebrow, Rik-pool added, "Perhaps he's not the real Scharr ben Fray after all."

"Of course he isn't." Wiping his tattooed arm across his brow, Weese looked out at the escaping carriage. "You think the real Scharr ben Fray would come bragging into Mad Sun's? He would know that the Aerial has eyes and ears everywhere."

But that driver, Weese thought. *He knew so much about happenings all across the Expanse. And it turns out he's a stonemaster.*

"Poor impostor," said Rik-pool as the man on the bridge was surrounded by angry drunkards. "He's gonna lose more than his fancy red costume."

"I think it's closing time." Weese pushed back through the swinging doors. Then he took the heavier front door—the sliding gate that would seal the bar—and mightily dragged it shut. Circling the room, he pulled down the shutters, then jumped over the bar to grab his best fightstick—the one with a concealed blade.

Out front, the red-robed impostor was howling through the herdsmen's assault.

Out back, to the crack of a whip, the longbeard's vawn was galloping away. *Gonna be an uncomfortable journey for that old fool's backside,* Weese thought.

Slipping out the back, he hurried to the bundle of blankets where Meladi was still, somehow, asleep. "It's time, my joy. I'm taking our carriage. I'm off to tell the Aerial that I've seen Scharr ben Fray."

A hand emerged from the blanket, waving him off. "Bring back that reward. We've got spawn to feed."

In moments the wheels of Weese's carriage were grinding through the sand. Even though the vawn groaned with effort, their progress was slow. The carriage seemed heavier than usual. Weese noticed this but did not investigate. His thoughts were distracted.

"Saw him," he sighed. "Finally. With my own two eyes."

Then he fell into fantasies of collecting his reward from the mages, taking Meladi and the children, and escaping to Wildflower Isle, where he could train up young rioters for the day when the people would take back House Jenta and bury the mages for good.

"Freedom."

2

THE EVER-WOVEN WORLD

The only place finer for swimming than water is light.

That's what she whispers, this woman draped in a shining shroud.

On the smooth stone shore of a river far below ground, she sits with him in a circle of shimmering phantoms, specters who carried him upstream all night. Their boat waits, rocking slowly, tugging at its tether. His mind is in pieces—he cannot remember what happened or where they are going.

The only place finer for swimming than water is light, she says again. *You'll see.*

This strange, weightless sheet they've cast over him is sticky as a spider web. Through it, everything is coming into focus.

Creatures leap and dive, wriggle and splash in the river—eels and frogs, padbellies and wrigglebeaks. Vines shine, their leaves green and broad. The water casts steam thick as cream into the cool air, and he does not know where he ends and the vapor begins.

"You have no oars. But we moved upstream." He says this, but there is no sound.

She hears him anyway. Who is she?

Yes, it takes time to get used to such things. Where we live, boats tethered to their destination can be drawn against the current by a thread.

Frail wires like kite strings trail from the translucent sheet that covers him.

They reach back into the dark. The boat in the water may be bound to their destination, but he—whatever he is now—is still bound to some kind of anchor downstream.

He looks back. He remembers violence. Desperate endeavors. Failures. He was trying to rescue someone.

A shape returns to his memory. He glimpsed it as they cast the sheet around him and took him onto the boat. A boy's body—lying on a mat of weeds and branches that turn slowly on the water in a whirlpool. Arms outspread. Legs bent as if broken. Lips parted. Eyes wide and unseeing. Clad in nothing more than rags.

"Who was the boy?" he asks. "He fell, didn't he?"

The strange company is whispering stories to one another, testimonies of things they've witnessed. But the woman beside him answers. *His work was done. His sufferings are over. He did such great things that stories of his courage are already told on the mountain.*

A word is restored to his mind. *Northchild.* He cannot raise his hands as she does. He is like a balloon, a swirl of cloud in a sheet. "Are you Northchildren?"

It's what some people call us. She does not speak with a voice. It's a wave of sensation between touch, taste, sight, scent, and sound. *Like you, we grew in the Expanse. Our shells shattered, as they all do. We consented to be carried home and restored in an uncorrupted form.*

"Mother." The word escapes him even before he knows what he's saying.

I'm here too, son, comes a voice from the circle. His father? He reaches for their names and for his own.

We were sent to find you, says his mother. *Your sufferings are over. No more fear. Only mercy.*

"You unstitched me. Just as you unstitched Auralia."

We untied cords that bound you in a broken shell. Don't be afraid. On the mountain we'll take you to the garden, where you'll be refashioned. Your body will grow back from your spirit. And you won't suffer any poisons from the Expanse. You'll be free in the light to move from here to there, from past to present. Free to witness so many amazing things. And we'll be together.

"What do you mean—my 'broken shell'?"

Think of a soldier casting off battered armor after a war.

"I was a soldier's son." He looks to the radiant figure of his father. "I was an errand-runner. I did simple things."

You were an ale boy. And more. From long before that, you were extravagant.

He remembers it now. Their gloved fingers passed through him to loosen threads. As he floated among the river weeds, he felt a pain like a needle in his head. But the knot it touched would not unravel. Another at his center held.

You're a stubborn one. Her thoughtspeech feels like laughter. *But you'll let go in time.* She gestures to the kite strings that run back into the dark. *You'll feel such relief when you do.*

"How is it I can see you? I have no eyes."

The borders of your senses have blurred. Knowing is easier now, and you'll remember so much. Beyond your time in the Expanse.

With her hand on his veil, he feels her memories fill him up. He begins to understand. These witnesses have come to this place, this time, like birds through air, like fish through water, coursing through the fullness.

The only thing better for swimming than water is light, they like to say.

He remembers now what they mean. Maybe that's why he loved to float on a raft across Deep Lake under the stars, why he held his breath while swallows weaved in the air over the water, why he thrilled to run through House Abascar's corridors. These pleasures remind him of how he first flew, how he'll fly again.

Among his mother's memories, he learns how these Northchildren came for him. They drifted like snowflakes between innumerable stars. The stars are bells, resonant with sound. The bells are made of cords, tightly woven, lines that swirl and tangle and rush like ocean currents. The cords are made of threads, twisted and braided. The threads are other histories, other worlds.

As the Northchildren slid between the threads, the edges of their wings brushed against them, and the sound the bells made was gratitude. A song. Drawn by the gravity of a particular thread, like leaves drawn into a rushing stream, the Northchildren tumbled suddenly into a waterfall, long and cascading, which delivered them into an underground river, the same water that runs beside him now.

But the Northchildren did not stay. They rose up through a break in the ceiling, emerging from the mouth of a well, where blue flowers bloomed between the stones. This was the Expanse, a place of peril and poison. But they were safe from such corruption, swaddled in their shrouds.

They ran, feeling the world's rough textures against their feet. Colors—the hot white of the mountain peaks, the lush greens of the Cragavar forest, the gleaming emerald of Deep Lake, the rust-colored dust and coal black rocks of the high southern plains.

They gathered in a glen. One placed a candle at the heart of their quiet circle. In its luminous bloom, they shared stories of what they had seen. They spoke of events they hoped to witness in this world's history, to see how all sadness, surprise, triumph, and mystery are drawn together into a whole.

They laughed. They laughed a lot.

If this is what I'll become, I'm glad, he thinks.

In their candlelit circle, the Northchildren watched a stand of cloudgrasper trees stretch, soak in sunlight, raise arms and hands in praise, hum with the blood of sap, tremble with birds. They observed this as if it was as rich as any human story, seeing so powerfully that he felt as if he had stumbled through his earlier years in a half sleep.

He realizes now that all he's known in the Expanse has been a song. Everything he's seen, everything he's overlooked—a testimony, inviting him to answer.

When mystery sent you into the Expanse, his mother tells him, *you were invited to follow the questions. So many people cling to what's not theirs and resist the invitation. But you've recognized the endless song, the golden thread, verse by verse. You've run after it. And in doing so, you've expanded the richness of mystery.*

"I'm ready," he says. "I'll surrender these knots now. I'll go with you to the mountain."

You're very brave. This isn't the first time that the Northchildren have come to unstitch you.

"It isn't?"

Here. She touches his delicate garment. *Remember.*

The images awaken within him, memories from someone else.

As purple storm clouds collide over the forest, a man in a soldier's riding jacket steps through a break in the wall of an abandoned barn. He holds an infant bundled in his own riding cape.

A woman, wrapped in a blanket, follows him. She's exhausted, and she takes his arm as they move to an empty horse stall. Kneeling on the thin scatter of white-grass, the man helps the woman lie back against the wall's wooden planks, then scoops up enough grass to make a soft nest for the child.

"Brona," she whispers, her voice breaking. "I thought that we would—"

"I know," he sighs, embracing her. "I was frightened." His wild eyes speak of fears not yet put to rest.

"You were marvelous," she sobs into his shoulder.

"You," he replies, "had a harder battle to fight than I." He strokes her hair. "It should never have happened this way. In the wild. So many weeks early. Your mother will be furious that she missed it. She'll make it my fault somehow."

"But now that it's happened," says the woman, "I wouldn't have it any other way. I wouldn't bring our son into the world behind Abascar's walls. That glen was a beautiful place. The leaves were like incense. And the birdsong...the birdsong."

"I'm just grateful we found a well. And one with such clear, warm water to bathe him." He offers her the water flask. She drinks some more.

"We should live there," she sighs, "and drink this every day. As water goes, it's wine."

"If it's water at all."

As the storm continues without pause outside the skeletal shelter, the man wipes tears from the woman's face. "You're trembling. Give your hands something to do." He opens the pouch at his side and gives her a folded cloth. She unrolls it, revealing a cushion full of pins and needles, two unfinished shoes, and scraps of cloth and grawlafurr hide.

He touches the child's cheek, then pokes a fingertip into the boy's delicate grasp. "Our son will never be a soldier. He's small."

She tries to sit up. "If you speak any words against our boy, Tar-brona, I'll run this needle into your ear." Exhausted, she rests. "You're not a tall man yourself, and you're the captain of Abascar's guard. Even if he's not meant to be muscular, he'll have a remarkable mind. For he is our child. And I cannot wait to know his name and see what he will become."

Wind lashes the trees outside, and thunder shudders the shelter. The man takes the baby and presses his grizzled cheek to that small pink forehead. "Would that he might inherit your gift for craft," he says, watching the woman work with the needles and hide. "The spells that you know. To craft gloves like mine. Or a scarf."

"We will give him the best tools, whatever his passion." Her voice fades almost to a whisper, as if she might fall asleep. "Like these." Her hand still trembling, she raises up a fistful of long needles of varying thickness. "Each thread-pin has its own name. Each one stitches a particular cord. The larger ones can pull thick, binding lines. But the tiny ones, like these..."

"They have names?"

"The green one, that's Patcher. The red, that's Key. Yellow's the Stitch. Brown, that's Thorn. These two, they're thicker. I call them Knife and Spike."

"And the thread-pin with the bright blue gem?"

"Don't you love how it gleams? Azure. Like the sky after a storm. It's my favorite. I use it when I do the heavy stitching and weave things into a whole. I just call it the Pin." She smiles and shrugs. "I..."

"Shhhh."

"What is it?"

"Look, my love."

The infant's eyes have gone wide, and where he has been gazing without seeing, as if into a fog, he suddenly seems alert, attentive, staring at his mother. New tears spill from her eyes. "He looked before," she says, "but this time he really sees me."

And then the child's hands open. He reaches with his tiny arms as if to grab what his mother is holding suspended in the space between them—the colored caps of thread-pins that bristle from the cushion.

"He's reaching," the man whispers. "He's reaching for..."

"I see that."

"Which one? Which one does he want?"

"Make this memory stop!" cries the boy made of cloud.

He knows already what his parents will name him, but he cannot bear to see them decide. For this is the name they called out as their Abascar home burned around them, taking both of their lives.

Northchildren saved you from the fire that claimed us, says his mother. *They bathed you in this very water. It awakened your gift of firebearing.*

"I remember. Northchildren stood around my cradle as the fire..."

Yes. They came to unstitch you. But the plan changed.

"Captain Ark-robin. He rescued me."

The Northchildren look back through the fog, anxious. Something is wrong.

"What's happening?" he asks.

I don't know, she whispers. *We've never been inside this strand before.*

He concentrates on the strings that trail back and anchor him to his broken shell. "Someone's in the water," he says. "He's found my shell. He's calling for me. A friend. He wants me to wake up."

Let go, Son. Let go.

"I'll let go," he says, "if you'll take me to Auralia. I've missed her."

His mother is silent.

"The Keeper and the Northchildren took her away," he says. "I want to follow her."

Auralia did not stay on the mountain with us, says his father. *She said something was unfinished. So she gave up her memory and her safety. And she...*

"Auralia's come back? Father, where is she?"

He's suddenly pulled from shore, swept downstream, cords drawing him back to where he fell.

He hovers, watching, while a groaning giant lifts and cradles the boy's crooked body.

I recognize him. But he cannot see me.

He descends over the boy's broken form. Hoping the body will breathe him back in, he touches the open lips. The skin quakes.

Spare yourself, says his mother. *You've suffered enough. I can't bear it.*

His father speaks to soothe him. *The world is not all yours to mend.*

But it is too late. He has decided. *Breathe,* he says to the broken body, just as his father had said in the moment he was born.

The giant lifts an open flask and pours water into the boy's mouth. He recognizes the flask—it fell with him from the bridge.

"rrBreathe." That growl—it's familiar.

The boy's body jerks, folds up as a child in the womb, and inhales a feeble breath. He's drawn in. Stitches tighten, binding him fast.

He cannot see the Northchildren anymore. He feels the cradle of the giant's strong, hairy arms. They smell like a wet dog.

His friend's name flares in his memory like a lit candle. *Jordam.*

The body came alive, choking a spray of water.

Jordam pressed his bristled cheek against the boy's scarred red face. "Oh. Good. Good, O-raya's boy." His legs folded beneath him from exhaustion, from the strain of his fears that the child was dead. On his knees he held the boy above the water.

Searching for Cal-raven and the boy in the Cent Regus Core, Jordam had stepped onto the broken arm of the bridge that had once spanned the abyss. Could the boy have fallen? The very thought of that small body dashed upon these rocks made him feel as if he too were falling. But he descended nevertheless.

The climb had nearly defeated him. A voice—a groan like subterranean continents breaking apart—quaked in the recesses of the earth. A voice that sounded like the Curse itself. Sickened, he was seized by the urge to climb back out of the chasm. But then he heard the river.

Arriving at its edge, Jordam saw the boy's sprawled body and pulled it from the floating weeds. His roar of anguish was drowned out by another wave of misery from somewhere beyond the walls. He wanted to fall into the river, to let it carry him away. He had lost too much, failed too miserably.

But then he found the flask. It contained some water from the well where he had first met Cyndere. The water that had helped him escape the firm grip of the Cent Regus Curse.

After staggering to shore, Jordam slumped to the ground, cradling the body. He raised a glowstone, and as he looked into the boy's face, his vision blurred. Tears slid in cool lines down the rough skin that had shed its mask of hair and splashed onto the blaze-scarred boy.

"Jordam," the boy gasped again. "The others. The slaves."

"rrSome got away. Others killed by Cent Regus. rrFound them up there. Bad. Very bad. rrOne man hiding...alive." He gestured to that dark shaft in the ceiling. "He waits. Guards a boat for us. He is very afraid."

"It's not Cal-raven waiting...is it?"

"rrNo."

"And Jaralaine?"

Jordam closed his eyes, choked by his shame. During the escape attempt, the chieftain had caught him and forced him to swallow a bellyful of Essence. Overcome by a violent rage, Jordam had slain the chieftain and gone on to attack Jaralaine's captors. One of his victims had fallen upon her, running her through with a spear. Cal-raven had held her as she died, and in his grief and rage, he had blamed the Keeper. Jordam had remained silent, too frightened to admit his mistake.

The boy reached up and touched his face. "You're changing. Your face isn't so hairy. Your arms don't look so much like a beastman's arms anymore. Well, they're huge. But they're not so scary."

"Arms not so strong as before," Jordam sighed, looking up through the dark. "Strong arms would be good. For the climb."

"But your heart—it's stronger than ever," said the boy. "You came back for me."

He turned away. "Not so strong."

The boy was quiet. Then he said, "We should go. We can't let anyone find us."

"Strange," said Jordam. "No chieftain. Cent Regus scatter. Can't find the Essence. They are thirsty. Angry. rrFighting each other. Weakening. Keeper burned chieftain's throne room. Burned the throne. All ways to the Essence are closed. For now." He shook his head. "End of Cent Regus like me maybe."

"None of them are like you."

Jordam set the boy down on the rocky bank and watched the whirlpool spin in a strange, slow current so far below the other river on which they had planned to escape.

"So," said the boy, "we must finish what we started. We'll rescue the rest of the slaves, Jordam. All of them. Bel Amicans, Jentans, whoever's left." He smiled, and pretending to growl like Jordam himself, he said, "rrrrRescue!"

Startled, Jordam laughed—a series of puffs through his teeth, a sensation that was still very strange to him. "rrNot how O-raya's boy talks."

"I'll need your help. I can't move very well just yet."

Jordam looked back up into the dark, then pounded a closed fist against his chest as if it were a salute. "rrBig fall. You should be dead."

The boy sighed. "I think I was. A little."

3

The Bird Kite

A*re you sure you want to do this?* asked a Northchild.

Yes, said another. *My son is there.*

While rain clouds flooded the sky from the west, the two Northchildren walked across Deep Lake's darkening water like stray flares from the sun stranded beneath the storm's curtain. They passed through the eastern span of the Cragavar forest to the edge of House Abascar's ruins, where they wrapped themselves in whirlwinds and wisps of ash.

The ground, shattered by the quake that had ruined the house, was a maze of pits, spoiled structures, and crazed cobblestones blackened by fire. Greedy ivy and brambles clambered across it, reclaiming it for the wild, and the hot wind from the east stirred up dustclouds.

House Abascar's palace was gone, collapsed like a cake, sinking into the foundation that had dissolved from stone to sand. Its towers had smashed into one another, its walls ripped open to expose royal chambers and stone stairways.

One by one, the troubled clouds dissolved, raining down in sighs.

The crater where Abascar's palace once stood and the canyon of breaks in the stone all around it whispered with tiny waterfalls that trailed like traces of spider webs down into the catastrophe. They splashed across walls that had fallen to floors, soaked the wood of wardrobes and library shelves, saturated scraps of old scrolls that had once told the histories of House Abascar, and carried them away like so many autumn leaves. And so dissolved the tale of Abascar's kings—Cal-marcus, Har-baron, all the way back to Tammos Raak himself, who brought the children out of captivity north of the Forbidding Wall.

Observing this, the somber witnesses crossed the wreckage, making their way along broken trails, down slanted shards of wall, and into the spectacular labyrinth. They could see across chasms into the remaining halves of great halls, into small cavities of chambers once private, into dining rooms opened like eggs. Furniture was scattered, scorched, and overturned, half-buried in spills of earth or caught in dangling creepervine.

As they descended, spiderbats fluttered around them and hissed. A saucer-eyed lurkdasher, the red fur on its back standing on end, stared after them, and then it darted back into whatever tunnel had given it safety.

Across a yawning space, they saw a box upon a promontory—two walls and a sheltering ceiling. The coil of a stone stairway, which had once wound its way up inside a tower, now stood exposed, spiraling up to the mouth of that room. It was still sparsely furnished—a bed, a dresser, even a rug had somehow been spared from the fire. A torch beside the bed revealed that the blankets were moving, the sleeper restless.

Let's go to him.

The music weaving through their thoughts gave them no permission to reveal themselves. They were careful to trust the music. The more they attended to every scene, restraining their impulses to intervene, the more they found something richer than narrative—not just a chain of this, this, and what happens next. Life was poetry, each scene woven through with innumerable threads. They could find glory in moments that might seem like defeat to someone of lesser vision. This was one of those moments.

Your son has fallen so far, Cal-marcus.

Look. His hand is stretched out for help in the night. I wish I could hold that hand.

They walked across the room's rough ceiling and lay down upon the wall.

Bats. Beastmen. Deathweed. So many dangers here, Cal-marcus. Why doesn't he go back to his people in Bel Amica? This is just a graveyard.

He is his father's son. He doesn't want comfort. All he thought he understood has collapsed. He's distraught. He wants to wrap the night around him. He's disappointed and ashamed, as I was, but he will not rest until he's made sense of mysteries.

Then he will not rest.

No, Ark-robin. He won't. My son has seen the beacon from the north. He's seen the towers of Inius Throan. And more. Colors shine from beyond the Forbidding Wall. Now if only he would lift up his eyes from his troubles. And remember.

Cal-marcus, what is this? A tiny bird of color and light.

They're everywhere, but so few ever see them. This is just like the one my sweet Jaralaine described. She said it flew into her chamber when she was a girl. She thought it was made of light. And she sought it ever after.

Hush. Trouble.

He's waking up.

Cal-raven felt a touch on his brow, and he flung himself from the bed. Dust exploded from the blankets that he had dragged from the rubble. Landing in a crouch, he snatched up his sword from the floor and swung it around at the shadows. "Get out!"

When the dark did not answer, he took the torch and dipped it in the barrel of torch oil. The room reddened.

Scanning the sparse, scorched furniture, he saw scattered figurines, a dark lantern, a clay goblet. There was the bag he had woven from shieldfern leaves and filled with seeds and roots, should he have to flee into the forest again. Everything was where he had left it.

But there were smudges like footprints in the dust beside his bed. He knelt, pressing the sword—the one he had trained with as a young man and kept concealed within a hollow bedpost—point-down against the floor.

Bare feet.

And then his gaze alighted on the bird kite.

He had left it on the dresser, but here it perched on the edge of the platform as if it might fly away as easily as it had flown in.

Several days had passed while he languished in a half sleep of nightmares, too weak to weep any more tears, and then this gliding fragment of light had come fluttering through the darkness.

He had watched it, certain he was losing his mind. The idea did not trouble him. Better to be a fool here, alone, than among people who depended on him for guidance.

I led the remnant of my father's people in the footsteps of some half-imagined creature. I trusted a being made of little more than hopes and dreams. And now I must swallow the truth. There is no Keeper. There are only myths. Delusions inspired by untrustworthy monsters. They lure us into admiration and awe, and then they fail us. One by one. They tease us with kindness. They've been captured and caged. I saw it with my own eyes.

Devastated by his discovery of the creatures that the Seers had captured, Cal-raven had collapsed. Someone had lifted him and carried him away.

He had thought it was Jordam the beastman who took him. But when he woke alone at a campsite north of the Cent Regus wasteland, he saw saddlebags beside the fire and a mule staring dumbly at the grass. They did not belong to Jordam. The one who had carried him was nowhere to be seen, but by the look of the fish cooking on a spit, the man would return soon.

Cal-raven, afraid and confused, had run north and east, drawn by a strange gravity. Beyond those hills and trees lay his home. Or what was left of it.

He did not want to be recognized. He did not want anyone to find him. So he had gone down into the ruins of his father's kingdom to hide in a hole and give no thought to any future.

But this tiny, colorful bird had fluttered past him, and he had snatched it out of the air. It struggled only a moment and then surrendered. It was a tiny thing of sticks, paper, and string. A toy.

Someone above ground was teasing him, and he had answered, "I'm not coming out!" But the toy had fascinated him ever since. How could such a fragile invention fly so gracefully? And what were these silver strings anchored to its wooden frame, as if someone had once flown it like a kite?

Now, lifting it from the precipice, Cal-raven considered it again. "Thinking of throwing yourself into the chasm? Me too. You go first." He cast the paper toy from the chamber.

It fluttered in a circle and returned promptly to alight on his shoulder.

Amazed, he raised it to look for hidden wires, to try to solve the mystery of its mechanism. The bright daylight above made him wince, and the white scar in his left eye flared up again—the burn he had suffered while staring through a farglass at a beacon from the north.

Through the mist that wafted from the rainwater falls, he saw a faint patch of shifting light and passing clouds. An angular shape like a kite appeared in the sky over the crater.

"No," he said again. "I don't care who you are. I'm not leaving my kingdom."

With that, he cast the bird again—harder this time. It fluttered, then fell, twirling like a pinwheel past the spiraling stair. The sparks of its colors disappeared in the chasm.

From the darkness came a sound like someone dragging branches across rocky ground. Then he heard a spill of pebbles from the stairway just beneath his chamber.

Raising the torch, he peered over the edge.

The torchlight revealed a twitching, bristling branch—the vinelike scourge that had driven his people from hiding in the Blackstone Caves. The Deathweed tendril had wriggled its way to the top of the stair. Its sharp, twiggy fingers spidered across the threshold of the half-walled chamber, groping for the prey it somehow sensed.

As if following this tentacle's tentative lead, a wave of crackling branches, black and oily, surged up behind it, coiling around the stair, spilling over one another like a swarm of snakes.

Cal-raven had sensed the Deathweed's presence even in childhood. He believed his father had too. Guards had spoken of a terror in the Underkeep. But no one wanted to dwell on such thoughts.

Who can hope to build a house that stands when such a destructive force can sprout up through the floor?

Eager, twitching tendrils jostled the empty marrowwood dresser. Cal-raven's stone figurines shifted and toppled and rolled across the dresser's flat surface as the predators slid beneath it. They tumbled into open space—Lesyl, Jordam, Emeriene, Tabor Jan, Cyndere, Partayn, and the figure of his teacher, the one man in the Expanse that he believed could save this world. Scharr ben Fray.

Cal-raven reached out and caught the last piece as it fell off the dresser—a stone he had once lifted from a riverbank and marked with an image of the Keeper's footprint—and stuffed it into his shoe.

Fingers of a single hand directed by a single will, the tendrils spread out to cover the floor and prevent his escape.

"You want to fight the king of Abascar?" He overturned the bucket of torch oil and flooded the oval-shaped carpet. Then he knelt and lit the edge.

Flames erupted before him and spilled down the stair, igniting the weeds. Branches thrashed, writhed, and hissed until they burst into smoke. The arm from which these fingers grew uncoiled from the stair and slunk back into darkness. Smoke billowed up from the oil burn as if this were an altar for some dark ceremony. It wound through the crowded chasm of the earth's raw wound, all the way to the sky. He collapsed on the bed, coughing.

And again a pillar of smoke rises over Abascar. But no one stands on the highwatches anymore. No one looks this way for anything but a troubling lesson.

There it was, that angular silhouette gliding through the smoke in a sweeping curve. He was almost certain it was a kite. But who would fly kites over Abascar's ruin? Its shape resembled a blue-winged crane. Skittish, cautious birds. Some said that if one flew into view, it would mean good luck for the witness, for he could be certain there was no danger for miles.

"Another myth," he muttered.

As he watched it circle again, he felt a strange change, as if a trusted friend had placed a hand upon his shoulder.

Remember how you were shielded from the enemy at Barnashum.

He was alone. Yet the haze felt charged with energy, just as it had when figures of light stepped out of the air and watched him trying to save his mother.

Remember how you were given all you needed.

"Go away. You're not welcome here."

Remember how you were saved from slave traders. How you returned from captivity to lead your people again.

The room rocked. He fell forward, almost tumbling into the slick of sizzling debris. The empty barrel hurtled off the platform into space. There was a sound like boiling stew below, intensifying.

He clambered up the tilting floor. Gripping the edge of the bedframe with one hand, he seized the sputtering torch with the other.

The Underkeep was alive with motion. Limbs flailing over limbs, a rising flood of Deathweeds climbing up to tear him like an injured bird from its nest.

"Why do the worst rumors always prove true?" he muttered.

As Deathweeds coiled again about the stairway, their bristles and thorns scraped against each other with a searing sound that made his teeth ache. He gripped the torch and readied for the onslaught.

The stairway shattered, disappearing in the sea of oily tentacles.

The platform groaned, tipped, and began to tear from the wall. He lost his footing. The back of his head hit the floor. Stripes of light crisscrossed his vision. His boots kicked at the oil slick. Furniture slid toward the edge, the bed pushing him into the swath of oil. Deathweeds thrashed, rising to seize him.

Something struck the floor beside him. He felt a firm grip on his forearm. He lashed out with the torch, but a hard kick struck it from his hand.

An aroma of damp leaves and treebark, the scents of deep forest, enfolded him. Those perfumes thrust a distinct memory to his attention—Obsidia Dram, the woman who had governed Abascar's breweries.

But it was a man's arms that embraced him, and a brusque voice said, "Will you let me carry you?"

Cal-raven's body answered before he could speak. He wrapped himself around the stranger. The man—sturdy and almost as stout as he was tall and clad in rough garments that were, indeed, the stuff of the forest—reached up and tugged twice on a silver line.

The floor fell away. They rose swiftly.

Cal-raven heard his chamber disintegrate below.

They ascended through the pillar of smoke. His thoughts lost their outlines. All he could perceive was the costume of his rescuer, the thin cord that drew them up, and then the heron shadow sweeping against the light of the afternoon sky.

A rain shower later, beneath a canvas shelter draped between open-armed cotton-beard trees, Cal-raven held his hands out to the crackle of a smokeless fire and tried to absorb what had happened.

I've heard children speak of a sky-man. I never gave it more than a laugh.

The sky's grey shell was cracking. Streaks of blue shone through. Rainwater, falling from the leaves and the ladders of branches above, drummed the canvas until the ceiling hung low.

An enormous kite the shape of a blue-winged heron slumped on the grass in front of him. Rain pinged against the heavy fabric stretched tight across its frame. Its body was an intricate spring-rigged mechanism—a coil of wire connected to a harness of leather belts.

Clearly it came from the same inventor who had designed the tiny paper bird.

Old Soro.

This kite had suspended Cal-raven's rescuer, and its coil had retracted the lines, pulling both men up into the sky. They had flown in a graceful escape from the crater, soaring off the edge of Abascar's stone plateau and descending toward the Cragavar forest, which was green and gleaming in the morning light.

"I knew you were a kite...a kite-maker," Cal-raven stuttered. "The woman you were helping at Mawrnash—I don't even remember her name—she said you made kites. I saw the materials. But I had no idea. You. . .you built that?"

Old Soro snorted, shaving curls off a beam of wood with a broad, sharp knife.

"You helped me climb the tower of Tammos Raak at Mawrnash. Now you're all the way out here. Why? Why follow me so far?"

Soro put the plank down, and a sigh puffed through his wild, bristling beard. But his face—it seemed a wooden mask of intricate engravings through which he stared with otherworldly eyes—gave no clue to his thoughts. He slid a hand beneath the bristled treebark vest and withdrew a small loaf of hard-crusted bread as if pulling out his own heart. He broke it into three pieces and offered one.

Cal-raven took it and began to gnaw at it. It was tough but full of seeds and flecks of dried lamb. The piece was difficult to swallow, but he hadn't eaten more than a couple of flavorless roots in the last few days.

He choked and muttered, "So you left the woman at Mawrnash. Just as I did." Shame burned his face. He had promised to go back and rescue her, and now he could not even remember her name. "You left her there in order to follow me?"

The old man offered him a flask. Cal-raven sniffed the spout, then swallowed the sour wine.

"Was I so lost and desperate that you thought I was in more trouble than she? You should have stuck with her." He paused. "Gretyl. You should have stuck with Gretyl."

Soro silently regarded the kite resting on the grass.

"Poor Gretyl," Cal-raven sighed. "Yet another promise I failed to keep."

Soro glowered at him, then shook his head.

"What are you doing here, Soro? You're not from Abascar. I've no idea if you're a merchant or a farmer, a Bel Amican or a Jentan mage. Did you ride from. . ." He heard the splash of footsteps across rain-soaked soil. "Someone's coming."

Soro glanced at Cal-raven, amused.

A skeletal man wearing a rough beard, ragged trousers, and an array of scars and bruises staggered into view. He cast down a pile of branches, green boughs like those that Soro had whittled into straight, precise planes.

"You think he came here for you?" The newcomer's voice was tarnished and thin as a rusty razor. He sat down and folded his arms across his jutting ribs. He was a bald man, and his wide round eyes regarded Cal-raven fiercely. "This marvelous fellow found me, helped me get my strength back, and carried me up out of the ruins, and along the way we noticed you. He was ready to move on. He asked me if you looked like you needed help."

Cal-raven's eyes narrowed. "You asked Old Soro to take me out of there?"

The man lowered his eyes. "The least I could do, my prince. My *king.* I failed your father. I thought the pillars of the Underkeep were strong."

"Pillarman." Cal-raven ran his hand across his chin. "Nat-ryan. I didn't recognize you without your tools." Nat-ryan, the "pillarman," the mad architect of the Underkeep. His task had been to routinely examine the columns that kept the Underkeep secure—a dangerous affair involving scaffolding, wires, and ropeladders. "You've been hiding down there all this time?"

"I thought...I thought the pillars would hold." Nat-ryan sucked his lower lip between his teeth and bit down as if he'd chew it right off.

"How did you fight off the Deathweed?"

"I kept a fire burning. Deathweed—is that what they call it? It doesn't like fire." He was staring into memories Cal-raven did not want to understand. "But it waited for me. It wanted me to sleep. And it should have taken me. For how I failed."

"Failed? You did what you could to build something that would last. It wasn't your fault, Nat-ryan. The fire. The Deathweed. Let it go."

Soro laughed again, shaking his head.

Cal-raven glared at him. "I should heed my own advice. Is that what you think?"

Soro took a long strand of reedstring and began binding two of the wooden beams crosswise and then wove the reedstring through a flat of canvas. Another kite, Cal-raven realized.

"It's been a year," said Nat-ryan. "A year, master. You cannot build something in haste if you hope for it to stand." He watched the kite-maker work. "Soro. That's your name?" He frowned at Cal-raven. "If you know him, why did you run from his camp?"

Cal-raven blinked.

The pillarman continued. "He says he knew there was trouble in Cent Regus's territory. He went in there and found you half-dead."

"Soro? He carried me out of there?" Cal-raven closed his eyes. "I woke and thought I was in a slavers' camp."

Soro gave the rest of the bread to Nat-ryan. He devoured it, his jaw working hard as an animal fighting for its life.

Soro got up, and the sight was something like seeing a misshapen shrub grow legs. Cal-raven watched the brusque hunchback hobble awkwardly across the grass.

Left alone with the rain and the emaciated pillarman, Cal-raven felt as if he couldn't breathe. He glanced up at the three shadows on the canvas ceiling, and their strange dance was all the persuasion he needed to step out into the air.

The veering shapes in the sky hypnotized him. They were kites—more kites, smaller and bound to strings that were tied to the tree branches. And yet they flew in concert, darting left and right, diving and rising, dancing in the sky.

"They're learning," said Nat-ryan from behind him.

"Learning?"

"Didn't you see the kite that carried you out? The old man calls that one 'mature.' It flew on its own, master. He builds them, and then he trains them to fly but never to wander away. And if he takes their strings, they respond to him." Nat-ryan shrugged. "Sometimes they fly off on their own, but eventually they fall and break. He runs after them, puts them back together. He says they're humbler after they're repaired." He coughed suddenly, pressing his hands to his chest. "He may be crazy, but he brought me out of the pit." Then he coughed again, clearly pained by the turmoil in his lungs.

"What happens now, pillarman?"

"Soro's taking me to the lake. He says there's good water there. And you don't want to know what I've been drinking here."

Soro seemed to be adjusting the rods of the heron-kite's frame.

"Shall we take you along, master?"

"I don't think you're equipped to take me on any journey. What do you have here—a mule?" Cal-raven shrugged. "And I can't say I'm comfortable around Soro. I don't know what he wants. I need somebody who can answer my questions. Somebody I trust." He looked off into the Cragavar. *Where is my teacher now? I wonder.*

Old Soro trudged to the mule at the edge of the trees and lifted saddlebags over its back. Then he paused, distracted, gazing skyward.

A magnificent rain cloud moved westward on high winds, its bulk like the hull of a ship, its highest reaches white and wind-swept like sails. Sunset's rays beamed along beneath it. The sight lifted Cal-raven momentarily from his distress. He longed to go back into the sky. To forget everything that burdened him.

Soro buckled the saddlebags and began untying the mule from the tree.

Cal-raven walked down toward him. "Where do you plan to take Nat-ryan?"

"Where does an Abascar man belong?" came the bearded man's reply.

The barb in the question snagged him. "I'm not going with you." He turned back toward the ruins. "I can't."

Soro finished strapping the bags to the mule, then clapped his hands three times, and the animal turned and trotted dutifully into the woods, its ears swiveling as if already watching for predators.

"What are you..." Cal-raven pointed after the animal as if Soro hadn't noticed. "It's off with your things!"

Soro ignored him and marched back to the large kite. He began bending the beams of its wingspan. Then he unclasped small latches along those beams and unfolded greater extensions of canvas, doubling the stretch. It began to beat those wings against the air, eager as a hawk for the hunt. He lifted it then, turned, and waited as if listening for something.

A wave of wind poured over the ruins, stirring up a dustcloud that rushed toward the forest.

The hunchback cast the kite up, and it caught the current, fluttering and rising. Its master walked backward, giving it more and more of the cord. "Nat-ryan?" Soro called. "Ready?"

Cal-raven glanced back to find that Nat-ryan had untied the canvas shelter from the trees. He was holding the canvas just as Soro had held up the kite. And then he cast it up into the wind. It caught and rose, trailing a cord of its own, which, Cal-raven saw with surprise, was anchored to Soro's belt.

The two kites began to ride the wave of wind toward the forest, and their combined force pulled Soro into a heavy run. Cal-raven saw now what the man meant to do, and even so he could not bring himself to believe it would work.

But before Soro had reached the trees, he was bounding in long, elevating steps. And as he reached the tree line, he steered the kites sharply to his left, and they wheeled about and lifted him in another long and sweeping curve. Their spools began to retract. Old Soro ascended, soaring over Cal-raven's head. His laughter as his kicking boots passed by seemed a response to Cal-raven's incredulity.

Then Soro flung out more cords, and they trailed below him. Nat-ryan reached out and caught them and quickly bound their hooks to the strange harness that he wore. As he did, he began to run forward, a frantic stumble, until the cords pulled taut and he too was lifted and swinging through the air just behind Old Soro. Now he was laughing as well.

The kites ascended to the tops of the trees, then higher and faster, in wide circles around the clearing. Cal-raven found himself turning in place, open-mouthed. And then they began to pick up speed, gliding swiftly on stronger currents, straightening their paths, and moving north and west, their backs to him.

"Wait!" He began to walk forward. "Wait! Don't go yet!" He started to run. And soon he was dashing hard and anxious after the rising kites and their passengers. "Take me with you!"

The three kite fliers gripped the cords and gazed wide-eyed at the forest beneath them, the trees painted gold by the sunset's flood of light.

Cal-raven, strapped in a harness Soro had drawn from his pack, had already forgotten the first sight he had seen in the moments after the cords pulled sharply and broke his run, lifting him in a graceful curve over the ruins of House Abascar.

The crater in the stone below had seemed an open mouth, a throat, a devouring emptiness swallowing all that Abascar's people had built to make themselves the world's glory.

Abascar seemed so small as Cal-raven was carried up toward the low, streaming clouds. And as they turned and accelerated westward, he marveled that such simple constructions—wooden beams fixed crosswise, with canvas stretched to catch the invisible forces around them—could lift him so easily above his troubles and give him hope, could raise him to such a staggering view.

It was as if he could see the whole world.

As they rushed across the Cragavar, he saw highwatches far below, the platforms he and his soldiers had built to send messages over the trees. They were small wooden squares, tiny pieces from a game he had played long ago. When the mist of the low clouds moistened his brow, he found himself laughing. Nothing—not even the fastest charge on a horse—had ever given him such a thrill. He felt as if he were escaping the world to touch the fiery sky. He was free in a nameless country. Anything seemed possible now.

The world blurred—colors, motion. They moved in a cool dream, a concert of whispers, and the wind told the kites just where to fly.

Cal-raven watched Old Soro, admiring the way he could steer the kites with the slightest tugs on the line. It was as though they were knives and he was sculpting the air, finding the right contours.

When the gleaming lake came into view—a pink mirror of the evening sky—they began to descend.

Hearing the kite-maker's instructions, Cal-raven and Nat-ryan raised their feet and then landed in a run. Soro guided the kites to gently scud along the pebbled beach until they stopped, their canvas sagging wearily.

The beach ran along between the rippling lake water and three dark cave mouths at the base of a cliff that rose high and smooth above them.

The high stone wall gained his full attention, for it was painted in grand, vivid stripes of color.

"Auralia," he whispered.

4

Awakenings

As the ale boy emerged from the earth's crooked mouth, he breathed deep, relieved to escape the stagnant air of the maze below. Any light, even the sickly glow of the sun's cold coin over a world drained of colors, was better than the subterranean dark.

Auralia's out there somewhere.

He looked down at himself, an unfamiliar clown. The tunic and torn trousers that Jordam had found in the Cent Regus's plunder did nothing to muffle the bite in the breeze. Had winter lost its patience and pushed autumn aside?

How he longed for a hot bath. He thought of the wine barrel that Abascar's brewer, Obsidia Dram, had given him for a washtub, where he could bathe after carrying heavy harvest from the forest to the Underkeep. The steam had smelled faintly of the wine that had once filled it. Obsidia would hunch over the barrel—she was always hunched—and redden his back and shoulders with a harshbristle brush while she sang a strange, comforting melody fourteen notes long.

He sang it now, limping along the river's slick bank on his half broom-handle crutch, his body slow in remembering how to walk.

The river slithered past, its skin opaque and filthy, spilling down into the Core. Brascles crazed the sky's brown haze, waiting for the beastmen they served to come out of their burrows and take them hunting. He could see their beady eyes.

"Sometimes," he said, "I miss the Underkeep."

His words startled a heap of branches. It leapt from the riverbank, shrieking. The ale boy dropped the crutch and slid on his backside down the incline to the river's edge.

The branch-tangle pursued him, snatching up the crutch as a weapon. Then it stopped. Amid the thicket costume, a bearded face peered down at him.

The ale boy noticed the tall forehead and the wiry grey hair. A name found his voice. "Kar-balter?"

The man in the suit of twigs paused. "Rescue? Is that you?" He turned the crutch to offer the blunt end.

Relieved to recognize the former Abascar guard, the ale boy took the offer. Upright, he nearly fell again under a barrage of anxious words.

"That beastman, the good one, he went to look for you, boy, and he hasn't come back and—forgive me—I told him you were shot or eaten or ruined, in some way dead like the rest of our people, and it's true about them, I've seen them, just back in there, downstream, where you came from, but shut my jaw like a window! You're...you're not dead! Where've you been?"

"Far below," the boy whispered. "On a different river. Jordam told me to bring you back in."

"Go back? No, you have it wrong. We're leaving."

"He told me he asked you to watch over the dead."

"You came out of there, so you've seen them, the bodies, back there beside the river where we started our escape. Awful, how they're piled on top of one another, like firewood. You, you're lucky, only a bad leg to show for it all. But, oh." He leaned in closer. "Oh, you're burnt like bacon on the spit too long."

The ale boy hobbled toward a rowboat that someone—probably Kar-balter—had half covered with dead reeds. "Beastmen're distracted for now. They're fighting each other and digging for Essence. When they find it, they'll be dangerous. And hungry."

"Sure as vultures." He brushed the reeds away. The rowboat's sides had been smashed, but the remains still worked as a raft.

"So we gotta finish what we started."

"Finish?" Kar-balter glanced over his shoulder, then followed. "Maybe you've not noticed, Rescue, but our adventures here are over. Beastmen are swarming back to the Core like flies to...well... We'll be lucky to get away alive. The Strongbreed have arrows as thick as tent stakes and spears heavy as flagpoles. They came over the rise and attacked. Thought sure I was dead, but Nella Bye, she..." He paused, trying to wipe at tears, but poked himself in the eye with a twig glued to the back of his hand.

The ale boy clutched at his chest. "I don't want to know."

"She stepped in front of me. Arrow hit her hard." Kar-balter pointed to a purple lump over his left eyebrow. "Back of her head knocked me overboard. *Splash! Splat!* Arrows. Arrows everywhere."

The ale boy knelt and pushed the makeshift raft back into the stream.

"You were an Abascar ale boy, weren't you?" Kar-balter stepped carefully on and crouched down, ten fingers splayed on the raft's wet wood, while the boy lifted his long, spiked pole from the bank. "Know where I could get a drink around here?"

"Nothing fit for us to drink."

"Remember those days? You'd bring juice to the top of the wall. I'd bother you for something stronger."

"I remember."

"You were a torment, flaunting wines and liquors and even the king's blasted hajka. Thought I had it bad back then. But now...to have just one more day pacing Abascar's wall—that'd be grand as a birthday party. Wish I could stuff King Cal-marcus's skull with—"

"Don't go blamin' the king for Abascar's collapse," the boy growled.

Kar-balter quieted for a moment, then cupped his hand into the dark soup, sniffed it, and cast it back. "Ballyflies! I'd suck down water like it was sweet cream if I could find some."

"Throw yourself into the abyss, and you'll find some."

"What's that, boy?"

"If we stick together, maybe we can find some."

They drifted along the river's edge, leaving daylight behind. Kar-balter began to weep. The ale boy understood. This was like falling back down the throat of a monster that had just coughed them out.

"Tell me again why Jordam can't come to us."

"He's at the dock collecting what we need to save the rest."

"The rest? They're dead! The only slaves alive in this hole are Bel Amicans and..." Kar-balter pulled his hat of branches slowly off his head. "No. We're not gonna risk...no. We couldn't even save our own!" Kar-balter sank lower. "Not even Cal-raven could manage a rescue."

"It wasn't Cal-raven's fault!" the boy shouted. "Don't ever say that!" Then he seized the pole and attacked the water as if it had offended him. "It was me. Don't you remember? We'd almost escaped. The rafts were moving out. I tried to slip away. I didn't expect Queen Jaralaine would come after me. But she wasn't right in the head. She thought I was her son."

The raft spun slowly.

"Then Cal-raven came after her. And you all got caught by beastmen. Everything was spoiled except for them that got away in time. And now..."

Kar-balter awkwardly embraced the boy, branches on his arms and legs crackling and poking. "No, no, Rescue. It's not your fault. Sometimes your heart's so big it gets in the way, that's all."

The raft carried them quietly until a soft splash turned their heads.

The river's skin, barely visible in the soft shine of glowstones, seemed troubled to a cold boil. Waves splashed the banks. A tentacle broke the surface, spiny and tall as a cloudgrasper. It strained to touch the ceiling, then slid down the wall until it slapped the stony bank opposite them.

"Prowling," said Kar-balter.

"Shh," said the boy. He could almost swear he heard it sniffing. *Beastmen aren't guarding the Core anymore. So the feelers are rising to protect this place.* He grabbed Kar-balter's wagging beard and held a finger to his lips.

They let the current carry them.

The tentacle slowly retreated into the water. Then a swarm of limbs rose and slithered against the current back toward the tunnel's entrance.

The raft rounded a bend. Kar-balter reached into the sludge and hauled up a two-ended oar. He snapped it over his knee and gave half to the boy. Without a word they paddled, propelling themselves into the Core.

The river broadened, and they drifted into a swirling pool, then came to rest against the edge of a stone plate that jutted out over the water. Jordam waved a torch from the edge of it. The ale boy could see that the beastman had recovered two of the damaged boats from their failed escape.

He kept his eyes on his scowling friend. He did not want to see what torchlight revealed in the shadows. As Jordam had carried him up from the river at the bottom of the abyss, he had glimpsed the stacked bodies of those who had fallen when the red-armored Strongbreed attacked.

One image burned in his mind's eye—a white face and a white arm, fallen outward from the bodies as if reaching for him. Nella Bye's golden hair spilled down. Nella Bye, who had moved among the Cent Regus slaves as a gentle comforter.

He had seen her arrested in House Abascar. He had come to collect hajka peppers from the garden alongside her house, only to find a duty officer stuffing his pockets with them. The officer fled, but Nella Bye pursued him, demanding that he empty his pockets in front of onlookers. Instead, the officer arrested her for growing the peppers in plain sight—he insisted that the colorful array was an open act of rebellion against Abascar's "wintering." Due to his high rank, he was given permission to cast her outside the walls to live as a Gatherer, condemned until she could earn her way back into safety.

Living among the Gatherers, Nella Bye might have withdrawn in bitterness. Instead, she had served the others with motherly grace. Now she was cast aside like rubbish.

As Jordam secured the raft, he saw their anxious backward glances. "rrTrouble?"

They heard a rumble like an avalanche upriver. Black dust wafted downstream, and they shielded their faces.

"Feelers," Kar-balter squealed.

Jordam's teeth gleamed in the torchlight. "rrNeed a new way out."

A feeble sound like a cough silenced him. Kar-balter turned and squinted toward the darkness where the dead were piled.

"Don't look at the bodies," whispered the boy. But then the cough recurred, and there was a rustle of cloth.

Kar-balter's emaciated face twitched as he tried to make sense of what he saw.

Jordam knelt beside the boy. "rrDon't run."

"Nella Bye?" Kar-balter said.

When a feeble voice answered "Yes," the ale boy turned, astonished.

Like weary travelers rising before dawn, shapes were crawling from the pile. Nella Bye's hands were flat on the stone, her hair trailing to the floor. As she crawled toward them, she patted the floor before her cautiously, unseeing.

"It's the Curse," hissed the boy.

"No," said Jordam.

Nella Bye raised her head. Her eyes were bright, and while her face was still grey as a fish, a thin and ragged breath escaped her lips. Then she came to her knees and clasped the arrowshaft protruding from her belly, looking surprised.

"rrWait!" Jordam shouted. He thrust the heavy torch at the ale boy, then hurried to kneel beside the struggling woman. "rrWait."

"Beastmen. Arrows." Her hands closed on Jordam's forearm. "Save us."

Others—the boy counted eleven—squirmed and wheezed, trying to rise. They stared in confusion at the arrows bristling from their bodies and their bloodied rags. They fingered the edges of deep gashes. Some sucked in air as if they had been drawn from drowning. And they looked about with the bewildered expressions of infants trying to make sense of the world.

"Jordam," said the ale boy. "Jordam, what's happening?"

The beastman lifted something, then sent it skidding across the floor to the boy's feet. It was the flask that had contained the well water from the Bel Amican bastion of Tilianpurth.

"How..."

Kar-balter picked up the flask and shook it. It was empty.

"rrGood water from O-raya's well," said Jordam, shrugging. "Woke you up."

For a moment the boy had an unsteadying sensation. A flicker of memory—of being slipped back into his body as if it were an old set of clothes.

The waking bodies reached for one another, voices faint in whispers, groans, and laughter. One had a hard case of hiccups. Jordam lit torches he had collected and gave them to those who could hold them. The ale boy felt sick. "Jordam, what have you done?"

Jordam took hold of Nella Bye's arrowshaft with one hand, raised a heavy knife with the other. "rrBreathe out," he growled softly. As Nella Bye exhaled, Jordam reached around behind to where the sharp end had emerged from her back, and brought the knife down hard. The barbed end of the arrow clattered to the floor. Without hesitating, Jordam pulled hard and fast, and the arrow came out of her belly with a splash of blood. She shouted, then slumped against him, shaking. He put his hand over the wound.

"rrPromised," said Jordam through clenched teeth. "Promised Bel. Promised Abascar's king. rrBring prisoners free."

The boy heard a squeak of disbelief, then a thump. It was Kar-balter's turn to sprawl silent on the floor.

"Jordam," the ale boy gasped. "Where's the queen? If we—"

"rrGone," the beastman moaned. "rrSearched everywhere."

Shuffling barefoot from the crowd, a man stout as a wine barrel, lumpy and bald as a toad, with an arrowshaft jutting from his neck like a flagpole from a tower, passed the ale boy. He knelt and lifted Kar-balter's head and shoulders to wake him. The ale boy recognized him at once—Em-emyt, who had often argued with Kar-balter on Abascar's wall.

Kar-balter's eyes fluttered open, and when he beheld Em-emyt's grinning face, he leapt up. "Get away! Get away! You're dead!"

"Am I?" Em-emyt opened his arms, standing. "Amends. Gotta make amends."

"A-what?"

"I got you arrested. 'Member, Kar-balter? Back in Abascar. I revealed your drinking to the captain. He beat you worse than you deserved. Sorry 'bout it all."

Kar-balter shook his head. "I saw you die."

"And I tell you, just after I stepped into the air, it hit me hard. Regrets. So before I slip like a butt-gust into the air again, I gotta set this straight. I don't expect your pardon. But I'm sorry for all of it."

Kar-balter covered his face with his hands. Em-emyt guffawed. "Lookit you. Scared like you're seeing a ghost."

"Aren't I?"

"I know just what you need, brother."

Kar-balter's face brightened with feeble hope. "A drink?"

"And if I had one, I'd sell it to you!" Em-emyt punched him in the shoulder.

He remembers being dead. The ale boy was amazed. He closed his eyes as that dizzying feeling returned. Whatever had happened to him, he was forgetting. *There's a reason I came back. I found out something. What was it?*

Cold hands gripped his shoulders. "Rescue?" It was Nella Bye, remembering him and pulling him close. He knew her by the smell of her hair and skin. Her cheek was warm against his. "It's so strange," she whispered. "I was somewhere. . .somewhere easier."

All around him the murmurs were growing clearer. Rumors of boats, of Northchildren, of strange lights and a feeling of flight. He put his arms around Nella Bye. "What's happened to us? We were somewhere else. I saw shining people. Gentle, shining people. We were telling stories."

"I didn't ask to come back," she said. "Help me. I can't see."

Jordam was at her side to catch her, to ease her back to the stone. "rrMust get stronger." He turned to the ale boy, fear in his quivering features. "Where did they go? Was Mordafey there?"

The chamber shuddered. Dust and crumbling stone rained down all around them.

"Feelers will find us," said the ale boy. "We need another way out."

He looked out across the rising, at these bodies learning to move, these legs struggling to stand, this breath finding a rhythm again. And there was laughter, a regretful sort of laughter, as if they had all awakened from the same glorious dream and wished they could get it back. He closed his eyes. Behind his eyelids he saw faint, swirling lines of light like fraying threads of color. He felt again as if he were floating. He heard the sound of distant, crashing water.

"I think I know the way out."

Jordam shook his head. "Nowhere is safe now."

"You're forgetting the deep river. Jordam, we were alone down there. The air was better. The water was cleaner. This river won't help us, but if we follow the deeper river upstream, who knows where it will lead us?"

Jordam looked too exhausted to lift such heavy hope. "How? Can't carry them down. Too many. Too far."

The ale boy stared at the far end of the cavern where the pool narrowed and became a flowing stream again, pouring into a lightless corridor. Slender wisps of mist wavered all about that passage. "Jordam, when we were down on the deeper river, we heard waterfalls. Do you see the fog there, in that tunnel? If this current eventually falls into the river far below us...you can keep your promise. We'll get them all out of here."

"But...when the river falls...how far will it fall?"

The boy smiled feebly. "One way to know."

5

Warney Fights a Woman

Warney remembered how the stories had whispered through House Abascar's streets, implausible as they were. Krawg the Midnight Swindler of House Abascar could break into the king's unbreakable vaults. He could make off with treasure even if all who knew its secret location had died. He could be in two places at once. Nothing could stop him.

Lonely, desperate, and wanting so much that was out of reach, Warney had come to see Krawg as a figure of hope.

When the two had become partners in robbery, most of those claims had proven untrue. Krawg was an awkward, anxious, aging thief; he looked like a fool and sounded even worse. But the myths had worked in his favor. People did not see the legend when he walked into the room, and they all but handed him their belongings. Still, the legends lived on in Warney's mind, increasing his courage.

His days of thievery were ancient history now. But on the morning of the day that Tabor Jan and the Abascar company set out from House Bel Amica, Warney found himself the victim of a theft. Consumed with rage and desire, he set out to regain what was taken. He forgot all about Krawg until it was too late. Captain Tabor Jan's company had gone, leaving Warney lost for days in a world of trouble.

This is how the story unfolded: Jes-hawk the archer—who would depart later that day with Tabor Jan's company—woke Warney in the dark before dawn and asked for help. They crossed the long floating bridge, leaving the rock of House Bel

Amica behind in the Rushtide Inlet like a mighty ship tethered to a dock. The sea-wary Warney felt a deep relief as they passed through the elaborate Arch of Welcome and set foot on the mainland. But then he saw the guards, tense and quiet, standing ready.

"Why'd you drag me out here before the sun's done snorin'?" Warney sulked.

"You've got sharp eyes."

"Eye." Warney tapped the new glass sphere that filled his long-empty socket.

"Also, I need someone who'll recognize her." Jes-hawk stood on his tiptoes, anxious.

Warney looked past him into the fog-thick gloom where the raised torches that approached them bloomed like red flowers. These were miners coming from Mawrnash, the mine run by the Seer called Panner Xa. Queen Thesera had closed it down, furious over the way the Seers had betrayed her. Now the disgruntled fortune seekers were coming home, so Warney concluded that this armed host was assigned to comb the crowd in hopes of arresting Panner Xa herself.

"Panner Xa," he shuddered. "A frightful beard she had. And that...that head. I'll recognize her."

"Leave Panner Xa to the soldiers," said Jes-hawk. "We're looking for someone else."

Warney tapped the spot between his eyebrows. "Your sister. The barmaid."

"Lynna's got nowhere to go now that Mawrnash is closed. And she's not my sister anymore. She betrayed us. She'll pay."

In the flame-scorched dark, dusty passengers emerged from arriving wagons. The archer wore an expression that Warney recognized—the look of a hunter determined to shoot down prey. His thoughts were almost visible. Lynna's betrayal had brought Bel Amica's Captain Ryllion upon the Abascar travelers, and he had beaten and humiliated Jes-hawk in front of the crowd.

"Take that joke off your head." Jes-hawk pointed to Warney's knitted cap. "We don't want attention."

"Auralia made this for me." Warney removed it, checking to make sure that its green feathers were undamaged, and then folded it into a cloak pocket.

As the dark became dim, and the dim became blue, Bel Amican guards searched the travelers' bags, pockets, and shoes, filling crates with the chalky mawrn stones. Meanwhile the miners' eyes widened as they looked across the water at House Bel Amica. The view was strange to them after their long absence, for the Rushtide Inlet had been emptied of boats, and the festive, crowded waters that had declared Bel Amica's prosperity were now a chilling, lifeless scene.

The city's walls still coiled about the island of stone, and gleaming structures still crusted it like barnacles. Great shells still domed its auditoriums, and promontories bustled with the daily markets. The towers of the royalty still pierced the blankets of fog. But the waters were troubled by something more than wind. The same Deathweed tentacles that preyed on forest travelers had smashed ships in the harbor and battered Bel Amica's foundation.

Jes-hawk gestured to guards seizing and emptying packs from aggravated miners. "Take a look at those arrivals."

"You know the new rules," one guard shouted. "No more potions."

"But my elixirs!" a woman shrieked. "The queen's gone mad. She's cast out Bel Amica's saviors."

"If you can't live without elixirs, you're a slave," growled the soldier.

"I'd rather feel young and beautiful than achy and old," the woman shot back.

"I need this potion to keep me awake," a burly miner complained. "If I have to go back to sleeping at night, I'll lose half my pay."

Warney stayed at the crowd's edge, counting more than fifty aggravated miners. But one held back, cowering—a woman of shifty eyes and long, matted red hair.

He shouted the name: "Lynna!"

The crowd paused, looking at him in surprise. He turned around as if he too was seeking the shout's source. But when he glanced back, he glimpsed the woman's matted red hair again. Small enough to make Warney feel tall, she seemed to fit his memory of Lynna. But he remembered her as young and flirtatious; this woman was burdened and tired, her skin hanging loosely on her skull as if only a mask.

An officer approached her and grabbed her bag, but she did not let go. It tore. A heavy chunk of mawrn tumbled out. "If I have to pry those stinking rocks out of another miner's hands," the soldier snarled, "I'm going to chop his hands off." The woman shrank within her cloak. And when he carried the stone away, she seemed to wither.

While soldiers gathered the confiscated mawrn into a barrel, which they would later cast into the sea, the miners sulked down to the bridge where antlered sandbucks waited to pull them home in wagons. The woman limped along with them, silent and cowering.

Warney seized Jes-hawk's sleeve. "Might be your sister."

Jes-hawk snorted. "She moves like an old woman."

She wedged herself between two muscular miners on a cart. They cringed and slid away from her as if from a foul smell. The sandbucks whinnied, shaking their antlers, and pulled at their harnesses. Then the carts rumbled onto the floating bridge.

Jes-hawk stood in torment, watching the diminishing crowd. "Follow her. Make sure. I'm staying."

As gold brush strokes streaked the sky, mirrored on both sides of the floating bridge, Warney took no comfort. He hated this bridge, knowing that Deathweed might lunge for him at any time. "Today we'll leave this place for good," he said, pulling his cap back over his head and hurrying after the wagon. "We're going to New Abascar. Where everything'll be fine."

The main gate was made from the wide jawbone of an enormous ocean-dwelling fish, and the prongs of its raised portcullis jutted down like teeth. Beyond it, passengers disembarked and scattered. Families embraced. Merchants besieged them. Cart drivers unloaded the miners' bags, casting them into a pile on the edge of the welcome yard, where squawking netterbeaks swarmed over the spread, pulling at straps and pecking at the canvas covers.

Warney slumped on a bound-up bedroll, catching his breath. His gaze strayed to the vagrants who picked at crumbs on the cobblestone plaza, their bodies permanently hunched as if the weight of the rock's collected wealth had bent them. But what could be done? They were human wreckage, blasted apart by their indulgence in the Seers' potions.

"In New Abascar," he murmured, "we'll all have supper. We'll all have shelter. We'll all have everything. Nobody's gonna sleep in the cold. Nobody'll get thrown outside the walls for the monsters. And colors...Auralia's colors will fly over it all like a flag." He craned his neck, tower-seeking. "Now that the Seers are surrounded, maybe the queen'll help these poor crumb-pickers."

One of the beggars skulked toward the luggage pile. "I know that sneaky step," he muttered. "You mean to steal somethin', don't you?"

She lifted her head, and he looked right into that familiar face framed by greasy red hair, the eyes wide and furious.

"Lynna!"

She was off, straightening and running, transformed from a burdened beggar to a crook caught in the act. She fled as swiftly as Krawg and Warney had ever run from the scenes of their own crimes.

Warney, warming with anger, came to his feet as if answering some unspoken call.

He followed, weaving through a parade of fish-packers, nearly knocking down a white-aproned cake-carrier, and then dancing his way through a crowd of kneeling children as they snipped marbles into brackets to win piles of colored chips.

The woman leapt onto a passing rail train that carried her away down a long curve and slid into a tunnel at the base of Bel Amica's rock. Warney reached the edge of the rails just before the train's end—an open flatcar—rattled past. He dove onto it, landing hard on his fragile knees.

The train coasted to a stop, and he waited, lying low and watching those who disembarked. She didn't appear. If she were smart, she'd stay on board until the train was lifted up the long shaft to the very top of Bel Amica's rock, where it would start its spiral descent again. There she'd have so many routes open to her that she'd be almost impossible to catch.

"That's what Krawg would do."

The lift mechanisms carried the cars two by two up the shaft. Warney's ears crackled and swelled as his own car was raised far from the ground. When they reached the top of the city, mechanical arms lifted the cars, carried them into the morning's bright white fog, and set them down on a rail line.

A bundle of dark robes flew from the train and made a frantic dash into an alley.

Warney was off, down the alley between the glittering turtle shell of Myrton's greenhouse and the tall Seers' Keep. Misshapen as a pile of ice blocks half-melted in the sun, the Keep was circled by archers—some on the ground, some poised in the windows of the five surrounding towers—all day and all night. Jaw-dogs slunk around the base of it, sniffing.

Rumors had spread that the Seers were already gone, escaping with an invisibility potion. Warney had feared the Seers ever since he'd learned that they'd sent beastmen to kill Abascar's people in the Blackstone Caves. He had feared them even more after seeing Panner Xa threaten to crush Krawg's throat for telling a story that offended her. Now they had sought to slaughter Bel Amica's royal family. He did not like the idea of such villains lurking unseen in the fog.

The escapee jerked to a stop, startled to see the archers and the dogs. She slipped between two rubbish bins against Myrton's greenhouse. Warney seized his moment. He stepped in front of her, trapping her there.

"You're a tad anxious," he said. "Don't know why you'd run from me 'less you got somethin' to hide."

The woman tucked in her chin like a chastened child.

"I was part of a company that camped in the woods with a woman who looked just like—"

"Stowey," she murmured. "My name. A stranger."

He was surprised that she did not fight or run. She seemed to have forgotten the chase. And one eye was staring at his feathered cap. His words went sideways in his throat, for the woman's eyes were wrong; they were open too wide, and they did not align. She grinned fiercely, her teeth too big for her mouth. If this was Lynna, she was diseased beyond repair.

"That's...strange," she whispered, raising a pale hand with a long, curling fingernail. "Your hat. Tell me."

"A friend made it," he said, suddenly feeling as if he were the one cornered.

"From where?"

"Abascar," he snapped, wondering why he even answered at all. "Well, not really. She came from somewhere else. Why?"

"Those colors. Those feathers." She spoke to herself, and something like fear flickered in her eyes. "Impossible."

As Warney's next question sought its shape, the woman snatched the cap from his head. Reflexively, he grabbed hold of it. She tugged. He bared his teeth. She seized it with both hands. "Not...allowed," she growled, her grip tightening.

As they grappled, he noticed her hands—rather, her left hand in particular. It was far too large for the small woman. It was ash grey. And it, too, was familiar.

"Those runes on your knuckles," he grunted, straining.

Her eyeballs, rolling as if they might tumble out, swiveled to see the marks as if they had only just appeared.

Even as Warney realized what he was seeing, he found his conclusion to be madness. He had seen that hand severed from the wrist of a drunkard in the Mawrnash revelhouse and cast out the window. Later, finding a hand on the ground below the window, he'd bent down for a better look and seen that it was a different hand altogether.

He dropped his cap and took hold of her wrist. "Did you...trade your hand for this one?"

She flung herself away from him. But his grip was still fixed on her wrist, and the rune-marked hand tore right off.

She tumbled onto the road, then propped herself up on the bloodless stump of her arm. She clutched Warney's cap in her remaining hand.

Warney looked at the severed hand, then threw it down. "What... How could..."

She dropped the cap and launched herself at his face, shrieking. A long curling nail on her right hand's forefinger sliced like a spoon into his eye socket, gouging out his glass eye and dropping it into her closing fist. Warney cried out at a flare of pain deep in his head. He doubled over, covering his empty eye socket. She grabbed the cap and dashed away.

Warney's anger blazed hotter than his injury. He went after her.

She ran into the open, straight at the wall of the Keep. She did not stop. A break formed in the wall like a fracture in a window. It widened just enough for her to slip through.

Warney threw himself at the wall. It slammed shut, and he staggered backward, clasping a new bruise on his forehead.

Looking up, he saw a hundred arrows from nearby walls and windows aimed in his direction. He crawled on all fours away from the wall, back between the trash bins, and curled into a trembling huddle, covering his empty socket and sobbing curses at the Keep. A guard appeared with furious questions, but Warney's story was so bewildering that he retreated.

Exhausted, Warney quieted to a sulk, glowering at the impenetrable wall.

"You'd better hide," he muttered. "I'm comin' in there."

The train rumbled past ten times while Warney muttered insufficient plots for entering a building without windows or doors. He considered the strategies he and Krawg had devised in the past.

They'd stowed away in wagons loaded with bait. "But these tricksters don't want anything, save Auralia's colors." They'd cut doors in walls by night and sealed them up by sunrise. "But nothin's cuttin' through that wall." They'd blocked locks when doors were open so they'd fail to latch when closed. "These cowards won't open a door unless one of their own comes knockin'."

They had tried disguises, but how could Warney make himself look like a Seer? They'd gone down chimneys, but no smoke rose from the Keep's heights. They'd burrowed under homes, but this was rock that needed blasting.

"It's imbreakable," he said. "No, that's not right. It's unsolvable. It's..."

"Impregnable?" said a voice behind his shoulder.

Warney leapt as if he'd been stung.

"Unassailable? Inviolable? Puzzle, puzzle. Ah, but you're wrong. If you had another season, you just might solve it."

A soot-smeared, grass-stained man stood fidgeting in a doorway that had opened quietly in back of the greenhouse. He clutched a smelly crate against his apron-draped belly while he noisily gnawed the end of a sweetstalk. What hair he had left stood out from his head like quills.

"Took me many seasons. Several years. A long time." He spoke out of the corner of his mouth. "A long time of staring out the greenhouse windows..."

Warney waited. The old man seemed to have forgotten him already. It was as if his attention had retreated into an engine of whirling gearwheels at the back of his mind.

"Took you a long time to what?"

The old man blinked, a stone catching in the gears. "To see what no one else sees. Puzzle, puzzle." He turned to one of the trash bins, lifted the crate, and dumped a pile of rotting roots. As he strained, muscles bulged through the slack brown flesh of his arms. He almost seemed a man made of roots and branches himself. Above him, netterbeaks gathered on the greenhouse roof to see if he was disposing of anything edible.

"You're Myrton," said Warney. "The gardener."

"Gardener. Cure-maker. Chemist. Scientist. The more I study, the more mysterious the world seems. Puzzle, puzzle—I like mysteries. Well, well." He shrugged and tossed the crate aside, then turned, and a wispy smoke-reed had replaced the sweetstalk. He puffed thoughtfully.

"You fix people."

He sighed. "I've been known to try repairing a thing or two that's broken. Repair. Reconcile. Restore."

"You're workin' on a cure for them beastmen."

"Puzzle, puzzle. Better to say I pay attention to what helps green things grow healthy. Still, sha-woof! It's a dangerous trade." He raised his fingers and wiggled them to show that more than a couple stopped bluntly at their knuckles. "Perilous. Life-threatening, even. Broke my daughter's leg, you know. Blam."

"Can you make this right?" Warney pointed to his empty eye socket. "Now don't get me wrong. It's just a glassy. But it was a gift. And that's not all the blasted thief took. She's got my cap, the one Auralia made for me. And she took it in there." He pointed at the Seers' Keep. "Time's short. I'm leavin' this house today."

"Puzzle, puzzle." Myrton rubbed his hands together as if this were a game. "Eyeballs. I'm no good with glass. What else could an eyeball be? A berry. A swatter-ball. Do grapes grow big enough?" He frowned. "I've never told anybody how to get inside that Keep. Whoof! Nobody's asked. I doubt anybody who gets in will come back out alive. Perhaps as a cloud or a light or a burst of noise. Sha-wham! But not alive. Ho, no!" He spat out the smoke-reed and unpocketed a carrot to crunch.

"You're talking to the One-Eyed Bandit," said Warney. Familiar resolve burned inside him. "I've broken out of places nobody knew had an inside. But I saw that wretched woman walk right through the wall. That's some trick. How'd she do it?"

"Oh, I haven't solved the Seers' magic. Strange. Foreign. Unnatural. Yeeps! I doubt anybody born in the Expanse can rightly figure them out. Not from around here, those monsters."

"Not from the Expanse?"

"Wouldn't bet a bellflower's bud on it, Bandit!" Myrton looked down and kicked the severed hand aside. "Puzzle, puzzle. You see that? Body parts. The Seers leave a trail of them. Ever since they set foot—set foot, ha! Ever since they slithered into Bel Amica, they've been giving us potions to unbalance our wits. They distort. Dismember. Poison. They meddle. Like they have some kind of grudge. They tinker with us, like I tinker with mosses, weeds, and ivy. Except I'm trying to plant things that live, so ripe fruit falls in piles. The Seers pull up our roots and shove our stems into vases full of sweet poison."

Myrton shivered, then reached under his apron, pulled out an enormous moth, and cast it into the air. "Whoof! And here's the thing, Bandit. I think the Seers are enjoying it. Bel Amica's fools just keep coming back for more. I'm glad the queen finally drove them into hiding. But trust me, Bandit." The carrot's nub disappeared with a crunch. "They're still dangerous. You don't want to go inside that place." He tucked a celery stick between his teeth and muttered, "Six vegetables for every smoke-reed. Six."

"Auralia made that hat," Warney groaned, slumping back down to the ground and knitting his fingers over his bald head. "It's all I have left of her colors. If you had a daughter, you'd understand."

"I do have a daughter," said Myrton. "Surprise! Wow!" And then he sighed. "And I almost lost her due to my very own foolishness."

Warney glanced up at him. "Oh. Right. Sisterly Emeriene. What happened?"

"Emmy liked secrets when she was young. Wanted to be the first to know important things. Probably why she stuck close to Cyndere—to learn what went on inside the castle. She'd watch my experiments and write about them. And she happened to be there one night when my curiosity took me off the path of wisdom."

Warney listened, hoping to relay these details to Krawg so he could craft them into a fireside tale.

"It's good to want to heal broken things," said Myrton, "and of all creatures I know, nothing heals its own injuries like a shockwyrm. It's the flash that ripples through their bodies. Zzzark! I tried to catch that flash by cutting right into it. Puzzle, puzzle. Something sprayed out and hit my lantern. It blasted windows off my greenhouse. Boom! Shot fire into Emeriene's leg." He chewed the celery, lost in the memory. "Burnt the bone to breaking in three places. She'll never walk right again. Not a day goes by I don't thank the world's great mystery that she's still alive."

Myrton rubbed his hands together again as if he could clear the muddy stains. "A shockwyrm's a rare and wonderful beast. I was wrong to cut into it for curiosity. But the Seers, they're cutting into people. Rumors say that...well..." A shadow passed over his face. "Let's just say that I've seen more than one woman who was carrying a child go inside, then come out carrying a lesser kind of wealth in trade."

"They've bought—"

"Look, Bandit. Look." Myrton pointed up into the fog that roiled about the roof of the Keep. "What do you see?"

"Fog. Wait, sky. Nothin' else."

"Oh, there's something else. Puzzle, puzzle."

Warney squinted. Through a rip in the vapor, a sharp white thorn pricked the blue sky. "The moon!"

The moment the moon sailed into view, a burst of birds flew up from the roof of the Keep. They flapped about, cawing and crying, until another wave of fog rolled over the patch of sky again, and they settled.

"So?" Warney asked. "The moon's still up."

"Yes. But what else did you notice?"

Warney chewed his lower lip. "Birds?"

"Why did the birds rise, Bandit?"

Warney squinted again, staring at the same spot of sky. The white curtains parted to reveal the sliver of moon again. Birds flung themselves up.

"Them birds, they like the moon?"

"Do birds usually get excited about the moon? No. But who does?"

Warney came to his feet. "Seers. They're always goin' on about moon-spirits." He pointed at the rooftop. "The birds, they're scatterin' because something happens to the roof when the moon's in view."

"You ever heard of moonpetals, Warney? I could show you some inside. They're flowers that open only when the moon's in the sky. Puzzle, puzzle. They get some kind of cold nourishment from that pale light." Myrton swallowed the celery. "Tell me. Have you ever seen a Seer eat anything?"

"You're sayin' the Seers need moonlight." Warney's bony hands made fists. "You're sayin' that when the moon comes shinin', they let in the light."

"Poom! Surprise! If you really mean to go inside, that's all the help I can give you."

"Maybe not." Warney grinned. "Got a ladder?"

6

The Secret of Auralia's Caves

Kite sails and pieces of driftwood became tents as if Soro had designed them for that very purpose. But as Cal-raven helped raise these uncanny lakeside shelters, his attention fractured. Those caves at the base of the colorful cliffs called to him.

"We should have a look inside," he said as the sheer, smooth stone face purpled with the sunset's hues.

"Must I, master?" The Abascar pillarman lay on the shoreline stones staring skyward as stars awoke. "I've spent too much time in the Underkeep's dark. I'd like to lie here and look at the sky." He wore a smile of happy exhaustion. Their flight with Old Soro's kites had left them both dizzy.

Absently, Cal-raven pinched the line of lighter, smoother skin that circled his ring finger. *The colors on that cliff face... I've only seen colors like that in things that Auralia made...*

Soro, spreading a canvas to sleep on, said, "Shouldn't you get some rest before you wake the cave's trouble?"

"Trouble?" said Cal-raven. "I have to see what's inside."

Nat-ryan sniffed a deep breath of the lakeside air as if drinking from a glass of chilled plum wine. "Think I'll sleep in the open for the rest of my life."

Cal-raven shrugged and marched up the scree-strewn slope to the mouth of a cave, then pressed on into the shadows.

Bird nests of twigs, leaves, and strands of luminescent string perched on stone outcroppings. Scattered shreds of fabric, clumps of crumbling chalk, fading lines of wall-sketches—each chamber was filled with echoes from a vivid symphony. What figures remained were abstract and strange, the traces of a half-remembered dream.

Could this have been her workshop?

He passed through a high-ceilinged chamber with a waterfall wall of luminescent blue, then moved up a tunnel to pull back a dust brown curtain. Faint light fell on a slender arm of vapor that reached out and rested its fingers on his shoulder. Beyond, a small bowl of a cave rippled with shallow water. Beside the pool a blanket of sewn leaves was cast back from a bed of dry sponge-bark.

Looking up, Cal-raven found what seemed another pool of water suspended on the ceiling. Glowstone stalactites, wet from the rising mist, punctured its shimmering surface, dissolving the illusion. Cal-raven was looking at a canopy of cave-spider webs. The thickly woven mesh rippled in the currents that wheezed through the wall's intricate fissures. He shivered, even though he knew that cavespiders are as gentle and fragile as they are enormous and long legged. If he stared, he could glimpse them there, picking their way nimbly through the nets in search of tiny flies and beads of water.

He let the curtain close and knelt beside the rumpled leaf-blanket, cautious as if he might wake some invisible sleeper. A square platter of thin, broken slate held a rough crust of bread. He sniffed it, then laughed. It was not bread at all but a brick of brown clay that warmed in his hand and emanated the scent of a freshly baked bun, which only made him hungrier for the real thing. *Toy food,* he thought. *When hunger woke Auralia, she crafted what she could not reach.*

A sound like oars splashing came from far away, a distant echo from a world below. This pool, he realized, came not from seeping rain or springs but from fog that rose from a deeper reservoir; the mist dampened the webs and stalactites until they dripped a slow rain. He cupped a hand to the pool, touched the water to his tongue, then drank several handfuls.

The water was warm and invigorating, but it awakened the white pulse behind his eye. Weary of his vision's bright stain, Cal-raven lay down, rested his head on the feather-weave pillow, and looked up into the ceiling's shining spikes.

Waking dreams filled his mind as if the pillow were soaked in them. "I want to pick berries. I want to catch fish from the lake for my lunch. And I want my dog."

Dear old Hagah. He'll forgive me anything, no matter how often I disappoint him.

He drew from his shoe the pebble of the Keeper's footprint and began to soften its edges, flaring them out into a star-shaped ornament. He did this without thinking—had done so since childhood at Scharr ben Fray's urging. "Practice until you don't know you're practicing. Practice until a day is not complete without a new sculpture. Keep the power hot on your fingertips." The work calmed him.

"I want to sculpt something new. To return from the day with soreness in my back and find a feast waiting at the fire. I want storytelling. And music." He began to hum the verses of the Abascar hour songs.

I need these songs. I need the order of an Abascar day, an Abascar night.

Drunk on the strange water, he sang his way back through ceremony songs, ballads of history, poems of epic romance, as many as he could recall, rediscovering a tapestry of memories.

He was eight years old, kneeling beside the River Throanscall, pressing the mark of the Keeper's footprint into this pebble. The white scar pulsed brighter, as if from the stone.

He was a young soldier in training, riding a vawn alongside Tabor Jan, driving beastmen from the Gatherers' harvesting ground. But a girl among the Gatherers drew his eye. The white scar blazed from her forehead.

He was leading a charge in a fangbear hunt, a hunter's chant on his tongue. But Forbidding Wall peaks snagged his attention, gleaming like the serrated jaw of a flay-fish, while Tabor Jan turned and, without hesitation, cast an arrow into the prize. The scar flared so sharply it hurt.

As he sang, he began to see a subtle golden thread that bound these memories into a story—a thread of longing that had led him from mountains to fields to faraway city walls. The cord stretched into mystery, and his restlessness burned strong as ever.

He stared into the canopy of glowstone spikes and sparkling webs, which glistened like a clear night sky. *I want to know where Auralia's colors come from.*

He was back in Barnashum's Blackstone Caves, in a chamber where his people had assembled pieces of Auralia's art. The gallery's aura enveloped a figure playing soft, sad notes on a string-weave—a song of lament for House Cent Regus. Cal-raven thought of Jordam, of the faint hope that the beastman represented.

In my hatred I almost killed him.

In the singer's final verse, the dissonant chords resolved into a hopeful, ascending anthem. She sang of a fallen tree, its branches filling with birds that lifted it up and carried it away. Something might yet rise from the ruins of failing houses. The last note floated into the air like a firefly.

The singer looked up, and he knew her. *Lesyl.* He let go of the music's golden thread and reached out, instead, for the freckle-faced singer. *Leave Bel Amica, Lesyl. Forget about Partayn. Come with me.*

At once the pulsing light faded. Lesyl smiled softly, and Cal-raven felt a cold knife against his neck. He gasped, falling back against his attacker—Ryllion, with blood on his teeth.

Cal-raven woke beside the pool, water dripping against his neck. He choked on Ryllion's name.

"Fallen tower of Tammos Raak!" he gasped. "Cal-raven, you fool's fool, you've forgotten!"

Hiding inside a statue before the throne of the Cent Regus chieftain, Cal-raven had listened to a Seer describe a plot against Bel Amica, a trap about to spring. Had it happened? Had Captain Ryllion killed Queen Thesera, Partayn, and Cyndere? Or had the rebellion failed?

"My failure made me forget," he growled, as if making an excuse to himself. He rose and stepped into the pool, took hold of a glowstone stalactite, and snapped it loose from the ceiling's webbed hold. Sculpting a hilt and a blade from the long stone spike, he cringed at the bloody images that filled his imagination.

Ryllion's slaughtered my people or thrown them in prison. Tabor Jan, Say-ressa, Lesyl. . . I'm not fit to be their king. And what of the Bel Amicans? Emeriene. . .

Leaving the pool behind, he found the corridor dark. The sun had set.

Through the strange echoes of wind and trickling water, he heard a distant footfall on the lakeside pebbles. As he moved quietly down the steep tunnel toward the sound, his knuckles brushed against a velvet curtain. He paused. He had not noticed this doorway on his ascent. He pushed it aside.

A fading glimmer caught his eye, as if someone carrying a lantern were hurrying away. The space was heavy with the air of decay. As he stepped through into the dark, something rolled and cracked underfoot like dry kindling. His grip tightened around the shining stalactite sword.

"Is someone there?"

A splash like an oar in a lake. There was water, deep water, nearby, perhaps on the other side of this chamber's wall.

But the sound faded, and the air was still, like a predator waiting for the right time to strike. He felt strangely cold. He felt observed. His throat went dry. Holding out the glowstone sword, he looked down.

Bones were strewn all across the floor. Bones of animals and beastmen. But this was no accidental scattering. The figures below—a wild, violent struggle of twisted bodies—were all turned toward the same subject, their white skulls gaping.

Fighting a wave of revulsion, Cal-raven stepped through the bonefield toward the goal of their skeletal reaching—a pinnacle of black stone. In the sword's faint light, he could see a shape. He ran his hands along contours too symmetrical to be accidental.

A statue. A young woman.

Cal-raven climbed onto the carved sweep of the figure's trailing cloak and worked his way around to stand before her. The cloak and hair were littered with bones, twigs, leaves, and pebbles in wild whorls and patterns.

Cal-raven's questing hands found a gob of wax—the stub of an old candle—resting on the figure's outstretched arm. He found crumbs of broken sparkstone beside his feet and molded the fragments together until they were large enough to break against a sharp edge. In a moment the candle was lit, the light swelling to illuminate a small sphere of space.

He had seen her once a long time ago, deep in Abascar's dungeon, only moments before he rode out through his father's gates for the last time. But he recognized her even though the sculptor had given this Auralia a posture of anguish and desperation. Caught in midstride, she strained to escape her pursuers, the ghastly swarm of bodies and bones that clutched at her garments.

More candles waited around the ripples and wrinkles of her cloak. Cal-raven lit those too, freeing more details from shadow. The ceiling's stone had been molded into vicious expressions, and hands clawed at the hair as if reaching for the girl.

You saw a world of death and desperation. It made you lonely. Cal-raven thought of some of the horrors he had sculpted—monsters that had troubled his mother by their violence, figures that had offended his father by their ugliness. *This was the safest way for Auralia to scream. To wring light from the darkness. To name her fears, know them, and leave them behind. She knew if others saw this, they'd condemn her as a danger.*

He touched her outstretched hand, the figure's most complete detail—small, fine boned, and pointing forward through the dark. As he squeezed her hand in sympathy, his fingertips found the ridge of a ring on her finger, and he felt a pang of shame.

Something in her hand shifted, like a lever giving way. He looked ahead into the shadows, for he heard the sound of rusty hinges flexing in an adjoining chamber. Slowly he discerned faint light on the outline of a narrow door.

"Full of secrets, aren't you?" He stepped down and moved toward the hinges' fading echo. As he did, he glimpsed other faces gazing from the wall. Even there, sculptures waited, watching Auralia. But these figures were not reaching out to her. They were forbidding her to reach her destination. One had a stone mask sculpted like a sneer. Another had a jaw that hung open in derision.

Out of the corner of his eye, he saw another statue with lifelike detail. He turned and leaned in closer to study it.

It looked like Ryllion with a dagger drawn.

It was Ryllion.

Cal-raven swung his makeshift sword, but Ryllion seized his wrist with astonishing speed, halting the blow, and drove his dagger's tip up beneath Cal-raven's jawbone. He dropped the stalactite. Ryllion kicked it away, then pushed Cal-raven back between two of the towering figures carved into the wall.

"Are you alone?" he hissed.

"Well," Cal-raven gasped, "there's you..." The blade bit into flesh, and he felt warm blood trickle down his neck. "Two men," he whispered. "By the lake. They'll come at a run if I shout."

"It would be a short shout," said Ryllion. "And your last."

Cal-raven sucked in two deep breaths, then relaxed, as Scharr ben Fray had taught him to do. *It would be funny, wouldn't it? Auralia, imprisoned by Abascar, dies in its dungeon. But Cal-raven, new king of Abascar and free, dies in Auralia's cave.*

"These are my caves now. Take your men away, and never come back."

"They're not my men," said Cal-raven. "They only brought me here."

"Tell them the caves were empty. Give up the hunt."

"The hunt?" Cal-raven's mind raced.

As he gained a measure of calm, he could see his attacker more clearly. Ryllion was bruised, battered, ugly with scars, as if he'd been mauled by a fangbear. Teeth were missing from his distorted mouth, and his eyes, once blood red, were pale, as if he were half-blind. The crimson mask around his eyes from a burn he'd suffered was painted with purple bruises. Scraps of a timeworn bandage clung to his face. Patches of his striped mane had been ripped from his scalp, leaving scabs of dried blood. He held his knife with only three fingers, the others crooked and useless.

Beaten half to death. And hiding. Ryllion's on the run. The plot failed. Cal-raven felt a thrill of relief.

"Who are you?" Ryllion demanded.

Thinking fast, Cal-raven replied, "An Abascar survivor. Trying to make it through another day."

"Do you know who I am?"

"I don't," he lied.

Ryllion leaned in close, and his breath caused Cal-raven to recoil. He had been eating fish from the lake. "I'm a survivor too." Cal-raven heard something more than anger in that voice. He heard bitterness and despair.

"You're not from Abascar." Cal-raven spoke tentatively. "The accent's wrong."

"What does it matter where I'm from? World's been poisoned. We're all going to die."

"Bel Amica." It was a risk, but Cal-raven took it. "I heard rumors of trouble there. Something about the Seers."

His captor, in a rage, threw him into a scattering of bones. Cal-raven fumbled backward on all fours, gathering his thoughts. If he could press his fingertips through the debris to the stone floor, he might gain an advantage.

Ryllion sheathed his dagger, picked up a tree-branch spear he had fashioned, and thrust it at Cal-raven's face. "Seers are liars." His voice was like ice breaking. "You haven't heard? They betray anyone. Even those who gave up everything for their promises. Tried to kill me." He spat out curses.

"We agree then," said Cal-raven. "The Seers planned a slaughter for Abascar's people, even as we struggled to survive."

"Look what they did to me!" Ryllion turned the spear upright and spread his arms. "I was their servant. They promised me a throne. And they made me half a monster."

"But you're free now," said Cal-raven. "Free of a lie. And you're not alone. I hate the Seers as much as you do."

Ryllion stood still before the candle-ringed statue of Auralia. Panting like a frustrated hunting dog unsure which path his prey has taken, he narrowed his eyes and said, "Get up."

For a heartbeat Cal-raven considered melting the floor to bring down his assailant. But Ryllion still held that spear, and Cal-raven knew, in his weariness, that he might not have the strength.

"I'm not going to hurt you," said Cal-raven. "We can talk."

"Don't presume to instruct me." Ryllion's eyes flared, but his legs were shaking, and his arm wavered. He was weakening.

"I would never instruct you," he said, making an appeal to the soldier's pride. "You're the most powerful soldier in the Expanse. Yes, I recognize you now, Captain. The Seers may have cast you aside, but they've underestimated you. You'll surprise them someday."

Ryllion grinned. "I'll surprise everyone."

Cal-raven stood, holding his hands open before him. "Let's surprise them together." He advanced slowly, unsure where this courage was coming from. The scar in his left eye burned bright as a star. "No man in the Expanse is in a better place to help you strike back at them than me."

Ryllion raised the spear again.

"Test me. Let me prove it."

"Who are you?"

"I have Partayn's ear. Cyndere trusts me. They know the Seers are deceivers. I can win your pardon." Every word was a step on a razor-thin wire. "I'll tell them that you're with me and that you're ready to pay every debt. You'll become Bel Amica's champion again. They'll listen to me."

Ryllion nodded slowly. Then he pushed the tip of the spear between Cal-raven's ribs. "You're clever, King of Abascar, but you're wrong. Cyndere might play along to bring me within reach. Then she'll feed me to the Deathweed." He laughed, and every bark struck Cal-raven like a slap. "She'll kill me and enjoy it."

"Cyndere forgives beastmen, Ryllion. Imagine what—"

"I murdered Deuneroi!" Ryllion drew back the spear and raised it over his head, then snapped it in two and cast it aside.

Cal-raven was stunned. "I...I didn't know."

"Neither did Cyndere for a while. But she knows now. The hunters are out. What kingdom would ever give me better than prison?"

"Mine." Cal-raven stood very still, astonished at his own answer. "New Abascar will be a safe place for you, Ryllion, if you'll leave your old ways behind."

Ryllion glared at him.

"You're sleeping beside Auralia's pool, Ryllion. You've heard her story. You've seen her colors. I know where they come from. I'm taking my people there. We need all the help we can get. We'll set up a refuge, safe from the beastmen, safe from Seers, safe from Deathweed."

"I can't risk it."

"It's your only chance to have a new life, Ryllion. If I had my Ring of Trust, I'd offer you that." He glanced toward the candlelit statue. "Abascar's a house of failures and crooks who want a second chance. I'll see them all safely to a strong foundation or die trying. I know what it's like to fail, Ryllion. To raise a house is to fail much and succeed on occasion. But that is how the best things are built."

The despondent Bel Amican's attention shifted. He looked toward the dim adjoining chamber, and Cal-raven could see light reflected in his eyes. Cal-raven turned and walked into the brightening room.

The room was small with a broad wall spread before him like a canvas. Through the ceiling window that the statue's trigger had opened, the sky was pink with clouds. Light spilled over him like honey.

Approaching the far wall, he discerned a painted scene, and a sculpted man stretched out his arms between him and the painting.

Cal-raven stopped. His scar flared faintly, but it was not just in his left eye anymore. He touched his temples and blinked. The image flickered in both his eyes now. And it was brightening as the sunrise brightened. Even stranger, when he tilted his head, it remained in place, shining.

The white flare was not in his eyes at all. It was a shape painted on the wall—the very shape that had burned in his vision since Mawrnash. A magnificent snow-white peak. The mountain's slopes spilled down to empty space, a span of unpainted stone above a jagged line of green treetops that had been painted to represent a forest.

Auralia never finished this picture, he thought. *But it's important. Look how the man stares.*

The statue's face was blank, a question, as he leaned toward the blaze of the mystery, the white mountain, before him.

Looking over his shoulder, Cal-raven could see Auralia reaching forward, flickering in her circle of candles as if sparks had fallen to bless her. *She's not fleeing from death and darkness. She's trying to drag the world with her. To the mountain.*

"Cal-raven." Ryllion's voice from the darkness behind him bore a note of unease.

Sensing his time might be short, Cal-raven drank in the sight of the painting. Daylight increased, the mountain gleaming as if it were painted with the dust of crushed diamonds.

"This is what I saw from the Mawrnash lookout on top of Tammos Raak's tower," he said. "This is what caught the light and marked my vision. This is what Auralia hoped we would find." He touched the gap between the painted forest and the high mountain. "If only you'd finished the painting," he whispered. "You didn't show me how to climb there." Even on tiptoe he could not reach the lowest stroke of the mountain's chalk.

Fetch me a ladder. I'll get there.

Something momentarily obscured the light. Cal-raven looked up in time to see an array of kites pass over. "Wait!" he cried.

A blast of shattering stone from the cavern behind him shook the ground.

"Cal-raven!" roared Ryllion. "Deathweed! Breaking through!"

He heard a wall crumbling behind him and a flood rushing in.

Ryllion leapt into the chamber. Beyond him, the candles went out around Auralia's statue as a massive, dark arm wrapped around it. The bone-littered ground rose as if someone were shaking out a blanket. Water poured toward them, carrying a chaotic clamor of debris.

Ryllion sprang to balance shakily on the arm of the unfinished statue, staring toward the ceiling. Reaching down, he seized Cal-raven's hand and pulled him up onto the other arm.

The wave of sludge broke against the painted scene, surged back to splash against the statue and rise as high as Cal-raven's knees, battering him with branches and bones.

Ryllion twisted Cal-raven's hand sharply, and he cried out in alarm. "I'll play along with your game," the Bel Amican growled through unnatural teeth. "For now." Then he bent his knees and jumped straight for the opening, caught the edge and, grappling, pulled himself through.

The Deathweed snaked in, thick as a tree trunk, spiked and smashing at the cluttered tide, searching. As it struck and broke the statue, Cal-raven leapt for the wall, sank his fingers into the stone, and pulled himself up like a spider.

A tree branch came down through the window. At first Cal-raven thought it was another Deathweed tendril. But then he grasped it and heard Ryllion groan. He was raised up through the window and out into the day. Behind him, Deathweed struck the walls of the chamber.

On a grassy hillside, Cal-raven lay shaking at Ryllion's feet.

"I'm not safe out here." Ryllion watched the edge of the forest.

"Nobody's safe anywhere," said Cal-raven. "Not anymore."

"What do we do?"

"We go on. Together. Two failures beginning again."

"It's not just Bel Amicans who want to kill me." Ryllion's eyes narrowed. "Your own people sharpen their arrows when they hear my name. Do you mean what you've said? About protecting me?"

"If the word of Abascar's king is worth anything," said Cal-raven, "you have it."

7

Down to the Deeper River

The underground river writhed and turned, an angry snake seeking to shake off its anxious riders. But the ale boy clung to the raft behind his companions, who held to their battered boats as the line of crowded floats descended. Karbalter shouted from his vantage point at the front, informing them all of what little he could see ahead.

Between them, the awakened Abascar dead murmured as if rousing from a dark dream. When they spoke, such strangeness! They described vivid visions of threads, lights, and boats that had carried them north through the earth. They claimed encounters with Northchildren in luminous veils. And the ale boy was troubled, for it seemed like a beautiful song he'd forgotten.

Striking stone wedges that jutted from the walls, the floats spun and sailed around bend after bend. The passengers were dismayed at how far and how deep the beastmen had burrowed. Steep riverbanks rose to fissured walls where broad-backed toothbeetles clung in clusters, scrabbling and chewing at the earth's oily seepage, their scalloped purple shells aglow. And in the scavengers' pale light, a sickening spectacle was revealed—beastmen in a cacophonous travail, desperate to break through the walls, panting like dogs beaten bloody.

We can't slip past unnoticed, the boy worried. *Some see in the dark, like gorrels and viscorcats.*

And yet, the beastmen gave only weary glances to the passersby. Spread along the base of the walls, they bashed at the earth with pickaxes and stones, even with their bare and bloodied claws, single-minded, desperate as men drowning beneath a layer of ice. Their chieftain was dead, and the Keeper had burned his ghastly throne to ashes. The veins through which he had poured Essence for his servants were gone. Cut off from the source of their strength, they dashed their bodies against the rock, seeking to restore their spoiled illusion of power.

They might be helped, the boy thought. *If only we could lead them to the well. . .*

As if reading the ale boy's mind, Jordam said, "Bel's well. Gone."

"What do you mean, gone? We need that water. Look what it can do."

"rrGone. Stones, scattered. rrRiver, dry."

"Did Bel Amicans destroy it?"

Jordam shrugged. "No water. Do rivers. . .move?"

As the raft rocked and spun, Mulla Gee, a Gatherer woman the ale boy had known from their harvest work together outside House Abascar's walls, struggled to bind a sling around her broken arm with a roll of rag-strips. "I miss the sky," she said to herself. She seemed bewildered to find herself here and touched the dark patch of dried blood on her temple where an arrow had gone in. "The sky was so near, I think. And the bright ones, the Northchildren. . . Where have they gone?"

Several of the riders turned, but instead of mirroring the ale boy's bewilderment, they seemed to share the old woman's longing.

The floats surged quietly along through the earth, carried like dry leaves through an unmapped world.

If I'm right and this river falls to join the deeper river, it will happen soon. What will we do then? These people are weak, unfed, and hardly capable of rowing north against the current.

"O-raya's boy is sad," said Jordam, watching him warily.

"If I escape with these from Abascar, I doubt I'll ever make it back to help the Bel Amican prisoners. And I promised I'd see them all to safety. But it's too far. And I'm too tired."

Jordam huffed a sigh. "rrMany promises. Too many promises. O-raya's boy can't do everything." He splayed his large right hand across his chest. "Bel says heart has one hand." He shrugged. "One. . .not big enough to catch everybody."

The boy looked over his shoulder at nothing but coursing water and darkness.

Wisps grew into a thicker fog, concealing what lay ahead, and the torches hissed and sparked. When the current slowed and the waters quieted again, the parade glided steadily, and the passengers relaxed their grips, catching their breath. Jordam dipped the torches in the bucket of pitch, letting them flare.

Their relief was short-lived. The torchlight found two beastmen crawling along the nearest bank. The creatures saw the floats just as the passengers saw them.

One was a female, resembling sketches the ale boy had seen of stout, tree-dwelling Fraughtenwood trolls. She struggled along, one arm embracing her red and swollen belly to keep it from touching the ground. The other—a chalk white, hairless male—moved with a wolf's predatory stride. His face was marred with a toothy grin, joyless and drooling, more a muzzle than a mouth.

The creatures overcame their surprise and sounded shrill appeals for help.

"rrDying," said Jordam.

The creatures' anguish was clear; rib bones jutted out through translucent flesh. The female's belly bulged with the effort of something struggling and unborn. The male's canine grin groaned a wretched spray. But when his baleful gaze met the boy's, he turned his head, and a second face, this one more like a man's, appeared on the side of his head, a visage that seemed to have been melted down by a hot iron. This second mouth spoke, pleading in the Cent Regus's rough, barking speech.

The ale boy held up the empty water flask. "What can we do?"

Jordam steered the raft closer to the shore. "Won't hurt us," he said. "rrCarry them for a while. Find help. Somewhere."

"We're bringing them with us?" exclaimed Kar-balter from the front. "Did you drop your sense in the river?"

Jordam turned to the boy as if to ask for a better suggestion.

"They're still dangerous," said Kar-balter.

"rrYes," Jordam agreed, and then he sighed. "Like me."

The other Abascar riders did not protest as Jordam helped the beastmen climb aboard his raft, but they did crowd onto other vessels to make room, while the ale boy, Nella Bye, and the young man Jaysin, who was quietly singing through Abascar's hour songs, bravely stayed. The ale boy could see in the company's expressions that old fears were returning like a fever.

Jordam barked warnings to the two new riders. They cowered, fretful. But then the male's ferocious face fixed on the ale boy, and he licked at the crimson stains of his fangs. Jordam growled again, and the monster turned to gaze instead at the ripe flesh of the female's hairless belly. She whimpered, covering it with her red-fleshed hands. It rippled as if the unborn could sense danger.

"What will we do if..." The boy held back the question. Then he wrapped his arms around his knees, peering anxiously ahead.

Moments later he felt a brush of cold, damp feathers against his face. Strands of luminescent lichen swayed through the fog, trailing across the passengers' heads. In the quiet the passengers all faced forward, helpless in the river's swiftening momentum.

The two-faced beastman howled a bloodcurdling lament from his dog face. Jordam snatched the last length of the rag-strips and bound it tightly about the creature's muzzle, while the expression on the other, more human face seemed almost apologetic.

The ale boy's gaze shifted to the female, who seemed weaker, almost asleep, while her belly quivered.

She's dying.

He put his head in his hands. *This river. It's endless. What if I'm wrong? What if we have to go all the way back?* As they rounded a curve, he could hear a new sound—the thunder of crashing water.

They raced toward a wall of vapor.

"This is it!" shouted the boy, clutching the side of the raft just as the river, which had widened, plunged them down a rugged stair, threatening to break the bonds that kept their feeble vessels together. He yelled to hold on tight. The passengers needed no such instruction.

Jordam jumped across to the foremost craft and swiped at the fog as if he could pull back its curtains. In his absence the two-faced beastman snarled and turned his savage face to the boy. The boy clutched the torch with its tremulous blue flame.

The floats jerked, crashed, tipped, spun, and slammed against one another. One split almost in two, and passengers reached for each other.

Boom, boom. . .boom.

The beastwoman shrieked. The boy saw her try to leap from the raft as the male seized her by the leg. He dragged her back from the edge so that she fell, his claws digging ruts in her skin. She kicked and roared. His human face, wide-eyed and afraid, looked desperately about as if seeking an escape from its own body's mad intent.

Boom, boom!

Jordam leapt upon the vicious beastman. The raft dipped sharply, its prow striking stone. Just as the beastwoman struggled to her feet, it spun around and flung her into the water.

With the change in weight, the raft flipped sideways. The boy lost the torch and fell headfirst into the stream. The rush cast him against sharp stones again and again.

Boom, boom. . .boom.

Choking on sludge, he struggled to find a foothold. The river rushed over him, roaring in his ears, pummeling him with debris. His left hand was still closed fast around the strap of the water flask. He fought to get his head back above the tide. He heard muffled shouts. He saw nothing. A wave pushed him back under.

A firm hand gripped his wrist. He was lifted up, trailing strands of sludgeweed, and laid across the raft. The beastmen were nowhere to be seen, but he heard screams fading quickly behind them.

"Are you hurt?" Nella Bye was shouting as the raft scudded and bucked along the river's descending stair. Blindly she reached for him, but he could not answer. He was still choking out mud and slapping at his tunic, for something wriggled against his chest.

Boom, boom. . .boom. And then they sailed into open space, fell, and landed with a splash.

He tore open his shirt, and the hot, slimy worm wriggled out and splashed into the water. He leaned over the edge and emptied back into the stream the sludge he had swallowed.

Eventually the raft slowed, and he realized that the thudding had stopped. Nella Bye embraced his aching frame. The fog had thickened again, and he could no longer see the other passengers.

With a jerk, the front of the raft tipped up as a heavy hand seized the back end. Jordam's face appeared, dripping black sludge, his teeth gleaming through it. He pulled himself up among the other passengers.

"Jordam," the ale boy coughed. "The deeper river. We found it."

Jordam's right arm was folded, cradling something that squirmed and kicked against his chest.

It was a hairy, bloodied figure. A newborn creature. And Jordam's furious expression made it clear that no questions would be welcome.

The light began to change. The fog was warmer and painted with flickers of red light. Torchlight.

Red faces emerged, ghostly in the mist. Figures standing on the riverbank. And then he heard glad voices, shouts, and other voices answering farther away.

"rrBel Amicans," Jordam whispered. Then he uttered something like a laugh. "Look, O-raya's boy! They made rafts!"

The rafts of the escaping Bel Amicans—eleven of them—were spread across the bank of this vast, swirling pool under a high, arched ceiling. They were larger, stronger, better, built by prisoners who had learned the craft back at their home in the Rushtide Inlet. The slaves had patched them together from wagon planks and scraps they had collected from the Cent Regus plunder.

Some Bel Amicans had found this place during their years of labor, and the idea for a daring escape had begun. After the ale boy and Jaralaine had visited them, their courage had grown. They had collected the pieces slowly and buried them until rare occasions when they could work unobserved. In the Cent Regus Core's unrest, their guards long absent, they had dared to make a hurried descent to the water, hoping it would offer them a way to escape.

"This water," Nella Bye sighed. "It smells like high, snow-crowned mountains." Others agreed.

The ale boy watched the frothy spill of the falls that had delivered them here. Behind that rushing curtain, there was a deep and echoing darkness—a wider river pouring out into this pool. Those waters were warmer and cleaner than the current that flowed from above ground. And he was certain that if they could move upstream, they'd pass the place where Jordam had found him at the bottom of the abyss.

One of the Bel Amicans had even caught a fish that almost looked fit to eat; he was pulling off a few scales to see if the meat might be good.

More than fifty Bel Amicans, clad in rags and skins as frail as autumn leaves in midwinter, welcomed the Abascar survivors into their midst as if they were old friends. Though the beastmen had kept them separate, their sufferings united them.

Some embraced the boy who had visited them with food and water in days past, and their leader, Mad Batey, tousled his hair. Batey, a muscular builder who had been captured with Partayn several years earlier, also opened his arms to embrace Jordam, but the beastman turned and moved to the edge of the crowd, settling by the swirling pool with the fussing newborn.

Mad Batey rubbed at his chin. "Shouldn't he kill that thing?"

Kar-balter agreed. "It'll be bloodthirsty. Or miserable. Both, probably. That is, if it doesn't die by morning."

Batey's mind was an engine of perpetual plotting, seemingly powered by the fitful flexing of his grey-stubbled jaw. Chewing problems apart, he had planned his way out of circumstances that would have made anyone else despair. When he got an idea, his eyes went wild and white, all the brighter for the blue stripes tattooed beneath them, and the scar lines from his left eyebrow to behind his left ear deepened. "We could send it on ahead to test for traps and predators."

"Jordam knows what he's doing," said the ale boy, eying the Bel Amican rafts with rekindled hope. The Bel Amicans had pillaged the abandoned loot in the

Cent Regus's unguarded treasure caves. He saw crudely fashioned spears, quivers of arrows, and old shields emblazoned with symbols from both Bel Amica and Abascar.

"These are some of the best Cent Regus spoils." Batey poked through a pile. He explained how back in Bel Amica he had made a name for himself as a metalworker, buying scrap and crafting it into something useful. "In the Core," he said, "I've learned more about building things than anywhere."

He stopped with an exclamation of delight and, pawing through the salvage, pocketed a few coins, his mustache twitching. "Very rare," he muttered. "Fetch a fortune back home. They'll buy me and my lady Raechyl a nice place with a view of the sea." He glanced over his shoulder and exchanged a smile with a tall, elegant woman.

Batey went on to describe with pleasure the weapons they'd collected—stone-flingers for heavy stones, primitive arrowcasters, wrist-daggers for close combat, and decoy daggers with hilts that would bristle with razorpins when seized.

"It's hard to believe you found us in time," he said, sitting down to scratch his chin's grey grizzle and comb his thick mustache. "We were almost on our way. We might not have dared it without you, Rescue." He opened his broad, hardened hands in gratitude. "You walked through fire to help us." He nodded to Jordam. "Beastmen bow to you. The queen of Abascar asked you for counsel. And they say you called down power from the sky that ruined most of the Strongbreed army. We were all too afraid, too beaten down for hope. But you…" He paused and cleared his throat. "You brought us enchanted waters. You gave us dreams of what might yet be possible. So tell me, what do we do now?"

The question astonished the boy. He looked around at the talkative crowd and began to notice that all of them were glancing in his direction as if sure he was about to make some kind of speech. Even Jordam turned to watch him.

Mist swirled around the falls at the dark mouth of the warmer river.

I have nothing to say, he thought. *I'm not a leader. I don't know how. All I knew was to find the people in trouble and help them out. What more can I do?*

"This," he heard himself say. "This deeper river—it's warmer."

"Yes," said Batey. "Yes, it is."

"And slower. Shallower."

"Seems that way."

"So...we can probably row against it."

"In shifts," said Batey, "yes. But why not go downstream? It must reach the sea eventually, and then we can travel up the coast."

"Well." The boy felt himself straining for words. "This water is warmer. And cleaner. It comes...from somewhere else. A better place. Probably closer to Bel Amica."

Batey nodded. "Harder work, but it could take us home faster."

The boy considered the debris-strewn bank. "There's green on these branches. And there..." A dark cavebird hopped onto a rock and ogled him with bulging eyes. "What do cavebirds eat?"

"Berries. Green leaves. They must have ways to get out." Batey grinned, his eyes flaring. "Oh, to bring my Raechyl back up to the sun-touched skin of the world."

"So," the boy continued, "that bird probably came from above ground, somewhere north of here." He pointed to the flow that came from beneath the falls.

"If we go far," said Batey, "we might find water clear enough to drink."

"Or bathe in," said Nella Bye. "Trust me, if we're going to spend much time crowding these rafts, we'll all need to wash up soon."

The cheer in their voices encouraged the ale boy, and they began to push the rafts out into the water. But then he caught sight of Jordam. The beastman was muttering to himself at the water's edge, the newborn in one hand, the other hand pressed to his forehead where the browbone scar remained. The boy went down to sit beside him.

Jordam lifted the perfect skeleton of a strange eel.

"The baby... It ate that?"

"rrFast."

The boy was amazed. "He looks like a normal baby. Except for the webbed toes. And the grey stripes." He frowned. "And the face. Kinda like a frog's, I guess. A frog with a striped, fuzzy mask on. Those teeth look sharp. But otherwise..."

"rrFast," said Jordam again. "Go fast, O-raya's boy. rrKeep torches fired. Watch for feelers."

"Of course. But you'll help us with that."

Jordam looked away at nothing but shadows. "rrMust find Abascar's king. Must...must...say things."

"You're...not coming with us?"

"rrMust find the Abascar king." He pulled his hand from his forehead and touched his chest. "It burns. Here."

"You come with us." The boy spoke it like a command. "You can find Cal-raven later."

Jordam looked at the striped face peering up at him. "Bel might have water. Water from O-raya's well. rrMust try to help...help this."

The boy looked at Jordam's face as though seeing it for the very first time.

This was the beastman who had hunted him on Baldridge Hill. But that creature had worn a fearsome and furious mask of appetite and anger, rough with scars and framed in bristling black hair. That face seemed to fade before his eyes. In its place he saw the broad, rugged visage of a powerful man, his flesh a map of islands red and brown on a grey sea. Those eyes, once blazing coals, had cooled. Bulging tusks had crumbled and fallen away. The hands that held the mewling infant were not the clawed and hairy hands of a forest ape; the barbs and bristles had disappeared, revealing large, soft, red flesh that held the newborn with tenderness.

A flicker caught the corner of his eye, and he looked up. High on a jutting ledge, shimmering figures gazed down at them. *Northchildren.*

On an impulse, he spoke a strange name aloud: "Deuneroi."

The figures faded at once, as if alarmed they'd been visible.

"rrWhat's that?"

"Nothing," said the boy, but now he was anxious. And angry. He could sense a change coming, and he did not like what he felt.

A shout drew his attention. Kar-balter, having climbed up on the pillage, brandished a bottle in the air like a prize. "I don't believe it!" he crowed. "Abascar ale!" The scattered prisoners began to crowd around him.

The ale boy put his arms around Jordam. "Don't go," he whispered.

He felt the familiar brush of the beastman's hand upon his head. "rrNo sadness," said Jordam. "You know the way now. You've...grown."

"Jordam, I haven't told you. Auralia. The Northchildren told me that she's come back. When I get above ground again, I'm going to find her."

"O-raya?" Jordam's eyes grew wide. "The caves. rrBy the lake."

"Yes," said the boy. "Will you look for her? If you find her, will you keep her safe?"

"rrFind O-raya. I keep her safe. Never leave her."

"I'll look for you there. When I've fulfilled my promise to them." The ale boy, eyes closed, felt a tremor run through him. In his memory the Keeper loomed in a whirlwind beneath House Abascar. It was taking Auralia up in its hands, lifting her while the Northchildren watched. He grasped the edge of Jordam's wrist so tightly that the beastman grunted. "I've gotta tell you something. In case...in case I don't see you again."

"rrNo bad talk."

"Listen."

Clutching the bundle to his chest, Jordam leaned low to the ale boy's ear.

"Not even 'Ralia knows my real name," said the boy. Then he pressed his forehead against the rough bristles above Jordam's ear and whispered.

The beastman grunted. "But...why?"

As the boy began to whisper again, Nella Bye arrived at his side and took his hand. "Come along, Rescue. You were an ale boy once. If anybody knows what to do with this bottle that Kar-balter's found, it's you."

Pulled toward the crowd where Kar-balter still held the bottle high like a trophy, the ale boy took one look back to wave farewell to the beastman.

But Jordam was already gone, beginning his long, last climb through the dark of the Cent Regus Core.

8

FRAUGHTENWOOD

"You lookin' to die?" came a boy's voice from the base of the tree. "Everybody's in except you."

Losing his balance on a high bough, Krawg caught the branch above his head and held on, wheezing. His shoulder bag full of knuckle-nut shells clattered as it swung against his side.

"The whistle's blown." It was that bothersome merchant boy Wynn, standing with his hands on his hips. His younger sister, Cortie, one of the few who had narrowly escaped slaughter in the calamitous escape from Cent Regus slavery, was strapped to his back. "Everyone's waiting."

"I heard, you intolerable skeeter-bite."

"You're ungrateful," Wynn growled. "I single-handedly saved House Bel Amica from a swarm of beastmen. Or have you forgotten?"

"Forgotten? It's the only story you know how to tell. Bigger every time too. A swarm? Single-handedly?"

Since his heroic burst of courage in Bel Amica that had put rampaging beastmen to sleep in an instant, the boy had become increasingly unruly. Praise had inflated his pride. He objected when he was denied a place in secret conferences, when he was not given assignments with soldiers, when he was named among "the children." Tabor Jan had assigned him to protect the Abascar people who remained in Bel Amica while this small company set out to find Cal-raven's foundation for New Abascar; but Wynn had sensed the charade. Insulted, he'd taken Cortie and stolen an Abascar colt from Bel Amican stables to make a reckless escape and catch up with Tabor Jan in the wild.

Most of the travelers had scrounged up sympathy. Wynn and Cortie had been orphaned in a beastman attack, after all. But Wynn's experience as a merchant's child made him see all encounters as competition, all people as threats, all exchanges as challenges to gain the upper hand. *Poor fool,* thought Krawg. *So unlike Auralia. Did no one teach him how to play?*

"What're you pickin' knuckle-nuts for, old man?" Wynn barked. "There's nothin' worth eatin' in these krammin' woods."

"These krammin' woods," repeated Cortie, always amused by the rough speech of her elders. She rode in her brother's pack because her legs were still healing from her ordeal in the Cent Regus Core.

"They're not for eatin'," said Krawg. He split another nut between his teeth—*crrak!*—and spat it into his hand. The nut inside was rotten like the rest.

"Is the storyteller stuck?" asked Cortie.

"Of course not," the old man lied, edging his way along the bough toward the trunk. All the tree's branches were dry, dead, likely to snap. Rather than climb down to fetch the picker-staff he had dropped, he took to snatching clusters with his bare hands. He'd always found it a thrill to climb up to a view and a panic to climb back down.

He dropped the shell halves into his shoulder bag, then leaned to embrace the tree trunk and eased himself down a branch. Something squirmed underfoot. Flame engulfed his leg as a squealing puffdragon sprang from the branch.

Krawg seemed to take flight. His cloak billowed out around him, and he landed hard. The pop from his knees was as loud as nutshells cracking.

"Ow," he said.

"Ask him, Wynn!" Cortie whispered.

"Cortie's scared of Fraughtenwood," said Wynn. "She wants one of your stories."

It wasn't Cortie who looked scared. "Leave me alone, boy," Krawg muttered, "and I'll think one up for her."

It was unexpected to find his attempts at storytelling welcome, to learn that they were meaningful to some beyond himself. If this journey came to nothing else, and his name was known by few and soon forgotten, he would be grateful for having provided something that was, for a time, wanted.

"Tonight, Warney, I'll finally finish telling my very best tale," he murmured. "And you won't be here to learn it. That's a shame."

He'd been gnawing on the narrative since the tale of six tricksters had first appeared, unfurling like a scroll within his imagination, during a storytelling contest in the Mawrnash revelhouse. The story had surpassed his expectations, burning his voice to a rasp as his characters led him breathlessly along. But he hadn't reached the end. That Seer called Panner Xa, strangely enraged, had seized him by the throat as if he were revealing secrets.

At times he'd grumbled over missed opportunities, ways he might have told the story better, giving characters more time to emerge in detail. There was no going back. Either the story would live on for those hearers, or it wouldn't.

But here was an audience who had not yet heard the story. Tonight he could tell it again and tell it better. There were no Seers here at the southern edge of Fraughtenwood to forbid him to reveal the story's conclusion.

Wynn led Krawg through a patch of trees that soldiers were tapping for flammable pitch—men and women of the Bel Amican escort sent by Queen Thesera to protect the company. "Evenin', storyteller." One of those archers—a high-spirited woman named Deanne—nodded to him as if he were someone of importance.

"Told you they were waiting for you," grumbled Wynn.

The travelers gathering around the fire looked in Krawg's direction with some admiration. Bowlder, his chin set on the heavy firewood pile he was carrying into the camp, grinned at him like an excited child. Krawg's frustration with Wynn dissolved. He gripped the picker-staff as if to wring courage from it.

As they settled in around the smokeless fire, he noticed that almost everyone held an unlit branch or torch. Fear of Deathweed followed them like a cloud of skeeter-flies. The deadly tendrils had remained unseen since they left Bel Amica behind, but the memory of sudden attacks and lost companions was still blood-red in their minds. Gashes like scars from a lash marked the ground in places, assuring them that they were within reach of the scourge. They would be ready with fire should it come.

"Not yet, Krawg," said Tabor Jan, a shadow at the edge of the firelight. "We're still missing one."

He wondered if Milora was the straggler again, but no. From the captain's distress, Krawg sensed it was Brevolo. Many had rumored that the captain would marry that formidable woman back in Bel Amica. She'd been quiet and disgruntled on this journey, and Krawg had heard her complain about leaving.

But there had been other rumors too—rumors that Tabor Jan was looking back toward Bel Amica too often.

Brevolo had only spoken to Krawg once, at the conclusion of his last fireside story, a dramatic tale of a girl whose kindness helped merchants survive a hard winter. The character's tricks and tactics in foiling monsters and thieves had delighted Brevolo. But Krawg had concluded it without resolving all of its questions, including the fate of its hero. This bothered Brevolo. But Frits, the master glassmaker, had patted Krawg on the back, perhaps a little too firmly. "Not bad," he had said. "And don't give in to those who want explaining. Questions are the life of the story. They keep us humble."

Frits sat on the other side of the fire beside Milora on a broad, flat stone. "We all thought she was his daughter, Warney," Krawg whispered. "But now I know different." He wished he could shine the shadows from Milora's downcast face.

"Did I hear a button wren?" mused Frits. "We must be close to home."

"Button wren, button wren, sing us back home." On the ground by Frits's feet, his granddaughter Obrey leaned back against Milora's shins. "When we get back, we'll have to make something for the forest. Something to, I don't know. . .brighten it up."

"Why bother?" Milora's question had a bitter tone, and she stripped the seeds from a reed. Frits looked as if he'd been stung. His shoulders sank, and he looked very old.

"Well..." Obrey scowled, searching for a reply. "Button wrens don't say 'why bother.'"

Milora tied the reed in a knot. "A song like that makes no sense in this dead place."

Obrey didn't want to have this argument. She started whistling to herself, playing with silvery vawn scales, poking holes in them with pins, and threading her long yellow hair through them so that her braids sparkled.

"So like Auralia, Warney. In some ways. But she's too young." Instead of sitting down in the space others had cleared for him, Krawg half circled the fire, lifted his shoulder bag, and scattered some scraps he'd pulled from the knuckle-nut tree on the blanket draped across Obrey's lap.

The girl stared at the nutshells, moss-ribbons, and lace-leaves, then looked up. "What're these for?"

He shrugged. "Thought they looked like pieces to a puzzle."

"She's not a trained monkey," Milora muttered. "Obrey plays when she's inspired."

"I'm not givin' her a job," he said. "But if she can make Fraughtenwood look a little better... Well, it's such a grim and shivery place. Maybe a spot of beauty would do everybody some good."

Obrey jumped up and set about bouncing. "Make something with me, Milora!"

"Beauty," said Milora, "is very laborious."

Krawg leaned in close. "It'll come back to you."

Milora's eyes narrowed. "Is this some kind of test?"

Yes, Krawg thought. "Never," he said.

As Obrey offered her some of the nutshells, Milora's hands tightened into fists. "I'm not a child," she murmured, looking away so that he was left studying the short silverbrown hair on the back of her head.

Maybe I'm imagining things, he thought. *Maybe I just miss Auralia too much.*

"Obrey," said Frits, "come here. I'll play with you."

"Nah." Obrey dropped the pieces on the flickering dust. "Now I'm not in the mood."

"Brevolo's here," somebody whispered. And there she was at the edge of the light, holding the leash for King Cal-raven's woodsnout, Hagah, who panted and whimpered anxiously.

"Story time," said Obrey, and in her eager gaze he could sense how badly she wanted to escape all of this tension.

Relieved that Brevolo had emerged from the trees, Tabor Jan stepped into the fireside circle.

He addressed the travelers with feigned confidence, encouraging them to retreat to their tents as soon as sleep seemed possible. The next day's road through Fraughtenwood would tax them. They'd push through the dense undergrowth that had given these woods such a troubling name. There would be leech-bogs. Tree-trolls were very rare, but thieving rat-monkeys might pester them from hanging mosses. "If the chatterflies buzz in your ears," he said, "Say-ressa can give you oil to discourage them."

Even as he spoke, he was mightily distracted. He'd assigned Brevolo to the team that would sneak back along the trail to ensure they hadn't been followed. She'd gone farther than he'd intended, perhaps tempted to return to Bel Amica.

"If we make good ground," he continued, "we'll be free of Fraughtenwood in just a few days. We will be walking where no one from House Abascar has walked in generations."

He bowed to Krawg, backed out of the circle, and sat down against a fallen tree. Brevolo bound Hagah's leash to a low tree branch, then leaned against Tabor Jan. He draped his arm around her.

As Krawg began his story, Tabor Jan gazed at Brevolo's fire-lit face and then down to the freckles at the base of her throat. She looked beautiful and dangerous, her dark, wild mane typically strewn with leaves and scraps from the forest. He traced her thick eyebrows with his fingertip. She did not look at him. Her eyes flared with unspoken anger, as if she had hoped for a fight but found no opportunity.

"Remind me," she said softly. "What do we hope to find up there?"

"A house with King Cal-raven on the throne," he said without hesitation. "A house where these people can be safe enough to begin families again. A house with a solid wall that will keep out the troubles south of us."

"Yes."

"And a wall to the north to keep out any mysterious curse."

"Yes, again."

"I want to be safe, Brevolo. Safe so we can build without interruption. And I have plans of my own." He drew a slow spiral on her cheek.

She ran her fingertips down his arm. "Sometimes it seems all you think about is getting Cal-raven onto a new throne. Have you imagined the events that come after?"

He was surprised.

Brevolo had always loved a good fight and reveled in a wild gallop on a vawn or a horse. But since Deathweed had killed her sister, Bryndei, in the Blackstone Caves, she'd become more mercurial. She wanted to punish somebody. During their Bel Amican stay, Brevolo had joined the patrols of Captain Ryllion, whose charm and violence had distracted and inspired her.

Tabor Jan had begun to feel he was fading from her attention. He was a part of a world full of painful memories and loss. She might leave him behind.

As Krawg went on, telling the story of the strange magician who had sewn up dolls with minds and wills of their own, Tabor Jan traced lines around the ridges of Brevolo's knuckles, where Abascar tradition would require a marriage tattoo. She would not miss this suggestion.

"So you do have plans." Her voice sounded suddenly fragile. Fearful. "Can it still be possible?"

It had taken some persuasion to get her to come along on this journey. He wanted to find a way back to the feisty, stormy romance they had shared before she lost Bryndei. He hoped to ask for her hand in marriage and create a bond that would make them both stronger.

But did he want this for her good? Or his own? Did he want it because it was the best plan or because any plan seemed a comfort in this disappointing world? The king's disappearance had raised so many uncertainties. Tabor Jan had led this party along Cal-raven's charted course, as if by putting that plan in motion he would draw the king out of the darkness.

"I will not let fear rule my decisions," he said aloud, surprising himself.

Brevolo released a shuddering sigh. "I had wondered," she whispered, "if your eagerness to lead this mission came from fear."

"I feared what would become of us in Bel Amica," he murmured. "Abascar was dissolving like sugar in...like salt in a..." He had never been very good with poetic turns of phrase.

"I think you were afraid of more than what was happening to Abascar. Something unsettled you there."

He pressed his fingertip more determinedly against the back of her hand as if he could engrave the tattoo on her skin by sheer willpower. He would not let himself think of Queen Thesera's daughter. Cyndere lived in a different world, with different demands and responsibilities. She belonged to House Bel Amica. He had been a fool even to consider the possibility.

He closed his eyes.

"I feared," he said determinedly, "that we would not separate ourselves from the Bel Amicans. I feared we'd never see all that we had fought for. Consider what you and I might do for these people, Brevolo."

Our family could rise as a pillar of New Abascar.

"And you?" he asked hesitantly. "What would you hope to find up there?"

"Room to raise an army," she said. "The great army that you deserve to lead, Captain."

He looked at her, half expecting to find that she was joking. But before he could see her expression clearly, she was kissing him. Then she whispered, "Forgive me. I let myself become distracted by a liar. I feel like a fool. I've just been so...so helpless since..."

"I know." He touched her first tears as if they were rare gemstones.

"I wanted to be part of something strong. But when I saw you walking with the Bel Amican royals after you spoiled the conspiracy, I woke up. And when I heard you were planning this journey, I remembered how rare it is to find a principled man. A man faithful to his friends and to his house. A man who suffers so that others will be safe. A man who is everything my father failed to be. I saw that I still have something to lose. Someone I want to protect."

Krawg's story went on. He spoke of the girl sewn by the magician, the girl who came to life and flew. The listeners were enthralled.

Tabor Jan looked at the glassmakers. Obrey was grinning as if the story were coming true before her eyes. But as she listened, her hands were busy. She'd taken a branch and planted it in the ground. In each rising, coiling offshoot, she had set a stick of wax, making a candlestand out of materials she'd found in the Cragavar.

What would it take to bring these artists to Abascar? To give them enough peace that they could remember how to play?

Milora was distracted—transfixed—by Krawg's narrative. Her face seemed bruised, troubled as the old Gatherer went on. When Krawg spoke of the girl flying back into her maker's arms, she stood, face wet with tears, and slipped away. Frits watched her go, visibly worried.

Tabor Jan did not go after her. Brevolo was asleep on his arm, and she was warm. He decided to wait awhile and quietly pulled bits of bark and insect wings from her hair.

Just as Krawg reached the part where the disgruntled young boy rebelled, breaking away from his maker and taking a group of children with him beyond the border of safety, a sound began to spread through the boughs over their heads. Rain. In this thick cover of branches, no one had noticed clouds coming down from the north.

Brevolo awoke with a start, and Tabor Jan stood. "Time for the tents, everyone. You'll have to dream the rest of the story." At the rising chorus of complaints, he added, "And I've said it before—Krawg needs shorter stories. A few characters we like, a few we don't, and the bad ones are beaten at the end. That would help us sleep."

Krawg growled and groaned. "Ballyworms! I'll never finish this story. And I want to know how it ends!"

In his tent Krawg tossed and turned.

Every time sleep took hold, he saw Cal-raven fighting a monster in a cave, Warney strung up by his ankles in trouble, and Auralia locked in a prison, waiting for rescue.

"Auralia!" he shouted. That drew the attention of Jes-hawk, who was on patrol.

"Help me," the archer said, restraining the excited, slobbering Hagah on a leash. "Frits says Milora's wandered off again."

Krawg knew Jes-hawk's deep distrust of strangers and his rage against deserters.

Jes-hawk gave him a crooked torch, and they decided to walk a wide circle around the camp, going in opposite directions. Krawg hadn't gone far when something stopped him.

"Pssst."

It was Obrey, hiding just out of the light, huddled at the base of a tree. "Don't tell the soldier," she said, "but I'm looking for Milora."

"Oh no you're not," Krawg insisted. "You're goin' back to camp. Leave the lookin' to me. What's she doin', runnin' away again? What's got her rotten as a winter plum?"

Obrey crawled out on all fours, cautious as a fox. "It's her memory. Sometimes it starts coming back. It scares her."

"Is that why she wouldn't play?"

Obrey sighed as if she were carrying the burdens of an adult. "She says it hurts too much—makin' things no one's got time to see. It makes her feel. . .invisible."

"I see."

Obrey stood, brushing off her hands. "And when somebody does slow down and really look, well...they always say nice things. But then they start askin' for stuff. Gifts and favors."

Yes, yes, that's how it was for Auralia. Krawg felt trapped. He wanted to back away, wanted to lean in and ask questions.

"One woman asked her for a statue. She was a small, scowling, jealous woman, and when Milora made the sculpture, it looked just right. The woman smashed it."

Krawg nodded, amazed. *It has to be Auralia,* he thought.

"Most of the time, though, she says that people are just waiting for her to find a man. As if that's all that matters." Obrey crumpled her face as if trying to imitate Milora's expression. "Why is it that way? And who made it so?"

Those two questions, spoken in that particular tone, struck Krawg like a slap in the face. He staggered, and sparks rained down from the torch.

"There's no man alive who deserves her," Obrey sulked. "Nobody lets her be herself. Nobody sees her."

Krawg remembered Milora's confession about Cal-raven. "Surely there's somebody."

Obrey scowled forcefully and turned away. "If there was, I wouldn't tell."

Krawg looked off into the darkness. "You're a special kinda friend, that she'd feel safe to say such stuff to you. Have you watched her make things?"

"She only makes stuff in certain...conditions."

"Like?"

"Quiet. No interruptions. Nobody payin' attention. Play, she says. It's hard to do."

"Is that why she wanders off?"

Obrey folded her arms. "You're just tryin' to spoil things, aren't you? I'm going back to my tent." She stomped away.

"I found her last time." Gripping the torch, he moved out into the dark.

At first all he heard was the occasional unsettling creak, like a door hinge, among the branches overhead. But then an unnatural clatter, like teeth shaken in a bowl, attracted his attention. He raised the torch and stalked through the tangled brush, cringing as his passage sent nocturnal crawlers—rabbit-sized crickets and hundred-legged serpents—scuttling and slithering through the ground cover.

What he found made him forget his purpose.

Hanging from a low branch, a mobile of seven crisscrossing twigs, carefully balanced, spun slowly. Krawg's knuckle-nut half shells hovered from strings at the end of all fourteen spokes. They fluttered on leafy wings. The shells were hung with the cavities down, and inside their concave shape hung tiny pebbles. Each winged half shell clattered like a bell.

Just below that, at the end of a blunt, eight-fingered branch, hung a scrap of twisted, textured bark. Yellow flower petals were pressed into the bark's swirling grooves to create bright spirals and lines. At intervals along the winding yellow line, the wood was embedded with gemstones as if to mark treasure along a trail.

Krawg had no idea what it meant. But it all seemed to hum with meaning.

He reached out to take the bark from the branch. The eight fingers of the branch tightened their grip on it. Krawg scowled. He took the piece by the edge again.

The wooden fingers opened, releasing the bark. Then they lunged forward and caught Krawg's forearm in a piercing grip.

He yelped and threw himself backward. The branch, holding him fast, broke from the trunk like an arm tearing free at the shoulder. But its clutch of sharp twigs tightened.

Krawg clawed at the wooden hand, trying to tear it free. Its sharp fingertips pierced his skin. He roared and rolled toward the smoldering torch, then waved the torn end of the attacking arm into its flame. The claws came out of his wrist, and he scrambled free, clasping his hand over the bloodied punctures.

Back at the camp, there was a commotion. Someone had heard him. Hagah began to bark.

Krawg took the torch and scanned the ground for his attacker. He did not have to find it—it came running for him, its fingers sturdy as insect legs, dragging its broken-branch body along.

He thrust with the torch as if the flame were a dagger. The aggressor reared up, twig-legs flailing, as fire engulfed its spindly wooden spine. It tumbled onto its back, and from its kicking legs came a high-pitched whine like the sizzle of a roast as something within burned into clouds black as oil smoke. Then the twigs curled inward like a dead spider's legs. The creature crumbled into ash, leaving a stench in the air.

Krawg looked up at the vast ceiling of interlaced branches above him. And now it seemed that all of them were restless, like fighters cracking their knuckles before a riot. He began to tiptoe back toward the camp. A few steps later he gave up any concern about quiet, hurrying in leaping strides.

9

Cesylle's Regret

Cesylle had never ascended more difficult stairs than those that led him up Queen Thesera's tower on this, the twentieth day since he became a wanted man.

Sought by soldiers throughout House Bel Amica's alleys, markets, and evacuated farms, and hunted by east-riding patrols in the Cragavar forest, he took every step with a growing sense that it might be his last. The air weighed heavy as water.

But ascend he did, with a bundle of maps—diagrams of the city's tunnel systems—rolled under his arm and the hood of a black wall-patcher's cloak pulled up to darken his face. His mind was set. He would visit the chambers he had shared with Emeriene and their sons. Risky, yes. Probably a death walk. But if he could warn them about the next stage of the Seers' plot, perhaps they would escape Bel Amica with their lives.

He passed a cacophonous corridor, a spring of noise fed by gossip that flowed from the sisterlies' chambers. As Thesera's attendants readied carts of supplies for her imminent tour of the new island colonies, he did not hear Emeriene shouting instructions—only anxious chatter about the recent tensions. With criminals on the loose, assassinations foiled, and a conspiracy narrowly averted, Bel Amica was in shock.

Someone had drawn curtains aside from the window at the corridor's end, affording him a glimpse of the morning fog that muffled the chants of protesters far below. Some Bel Amicans were outraged that Queen Thesera had pronounced the Seers' potions illegal. Their refrain—"Restore Bel Amica!"—was a demand that the queen make them comfortable, not a cry for real healing. They wanted to go back to a way of life that had pleased them, ignoring any damage such comforts had caused. So they eagerly embraced any lies about the queen's character. It was easier to slander and complain than to inconvenience themselves with the truth.

Many of these chanters had been forced into the city from their farms. Deathweed struck Bel Amican pastures and barns and disrupted trade routes every day. Herds of chumps and grazers vanished overnight. Traveling merchants failed to arrive for appointed trade.

So much dissension, Cesylle thought. *We'll fall quickly when the Seers unleash their final curse.*

In the neighboring spire, the Heir's Tower, a man and a woman sang a delicate harmony. Cesylle recognized Partayn's melodic tones. House Bel Amica had rejoiced to learn of the heir's return from slavery. He'd been freed by the beastman that his widowed sister, Cyndere, had befriended and reformed. He'd reclaimed his prominent place.

Thinking Partayn was dead, the Seers had positioned Captain Ryllion to be Cyndere's suitor and Bel Amica's future king. With Partayn's return, Cyndere was no longer heir to the throne. So the Seers had prepared a more violent endeavor, conspiring to unleash beastmen during a royal ceremony. Behind the scenes Ryllion would slay Queen Thesera, Partayn, and Cyndere. But then he would appear before the crowd and slaughter the rampaging beastmen in full view, thus presenting himself as House Bel Amica's savior. By merit of the people's gratitude, the throne would be his.

But this plan too had failed. Cyndere and Partayn, with the help of Abascar meddlers, had uncovered the conspiracy even as the knives were sharpened. The Seers had fled into their Keep, sealing it with sorcery, while soldiers sought Ryllion and Cesylle, whose lies and treachery were condemned.

The song Cesylle heard from the Heir's Tower was a love song—a sail-maker's lament. The sail-maker sounded distraught, for if he stitched a perfect sail, the ship would carry his true love far away to work for months on an island. But if he did not sew a binding line, storms would overcome his lover's ship. She might perish in the Mystery Sea.

The woman's voice answered. She sang of how every stitch in her lover's sails reminded her of his love. She declared her faith that these sails would carry her ship safely to the island and back. And then she sang that every wave breaking against the prow reminded her of her lover's sighs.

How long has it been, he wondered, *since I heard Emeriene's voice?*

Then horns and lutes! Stringed instruments strummed in steady percussion, simulating the incoming tide—a new, compelling sound.

What house has a king who sings in his tower when he should be attending to matters of state? Clods! When Partayn becomes king, he'll make a queen of some swooning admirer. A head full of barnacles, the fool.

Cesylle arrived at the doorstep of a suite, and he paused. The door was unguarded, which surprised him. What is more, it seemed unfamiliar. He glanced up the stairway. *Can I have forgotten? Has it been that long since my departure for Mawrnash?*

He and Emeriene had painted their door together, according to tradition, the morning after their wedding. Emeriene had chosen bright yellow. This door was a fierce shade of red.

A message, is it?

He wiped his sweating neck with his sleeve. Boot scuffs marred a dusting of sharpenweed scraps, where guards had pipe-smoked long hours while they waited for him to appear and justify their vigilance. Had Emeriene dismissed them?

They must assume that Ryllion and I are off at sea. Or hiding in the Cragavar. Or dead.

He slipped the flexible wire from his sleeve and shoved it around the door's edge. Its hooked tip caught the latch bar. He pulled the wire up, heard the bar release. He'd done this before, planting mawrn crystals in chambers throughout the house for the Seers' surveillance.

Clods, I'm a fool. They'll be waiting for me inside.

As if it suddenly recognized him, the door opened. Curtained chamber doors wavered in surprise. After a moment he stepped inside and closed the door quietly.

The song in the Heir's Tower continued while Cesylle took silent steps through the curtains and into the sitting chamber. The couches were clean, pillows neatly arranged, blankets folded. If Emeriene had replaced him, there was no hint of it. The mawrn crystals and the colorful liquor bottles in which he had concealed them were gone, of course—part of Queen Thesera's mandatory housecleaning to rid Bel Amica of the Seers' spy-stones.

Clever girl, Emeriene. You knew they were watching. I'm glad. I don't want to be watched anymore.

Even so, Cesylle could not relax. He had lived with the Seers too long. They had planned to fill the Expanse with mawrn, that they might watch the world. He had managed the mawrn mine's schedules and money, keeping careful records of how much mawrn was taken from the crater, believing he would earn privileges and power. Now he knew the value of a Seer's promise. He'd seen them disregard and abandon Ryllion, their most passionate servant, in an instant.

From the roll of maps, Cesylle withdrew the parchment on which he had scribbled what would probably be his last words to Emeriene and their sons: *Get out of Bel Amica. The Seers will release a new curse. Worse than beastmen and Deathweed. Sail away swiftly. I'm sorry.*

He folded it and placed it on the table, then shoved the maps behind the couches. Sitting down, he breathed deeply to quell the shaking.

The smooth stone floor was busy with chalk drawings. He recognized his sons' frenzied imaginations. But he saw no sketches of himself nor of the Seers he'd taught them to admire. Instead, he saw images of Cyndere with a flaming arrow set to her bow.

They hate me. And why not? I placed them in the care of liars and destroyers. He kicked a slippered toe at the image of a beastman, drawn in such familiar detail that it could only have come from Cyndere's hand. Who else would draw a Cent Regus monster as if it bore some dignity? *Maybe she can save my boys.*

And there—his sons had drawn their mother. Emeriene, her leg wrapped in a cast, held a bright red arrowcaster. She looked heroic.

He admired the likeness a long time. The large eyes beneath thin eyebrows. The tiny red mouth. Her stature, small as a girl, but seductive and strong. Her feisty smile. He had provoked Emeriene just to distract her from her tasks and to become the subject of her beautiful gaze.

It has been so long since I looked at her—really looked at her.

Ryllion had looked at Emeriene too. But Cesylle had fixed a card game and won the chance to woo her first. With the help of Seers' potions, he had dissolved Emeriene's resistance and replaced it with a passion that seemed to come from something outside herself. Tears had run down her face when they kissed, born of bewilderment rather than the joy he would have preferred. In less than two years' time, she'd given him two boys. But any love she'd had for him was gone.

"I meant to earn enough to make things better tomorrow," he said. "I lost sight of today."

In the remaining mirror—a tall glass oval in an ornate wooden frame—he saw a figure haggard and worn. How ugly he would seem to her now. His eyes were yellow as yolks in black eggs. His bruises made a bandit's mask, the marks of managing Mawrnash through a thousand nights, kept awake by the Seers' fierce elixirs.

In a feeble rehearsal he whispered, "Forgive me."

"You're joking."

She appeared in the mirror, standing just behind him, arrowcaster raised—an illustration come to life.

He laughed softly and leaned forward to grasp the mirror's wooden frame. "I thought you might be waiting."

The arrow went straight through his right wrist, pinning him to the frame. As he cried out, his knees buckled, and he hung from the spike, seething and shouting and trying to stand.

"Where's Ryllion?" roared Emeriene.

Blood burned down Cesylle's arm. "Clods! I've come to save you!"

"We're already saved! Where's Ryllion?" She advanced, notching another arrow to the caster's string. He felt the arrow's tip against his temple, and he closed his eyes.

"Ryllion's dead. We ran. He got ahead of me. I found him. He'd been tortured. Malefyk Xa had him out by the lake."

"The Seer?"

"Malefyk beat Ryllion. To death's edge. He would've killed the clodder. But I said I'd do it."

"You killed Ryllion?" One of her neat, thin eyebrows twitched.

"Threw his body off a cliff. So I could live. Live to make amends."

She laughed in disbelief. She had good reason. He was a weakling, and Ryllion was strong as a fangbear.

But it was almost true. The bloody scene had filled Cesylle with rage against the Seer and compassion for the Bel Amican champion. So, stepping between the two, he had asked to kill Ryllion. Malefyk Xa, perversely delighted, gave him a knife of mawrn crystal. But Cesylle had only pretended to run the blade through Ryllion's heart. Ryllion, perceiving the ruse, had suffered the shallow stab, flailed fiercely, and gone limp.

To the cold song of the Seer's laughter, Cesylle had dragged Ryllion away—no cargo had ever seemed so heavy—and vowed to cast the soldier to the rocks of Deep Lake's shore far below. "You must catch yourself," he'd whispered to Ryllion just before he shoved the heavy soldier over the precipice.

Had their deception succeeded? He had no proof. He'd seen Ryllion's body unmoving and bent at an unnatural angle while Malefyk Xa had hurried to look down upon it.

But that story would not help him now.

Emeriene's eyes narrowed. "If I ever see Ryllion again, I'm going to kill you both." She spoke each word neatly, as if clipping her nails. "Even our sons use your likenesses for target practice now. And they're not yet five years old." Then a sneer twisted her face. "Oh, did no one tell you? I've given them back their proper names—Cesyr and Channy. No one will again call them by the names that the Seers gave them. They have better teachers now."

So you're not going to kill me now. Cesylle felt darkness encroaching, and he wanted to pull it over himself like a blanket to escape the surging pain. "I would've run forever," he wheezed. "But I came to save you from the trap."

"You haven't heard?" She laughed sharply. "Thesera's banished the Seers. Tabor Jan and Cyndere spoiled their trap."

"Not that trap."

"Then what?"

"Malefyk Xa said that soon...they'll *turn them loose.*"

She drew back an inch. "Turn what loose? More beastmen?"

"No. Something else. Em, you have to let me go."

"Why?"

"They'll let me into the Keep. I can learn their secret plan."

"Why did you climb up here then?"

"To warn you," he gasped. "Go with the queen. Sail away with the boys. Get out."

Emeriene's lip quivered. "I can't trust you. Ryllion served the Seers, and he murdered Deuneroi. Who knows what you'll do?"

"I'm a fool," Cesylle wept. "A clodhead. I bet a bad gamble."

"No gamble as bad as your wager against Ryllion," she spat. "Your wager for me."

Cesylle recoiled as if she'd shot him again. "He...told you?"

"Know what's worse? I had no trouble believing him. I was just another prize. Then you sold our sons to the Seers for your advantage."

"Let me go."

"So you can take refuge in that Keep? And escape judgment? You'll be tried before Partayn and Cyndere. Nothing you can say will bring me back to you, Cesylle. Whatever bond we made, you broke it. I'll find a future for Cesyr and Channy. A life where they will forget"—she gestured to the window—"this place."

He slumped against the mirror frame. She was just a blurring silhouette. "Where will you go?"

"To find someone with a heart." Emeriene was staring out the window as if the wisping clouds carried new hope. "To see if that heart will still have me." Her steady grip on the caster gave way to a tremble.

"This heart," he sighed, "is failing. Before it stops, let me try to ruin the Seers."

Troubled waters slapped at the base of Bel Amica's rock, splashing one of the stone stages that had served as a loading dock until the harbor's evacuation.

"How long do we stay?" muttered a guard to Captain Henryk. He dipped an arrow in a pitch pot, ready to ignite it in the fire barrel between them if Deathweed surfaced. "Bel Amica's cut off. We can't survive here. We should go to the islands."

"This is home," said Henryk. "And if we can't stop Deathweed here, it'll follow us seaward."

The hood of his wall-patcher's cloak hiding his face, Cesylle listened to the officers as he waited at the foot of the stair that descended from the marketplace to this grim platform. As he gripped his bandaged wrist and fought to remain conscious, he watched the inlet's wavering surface.

Fire archers held a constant vigil around the rock, but the Bel Amicans' way of life was destroyed. The maze of wooden walkways and docks was gone. Seabulls, grawlafurrs, tidehounds—so many remarkable sea creatures had vanished, either snatched by the scourge or escaping to safer waters. His suspicions that the Seers controlled the Deathweed were growing into certainty.

"I hear that you can get everything on the islands," said the officer. "They're covered in fruit-bearing trees. Clouds of game birds darken the sky. We can live as we please. Might not even need any laws."

"I don't trust any society where people live as they please," muttered Henryk. "When people strive for such indulgence, they're speaking in greed—not out of concern for the crumb-pickers. Our new rulers are different. They know what we need."

"Some say Bel Amica's new rulers aren't fit for the task. Partayn's not training armies. He's helping beastmen and Abascar stragglers."

"Some say? Or you say?" Henryk rigged the cord of his arrowcaster. "If you want a fight, I'll give you one."

Their casters whipped up as a rootlike tentacle burst from the water. Unseeing, it lurched toward the harbor caves. A heartbeat later, it recoiled in spasms, scorched where the arrows had struck.

I should get myself on a boat and disappear, Cesylle thought.

Fingers of fierce cold burned his shoulder. Disguised in a sailor's raincloak, face wrapped in a scarf inside the cloak's hood, Malefyk Xa sat down beside him.

"I've no patience for delays," the Seer hissed. "I'm expected in the Keep. Did you recover the mawrn from the tower?"

"It was gone." That much, at least, was true. Cesylle pondered the lies that lay ahead. Malefyk Xa had a reputation as the most powerful and difficult of the six Seers. The others called him "the Rider," for he traveled the Expanse, making secret bargains. But here, deprived of the mawrn dust, he seemed weaker, anxious. The Keep would be full of mawrn.

"I serve my moon-spirit," said Cesylle, and this time that old refrain was bitter in his mouth. "And she won't let me forget—you promised me a winged steed. I told Emeriene we would fly. And I haven't failed you."

Malefyk's unblinking eyes searched him for dishonesty. "We've caged thirteen such creatures. One more remains. Our mawrn will spy it eventually. When we have them all, you might yet see the world from the clouds."

Cesylle clenched his teeth. "You failed to take Bel Amica's throne." His audacity was a gamble. He hoped to convince the Seer that he still clung to vain ambitions. Perhaps they would keep him alive like an old but dutiful dog.

Malefyk actually patted his head. "Come. See what I've captured in the wild. You've earned that much."

With discs of mawrn glass pressed to his eyes, Cesylle could see in the Keep's cold dark. And so he could discern the cold outlines of the Seers' laboratories. He felt as if his bones had turned to ice.

No fire or light was allowed in the Keep. The Seers hated fire, and light disrupted the distillation of their potions. The surfaces within this structure absorbed illumination, and he guessed they were stealing what they needed to maintain their mysterious adherence, then pushing out what was left. That would explain the nightly shimmer of the Keep's outer shell.

Cesylle, feeling bloodless, stumbling and afraid, followed Malefyk Xa through a high-ceilinged chamber that held nothing more than a spiky iron pole like an empty coatrack or a leafless tree.

Beyond this empty room, in a large vault of echoes, a great splinter of crystal floated like an icicle in a glass of water, suspended in the gloom by an invisible thread. Beneath it rested a dark, wooden box wrapped in wire.

Malefyk pushed him through into this space. Cesylle pulled the discs away from his eyes. Here, tepid light fell from a moon that appeared to seek escape from the fangs of a jagged window in the distant ceiling.

Malefyk Xa gestured to a facet of the crystal.

Cesylle had quietly studied the Seers' hatred of sunlight, their welcome of moonlight. It was why they valued him—his capacity for connecting one idea mechanically and usefully to another. Still, he remained mystified by the mawrn crystals and how they spoke to one another, invisibly connected so that the Seers could draw from one fragment the details of what occurred around another, as if every chip and fragment were an eye.

"A piece of the moon, our old watchtower," sighed Malefyk Xa. "We've created life, Cesylle. A living thing that obeys our laws and responds to our codes. We can cut it into pieces, crush it to dust, cast it across the Expanse, and absorb all that is worth knowing to increase the reach of our power."

A piece of the moon fallen to the Expanse. What a sight it must have been. Burning a hole in the Cragavar forest the size of that crater.

He looked at the Seer, then averted his gaze. *They are not like us. They are from somewhere else. Predators. Invaders. Bound to this, the source of their power.*

Malefyk Xa tapped the brightening facet with a fingernail. "I told you."

For a moment he had the strange sensation that the Keep had moved, settling in some faraway land, and this was a window opening onto a bizarre and unfamiliar scene. He saw the bars of three great cages. Behind them, three tremendous creatures—winged, horned, and wildly maned, more complex than any artist's speculation of ancient dragons—raged against the bars, striking them with their heads, breathing flame against them, clawing at the stone that anchored them above and below. One was serpentine, one lithe as a bearcat, and one scaled like something from the sea.

"We'll ride on their backs," said Malefyk Xa. "We'll rule the Expanse from the sky."

Cesylle forgot the pain paralyzing his arm. His imagination awoke, making connections as if it were made of shifting magnets. These fearsome shapes were familiar to him. He'd been made to feel ashamed of his childhood dreams, and he'd sought to stifle such visions in his sons.

"They fly above the clouds." There was awe in the Seer's voice. "They can appear as trees, as long grasses, as fire or storm. They are something altogether strange."

"Did you. . .make them?"

"We will," Malefyk whispered as if to himself. Then he growled, "We hunted them. We'll tame them and make them serve us. They've been nothing but a taunt. A scare. A nuisance. Interfering with our progress. He's just a braggart, sending these into the Expanse."

Who sent them? Cesylle's throat went dry. *They're going to kill me. Otherwise, he'd never reveal such things.*

"When we unleash our next surprise," said Malefyk Xa, grinning down at the box below the crystal, "those who live in the Expanse will wish they could go back to the days of the beastmen."

Cesylle would have asked about the box, but he was distracted by the scene within the crystal facet. A tiny shape had stepped into view—a hunchbacked figure, hands raised high, small as a beetle before the caged creatures. The creatures calmed, folding their wings, swallowing their fire.

"Who's that?"

The Seer shrugged. "Strongbreed. Such obedient beastmen, guarding our pests."

"Then why is he loosening the cage bars?"

Malefyk leaned in, teeth first, to breathe coldly against the crystal. His eyeballs swiveled, seeking focus. Ghastly laughter, devoid of all amusement, sputtered from his throat.

"Stonemastery," said Cesylle. "That fellow's letting the cage bars fall. He's releasing—"

His voice stopped. He stood immovable, his feet feeling glued to the floor. He saw the silver cap of Malefyk Xa's staff shining as it scorched the floor beside him. The air went out of his lungs, and he folded to the floor.

10

IMITYRI

The vawn slowed to a trot, then jerked at the reins in annoyance and stopped. Jayda Weese sensed the approach. "Is the Aerial sending a welcome party?" The bartender strapped on his belt with the old Defender's sword. Then he quickly threaded two cast-arrows into the braid of his yellow hair so he could reach them with ease. "I'm keeping my end of the bargain. Let's see what's left of their honor." He took a deep breath and stepped down from the small carriage onto the cool sand, where the world had been reduced to shadows and silver in the moonlight.

A distant lightning flash gave him details of the approaching horse and rider. The man was frail, no better than bones, slumped wearily forward so that his black, braided beard wagged before him. His desert horse was enormous and proud.

"Must not be worried about Deathweed down here," Weese shouted to the rider, "or you wouldn't risk the horse."

The rider was silent.

"The password," Weese muttered. "Right." He made a horn of his hands and yelled, "Onvora."

The rider lifted a glowstone, which made bright darts out of the first drops of oncoming rain.

"You know why I've come, don't you?" Weese said. "You've made a full day's journey to meet me."

He heard footsteps on the sand behind him just as he saw the slingshot in the rider's hand. In a heartbeat he saw the stone. He felt something like a lightning strike, saw the moon fly across the sky, felt the back of his head hit the sand. Pain erased all else but muffled sounds.

In time he began to recognize words.

"Why didn't my brother greet me himself?"

This was answered by sad musical notes from a reed.

"It cannot be," said the first man. "Ryp, you haven't eaten since I left Jenta. And that was a hundred years ago. But then...why eat anything if you believe that all is meaningless?"

Weese blinked, then turned his head, trying to see the two moonlit figures clearly.

The rider, holding a silver glowstone, wore a robe as black as the empty caves of his eyes. Clusters of blue warts bulged from his cheeks. His fingers holding the reed had long, painted fingernails. He looked like an ancient desert tree, bleached white by the sun and withered by drought. As he tried to rasp a reply to his challenger, a yellow chip fell from his mouth. He wavered, then dismounted and knelt—a long, slow collapse—to pat the sand in search of it.

In that awkward moment, the other man—all Weese could see in the soft light was the back of his round head—said, "I didn't want to upset you, Ryp." His tone was different now, tender and sad. "I meant to slip past you. I meant no harm. I never guessed you'd be so afraid of me that you'd stop this driver so far from the School."

A stowaway! Weese winced. *I'm a fool. No wonder the wagon was slow.* Then the wonder of it overtook him, and his eyes widened. *Scharr ben Fray, the prodigal mage. He trapped the impostor on the bridge, then slipped from his carriage and concealed himself beneath my driver's bench before I departed. Three days and he never made a sound!*

Scharr ben Fray was on his knees now, his hand on his brother's shoulder. "Since my plan has already failed, let me be useful to you."

"Useful?" hissed Ryp ben Fray, shoving the tooth back into his gum. As he staggered to his feet again, he shoved his brother away. "You?"

Scharr shrugged. "Let me cook. I'll feed you back to the man you were."

"You swore you'd never return." Ryp's voice was as rough as volcanic rock.

"I was only two hundred then, Ryp. Just a brash and arrogant boy. I've grown up. Deathweed changed my plans. I've returned to find hope for the Expanse."

"Too late. Deathweed will pour down on the School like brine into a bowl."

Scharr ben Fray's shoulders slumped. "Bad poetry spreads like gossip out here."

"Deathweed is a gift." The older mage raised his arms as if to present himself. "It will set us all free. Reject that cage you call a body. Learn to let it go. It imprisons you. Only a few remain in the Aerial now. We are set free in greater numbers all the time." He gestured to the faint outline of a leaning spire not far south of them. Even in the dark Weese could see the heap of gleaming white rubble at its base.

Bones, he realized.

"Throwing themselves off the Epiphany Tower, one after the other," sighed Scharr ben Fray. "Goat brains, all of them. Why haven't you joined them?"

"Every day I draw closer. But the colonists need my teaching if they are to learn true freedom."

"So you stay alive to teach them how to kill themselves."

"Compassion compels me. We were meant to fly, Scharr. Never to suffer. These bodies are the remnant of a cruel joke."

"To look at yours, I might believe it."

The two were distracted as the rain grew stronger. Weese slowly reached behind his head to draw one of the cast-arrows from his hair.

"You rejected us. You lost your privileges. You are barred from the histories." Ryp turned and trudged wearily back to his horse.

"You think I want to read those sad stories? Three houses have fallen to the Seers."

"And Jenta remains."

"No. Cent Regus fell to the Seers' curse. Bel Amica was poisoned by Seers' potions. And you. . .you let the Seers' whispers make you fearful and proud. House Abascar may have suffered, but its people remain strong. And I will help them escape the Seers' worst invention. I've come for maps. Give me a few nights to study them. In my old room."

"Your room's an aviary now." In Scharr's stunned silence, Ryp grinned, and Weese glimpsed several ragged yellow teeth. Then the withered mage, like a dying soldier, struggled to climb back into his saddle. "Take the bartender's vawn," he growled.

Weese tightened his grip on the arrow. *I shouldn't have trusted a mage in any kind of bargain. Ryp will pay for this betrayal.*

"Don't be wicked." Scharr gestured to Weese as if to a lost dog. "This honorable spy promised you a report of my presence. He did more than that. He brought me to your doorstep. If you're not going to pay him what you promised, at least let him ride his animal back home. I can ride with you, as we did when we were boys."

Ryp scowled at Weese. "I should release him from his skull. It would be the kindest thing. Look. He's trying to decide whether to kill us or not."

Weese felt any advantage slip from his grasp.

"How did you know I was returning?" Scharr asked abruptly.

"Your old friend, the dust-owl. Found her waiting where you used to meet her a hundred and fifty years ago. My acolyte's stones couldn't chase her away." Ryp cast a glittering shower of coins onto the sand before Weese. "Twice what I offered, bartender. And worthless when it comes to things that matter."

"Speaking of worthless tokens"—Scharr drew a pouch on a string from beneath his shirt—"I brought you something."

Ryp leaned down and withdrew a slender red feather. "Onvora."

"Ever filled that gap in your feather collection?"

"Where did you find it?" A skeletal finger stroked the feather's edge.

"While I explored the Forbidding Wall, I found a lot of creatures we'd assumed were extinct." Scharr put his foot in the stirrup and climbed up behind his brother.

Ryp kept staring at the feather as if it were a talisman. "I've almost perfected my wings."

"You started those when you were forty. Still intent on learning to fly, are you?"

"I'll soar from the tower with the feathers of all birds. That rush will be the last sensation I suffer in this punishing land."

"Except for the crash," muttered Scharr.

While Ryp busied himself sliding the feather into his flute and binding the flute back into the braids of his black beard, Weese rose and staggered toward his vawn. His head began to throb again as if a heart were thrumming where his brain had been.

As he climbed onto the driver's bench, Scharr called after him. "I'm grateful, Weese. Not that you were going to sell me to my brother. And not for the ride—worst I've suffered in three hundred years. But your ale. It tasted so very. . . Jentan."

As dawn broke, Scharr ben Fray left the humble cell where he'd slept—the room of a recently "departed" mage—to walk the lesson labyrinth painted across the cranium of this sculpted skull.

In the Jentan School, the Aerial studied and slept in honeycombs of candlelit rooms within massive boulders. These rocks, once crafted to resemble the heads of the first Jentan mages, had eroded over the years. They were scattered across the sand within what was left of House Jenta's stone walls like pieces scattered on a game board, staring blankly at one another. They were named for their shape—the Skull Chambers.

Scharr ben Fray had sought sleep in that dead mage's cell but found only a heavy, haunting emptiness, a sense of hopes abandoned. Through the uncurtained windows, he'd heard the soulless song of night breezes as they played the Skull Chambers like pipe instruments. Raucous sandpickers had squawked all night from the aviary above him—the room where he'd studied as a young man.

He looked south across the grey sea, but the distant green swell of Wildflower Isle was reluctant to emerge from the haze.

Forgive me, Zhan ry Wren. It was a mistake that we ever struck sparks. We were wise to stop.

He thought of her, the only woman he had ever risked loving. She would still be beautiful more than two hundred years from the time they met as young mages in training. Envied by all for her longevity, Zhan would be the eldest of the Jentan colony. She'd still be tall and sad, hiding her beauty in the trailing gown of hair she had vowed never to cut when he left her to explore and study the Expanse.

I hope you've not been lonely. I hope you have loved. No, no, I don't. I'm a selfish fool.

Like Scharr himself, Zhan ry Wren was more than a mage. Many Jentans were born with a power inherited from Tammos Raak. Those who were blessed with two—mages—were rare and revered. But even though Zhan had been born with three—a rarity in the history of the Expanse—she remained indifferent about her abilities. Longevity—that most coveted of gifts, which Scharr ben Fray and Ryp both enjoyed—was hers as well. She would live in good health for centuries, vulnerable only to calamity. Another blessing helped her catch liars in the act, while a third enabled her to interpret dreams with frightening and often devastating insight. But she eschewed such advantages, applying herself to common things such as caretaking, feasts, gatherings, games. And she had walked away from studying at the School.

Scharr ran the flat of his hand across the labyrinth's rugged tree-branch rail, glowering at the other Skull Chambers. They looked like ruins, remnants of the culture that had flourished here two hundred years ago, back when he was still hopeful for their house.

Noticing a scrape of blood, he drew out a cloth to wrap his hand. He had found this colorful, half-finished head scarf hidden behind a bird's nest in Auralia's caves.

I needed to know, Zhan ry Wren. I still need to know. And tomorrow I'll have all the pieces to solve the mystery of Auralia's colors.

Arriving at the center of the maze, he turned to retrace his steps. But someone blocked his path—Ryp's ivory-skinned acolyte. In her shapeless shift, she had tiptoed barefoot right up behind him.

She held a long vine of sweetberries, and plucking them one by one, she was throwing them aside.

"Listening to me mumble?" he mused. "Will you tell Master Ryp how nervous I seem? How many times I paced this labyrinth?"

She would not meet his gaze.

"What in the name of Brother Ryp are you doing to those perfectly beautiful sweetberries?"

"It's the discipline," the young woman said quietly. "We're to practice rejecting what we enjoy and desire. We want only what we've been trained to want, and we must break free of such tyranny."

"But...those are ripe sweetberries."

"They're a distraction from—"

Scharr ben Fray snatched the vine from her hands. She flinched as if she'd been slapped, and squealed, "Your brother requests your presence at the stables."

"Ryp can wait. I need to correct a few false teachings first. Sweetberries are for eating, not wasting."

Bowing her head, the girl paused, and then she whispered fiercely, as if frightened she might be discovered. "Master Scharr ben Fray, I need your help."

"What's that?"

"I need...another way out."

"Out of what?"

She cringed as if his question had been a shout. "Please. Before the others find us here. I want to know... Why did you leave? I have only what they've told me. The Epiphany Tower looms closer in my mind every day. But I..." She watched as he put a berry in his mouth. "I like the taste of sweetberries too," she whispered. "And I don't..."

"You don't feel right casting them aside."

She trembled.

What a perfect honeyflower. And Ryp enjoys her company every day? Surely he hasn't rejected every pleasure.

At that moment the sun's rays cleared the mist, and Wildflower Isle appeared like a lily pad on the warm, blue horizon.

"Let me tell you a few secrets," said the mage.

As they walked the labyrinth, Scharr ben Fray stopped resisting the echoes of memory. Now he had a purpose in revisiting his past. A chance to strike back against those who had committed so much wrong.

He spoke of his first hundred years of study and of the Seers' first visit to Jenta.

"No one paid the Seers much attention," he said. "They'd come from a camp within the Mawrnash crater, carrying boxes of mawrn dust as if it were some kind of gemstone. Strange folk. Acted like merchants, bowing and flattering. They begged for counsel. But their questions were razor edged, designed to shatter the Aerial's certainties. They meant to discourage any serious thinking, to rob us of curiosity and hope."

"These are the same Seers that have ruined House Bel Amica?"

He nodded. "I believe they poisoned House Cent Regus first. That's where the decline began. Then they came to Jenta, but after a while the Aerial sent them away. We were all frightened of their ability to expose flaws in our philosophies. They injured our pride. We were so distraught, we barely noticed when the Seers began to torment other houses."

The memories came back to him, one after another—the mages turning against one another, each bent on trumping a rival's argument.

"We blamed each other as our theories collapsed. We kept records of each other's failings and divided into camps. We became consumed with pointing out contradictions in each other's teaching. We'd stir up rumors to discredit one another and revel in ridicule. The people's affections and admiration were the measures of our contests, as if wisdom could be judged by ovations. We stopped caring about what was best for Jenta."

"So when mother says the mages betrayed her ancestors, she's right."

"She's right to want justice. Imagine. My brother and his contentious clan came to see their own people—their own families—as inconvenient. A distraction. So they conspired to be rid of them."

The acolyte's gaze strayed toward Wildflower Isle. "That's why they sent us across the water to start a new colony."

"They convinced the people that the island would be a better home. Hunting. Gardens. And a wall made of the sea to keep beastmen away. Ships once designed for a future of flourishing trade were filled with families and their belongings. And off they sailed into that lush, green prison."

"The Aerial threw their own people aside."

"They spit them out like seeds." He handed the vine with its last few berries back to the acolyte. "But it was slow. The colony's early days were industrious, high-spirited. The mages returned to the School only occasionally, for what they called 'investigations.' Investigations became frequent. And long. The School devolved to what it is today—a place of isolation, where mages wallow in dissatisfaction and shame. It's a place to give eloquent speeches about the impossibility of true communication. Anything beautiful—like the orchestral halls that once drew people from across the Expanse—was neglected or torn down."

The acolyte absently fingered the last berry on the vine. "And families were forbidden to come back."

"That didn't stop them from trying. But the wildspeakers of the Aerial commanded ram-horned seabulls to batter approaching ships. And the stonemasters crafted reefs beneath the water. Reefs that ripped through hulls." He watched her lips curl in revulsion while the pulse at her temples quickened.

"The Aerial only accepted me to the School because I submitted to their authority."

"Authority. It's strange, isn't it? The Aerial teach that there is no trustworthy truth. There is only argument for the sake of distraction. All is meaningless, chaotic, accidental. So why teach at all? And where does their authority come from? I tell you, the Seers' questions are devouring the mages' minds the way rot-eaters hollow out trees."

"Yesterday as I lifted a spoonful of broth to my lips, I asked myself, 'Why bother?'" She blinked back tears. "Sometimes I doubt that I'm actually here at all."

"The broth they serve here would spoil anyone's joy." He laughed. "The meals, the roads, the walls—time and storms have stripped the School to its bones." He gestured to the chimneyhouse, the stout brick smokestack above the subterranean furnaces that had once powered Jenta's mills. Black clouds plumed above it. "Sculptures once surrounded that, and we marked the hours by the shifting of the smokestack's shadow. Now they call time an illusion and art a delusion."

The girl ate the last berry. Her expression suggested it was sour. "So why are you different?"

"I like storytelling." He grinned mischievously. "That's what saved me. I lived in the libraries. My head filled up with questions."

"But you said questions will chew up—"

"Some questions you ask to make sense of an enchanting world. Others you ask to tear things down so you can escape accountability. The more I questioned the histories that I read in the Aerial's libraries, the less sense they made to me. I had to find a more persuasive story. So I set out to discover just that. And the world came to life before my eyes."

"You counseled Abascar's kings," she said admiringly.

"And they gave me freedom and access that helped me find answers." He turned and whistled. A dustbird hopped toward him along the branch-rails of the maze, cutting across the winding path. He opened his hand and chirped an invitation. The bird thought it over. "Knowledge is power," said the mage. "So tell me, what frightens you most?"

"Your brother." The acolyte shrugged. "And the curse."

"The Cent Regus Curse?"

"No. The curse in the clouds beyond the Forbidding Wall. The one that makes children yearn for a Keeper that will save them."

"Listen to this," said Scharr ben Fray, dropping his voice so she would lean in. "Knowledge can give us the power to cast even that curse down. That's become my mission."

He scratched the bird's striped brow and remembered how Zhan ry Wren would tilt her head whenever she caught him gazing at her, as if his love were the strangest mystery. *But what could be mysterious about loving the most irresistible woman in the Expanse?*

Zhan slept soundly, and he had loved lying awake night after night, watching the freckles on her back rise and fall with her breath. But she resented waking to find him gone. She was hurt that anything had the power to draw him away. Her contentment to live slowly confounded him; he could not rest without being caught by another question that needed answering. To go on loving her would have meant living with questions while others sought answers. He would feel weak, common, diminished.

Beauty is best at a safe distance, he reminded himself. *Otherwise it traps you. Freedom is better.*

The bird hopped into his hand, nestled down, and sighed.

The chimneyhouse shadow had shifted. Soon it would fall across him where he stood. Flames flung themselves like flower petals into the sky. It pained him to remember how he had watched those flares by night while concerts flourished on the sand. Music had shaken the Skull Chambers. Oh, to hear those instruments again with their exotic names—preezner, zimmer, perys, bowey, hewson-pipe, rain-dog, keaggy strings. (All he'd ever played were stone whistles and a handmade mouth-spring that he loved madly for its strange, tiny voices. He called it the Scar.)

"We had so much to offer," he said to himself. "We still do."

The girl watched him, puzzled.

"I'd give you a message for Zhan," he chirped to the bird. "But then I would be thinking about her all through the coming winter. I cannot afford distractions."

The bird shifted so she could stare fixedly at the mage with one eye, then the other, delighted to find a man she could understand.

"I can help you solve your mysteries," the acolyte whispered.

"Then tell me this," said the mage. "If my brother is right and the world's so worthless, why does he continue to hide and protect the treasures within Raak's Casket?" *I will have them tomorrow,* he thought. *At last I will have them.*

"They preserve Raak's Casket because, unlike the other houses, Jenta was loyal to Tammos Raak to the end." Her answer faltered. "But...but this is just a story."

"Stories are power. Tammos Raak's story has shaped the Expanse. It led us to scatter into four houses. It will save us from Deathweed if we can find our way back to Inius Throan, a city built on stone that Deathweed cannot break."

That legendary city—he had tried to find it before, but the mountains had deceived him. He'd stumbled, furious, into maddening mazes that led to nothing but dangers and death. But in Mawrnash, through the Seers' farglass, he had glimpsed its towers. And so he had returned, finding at last the city's main gate. *Locked.*

If keys exist, they'll be among the treasures in Raak's Casket. He whistled to the bird. "You'll see something tomorrow that House Jenta has never seen."

The acolyte reached out to touch a tiny wing. The bird did not stir. She looked up at Scharr ben Fray with a radiant smile. "I came to tell you that your brother has something to show you. But what I really wanted to say was this." She put her small, warm hand over his. "I want to go with you. When you leave."

He knew that the girl was his if he desired. She'd grown up hearing the exaggerated stories of his powers and courage. She was enthralled. But the temptation was only intensifying his longing for Zhan. He smiled sadly, sitting down in the very center of the labyrinth's path. The sun was blazing down on them in earnest now.

Try not to learn her name, he told himself.

"I have a better idea," he said. "You were brave to risk your life, come to the School, and spy on these despondent old fools for the resistance. But if I've already figured you out, so has my brother."

She winced and withdrew her hand.

"Give up your studies here. Go back to your angry friends on the island. Tell them to stop sharpening swords for revenge. This wasteland's not worth dying for. But New Abascar will be a paradise. And I mean to invite the Wildflower Isle colonists to join us."

The acolyte rose and walked away, looking around, afraid.

And I'll bring you, Zhan, if you'll come.

Scharr ben Fray and his brother Ryp rode north and west through the evening and a night. These were swift Jentan horses; Ryp's was an arrogant stallion the color of coal, tattooed with runes spelling out a verse about renouncing the world, while Scharr's dun mare was plain but impressively muscular.

Ryp led the way in smug silence, while Scharr imagined a thousand possible purposes for this excursion. When the elder brother slowed them to a stop at a break in the earth, a steep-sided canyon on the edge of the Cent Regus wasteland, Scharr stared in disbelief. He had never imagined this.

"Behold," Ryp tried to say, but a tooth fell out of his mouth. He climbed down from his horse to sift the sand for it.

Across the dry streambed, in the opposite cliff wall of the canyon, a line of fourteen enormous caverns echoed as the hissing wind cast debris against soot-blackened walls. Before each cavern lay massive metal bars in disarray across the ground. Whatever had been caged was gone.

"The Imityri," he whispered. "The Seers captured the Imityri."

Ryp, his hand covering his mouth as he tested the tooth he had inserted, said, "They trapped thirteen." Then he gestured to a cavern that seemed unscarred, untroubled. "They needed only one more to complete their collection."

"And then what happened?"

Ryp shrugged, scowling.

"Why? Did they mean to tame them?"

"Perhaps they merely sought to remove the creatures' influence from the world. But as you can see, they failed." Ryp sounded almost disappointed.

Scharr ben Fray watched him closely. "You knew this was happening."

Ryp, avoiding his brother's gaze, walked to the very edge of the cliff, knelt down, and pressed his hand to the stone. Stonemastery poured out from him, and the rugged cliff melted, forming a smooth incline suitable for their horses.

As they descended, the smell emanating from the empty caves spooked the animals, but they would not refuse their masters.

Scharr dismounted and walked slowly around one of the empty cells. Its walls were burnt and cracked and intricately lined as if the beast within had ceaselessly clawed at them. The cavern floors were scarred and stained. Deep gouges, bloodstains, and shreds of scaled skin littered the hard pack.

Tears stung his eyes as he lifted pieces of teeth and tusks. *If only I'd been here sooner. I would have freed them. How could anyone torment such magnificent animals? And how could Ryp let them?*

When he saw his brother lift a wide curtain of castoff skin—something shed from a wing—he knew. "Seers promised to give you one. If you kept silent, they'd give you a chance to fly."

Ryp spread the wing scrap on the ground, then folded it up in reverence. "I thought you might have set them free. I hoped you had. But I see now that you had nothing to do with it. And I do not like what that tells me."

"I've never seen two Imityri in one place." Scharr remembered glimpsing the back of a winged creature as it vanished into clouds over the Cragavar. He'd found seven-toed footprints on Deep Lake's shores near the caves where Auralia had lived. Auralia, who said that the Keeper had sent her. "Unthinkable. How did the Seers capture thirteen, Ryp? How did they keep such a secret?"

"Beastmen guarded the Imityri while brascles circled above to watch for trespassers."

"But someone outwitted them, Ryp. Someone set them free."

Ryp was watching him.

"It isn't Cal-raven, if that's what you're thinking. He's strong but not this strong." Scharr ben Fray kicked at one of the fallen bars. It was so heavy he could not move it.

"This ends an age of questions." Ryp took on a lecturing tone, one Scharr had always hated. "So many have wondered if the Keeper that haunts their dreams might actually exist. But there is no such guardian—only thirteen or fourteen animals that remind them of that childish hope."

"These skins..." Scharr ben Fray lifted a blanket of scales as long as the train of a queen's wedding gown. "These bones they shed. It's as if they die and rise."

"But they're hardly invincible." When he turned, Ryp could not conceal his satisfaction. "You see, brother? You've been kindling Cal-raven's belief in an illusion. And he has been shaped by that. A potted plant knows only the soil it's been given. When he learns that you've taught him to embrace a falsehood, he'll either succumb to fear and cling to the lie, or he'll let it collapse and despair."

Scharr looked up into the evening sky. He felt weary and defeated. "We see the suggestion of a shape among the stars. We give it a name, even though that shape is only a fiction. It's how we've always assembled our myths and our religions. We do this to comfort ourselves about all we do not understand. But surely this isn't an empty pursuit. If it helps us face the day, why fight it? We all choose stories in which to root ourselves. Why not choose the story that enables us to flourish?"

"Because that is still a life built upon a lie."

They were silent, both immovable.

When they returned to the horses, Scharr ben Fray found it difficult to leave. "What will happen to them now?"

"The Imityri? They'll spread out again over the Expanse." Ryp urged his horse up the crude stair, but the stallion needed no encouragement. "They'll show mercy to those they choose, destroy those they wish. They'll be monsters to some. To others they'll be symbols of all we wish were true. Some will damn them. Some will strive to tame them. Some will worship them."

Scharr ben Fray did not follow him up the path.

Ryp looked back. "Don't you see? The world never ceases to disappoint us. Give up chasing mysteries. Come back to the Jentan Aerial where you belong."

"Where I belong?" he barked. "I see you still embrace certain worthless illusions."

Ryp went on, undeterred. "Ours is the only true path. Leave behind all these stories, these crutches, these blankets for frightened children. Cast off your burdensome body, your mind and its endless, meaningless excursions. Myths, maxims, proverbs, laws, principles, science...it's all cracked and useless." He gestured to the air about him. "Give me nothingness. So I can rest."

Wind coiled through the empty caves, stirring up the dust as if these cells were haunted tombs.

"You'll never solve your mysteries, Scharr. Not so long as we live in this. This world's a whore, all soaked in perfumes, and you're so easily seduced." He tapped his skull. "Break the eggshell. Time to fly."

11

Against the Current

"How I'd love a bath," sighed Nella Bye.

"Another one?" asked Irimus Rain with a smile.

A bath was what the escapees had experienced, though not the sort they had wanted, as they fought through the polluted waterfall, raft by raft, lifting shields to deflect as much of the foul torrent as they could. Each of the eleven rafts carried seven, eight, or nine passengers, and each was propelled by two oarsmen, although they were as likely to be steering with a spear or a branch as an oar.

In spite of the fact that he looked like an owl dipped in mud, Irimus Rain was surveying the rafts as if he were once again a king's advisor examining a royal procession. Dutifully he counted the eighty-nine passengers, and then he counted them again.

"You should be on the foremost float," said Nella Bye, reaching to read the ale boy's face with her hardened fingertips. "You've lived your whole life running through tunnels. We need your eyes and ears."

"I'm not a leader," he shyly replied.

Irimus laughed and knelt to take his hand. "With your ridiculous notions that we might escape, you kept us alive, boy. You held hope for us when we could hold none for ourselves."

Nella Bye nodded. "You and the beastman drew us back from death."

Ark-restor the baker, who had somehow remained corpulent through months of slavery, rose suddenly from half sleep, perched himself perilously on the edge of a plank, and tried to flap wings he didn't have.

"Some of you," said the ale boy, "I could only bring back partly."

Reluctant, he climbed to the first float and settled in among Bel Amicans. *I'm so weary of the underground,* he thought. *I want the forest. Deep Lake. Trees. Birds. Gatherers.*

It seemed all of them were daring to wish for things again. The Bel Amicans spoke in whispers like restless breezes, eager for food, clear water, and relief from the injuries caused by the countless days of grueling labor. Many wanted more particular cures; beastmen had made them drink Essence for strength, and Essence produced strange symptoms. Some scratched at blue patches of skin, while others sprouted hair in strange places. Some had grown distorted features, and one bled from flaring nostrils, while another bled from the gums where her teeth had grown larger. Limbs ached from unnatural growth; their skin cracked and blistered.

To distract himself from such strange company, the boy leaned over the front of the raft and lifted a white glowstone to study the tunnel walls. A wild variety of bizarre and crawling things flinched, fluttered, and scurried away from the light. He felt fitfully itchy and muffled the glowstone's shine, turning his eyes down to the water. "At least this river's more like soup and less like stew," he murmured.

Maybe Auralia is painting by the lake again, he thought. *Maybe we'll pass right beneath her. Didn't she say there was water somewhere in those caves?*

As the rafts progressed upstream and the passengers from Bel Amica and Abascar strained to see through the fog, the ale boy leaned into memory. The thought of seeing Auralia at the end of this journey would keep his courage burning. And yet, it made him long to slip away, find his way back to the surface, and search for her.

Auralia knows me, he thought. *No one else does. When I keep my promise and bring these people to Cal-raven, I'll go and find her. We'll play by the lakeside with colors and flames. . .if we remember how.*

Mad Batey puffed through his grey mustache. "We're moving steadily north, I think."

"Northeast, I'd say," said Petch, the big-headed, sparsely bearded Bel Amican youth beside him. "But northeast to what?"

Batey flexed his jaw as he scratched another mark on his arm, a spidery map of their progress. "I don't care, so long as we don't see any Deathweed."

"We may be too deep for the feelers," said the ale boy.

"Where do you get that idea?" Petch sat so close beside Batey that he was almost sitting on him. "Where's your evidence?"

The ale boy was already weary of this man, a fount of perpetual chatter. If anyone offered a thoughtful idea, Petch would pounce as if he felt threatened. He reluctantly answered, "Feelers push up through the ground for prey. Haven't seen them dig down here. Not yet."

Petch scowled. "You almost sound like you want to stay down here."

Stunned, the ale boy groped for some idea of how he'd offended the big-headed Bel Amican. But Mad Batey pointed suddenly to the tunnel wall ahead.

Arrays of twigs and mud bloomed from pores in the wall above. "Cavebirds," said Petch, stroking his early beard.

He thinks the gesture makes him look wise, the boy thought.

"If cavebirds nest here," said Batey, "then Deathweed isn't troubling them." He frowned at Petch. "Evidence."

"I don't see any birds, do you?" said Petch. "Those nests are empty."

Batey stepped to the edge. "Worth a look. Might be eggs."

They drew the rafts to a stop. Batey couldn't reach the nests, so he called for Aronakt. A long-limbed Bel Amican known among slaves for his agility, Aronakt leapt across the rafts, his ragged overcoat fluttering like crow's wings. He calmly studied the pitted wall, then applied himself to climbing. "Too late." He dropped shards of shell back down to the water.

"Coulda been Deathweed," Petch said softly.

"Ready the arrows we brought from the Core," said Batey. "Anybody sights a cavebird, we'll shoot fast."

This tunnel is strangely familiar. The ale boy strained to remember. *What happened after I fell?* "I think this leads to better waters," he said.

"More unlikely claims," snapped Petch. "Has it occurred to you that at any moment this river might take a turn and steer us farther from Bel Amica?"

Trying to ignore Petch's challenges, the ale boy said, "This doesn't smell like the Core anymore. It's like...like we're just outside somebody's garden."

"Birds like gardens," mused Batey.

"The breeze is blowing the other way," snapped Petch. "I don't smell anything." He spoke to Batey as if the scar-faced Bel Amican was the only one worthy of his respect.

I grew up underground, the ale boy wanted to shout. *I know a thing or two about tunnels and currents. There's something green and growing ahead.*

Batey sniffed the air. "Beastmen had us slaving in such thick clouds of stench, I think my smeller surrendered."

Petch changed the subject, steering attention away from the ale boy and rambling on like the river's flow, divulging every scrap he could summon from his tremendous head on boating, tunnels, and what might or might not lie in the darkness ahead.

To flaunt his expertise on underground materials, Petch lectured them on the varieties of dark and glittering stones he recognized in the walls' dense layers: kaystone, endelode, gormenpeake. He was certain that the rank and rotting weeds mucking up their progress were jenkan-tails and timmola hay. But when an Abascar man suggested that the air smelled of spicemoss, no, said Petch, it probably wasn't. Anything suggested by Abascars was bound to be worthless, it seemed.

"Hush," said Batey. "It's important that we listen just now. We need to hear the river's temperament."

"True, true," said Petch quickly, nodding too much. Then he spoke about how he'd learned about listening during slavery, how he'd come to know the footfall of differing beastmen so he could look busy when they passed.

Imagine what he'd do in Auralia's caves, thought the ale boy. *His talk would wear the colors off the walls.*

They rowed on until they reached a stronger current. The river ahead rushed through an archway shaped like a keyhole. The travelers pressed on through it, their rafts in single file, taking advantage of the close walls to drag themselves along with their makeshift oars. Up ahead, splashes echoed.

They glided into a vast, open space. The wide but shallow stretch of the river rippled beneath a high ceiling supported by porous pillars—some thick as Tilianpurth's tower, some thin as saplings. This covered country seemed to stretch on forever in all directions. The water was agitated, alive with tiny crimson frogs that flung themselves at the pillars and burrowed into the holes.

"If the boy hadn't held out his glowstone," said Petch, "we might have surprised them. Might have caught some and had us a meal."

Frogs from beneath the Cent Regus world? the ale boy wanted to ask. *You were just complaining about the water they swim in. Help yourself.* He sank into a sullen silence.

As the rafts grumbled against the shallows' bed, the Abascars laughed quietly at the frogs' frantic dance and marveled at the patchy colors of rust and red on the pillars.

On the raft behind the ale boy's, Em-emyt found humor in almost everything, croaking froglike deep in his own thick throat and casting jabs at Kar-balter. "Look at you," he chortled. "Lost your hair. Skin and bones. Anxious. You look more like a cavelizard every day."

"Look at you," Kar-balter barked back nervously. "A hole in your head from a beastman's arrow... Half your wits spilled out."

"True," Em-emyt answered. "Then, I was missin' a few to begin with."

"I don't know about bringing Abascars with us, Batey," Petch was whispering at the front. "None of them're right in the head. They'll spoil our escape. The rafts would be lighter and faster without them. Wouldn't drag along the rocks."

"That boy helped us build these," Batey growled. "Brought us food. Show some gratitude."

"You don't think he was winning our favor for a time just such as this when he can't get anywhere without us?"

One of the Bel Amican raftsmen struck the water with his oar-stick and speared a dead frog carcass, lifting it into the air. He offered it to Batey, and Batey pointed to the ale boy. He refused it with a polite lift of his hand. Batey cocked an eyebrow.

"Water's still foul." The boy shrugged. "I'm waiting for something better."

"The Abascar boy would have us starve," laughed Petch.

"He didn't say that," said Batey, exasperated.

"You'd prefer poison to hunger?" the boy asked, then wished he hadn't, because it meant that Petch would go on talking.

"Why is it the Abascars aren't speaking of hunger? What're they hiding?"

"Patience," the boy barked back. "They're hiding barrels full of patience. For something better."

"You don't think Bel Amicans know good eating? What we call a daily marketplace you Abascars would call a royal feast. Who put you in charge?" That Petch's smile could expand to fill such a wide, fierce face was unsettling. "Saved a few Abascar slaves, and suddenly you think you're a king."

The boy waited. Surely someone would stand up and defy this blathering fool. Petch seemed incapable of saying anything that didn't create a confrontation.

When no one joined the argument, Petch smirked at Batey. "You're talking to this boy like an equal. But the best Abascar apple may yet be full of worms."

Exasperated, the ale boy climbed from the foremost float back through the train of floats that followed, past the Bel Amicans, over the cargo of shields, spears, and ragged blankets, past the Abascar people, until he arrived at the eleventh. There, he slumped down between Nella Bye and Irimus Rain. They could guess from his scowl what was wrong.

"Some monsters feed on argument," Nella Bye whispered. "Feed them silence."

"But everything Petch says is—"

"Never throw dirt at a Cragavar monkey," Irimus mused.

"What?" Nella Bye laughed.

"An old hunter's saying."

"Why shouldn't you throw dirt at a Cragavar monkey?" asked the boy.

"You'll get worse than dirt thrown back at you." Irimus smiled. "And it's the monkey's idea of fun."

"You were never a hunter, Irimus Rain," laughed Nella Bye. "Where did you hear that?"

"Folks muttered it behind my back in the Abascar council. I never introduced a new idea. I just picked at the ideas of others. Quite the bull-bottom I was. Back then."

The ale boy relaxed, glad to hear some of the old, familiar Abascar talk.

"Ever seen a bull-bottom bother a Cragavar monkey?" Nella Bye murmured to the ale boy.

They laughed as Kar-balter's oar thrust steadily against the riverbed.

As the oarsmen dragged the floats along through the shallow water, the ale boy lay back against Nella Bye, watching the copper and cream-colored pillars go by and listening to her softly sing an unfamiliar melody. Crystalline clusters of salt drew flocks of frantic yellowmoths who chewed hungrily at the deposits, and Irimus traced one of the moths' erratic paths as if trying to translate some foreign script.

Having returned from the dark, what will these people become when they walk in New Abascar?

"What's that song you're singing, Nella Bye?" asked Irimus.

"I've been hearing it since before the water awoke me," she answered. "It's in the mist. Above me somewhere. Like bells." She palmed her belly where the killing shot had gone in. "It's like I've broken open, and there's more pouring into me. More for me to feel."

"For all the glory of Abascar's palace, I've never seen anything quite so beautiful as this," mused Irimus. "We opened the earth and stuffed it with what we called treasure. Never thought to look around at what treasure might be there already. Who knew that there were worlds such as this beneath our feet?"

As the course narrowed and deepened again, the rafts took a different order, and the ale boy's raft became second in line. Those with oars knelt down for deeper strokes. As they dodged stone spikes that poked up through the water, there were quiet remarks about how they felt like giants boating through a mountain range at sea.

After hours of difficult work, they found themselves moving against a calmer, smoother current. The walls, pulsing with glowstones, fell away. The rowers, their arms and backs aching, began to grumble.

"Batey," shouted the ale boy. "Look!"

In the faint yellow glow, the passengers could see a scrap of dry and pebbled shore on the right and a bank of smooth, timeworn stone on the left.

Batey nodded, pleased. Petch, waking in haste to assess the situation, stood and crossed his arms, posing like a captain surveying his fleet.

"Do you see why this is good?" the ale boy asked Batey as the rafts drew together. "We could move upriver faster if we took to walking on the shore."

"We'll camp here," announced Petch, ignoring the boy.

"The rafts are light," said Batey, his eyes brightening. "If we share the load, we can carry them. Or some might walk in the shallows and tow the rafts along."

"We won't find a safer place," said Petch immediately. "How many want to camp here and look for food?"

The ale boy bit his tongue as Petch won a chorus of cheers. A crowd that thought with their stomachs would never know wisdom. And yet he knew that if he'd been the one to suggest they stop here, Petch would have mocked him.

"Never throw dirt at a Cragavar monkey," he muttered.

"Say again?" asked Petch.

Batey took a coin from his pocket and spun it on a fingertip as if plotting a bet. Bel Amicans were already rowing to the shore and climbing out.

"Hallowed halls of Har-baron! Is that daylight?" shouted Kar-balter.

Far ahead along the flow, narrow fissures in the distant ceiling lined the walls in gold. Excitement spread, the survivors' gazes burning as if to rend the ceiling open.

But the boy, keeping watch on the water that flowed toward them, spotted a floating patch of green—a tangle of leaves and buds red and thick as apples. "Riverbulbs. Batey, if we find where this grew, we'll have food. Real food. Riverbulbs don't grow without—"

"Water," said Batey. "Good, clean water."

"Bel Amicans, camp on this side." Petch gestured to the wide, smooth shore. "Abascars can camp over there. That will help us keep things straight."

"Keep what straight?" murmured Irimus.

Some Bel Amicans began to draw together at once, but the Abascars seemed not to have heard Petch's instructions, and they steered their rafts to the same smooth shore.

"I like your idea," said Batey as the ale boy set his bare feet down on stone. "We don't want to sleep when there's a chance that daylight might show us a way to the surface. And if we don't find food soon, I'm not sure we'll have strength left to stand."

Irimus and Nella Bye, slow getting off their raft, looked back at the narrower passage. "Is it still following us?" asked Nella Bye. "I can't see."

"Is what following?" asked the ale boy.

"Irimus thinks he saw something."

"Thought it was just a tree branch at first," said Irimus. "But then I saw it moving against the current."

They watched together for a while but saw no sign of pursuit.

When he saw Petch showing an interest in their quiet concerns, the ale boy took his glowstone and walked up to the sun-painted wall. Moving along it, he left the crowd behind. At the end of the scatter of sun spots, a line of glowstones stretched on ahead. His steps were uneven and stumbling, and hunger tightened its fist, insistent.

Keeper, thought the boy, *you knew what you were doing. You let me fall so I'd find this river. So I'd learn it was safe. So I could fulfill my promises.*

A tumble of river rocks came into view on the strand before him. They had been arranged in a circle, and the dust around them had been recently disturbed. *A crowd gathered here. They sat in the sand and leaned back against the rocks. Not long ago.*

In the center of the circle, he found clumps of a melted candle. A scene flickered in his memory. "Storytellers," he said. And then, uncertain, "Northchildren."

Irimus guided Nella Bye up beside the ale boy, and she put her hand on his shoulder. He looked up into her unseeing eyes, and she spoke the words before he could.

"I've been here before."

12

A Song for Thesera

Partayn, heir to Bel Amica's throne, snored softly, his jaw resting against his sister's shoulder, and Cyndere winced as he exhaled a cloud that reeked of beer. "Since you escaped slavery," she muttered, "moderation has not been your strong point."

Across from them in this, the fourth carriage of the southbound royal procession, Queen Thesera did not notice. In the swaying light of a swinging lantern, she held a jeweled mirror and stared at her reflection as if studying a wrecked ship that she'd vowed to rebuild.

I can't believe we're letting her sail away, thought Cyndere. *I suppose she'll be safer on the islands. But I cannot lose her to the sea the way I lost father.*

Outside the carriage the vawn-riding soldiers called signals affirming all was clear. Then the night was silent again. It felt as though they were traveling across the bottom of the sea.

Cyndere scratched the long, silky ears of the hound, Trumpet, whose enormous head rested in her lap. With a fingertip she lifted the dog's lip and looked at the strong white teeth. The sleeping beast made her think of Jordam. The beastman had left Bel Amica to search for King Cal-raven, and so long as he was gone, her dream of gathering beastmen and striving to tame and help them was at risk.

"Worn-out." Queen Thesera contorted her face. The Seers had cut, sculpted, and soaked it in potions so many times that the seams were showing. "I look worn-out."

Cyndere seized the mirror's edge, pulled it away, and threw it out the window. Both her mother and Trumpet lunged as if they'd leap out after it.

"That mirror was a gift from..."

"The Seers, Mother. You said you'd thrown their mirrors away. They lie to you. They make you think you need them. You don't. You've defeated them."

"If I'm finally free of their strings," said the queen, "why am I running away?"

"We've been over this," Cyndere sighed. "We all agreed it would be best for you to distance yourself from protests and riots. Let Partayn and me bring the house back into...back into tune."

Her brother had bet her that their mother would change her mind and turn the carriages around. But Cyndere bet with her hopes, wagering her favorite seashells that Thesera would run from trouble, set sail from the temporary harbor south of the Rushtide Inlet, and leave them alone to restore order.

"The islanders will welcome you, Mother. It was your idea, and a good one. The Seers didn't ruin that head of yours."

"No. Just my face."

Partayn snorted, opened his eyes, and announced, "There must be a secret stair." His eyes closed, and the snoring continued.

Cyndere laughed, but the queen scowled and wrung her hands, so Cyndere reached out to cover them with her own and calm her. But Thesera was increasingly agitated. "Stop the procession!" she suddenly shouted.

Partayn lifted his head, blinking.

"And bring me my new goblet!" Thesera exclaimed.

"What?" Partayn was alarmed. "No, we're not to the harbor! And dawn is hours away."

"It's never a bad time for a ceremonial drink," snapped the queen. "I want to offer prayers to my ancestors under the night sky, the way my mother once did. And breathe some open air. Let's raise a glass in defiance of the moon."

The carriage slowed, and in a few moments they stood at the base of a hill, staring skyward at fields of stars. The carriage drivers and guards—forty in all—lit torches and spread out to keep watch.

"Where are we, Cyndere?"

"The Baalke Hills, I think. Where father made star maps for his voyages."

"I so rarely see starlight in Bel Amica for the fog." Thesera pulled her feet from her slippers and brushed the grass with her toes. "Constellations. Look at them, Cyn. The kite people. The herons. But I could do without that moon. All those prayers. The Seers convinced me they were heard and answered."

"But notice which prayers the moon answered—only those that worked to the Seers' advantage. They were tricking you, Mother. Stealing your house. They taught each follower to pray for her own gain. That's why the people are angry. As the illusion shatters, they remember they're weak."

As others disembarked from their carriages, Sisterly Emeriene limped up to take Cyndere's arm. The tightness of that embrace reminded her that Emeriene, who usually sought to support her, was in a terrible state. Cesylle's betrayals had come as no great surprise, but the proof of his depravity and the damage done to her young sons, Cesyr and Channy, had shaken her.

Another figure leaned against Emeriene, and Cyndere recognized Bauris's childlike grin. The old soldier who had protected them when they were both children was traveling with them again. Emeriene had taken to caring for him since his fall into the enchanted well at Tilianpurth had knocked his senses sideways. He smiled all the time, living with one foot in another world, speaking in riddles when he spoke at all.

"They're all around," he whispered excitedly. "They're so full of questions."

"Who, Bauris?" Emeriene's grip tightened. "Who's there?"

"My new friends," he smiled. "They've come up from the deeper river. Something's about to happen." He glanced up at the copse on the hilltop. "Those dying trees, they make my new friends sad."

"Hush, Bauris. Nothing's going to happen," said Cyndere. And yet she could hear murmurs among the guards, some of whom carried torches to ascend the tree-crowned hill.

We're not alone.

"We should go, Mother." Partayn was anxious and with good reason. In a procession just like this, he had been attacked by beastmen and dragged off into slavery. "The ships are waiting. We'll attract attention here."

Standing at Partayn's side, Lesyl cupped her hands around a glowstone. It was unsettling to see them together, bound by such obvious affection, as all of House Bel Amica had heard the rumors of King Cal-raven's feelings for this soft-spoken musician. The people adored Lesyl for more than her extraordinary music; seeing her with their future king gave them hope that another heir in the line of Tammos Raak might soon be squalling in the royal nursery.

Cyndere could see her mother considering that future in this surreal scene under the star-strewn sky. "Dear Lesyl," said Thesera, "will you watch over my son while he rules in my absence?"

"I must do my king's will," Lesyl answered solemnly. "King Cal-raven, that is."

"Of course." Thesera lost her smile for a moment, then fought to reconstruct it. "Son, perhaps you can have words with Cal-raven if he..."

"When," said Cyndere urgently. "*When* he returns. And he will return."

Emeriene embraced Cyndere's arm as if the possibility frightened her.

"There he is," said Bauris, pointing toward the dark hilltop.

"Who?" asked Emeriene sharply. "Who do you see, Bauris?"

"Where's my goblet?" The queen stamped her foot.

Captain Henryk approached from the back of the procession, his sad eyes downcast, and he quietly informed the queen that he had found the new crystal goblet's wooden case empty.

Thesera's eyes narrowed. "I was in the glassworks when Frits nailed the case shut."

Captain Henryk opened his hands. "We do not know who removed it. It could not have happened along the road."

"Someone stole it in the glassworks then," said Thesera.

"Perhaps there was a mistake," said Cyndere. "Mother rejected the first goblet Frits made for her, the one with Bel Amican symbols. She liked an unfinished cup she'd seen in the glassworks."

"It was simpler," said Thesera. "Clearer. Silverblue, and its stem was like a tree with a bowl caught in its branches. Something that would make me think of Bel Amica's future instead of its past."

"Perhaps someone misunderstood and thought the wrong goblet had been packed for you."

"It's been stolen." The queen spoke as if she were bringing down an ax in sharp strokes. "I'm going back for it."

"No, you most certainly are not," said Partayn. "If we show no sign of alarm, it will be easier for me to catch the thief when I return."

"Bring me a cup," the queen growled. "Can the queen of House Bel Amica be granted that much at least?"

Henryk offered a handsome goblet of clay speckled with slivers of glowstone. The queen winced as if it pained her, and then he produced the bottle of wine.

As ordinary cups were distributed, she shivered. "What's that noise?"

"Dawn-frogs, Mother," said Cyndere. "It's almost morning."

Thesera raised the cup, but Partayn interrupted. "Since you've asked to speak your ceremony here, allow me to share something I've...we've prepared for the occasion."

Thesera frowned, but the expression faded as Partayn began to sing and Lesyl drew out a small wooden flute to accompany him.

The leafless tree lifts her eager head
As her roots whisper the rumors
Of surprise that every vivid springtime brings
Geese take wing in the wintertime
There's a summons in the distance
And I've cast off my cocoon to spread new wings

If there's no feast for this appetite
No reason in nursery rhymes
Why can't I leave behind this glorious lie?
And if there's no dawn beyond this dark

No secret stair to climb
Where did I learn the song that's falling from the sky?

The bells in the towers are ringing
Notes splinter beneath a half moon
The closing chime is slightly out of tune
This tapestry's torn beyond repair
Unless help comes kindly from the air
To weave us true on some enchanted loom.

Lesyl joined him in a hushed and haunted harmony.

If there's no feast for this appetite
No reason in nursery rhymes
Why can't I shake this great and glorious lie?
And if there's no dawn beyond this dark
No secret stair to climb
Where did I learn the song that shakes the sky?

As the last note resonated, the stars seemed to brighten.

Henryk emerged again from the dark beyond Partayn's shoulder. Bel Amica's heir raised his eyes and unsheathed the sword that had seemed, until now, ornamental.

"Betrayed," whispered Emeriene. "Cesylle's betrayed us. I should go to my sons."

"No, it's nothing to do with Cesylle," said Partayn. "The archers have sighted a beastman. Mother, we must get you back to your carriage."

The queen cursed and threw her cup down, spilling wine on the grass.

As fear rippled through the assembly, Cyndere took a step forward, straining to distinguish one shadow from another on the hillside. She saw a figure standing in the open with no fear. She did not hesitate. Pulling free of Emeriene, she ran between the torchbearers and up the slope, crying out, "Put away your arrows!"

"Cyndere!" Partayn came after her.

"Jordam?" she cried, both hopeful and dismayed.

The beastman put a hand to his mouth, and the trill of a shrill-whistle sounded sharply.

Partayn seized Cyndere's arm, but she pulled way, ascending. The beastman walked toward her, and as her brother's objection rang out, she fell into Jordam's embrace.

"rrBel," Jordam sighed. Cyndere could feel his rumbling voice through his chest, his massive hands pressed against her back. He was unafraid, unmoved by the fiery array that approached.

"How did you know I was here?"

"rrComing from the Core to Bel Amica. Heard the song."

Partayn stopped. "Good to see you, Jordam," he said, suspicious, sword in hand. "But why have you come?"

"rrMuch to tell."

"Bring my sister back into the circle. We're in danger here."

"rrDanger, yes," agreed the beastman. He glanced over his shoulder toward the trees, and then, with Cyndere taking his arm and leading him forward, he trudged down into the assembly of awestruck and troubled expressions. And as he stepped into the light, she began to stare herself.

Jordam, you're still changing. You're less a beastman all the time. You're a giant. A broken, battered, scarred giant. But a man.

"What do you want?" the queen asked sharply, leaning back.

"Mother," Cyndere said softly, "remember, we owe him our lives."

"Perhaps, but surely we should not lose our caution."

"rrPrisoners," said Jordam. "Bel Amican prisoners. Free."

"What? Where?" Partayn looked back up the hill. "Are they here?"

"No. rrUndergound. River. Boats. Far, far below." To Cyndere he said, "O-raya's boy found them."

"The ale boy? He's alive?"

"How do we bring them up from the river?" asked Partayn.

Jordam shrugged. "rrRiver is strange. Runs that way." He pointed south. "But they come against the water." He pointed north.

"I know this river," Cyndere whispered, remembering strange lights and the voices she'd heard during her ordeal at the bottom of Tilianpurth's well.

A hiss turned the company's attention to two small boys who had come to Emeriene's side. Cesyr had a rock in his hand, and he looked as if he might throw it at Jordam. Channy had an arrow that he must have taken from a soldier.

"No, boys," said Emeriene, kneeling. "That's Jordam. He's helping us."

"He's a lying monster," sulked Cesyr.

"Beastmen are no good," spat Channy, who was almost as big as his older brother.

"Don't let them offend you," Emeriene said to Jordam as she tried to pry the rock from Cesyr's hand. "They've had some horrible teachers."

"rrMore," said Jordam to Cyndere. "King Cal-raven."

"Is he alive?" Emeriene stood up.

"Alive," said Jordam.

"Alive!" Emeriene pressed her hands to her mouth, and her eyes sparkled. Then she seized Cyndere's arm again fiercely.

"Where is he?" asked Partayn. "Is he safe?"

"Safe," said Jordam. "He has...a helper."

Cyndere watched his face intently. There was more to this than the beastman was saying. She was about to ask him to go on, but then Jordam looked back up the slope to the tree at the top. "rrSomething to give you."

"What is it?"

"Someone...she needs your help."

"She?" Cyndere looked up into the darkness, having no guess at all until Jordam returned from the hilltop with a warm, squirming bundle. She drew back a fold of cloth and saw moonlight glint in the dark eyes of a small, ferocious face.

Among the trees in the hilltop copse, atop a bold eruption of stone, Ryllion crouched like a predatory cat, straining to hear the words exchanged by the beast-man and the Bel Amicans in the torchlit circle.

His senses were still sharp from the Seers' influence, but the more time passed without Pretor Xa's potions, the more he felt as if his body were a separate animal revolting against him. Spasms shook his limbs, and flares of pain trumpeted in his head.

"Jordam's told them you're alive," he whispered to Cal-raven. And then he cringed to see and hear Emeriene's overjoyed response. He could not repress a jealous snarl.

"Can you still see Lesyl?" Cal-raven sat behind the same stones. "She's the one who sang with Partayn."

"She's weeping." Ryllion looked down at the singer with the corn-silk hair. "She holds Partayn's hand, and she weeps."

He watched Cal-raven dig at the boulder with his fingers, breaking it apart as if this answer upset him. "Who else is there?" the stonemaster asked.

"Henryk. They'll have made him captain now." Ryllion turned and spat on the tree roots. "There's Bauris." He closed his mouth. *Poor old fool. It would have been a mercy upon you if you'd died when I threw you into the Tilianpurth well.* "They've brought two children."

"Emeriene's boys," said Cal-raven softly.

"Oh." Ryllion swallowed hard. In his mind Emeriene was Bel Amica's most radiant flower, but he always ignored the children that Cesylle had given her. *How would things have been different,* he wondered, *if I'd won her?*

Cal-raven kept digging into the boulder, with purpose now. "There's spark-stone in this rock. We should collect what we can. Fire's our best defense against Deathweed."

"One thing I don't understand," said Ryllion.

"Only one?" asked Cal-raven.

Ryllion laughed at that. Laughed. When had he ever laughed at all? "Cal-raven, how does Jordam know you're alive?"

"He must have stumbled onto our camp," said Cal-raven. "If I'd been alone, he would have approached me. But you were there. That confused him. He must have followed us toward Bel Amica. And because we heard the song and discovered this. . .this procession, he did too. We've done him a favor."

If the beastman heard my confessions to Cal-raven, thought Ryllion, *then he heard me speak of how I led the attack on Barnashum. And he also heard Cal-raven forgive me.* Ryllion sighed. "What if Jordam tells them that I'm with you?"

"He probably doesn't know who you are, or he would have said something. What are they saying now?"

"They say the Seers are hiding in their Keep. It's surrounded." Ryllion felt dizzy with disbelief. *Does this make me safer?* He laid his head against the stone. His arms trembled, and his heartbeat stumbled in its rhythm. "I am sick," he hissed. "The Seers' poisons. . ."

"I'll get help for you," said Cal-raven, "when we get back to Bel Amica."

"Wait." Ryllion lifted his chin. "Cyndere says your captain has taken a company north. To follow. . .your map."

"My map?" Cal-raven stood up, daring to take a look down at the constellation of torches. "Tabor Jan's gone north?"

Ryllion tuned his powerful ears to the company below. "They're off to find. . . New Abascar."

"Our plans are changing, Ryllion," said Cal-raven. "Tonight, you and I, we go north." He tapped two pebbles together and struck a spark. "To Fraughtenwood. With fire."

13

The One-Eyed Bandit's Greatest Theft

Whispers rattled the shutters of Cesylle's sleep.

"He's a wretch and a fool, but he'll do anything we ask."

For a moment Cesylle thought the voice to be a delusion after a night in the Mawrnash revelhouse. His head pulsed as if it might explode. Had he ordered a mug of Six Hard Slaps?

But then the shutters flew open. He remembered. This was the hard, cold floor of the Seers' Keep. The voice belonged to Malefyk Xa.

"He did kill Ryllion, after all."

Cesylle willed himself to be still even as he tensed to find that the Seers were speaking of him. His lungs burned from breathing clouds of mawrn.

"Oh, let me sculpt his face and send him out unrecognized." That hiss came from Tyriban Xa, she who concocted their potions. "Let's disguise him. Send him after Thesera's arrogant boy to set fire to his beard. Have him cast Cyndere from her tower. Without rulers, these streets will fill with blood."

Cesylle parted his eyelids the merest slit, but he wasn't wearing the mawrn-glass lenses. He was blind in this dark.

"Trouble insssside. Good." That clipped accent, might it be Panner Xa, back from Mawrnash? Her voice had changed. She sounded younger, smaller.

A mosquito's whine stung the air, and a strange energy prickled Cesylle's skin. He opened an eye again and observed a luminous blue ghost drifting through the dark. The glow revealed the outlines of five Seers standing in a half circle around him.

He had never seen them all assembled—the towering, broad-shouldered Malefyk Xa, a secretive manipulator who was always moving about the Expanse; Panner Xa, the Mawrnash overseer; Tyriban Xa, potion-maker and poisoner; Palaskyn Xa, the counselor, a seducer of gullible masses; Skaribek Xa, the Moon Prophet, who made any event an occasion to speak of history and prophesy fearful tidings.

But Pretor Xa, the strategist, the Seer who had mentored Ryllion and coaxed Cesylle with promises and plots, was missing. Rumors claimed that Cyndere had killed the Seer when the conspiracy had been exposed, but he found that hard to believe.

The Seers wavered like puppets on unsteady strings, standing apart from one another without even the respect of a glance. This was a collaboration driven by necessity rather than respect. *Like Ryllion and me,* Cesylle thought.

"Bel Amica is a lesser concern now," said Skaribek Xa, his voice tremulous, arms outstretched. "Abascar survivors are losing their fear of the Curse and moving toward the Forbidding Wall. We must make them afraid again."

"If Cal-raven's stragglers reach Inius Throan," sang Palaskyn Xa in her low, seductive tone, "they may expose all we've sought to—"

Malefyk Xa struck the last word from her mouth, and her jaw came unhinged, sagging crookedly until she reached up and snapped it back into place.

"You whine like a dog that's been beaten," Malefyk sneered. "What was the purpose of our truce? That we might strive together and force the tyrant to surrender, to give us his secrets and spells, that he might have no advantage. We've hurt him. We've ripped open the seams of his beloved inventions. I mean to torment him further."

"Surrender," panted Panner Xa. "The spells."

Lynna! Cesylle remembered now. The pretty barmaid in Mawrnash he had tried to charm—here she was, looking several days' dead. At this point his mind refused to put the pieces together in fear of what would appear. Mawrnash drunks had raved madly about seeing Panner Xa cut off pieces of her own body and replace them with scraps torn from corpses. Such claims had only made him laugh.

But I am looking at Lynna's face, he thought. *It sags upon her skull, and the eyes loll loosely in their sockets. One of her hands has been severed at the wrist. And the voice. . .that is Panner Xa, or I never heard her speak a word.*

"Abascar won't expose anything," said Tyriban Xa. "They can't enter Inius Throan. The Aerial guards the keys, the arrogant fools."

"When Raak's clan scattered from Inius Throan, we scared them into staying far away for a reason." Malefyk Xa's voice grew quieter. "Now Abascar's back on the threshold. But while you fret as if they've beaten us at this game, I've moved some pieces on the game board. If they succeed in reaching Inius Throan, they'll find the trap I've set for them, and they'll die full of arrows."

The blue phantom seemed to shudder, sparks flaring in its aura.

"Still worried about Ryllion?" Malefyk snarled at it. "You're worthless." He prodded Cesylle with his boot. "I enjoyed watching this one throw Ryllion to his death."

The ghost jerked and twisted, its edges bristling with bolts of tiny lightning.

Malefyk hissed. "Don't speak to me of unfinished plans. I captured the Imityri. Thirteen of the most powerful creatures in the Expanse. Each one worth a thousand Ryllions. And what happened? You lost control of Bel Amica and summoned me. While I was gone, a stonemaster released my prizes. Who have we forgotten? What wandering mage slipped through our fingers?"

"No one this side of the wall is strong enough," sneered Skaribek.

"I will find him. Whoever he is. And I'll enjoy tearing out his stitches. Otherwise, we need only wait. I've abandoned the Curse, so he's starving. As he fails, the Deathweed will uproot itself into countless destroyers. And the viscorclaws will strip the Expanse to its bones. A few will escape the trouble, and it will all begin again. The scattering, the gathering into clans, the battles for power and authority, the deceptions." Malefyk staggered suddenly, clutching at his chest and wheezing as if he might collapse.

"We're tired," said Tyriban. "We need strength. Put down these costumes, and come to the mawrn stone."

"First..."—Malefyk's cold hand lifted Cesylle and carried him away—"I'm throwing this one out to the Bel Amicans."

Cesylle flailed in Malefyk's cold, strangling grasp as the Seer left the blue glow behind. He kicked and struck, but the Seer did not release him.

The Keep's outer wall opened, a tear in an invisible seam. A fog-thick, moon-silver street appeared beyond.

An arrow pierced the Seer's sleeve. Cesylle squeaked, realizing that he was about to be cast into view of the archers.

Malefyk Xa paused, then stepped back inside. The open seam sealed again. "You want to live, don't you?"

Cesylle's "Yes!" emerged as a gasp.

"Very well." The Seer cast him down, then dragged him by his heel along the smooth, cold floor.

Cesylle sucked in air, uncertain whether the bursts of color were lights in his head or flares of Malefyk Xa's temper. The Seer's stride was uneven, and at times he leaned as if losing his balance, his shoulder brushing the wall.

They're weakening, Cesylle thought. *They're making mistakes.*

As the Seer turned a corner, Cesylle's elbow struck something in the path. His hand came down on the mawrn-glass spectacles, and he quickly pressed them against his eyes. He took in the scene cast in dark, metallic outlines.

Malefyk moved between stacks of metal cages, some cluttered with bones of what they'd once confined, others troubled by restless spasms of scales, flesh, and fur. Pumps forced a noxious concoction through tubes into whatever cowered within, while other substances drained into coiling stems, extracted into bottles—sera that were clear, amber, and blood red. Unfamiliar creatures lunged at their cage bars as the Seer passed.

Arriving at the largest cage, Malefyk fumbled with a ring of strange keys to unlock it. Then he walked directly to a suspended ring of wood. Carcasses hung from the ring like hunting trophies, large and motionless, strung in a circle above a wooden table cluttered with metal instruments, bottles, and bowls of dark soups.

Malefyk raised Cesylle up by his feet and locked them into ice-cold shackles so that he hung down with arms reaching to the floor. "You can wait here." Malefyk staggered, panting for breath. "I'll come back in a while and give you something to make you more comfortable. As you get used to your new...your new neighbors."

These were not animal carcasses. They were men distorted by strange surgeries and mutations. They swung from their feet, arms dangling as if in hopes of grasping the ground. Their mouths gaped, faces frozen in ecstasy or anguish. Some had limbs deformed. Others were bloated as if dragged from a lake after drowning. Still others were emaciated, like gigantic geese picked down to their bones.

Test subjects, he thought. *Victims of the Seers' investigations.* He and Ryllion had known that the Seers tested their sera on beastmen, but these were not Cent Regus creatures. He recognized one of the bodies. Bahrage. The Seers had preserved his childlike body, even as they hastened the development of his mind, making him a half-mad, hypnotic manipulator until his charade collapsed and he vanished. The Seers had clearly lost patience with Bahrage, just as they had abandoned Ryllion. *Just as they are abandoning me.*

As Malefyk lurched out of the laboratory, he stumbled, fell, and then staggered again to his feet. He seemed desperate for some kind of medicine as he careened down the corridor, the cage door clanging shut behind him.

Cesylle coughed and spat, convulsing. Hatred took hold and shook him. He had felt hurt, scared, betrayed. But this power filling his frame—this was rage.

He did not understand what he had heard. Costumes? Watchtower? Who was "the tyrant"? Why had they referred to the Curse as "him"? And what were the "viscorclaws"?

But he did understand that he had wasted every moment of service to them, both here and in Mawrnash. They had never intended to help him as they'd claimed. They had never cared about Bel Amica. They were playing an elaborate game.

If they find me inside these walls, he thought, *they'll kill me. It's time to learn what I can learn. Break what I've built.*

The Seers had favored Cesylle for his ability to design structures and machinery. He had invented the mawrn drills, which helped them draw the crystals from where they were embedded in the earth.

To please him, they had set their arts to work, giving him a tongue as smooth as a hypnotist's, and with that musical voice, he had comforted Emeriene. Someone had broken her heart. She wanted security, and he promised her a future. When he won her, Cesylle's reputation improved throughout Bel Amica. Entering a room with this beauty on his arm, he heard his name whispered in the crowd, and he saw heads turn. He liked being recognized.

Even so, he had wondered what his efforts were earning for the Seers. He had overseen construction of so many drills, but only a few were used to mine the white stone at Mawrnash. Most of them were taken away for purposes he'd never wanted to know, though a warning bell rang to tell him that the Seers had dangerous secrets.

Now, after returning to Bel Amica, he had pieced together parts of the puzzle.

Jordam, the beastman that Cyndere was said to have tamed, had helped to rescue some Cent Regus slaves and bring them back to Bel Amica. They came with stories of blood and horror for many others who had died during the escape. But they also spoke of what they had suffered in their enslavement—of hard labor deep beneath the ground, pushing powerful drills to break open passages for the Deathweed.

He had scoffed at the claims, calling them preposterous. What else could he do? To have accepted such allegations would have marked him as an enabler of unimaginable cruelty.

With the spectacles on, he could see the stark, sharp lines of the furniture and the Seers' tools glinting, as if all was made of steel and the enamel of clean teeth.

One of the hanging bodies seemed old in the hands and rib-jutting chest, but the face was a young man's. His eyes were open, and Cesylle had the strange sensation that the body was actually looking at him.

Cesylle bent at the waist, trying to pull himself up to wrestle with the shackles.

"It's no use," said a voice. "Best if you don't hurt yourself. It only makes the wait more miserable."

Cesylle clutched at his thundering heart. "You're...you're alive?"

"I would not call it that." The man's voice—it was really just a rush of air through a swollen throat—scratched the silence.

"How long? How long have they had you like this?"

"Seventy, eighty years," the man said. "They'll keep me alive forever."

"Why? Why would they do that to you?"

"I asked them to." Yellow tears leaked from the captive's eyes and ran down his forehead.

"You volunteered for this?"

"They asked me if I wanted to live or die. My answer amused them. Here I am."

Cesylle examined the man's feet, which were shackled in the same metal as his own, but those ankles had grown and swollen around their bonds. "Can we get you down?"

"Only Northchildren can free me now. I see them sometimes."

"The Seers...they let you hang for eighty years?"

"They turn me around sometimes, to hang from the arms, or they strap me to a table. They've tested me so many ways. I've tried so hard...to die. But they keep giving me new parts."

"How do you stay alive?"

"They feed me something that feels good. It fools me into thinking that I still want this. But then it fades. And I'm still here. Alive, I suppose. But for no good purpose." He began to tremble with some terrible emotion. His hands twitched, and his eyes swiveled to the other bodies as if suddenly remembering the extent of the Seers' tortures. "Bring," he breathed, "the whole thing down."

Cesylle reached up again, but the shackles at his ankles burned his fingertips with cold. He collapsed, swinging and sobbing.

"Fire." The captive's body twitched in a spasm as if his bones were trying to let go of one another. "Please. Burn it. Bring the whole thing down."

Then a sudden motion made Cesylle shriek. One of the hanging bodies dropped as if its ankles had broken. A body crumpled to the floor. This one was most certainly dead—motionless, spindly, gnarled, one-eyed, and, unlike the others, still clothed.

But then it moved. It stood, flicking a sparkstick to see in the dark. It lunged at Cesylle.

Cesylle tried to scream again, but a bony hand covered his mouth. He struck at his attacker, but the other hand caught his wrist firmly. "Shush!" said the one-eyed assailant. "You're safe. I'm just hidin' here. Been locked inside for days. But look!" He knelt in the spot where Malefyk Xa had stumbled on his way out of the cage. "The monsters made a mistake. They finally made a mistake."

The old man introduced himself as Warney from Abascar. "The Seers took things from me," he grumbled, fumbling with the long metal key that Malefyk had dropped. "My eye, for one. And the cap Auralia made for me. Here, don't move." He seized Cesylle as if he were a tree and proceeded to climb him.

Cesylle groaned as Warney's bare feet clawed at his chest, and then he heard a sharp *clak!*

Now they were both sprawled on the floor. The light from the sparkstick went out.

"You," Cesylle gasped. "You were with that storyteller in the Mawrnash revelhouse."

"That storyteller was Krawg," said Warney with a boastful grin. "The Midnight Swindler. Now, hush, we don't have much time. You seen my belongings? The things they stole?" Warney began to feel his way around on the floor. "They should never've stolen from me. I'm the One-Eyed Bandit. I can outsteal anybody, 'cept maybe Krawg."

Cesylle gave Warney one of the two mawrn-glass lenses so he could see. At once Warney crawled to the laboratory table and pulled out a heavy object like an arrowcaster—a wooden crossbeam equipped with a spring-triggered spool of wire—from beneath it.

"That's a fisher-spring," said Cesylle in disbelief. "Going fishing?"

Warney smiled, seeming afraid and exhilarated at the same time. "Not even close. I brought that in here for a reason, and I'm glad the Seers never found it."

"You came in here on your own?" Cesylle scowled. "If that's your weapon, well, I hate to tell you this, but you'll never get out of here alive."

"Are the Seers in that room with the big bright crystal?"

Cesylle nodded.

"Good. Last time they went in there, they were busy for a long time. If we don't get out now, we won't get out at all."

As they fled the chamber, Cesylle choked, too distraught to look back again at that old, suspended prisoner, for it was clear that no one could help him. But as he followed Warney, a whisper followed him. "Bring the whole thing down. Bring the whole thing down."

They made their way back through the twists and turns until Warney paused, panting, and seized Cesylle's bandaged arm. As Cesylle whimpered, Warney pointed toward the silver slit of an open doorway.

"That's the mawrn-crystal room. We can't go in there."

"It's the only place I haven't looked for my eye," Warney growled.

The chill was so fierce that they stopped and leaned into each other for a moment. Cesylle had a sudden, almost irresistible itch to flee. In the room beyond, the crystal that Malefyk Xa had shown him had turned to a pillar of cold blue fire, sparkling and hissing. As it did, a strange and dissonant chorus of voices moaned inside the light.

The Seers...they're in the fire.

Warney seized Cesylle's chin and turned it. "Look."

In the strobing light, he saw again that strange, branching, metal tree—dark and spiked as an iron coatrack—in the middle of the room. And he stood paralyzed as his mind slowly pieced more impossible details together.

Caught on its hooks by the backs of their necks, the Seers' bodies hung suspended. Their faces were downturned, their eyes white and sightless. Their long arms were limp; the fingers of their mismatched hands were lifeless, like long-dead spiders dangling in dusty webs.

"Are they...dead?"

"No," said Cesylle. "They're empty."

This suspended confounding questions in the room. They listened to the crackle and spark from the adjoining chamber, then glanced back toward the crystal's silvery spray.

"So that's the nasty secret," Warney whispered. "Panner Xa's hand. I'd seen it before. Seen it chopped right off a drunken miner at Mawrnash."

"Stolen bodies." Cesylle's resistance collapsed. The rumors in the revelhouse had been true. "When pieces wear out, they steal replacements."

"That's why they hate sunlight. I heard the tallest one say so. Gotta keep them costumes cold when they're not bein' worn. Else they'll rot." Warney glanced toward the Seers' crystal chamber. "Don't want to know what that shiny rock is for. Nothin' good, I expect."

"Don't ask me to explain it, but I think they're getting stronger. Mawrn...it's like Essence to beastmen."

"If we go in there, can they see us? I mean, without their costumes?"

"The crystal shows them what any mawrn can see. Anywhere. They're probably scanning the whole Expanse. We should get out while they're distracted. And fast."

"Only one way out," muttered Warney. He pointed to the jittery light.

"That's how you got in? Through the moon window? No wonder you're famous." Cesylle backed away from the bright door. "We'll never make it."

"You wanna stay here forever like that poor old upside-down fellow? Look, they can't touch us when they're out of their bodies, right?"

Cesylle thought of the blue ghost that had hovered in Pretor Xa's empty place. "I don't think so. But they won't be out of them for long."

Warney reached into his pocket and pulled out another sparkstick. Then his eye went wide as a shrillow's egg. "Oh," he said, amazed by whatever thought was congealing in his head.

The Seers' deathly costumes burned quickly.

And as they crumbled into ash and ember, a cloud of black smoke filled the room.

Warney and Cesylle watched, cowering just outside the entrance to the Seers' crystal chamber. And it was all they could do to stay still as the blaze of the crystal's fire in the next room faded, and six streams of shining, shapeless mist came writhing into the antechamber.

The phantoms circled the smoldering iron tower, seeking some way into the burning bodies. Warney thought he could feel the vibrations of their voiceless screams, and he shuddered.

One of the burning costumes lurched out from the cluster. As it did, its blackening feet gave way, and it fell to its knees, which exploded, and then the whole body toppled and smashed against the floor.

From its shattering hand, a small orb came rolling across the floor, stopping right at Warney's toe.

"Imagine that," he said, snatching the sphere from the floor and rubbing it against his cloak. He shoved the eye back into its socket, then he seized Cesylle and dragged him toward the crystal chamber.

In spite of the inferno behind him, Cesylle felt a sudden thrill. He and Warney had dealt the Seers a serious blow and discovered their weakness at the same time. A strange giddiness filled him. These manipulators were not so invincible after all. He heard himself laugh out loud, a cackle of half-mad zeal. But his delight faded when he looked up and saw the fanged window closing around a star-shaped patch of moonlit sky.

"No problem," said Warney, fixing Cesylle with a crazed look, his glass eye staring upward. "I'm the One-Eyed Bandit." And with that, he raised the fisher-spring and fired it at the skylight.

The forked spear flew through the closing mouth and caught.

Warney flicked the recoil trigger and locked an arm around Cesylle's waist.

"Wait," said Cesylle. He broke free and dove to the crystal. He seized the marrowwood box that rested on the small golden pillar beneath the floating mawrn stone and then hurried back to take hold of Warney's leg as the old man ascended on the retracting line.

They clambered out between the closing teeth just as the fog-shrouded rooftop sealed and the fisher-spring mechanism splintered, cut in half.

Together they slid down the Keep's sloped, glassy roof as if it were ice melting beneath them and skidded to the edge, grateful for the mist that concealed them from archers in the surrounding towers. The Keep shuddered beneath them.

A bright light lit up the sky, and they looked back up the incline.

Five blue ghosts rose from the rooftop into the sky, pulsing strangely, gracefully, like jellyfish ascending through dark water. The translucent umbrellas of crystal dust made sounds like dissonant bells, glassy ribbons trailing and stroking the air.

In Cesylle's mind the chant continued.

Bring the whole thing down. Bring the whole thing down.

Sensing that the other Seers were gone, Pretor Xa dragged his frail ghost up from the floor and drifted back through the corridors of the Keep.

He felt something like an ache, something like cold—there were no words for what he felt, save those related to a body. How he hated bodies.

They reminded him of his own, cast off so many ages ago. He had not chosen that form, and thus he despised it. Some great mystery had forced him into being a part of a larger design. But Pretor Xa did not want to be part of anything. He wanted to consume and own all. To be sovereign. And yet he could make nothing except by rearranging, reassembling what that mystery provided.

So he trembled now, jealous, willfully bodiless, and miserable. One desire eventually rose up through the turmoil. Gleaming and simple, it gave him purpose.

I want to find my servant. And I want to find him alive.

Pretor Xa had sculpted Ryllion from a young and zealous soldier into something of his own design—something that reminded him of himself many ages ago.

If I find him alive, perhaps I can still use him. But if I find him dead. . .

An idea flickered, a rush of sparks in the blue gown of his floating ghost.

He drifted out through the Keep's wall, wound through the streets. Mistaken for glints of morning sunlight, for glimmers on the water, he reached the mainland and became a shimmer in the trees.

14

Raiders of Raak's Casket

No one but Ryp ben Fray heard the first tremor that pulsed through the hard, dry ground of the Jentan School.

Lying on a stone bed in his candlelit cell, he watched the feathers of his extravagant, wall-pinned collection twitch slightly without wind to stir them. Perhaps Deathweed had come at last to shatter Jenta's foundations. Perhaps the inevitable uprising from Wildflower Isle had reached the mainland.

Ryp rose and pressed his hand to the featureless outer wall of his chamber—the room in which he had studied and slept for centuries. Stone rippled as easily as a breeze-blown bedsheet on a clothesline, pliable from years of obedience to his touch. Rings like ripples spread from his fingertips. A window opened to the hush before dawn. He held the onvora feather out into the air, and it fluttered on a faint breeze as if eager to rise.

Acolytes in their gauzy grey robes patrolled what sections of the wall remained, lost in their thoughts, having long given up any expectation of visitors or disturbances. Submerged in their Skull Chambers like clams in their shells, the Aerial brooded and stewed. *So many fruitless searches.* A familiar shape marked a window in a lighted room across the yard, also watching. *The day will come when my brother will go out too, like a puff of smoke. Poor fool.*

He listened for another rumble, but all he could hear was the sough of the Mystery Sea to the south. On the coast, overcoat herons would be spreading the inky fabric of their wings, drifting along the shoreline in this, the world's waking hour.

The freedom to fly. To cut the cords that bind us.

What if he leapt from the Epiphany Tower and found himself adrift, awake and without any help for himself? What if pain awaited him, with no source of comfort? Out of habit, he batted away doubt's whispers. He had stopped heeding questions long ago.

There will be a certain satisfaction in being free from the temptation to try and fail again. History is an endless chain of failures. If I feel anything at all, I'll feel contentment. No decisions to be made. Nothing to regret. All will be determined. I'll have no choice but to accept what comes. Any and all responsibility will fall on whatever cruel power is behind these horrible games. Let that power accept my surrender as an ultimatum. No more chasing the illusion of meaning.

He heard his acolyte's footfall behind him. "Tenderly."

"Master." The girl, clad in an ankle-length robe, set a tallow candle on the new sill beside him. At once Ryp knocked it out the window with his elbow. *Learn that, acolyte. Do what you've been told, and it comes to nothing.*

Tenderly tucked her yellow hair behind her ear and went on with her errands. She smelled like clereus blooms opening in gratitude during a desert rain shower. *As if there was any sense in gratitude.*

Spreading a clean sheet over Ryp's stone bed, Tenderly said, "Master, your breathing. You should close the window."

For a moment longer the mage held the onvora feather out the window, letting the warm wind ruffle and bend its firm fibers. "Did you feel a strange quake just now?"

"Not at all," she said. "What is the feather, master? Onvora? Did Scharr bring it to you?"

"Yes." He loved them all—the glasswing's crystalline sheen, the peacock's size and pride, the pone's delicacy, and the skycutter's curve. And he hated that he loved them, just as he hated the desire that gripped him when Tenderly came to the room. Even more, he hated his regrets, hated his restraint, hated any suggestion that there was a right or a wrong. She would learn hard lessons in this life. What did it matter if he gave her one of them?

"I will leave the window open," he sighed. "My brother's up to something. We must watch him." He glanced at the moonlit shadow cast by the chimneyhouse smokestack, then turned toward the bell tower. "The bell-hammer's late again."

"Master?"

"The dawn arrives without a bell. Since our volunteer disappeared, so many tasks are done improperly."

The acolyte flinched. "Some say he wasn't well treated."

"We took in that hunched old beggar and gave him shelter." Ryp saw her ears redden as she took up the broom to sweep. "Best blunt your barbs, child. Most your age never see the inside of the School." He waited. Still there was no bell. "You've been wise to wean yourself from any desires, save for an escape into oblivion, the great sigh of death."

The girl slumped down on the edge of the bed.

"I know, Tenderly. The world is burdensome. We'll help you slip out of it. It'll feel as good as casting off your robe." He clenched his teeth, hating himself, and hating himself for hating himself.

"Why did your brother return?"

"Scharr found no end to his ridiculous questions. All pursuits led to nothing. He's back, empty-handed."

"Except for the onvora feather. Which is beautiful, no matter what you say."

Ryp fashioned a retort, but the morning bell suddenly pealed. "Too loud!" he shouted.

"Never mind," said Tenderly. "It doesn't matter. Nothing matters. Maybe you should work on your wings. To calm your temper."

Ryp wanted to carve out a fistful of stone and throw it at the girl. Instead, he walked to the corner and untied the cord around a bundle of rods and canvas. After unfolding the roll, he spread the wings and fitted together the rods of their frame. "Perhaps it's time to put the feathers on my wings. Scharr has completed my collection."

"What did your brother do to deserve banishment?"

Ryp laughed softly. "He tells everyone we cast him out. In truth, he rejected our order. He'd prefer to make himself a myth—a man who carries secrets, unbound to any house or authority."

"But why come back?"

"He wants to see the scrolls of Tammos Raak. Just the latest curiosity to distract him from the emptiness. He hopes he'll find something there to help King Cal-raven establish New Abascar up north."

"Why bother with Abascar?"

"Cal-raven adores him. Adoration is a powerful thing. Cal-raven is moved by a foolish children's story about the Keeper, and my brother can use that to his advantage. By setting up a kingdom in the shadow of the Forbidding Wall, he'll dwell on the border between all he does and does not know. He'll have resources—armies, even. He'll go over the Forbidding Wall and try to learn the truth about the curse that Tammos Raak fled. Then he'll set himself up as revealer of that truth to Cal-raven and the world. He'll shape stories that will shape future cultures across the Expanse to his liking. Stories and histories—they're just tools in his grand manipulation."

"So you mean to refuse him access to Raak's Casket?"

"He'll have to steal them." Ryp lay down and rested his head on the stone pillow. "It will be interesting to see him try. Try and fail."

The acolyte was silent at the window, searching night's last shadows.

"It's a burden, isn't it? Knowing that great secrets may be just out of reach." Ryp ben Fray pressed his hand to his chest. "You feel it here. A maddening desire to know what isn't yours to know. Imagine carrying that ache for hundreds of years. Now ask yourself which is worse—not knowing the secrets in the casket or learning that there is nothing inside the casket at all but ashes and dust? Either conclusion will lead to madness. We must waste our time with comforting distractions or death. Come. Lie down with me. I'll take your mind off your despair."

The alarm bell—with its weight, its metal, its worldly harshness—shocked him as if the hammer had struck his skull. The acolyte rushed to the window.

"What do you see? My brother, where is he?"

"He's still at the window."

"It cannot be." He joined her there. Stars shone fiercely in the storm-scrubbed sky. The air seemed charged with conspiracy. "That's not Scharr ben Fray. It's a statue. Rebellious as ever, my brother." Ryp spit two teeth into his hand, then shoved them back into their places. "Where is he then?" Drawing his heavy cloak around his shoulders, he trudged wearily to the door.

As he did, the floor shuddered under their feet.

"Did you feel that?" Tenderly gasped.

They both heard a thunderclap in the distance. Such strange thunder—it seemed to emanate from underground, far, far away.

Ryp frowned. "Another trick."

They moved up the stairs slowly and then onto the curve of wall that stretched out from his Skull Chamber. Ryp cocked his head to one side, holding up his hand to demand silence.

Again there was the roll of some distant, powerful drum.

"That," he whispered, "is a sound I haven't heard in almost three hundred years." His voice deepened to a growl through clenched teeth. "And I was certain I'd never hear it again."

"Are we being attacked?"

"It isn't an army." Ryp gazed out toward the horizon. "Oh, he's going to enjoy his surprise. But it will lead to nothing."

"What do we do?"

"Watch the chimneyhouse," he said. "And stay close to me." He reached out, seized Tenderly's shoulder, and drew her body hard against his, seizing the excuse to steal her warmth. "You're a lucky girl, Tenderly. We're about to witness something no one's seen in almost three hundred years. And it may be the last thing we see."

Against early morning's azure sky, the chimneyhouse looked like a fat, melting candle in the center of the yard, its east side faintly detailed by the dawn.

At another distant boom Tenderly tried to pull away.

"The creature that approaches," Ryp sighed, his doubts erased, "has been eating and sleeping in seclusion for generations. During those years its armored shell has thickened. Its muscles, which it flexes in its sleep, have grown strong. The ancients thought that it flew, for it leaps in strides as long as a man can walk in a day."

The acolyte's eyes rolled as if she were searching back through memories of studies.

"We thought they'd lost interest in the Expanse, moving away across the Eastern Heatlands," said Ryp, hating the jealousy in his voice. "But Scharr has lured one here."

Boom.

"If I believed in myths," said Tenderly softly, "I'd think you spoke of a dragon. Not a puffdragon. But one of the great Fearblind Dragons."

Ryp pointed to the brightening sky.

A shape—very like a grasshopper—launched into view, stark black against the blue. Its long, thick legs were extended beneath it. But it was still far off. And after it silently descended into the shadow of the dunes, they felt another reverberation, and dust mushroomed skyward. The wall rattled. A haze browned the air around the School.

"It'll destroy us," said the acolyte, her voice pinched with fear.

"Perhaps," said Ryp. "But Scharr's not bloodthirsty. Just arrogant."

Again the shape shot up into the sky, growing more distinct as it approached, its silhouette blotting out the moon at the height of its ascent.

Tenderly slipped from Ryp's embrace and buried her face in her hands.

As the dragon hurtled toward Jenta, Ryp imagined the patterns made by the serrated black shields layered across the belly, protecting the soft flesh. Somewhere in its shielded head, the burning spheres of its eyes would be scanning the scene for its target.

The dragon's landing sent a shock wave through the School, throwing Ryp and Tenderly down. Sand moved in waves. A plume of dust cast a canopy across the sky. Somewhere a section of wall collapsed. Screams rose throughout the School.

When it leapt again, there was a sound like a gasp—a rain of debris falling from its feet. Ryp looked up in time to see something like a snake wrap itself around one of the creature's feet. Caught in midleap, the dragon made a sound, like a shell scraping rock. Then it fell hard and fast, trailing a fiery lacework.

"Deathweed," whispered Ryp. "Deathweed on our doorstep!"

The dragon thudded to the earth. Then a sphere of blue fire erupted and went out. The dragon leapt again, trailing a strand of charred, crumbling tentacle. When it came down at the edge of the School, it sent a spray of sand gusting across the ground. There were more shouts—Aerial mages calling for arrows, calling for stonemasters to turn the ground to glue, calling for help.

Daring to unshield his eyes and lift his head, Ryp found himself staring into the dragon's face. It stared back and shook its armored head. Again—that sound like shards of broken plate grating against one another.

Aiming the sharp beak of its snout toward the chimneyhouse, the dragon twitched its tail, a chain of interlocking shields. Then it threw itself at the smokestack. Clasping the bricks, it climbed the tower like a mantis up the side of a well. At the top it thrust its long head down into the chimney.

"For the rest of his life, Scharr will boast of this. He found the only creature in the Expanse, other than a firewalker, who could bear the furnace's flames and steal what they protect."

Tenderly did not answer him. She had fled.

The dragon disappeared, wriggling down through the smokestack toward the vast furnace pit that burned now with no purpose but to preserve House Jenta's pride. The furnace chimney became a fiery fountain, and smoke spilled as if a dam had been unblocked.

What did he promise it?

Bursts of sound blasted from the smokestack, like hammers striking metal drums. Then the deed was done. Something unrecognizable climbed out of the fire. Cracking, disintegrating fragments of its shields slid away, shattered by the heat. All that remained was the glossy sheen of bright green bristles—tender skin newly exposed.

The dragon almost fell from its perch as it craned its neck and blinked its glassy eyes. It looked like something made of thistle-stalks. Barking in annoyance, the dragon licked its exposed limbs with a sinuous, vermilion tongue. It turned its face, which looked like a pricklecone, toward Ryp and stared hatefully at him.

"Our famous Jentan Defenders should be grateful now for the dismissal," said Ryp to no one in particular. "If they had been here tonight, they'd have been ashes in an hour."

The dragon did not attack. Instead, it shrank back as if humiliated by its nakedness. Then, growling, it ascended as swiftly as a hummingbird. Without the weight of the shields, it could move almost too fast for the eye to follow. As it launched, it tore out a wedge of the chimneyhouse wall and the blazing stew of the furnace spewed into the courtyard. Mages and acolytes scattered, some fleeing, others rushing in to fight the fire with stonemastery.

"Oh no," moaned Ryp.

The dragon dropped, landing on the distant, leaning spire of the Epiphany Tower. The tower did not break, but it moved, the ground at its base bulging as the foundation was uprooted from the earth with the sound of tearing fabric.

Ryp pulled a farglass from his pocket and saw that the dragon held the legendary casket, a massive stone box glowing from the furnace's heat, in its claws.

Strange emotions roiled within the mage as he turned to trudge along the wall toward his chamber. Awe, for he had never dreamed he'd see a dragon again, much less up so close. Rage, for he was ashamed of his reaction. And of course, jealousy. But what did it matter after all? Everything was meaningless in the end.

Farewell, my brother. You've had your fun. And you've only made my time in this world more unbearable.

Ryp paused in the doorway of his chamber and blinked.

The pillowstone was missing from his bed.

He staggered, his hand clutched at his chest. But before he could cry out, he heard a low voice in the dark room.

"Where are they?"

The pillowstone was in Scharr ben Fray's hands, broken in two to expose a cavity in the center.

"You boasted that House Jenta kept its promise to Tammos Raak and guarded his casket. But I knew you were lying. You took the keys to Inius Throan from the casket a long time ago, didn't you? I came to fetch them while you watched my dragon put on a show, just in case you'd been keeping them under your head." He held up the empty stone shells. "But you've removed them. Are you so afraid I'll find them that you're carrying them in your pocket?"

Ryp recoiled as if slapped.

"You say that everything is meaningless. But you are so concerned with protecting Tammos Raak's secrets that you've conspired to keep the truth from me. You've learned something that you'd rather the rest of us never discover."

The chamber shuddered as the dragon roared.

Scharr leaned toward his brother, baring his teeth. "And more than that, you've been there, haven't you? You've unlocked Inius Throan and walked inside. How many years ago? Fifty? A hundred? You learned something that dragged you to despair." His eyes were wild as he threw the halves of pillowstone to the floor. "You're hiding the truth from the world."

"Yes, I've been there. I've seen the stories painted on its walls. I learned that there is nothing worth seeking in Inius Throan. I learned that the four houses have been built upon a lie. We are all more lost than we knew."

"I'm taking Cal-raven and the remnant of Abascar to Inius Throan," said Scharr ben Fray, "where Deathweed cannot reach us. We will wait until it runs out of things to consume. It will die."

"Deathweed replaced the beastmen," said Ryp. "Something worse will replace Deathweed. The Aerial is departing, Scharr. One by one. We're going on to something better. Freedom from the body. Relief."

"You've never known any pleasure that wasn't bodily, Ryp. The sweetness of nectar. The recognition of truth through the senses. This world and the truth are inseparable. I mean to enjoy it as long as I can. Give me the keys, Ryp. Or better yet, come with me."

"Be quiet before I change my mind," said the head of the Aerial.

For a fleeting moment, Ryp saw something on his younger brother's face that he had never seen before. Surprise.

Then he handed over a rolled scroll of cloth.

Scharr unfurled it across the bed and laughed in amazement at the intricate map drawn across its snowy span. At the end of the roll lay a ring with three large keys.

Ryp stepped forward and laid a withered hand on his brother's arm. "I give them to you, Scharr, because to keep them from you would be to say something there is worth protecting. But Inius Throan is as worthless as a tomb. Go find just how much fuss the four houses have made over a lie."

"What lie?"

"See for yourself."

Taking the keys, Scharr ben Fray touched the chamber wall and widened the window into a doorway. Then he stepped through onto a stone balcony that spread before his feet.

"How did you find the dragon?" Ryp whispered, hating his own curiosity.

"Isn't she beautiful?" Scharr spread his arms as if the dragon were his own invention. "Her name is Reveler. Her kind have grown fat and lazy in the Eastern Heatlands. But a cleverjay I know—Ruffleskreigh—told me Reveler was feasting on creatures as they fled from Deathweed near the Forbidding Wall's easternmost end. So I persuaded Ruffleskreigh to deliver messages and strike my bargain with the dragon. I'll arrange to have herds of muskgrazers led to her doorstep so she needn't go out hunting anymore. In return, I'll have Raak's Casket."

"It's worthless. Dusty old scrolls. That's all. Now send your new pet away. And slip out quietly, or the mages will cut you to pieces for what you've done."

"Why would they care? Haven't you taught them that nothing matters?" Scharr shrugged. "Ah, but they won't catch me. You didn't just provide me with keys. You provided me with a means of escape." He reached down and thrust his arms through the straps of Ryp's unfeathered wings.

Ryp barely had time to cry out.

Scharr leapt off the ledge. The wings snapped open, and he glided across the chaotic courtyard.

"They're not finished yet, you fool!" Even as Ryp shouted, the wings sputtered wildly and dove.

Then another shape left the edge of the wall. The great dust-owl screeched, plunging through the air toward the glider. It caught Scharr's shoulders and carried him back up in a sweeping arc, then alighted on the stairs of the Epiphany Tower just beneath the dragon.

A moment later Scharr ben Fray was climbing onto the dragon's back as if it were a giant vawn. And then they were gone—the dragon, the man, the casket, and the keys to Inius Throan.

As silence settled in the room, Ryp felt something slip away from him. He could not name it, and his thoughts berated him for his weakness in wondering what it might be. He saw Tenderly running across the sand, waving her arms madly and calling out as if the dragon rider had promised he'd take her along. He trembled.

15

VISCORCLAW

When Warney emerged from the back of Myrton's greenhouse and opened the trash bin, Cesylle sprang up with a pile of reeking weeds hanging off his head and a rag pressed to his face. "I've been in here all day. Thought you'd left me to rot."

"I told you I'd come back," Warney whispered. "You unlocked my cage, 'member?"

Fog around the Seers' Keep had erased all visibility. There was only the sound of disgruntled archers marching around the Keep to ensure no Seers were seeking to escape. Gossip buzzed in the alleys, where anxious guards locked all possible exits. Cracks were spreading through the Keep's walls. A strange clamor, like shattering mirrors, clashed within.

The Seers have already escaped, Cesylle thought. *Who will believe me if I describe it?* He clutched his prize—the Seers' marrowwood box—to his chest. "This box...it rattles," he muttered. "Even when it's still."

Warney pushed him back down as a line of guards hurried past. One glanced at him but showed no further interest. "Prob'ly figures I'm just a crumb-picker," he laughed. "They're off to the glassworks. The queen's procession is back, and they're sayin' somebody stole the queen's goblet."

"Good. Keeps the guards distracted. Did you talk to Myrton?"

"Myrton'll take a look at the box. He's a good fellow. Trust my eye." He tapped his glass orb. "Got a head full of bees and a cloak full of moths, but no need to fear him."

Cesylle wiped the weeds from his hair.

"Gonna follow me?" asked Warney. "Or rot in the trash?"

"What's in here, they say it's worse than beastmen." Cesylle handed him the wooden, wirebound box. "Don't drop it."

Warney shut the greenhouse door behind him, and at once the bandit and the wanted man found themselves in a jungle.

"Could almost call this the Cragavar," said Warney, " 'cept that the trees are planted in pots and all."

When nobody answered, he looked around. Cesylle was shifting from tree-pot to tree-pot like a gorrel in a fangbear's lair. "Don't go hidin'," whispered Warney. "Myrton's not a Seer."

"You don't understand." Cesylle peered out from behind a tree, shaking like a child who expects a whipping—a feeling Warney remembered well from childhood. "The kindest child in Abascar would put an arrow through my head. There's no way out of the hole I've dug."

Warney advanced from the tree room into the daylit, high-ceilinged workspace.

In front of a blazing brick stove with a towering chimney, Myrton was scratching his head's wild spray of grey hair, shelling seeds, and fussing over a table. Without greeting Warney, he took a twig from a handful he had cast across the tabletop and held it in the fire. From the smoke came a high-pitched whine.

"Puzzle, puzzle." He stepped from side to side, crushing seed shells. "That's not natural either."

"What do you mean?" said Warney.

"It's not the right pitch."

"The noise?" Warney asked, oblivious. "It should be a different note?"

"No, pitch. Pitch!" Myrton withdrew the smoking twig and showed the ink-black syrup dripping from the end. "This muck's running like blood through the Cragavar's trees. Seen it before...draining from bones of dead beastmen."

Warney noticed that the chemist had the same cloak, same shoes, same mussed tufts of hair as before. "You live in this place?"

"Oh, from time to time I'll go home and sleep a bit. But I find my joy here." He smiled at the hanging baskets, the chandelier of twinkling candleflowers. "The marketplace...so much competition, so much shouting. That place is a prison. But here, Warney..." He spread his arms to the array of green and growing things in pots and boxes on tables, benches, shelves, and sills under those great tortoiseshell windows that spread across the domed ceiling. "Here you'll find the greatest freedom. Know what that is?"

"Solitude?"

"Humility." Myrton put a finger to his temple. "Surround yourself with things that amaze you, and you'll forget about comparing yourself to others. The marketplace is a world of masks. Everyone hides themselves for shame. Better to lose yourself in a passion. What's yours, Warney?"

"Puzzle, puzzle," said Warney, trying to speak the chemist's language. He glanced back over his shoulder.

"You said you were bringing a guest," said Myrton, carrying another stick to the fire.

"He's...he's a little slow."

"A little afraid," Myrton growled, and for the first time Warney sensed that the old man might know what he had meant when he said, "There's a stranger, and you don't know him, and he doesn't want to talk to anybody, but he wants to bring you a problem to solve. And he wants to make something for you. Something called a 'mends.'"

"Amends are hard to make," said Myrton. "I wish he'd come out of hiding and talk to me." As he walked, the greenhouse master absent-mindedly reached out and let his hand brush along the flower petals in the raised beds on either side. "Sometimes I rise in the morning and set to work pruning a berry-tree, and then suddenly

I'll realize—it's the middle of the night. So different than the pace of life out there. So different not to hasten from one thought to the next. Here each thought has time to settle in my heart."

Warney stopped himself from declaring what a hurry he was in. He glanced over his shoulder again and caught a faint blur of movement just beyond the door—Cesylle, slinking into the shadows.

"I began here as an apprentice after hard years of rules in the shipyard," Myrton continued dreamily. "It was Doeann. She was so enchanting as we unloaded the plants from the wild islands. I followed her back to the royal gardens and watched her work. So quiet. So absorbed. It was contagious. And when Emeriene was born, lovely Doeann tended to her with the same joy that she did these flowers."

Warney thumped the Seers' secret box down on the table, watching Myrton's reaction.

An answering thump came from inside the box.

"I'm guessing it's not a puppy." Rubbing his hands together as if to warm them, Myrton stared at the box. Then he lifted it gingerly from the table and carried it out of the green, flourishing workshop into a bare, sterile glass room that, like the green room, had a fire burning in a brick chimney that rose to the roof. He slid the door shut behind Warney and moved to a table with a glass dome in its center.

"Why are you opening it here?"

"We should have nothing to do with the unfruitful works of the Seers," Myrton sighed. "Instead, we must expose 'em to the light."

He set the box under the glass dome. The dome was a solid curve except for two thick gloves, stained with dark splotches and stripes as if they'd come from a slaughterhouse, which had been attached to the inside. Pushing his hands into the gloves, he could work with whatever was covered while the subject remained sealed.

"Caution, caution," he whispered, putting his hands into the gloves. And then he spoke in a hiss as if trying to inhabit the manner of the Seers. "Inventionssss... inventionsss...distortionsss...lies."

Warney glanced toward the furnace. "I think we should burn it."

"Yes, yes, practical and good," said Myrton. "But we need better than good.

We need wisdom. We must know the truth of this box's secret. It's the first step toward being free of its threat."

Raising the box with his gloved hands, Myrton set it on a device that looked like a mousetrap with a razor wire. He turned a crank, then threw a switch, and jerked his hands out of the gloves, which fell limp within the dome.

The lid of the box was sliced free, and it toppled to the side.

Nothing happened.

Myrton leaned over the dome and looked into the box. "Hmm."

"What's inside?"

"A branch. A dead branch. But it drips the same dark pitch I was telling you about. That pitch is a poison. And it's spreading through the Cragavar." Myrton's hands twitched as if he were thinking about putting them back into the gloves.

"They twisted men into beastmen," said Warney. "What'll they do to the trees?"

"There's a troubling family resemblance," said Myrton. "It looks like Deathweed, but Deathweed's anchored to the ground." He put a hand back into one of the gloves and flexed its fingers over the box. "Deathweed works like a puppet. All of its lines move with one purpose, to seize and destroy."

"So who's the puppeteer?"

Myrton blinked, then looked past Warney toward the glass door. "Is that your friend out there, hiding behind my starcrown tree?"

In half a heartbeat, everything changed.

The many-fingered branch leapt from its box and seized Myrton's gloved hand. He yelped in surprise. The branches tightened their grip like a snake's jaws slowly crushing its struggling prey. Myrton threw himself back, trying to pull his hand from the glove, but as he did, he pulled the glass dome with him. It slid off the table and fell, shattering against the floor. The empty box toppled aside.

Three moths skittered out of Myrton's cloak into the air.

Cesylle came to the closed door, wide-eyed, hands pressed against the glass.

The green-black terror tumbled to the floor in a bundle like a clenched fist.

Myrton, his hand spraying blood, dashed to the opposite side of the room beside the furnace. He picked up the ember-fork with his good hand and surveyed the room.

"Better bandage that," said Warney.

"I'll soak it in a blood-cure first," Myrton snarled. "But later. Warney, we can't let that thing out of this room. . .alive, for lack of a better word." He fixed Cesylle with a look. "So you really have brought me that traitor." He raised the ember-fork and shook it. "It's too late for apologies, wretch! You've poisoned my daughter's life and her children."

The creature sprang up on the sharp tips of its twigs.

"It can see me," Myrton cursed. "It doesn't have eyes. How can it see me?" Then he paused. "Warney, I'll distract it. Go close the other door."

"The other door?" Warney looked around. "What other door?" It was difficult to discern an open space from a transparent barrier.

"Fire." Cesylle had slid through the main door holding a stick he'd taken from the green room table. The end was lit. "Fire's the only thing that can stop a viscorclaw, Master Myrton."

"A viscorclaw?"

"Tree branches quick and vicious as viscorcats. I heard Malefyk Xa whisper about them. Never thought they'd be real."

Warney found the second glass door open and slid its slight wooden frame along the runners until its notched edge snapped into the groove, latching the room shut tight. *I should be on the other side of this door,* he thought.

Myrton looked at Cesylle. He looked at the twitching wooden spider. And then he moved to stand before the fireplace. "Chase it to me. I'll catch it and throw it in the—"

The creature threw itself at Myrton. He had time enough to turn, but it scraped his face before seizing the back of his neck and wrapping its sharp tendrils around his throat. He choked, clawing at its tightening grip, and fell. His chin hit the edge of the raised stone ring around the furnace, snapping his head back.

Warney cried out and dove to help the old man. Seizing the fork, he tried to pry loose the monster's grip. Hot metal seared the viscorclaw's limbs. It sprang away and scuttled toward the other door, its steps tapping sounds like the clatter of woodpeckers' beaks against a pipe.

"Father!" came a muffled cry.

Emeriene and her boys stood with their faces and hands pressed against the glass. Before Warney could warn her, Emeriene opened the back door.

She did not see the viscorclaw even as it sprang at her.

As Cesylle dashed across the room, he reached into the furnace with a bandaged hand and snatched a blazing coal. He leapt as Emeriene fell, and, screaming as the coal blazed through his bandage into his hand, he pressed the flames against the attacker's black spine while it tightened around her throat.

The creature reversed itself, its legs bending back. It leapt at Cesylle and seized his face, thrusting two sharp limbs into his eyes. Howling, Cesylle threw himself backward toward the fire, the coal falling from his hand.

"Father!" shouted the boys.

Emeriene scrambled backward, dark blood streaming down her neck and darkening her gown. "Cesylle!" she screamed as her husband dove into the furnace.

She flung herself at the flames, reaching in for Cesylle's feet. But he kicked at her and disappeared in the blaze. She called for help. Fire flared into the room as Cesylle became a thrashing storm in the inferno.

Cesyr and Channy backed toward the door.

Myrton rose, groaning, and grabbed Emeriene by the shoulders. "Get back, Em."

A hissing, sizzling spray burst from the furnace and shot black, viscous lines across the floor. Smoke billowed into the room. The viscorclaw appeared again on the floor before the furnace, its spine unfurling flags of fire.

"Get out of here," Myrton rasped to Emeriene. When she failed to respond, he said, "Save my grandchildren."

Warney opened the door, and as Emeriene fled, he followed, closing it behind them. "To the infirmary," he shouted at her, surprised at his own forcefulness. "Fast."

But Emeriene, taking the boys under her arms and pressing their faces against her, turned back to watch her father.

Blood-masked, Myrton faced the burning creature with the ember-fork. He took a deep breath, put his bloodied hand into a pocket, and pulled out a carrot. He crunched three quick bites of the root and swallowed them. Then he lunged at the viscorclaw, scooped it up, and flung it hard back into the furnace. They all gasped as they saw it turn and spider its way up the chimney.

"The roof!" gasped Emeriene.

Myrton wasn't finished. He reached for a lever on the furnace's side and pulled it down, sealing the chimney shut. The furnace filled the room with smoke, and the fire within shuddered and shrank.

In a flash Myrton seized a heavy brick of mossy earth from the platform beside the furnace, flung it inside, and then dove to the floor, covering his face.

The fuel exploded. They all felt the tremor as fire poured from the furnace's mouth and filled the closed chimney.

The smoke dissipated. Fire crackled steadily inside. And a ruined mass dropped from the chimney, hissing and spitting, then crumbling into ash.

Myrton picked himself up, a man painted black and red. Coughing, he staggered to the door and slid it open.

"It's over," said Warney as Myrton embraced his daughter and her children.

"No," said Myrton. "No, it isn't. What we saw today... Viscorclaws'll be crawling over the Cragavar like flea-mice on a muskgrazer. Panic, panic... It's all going to come alive. For lack of a better word."

Cesyr and Channy clung to their mother, shaking, staring wild-eyed back through the windows at the stove's hot storm. Their sparkling eyes reflected fire and darkness.

Emeriene whispered a name. "Cal-raven."

The morning fog muted the sounds of the city as Cyndere followed the bounding hounds along the suspended arch between the Royal Tower and the Heir's Tower. She looked out over the domes of the auditoriums, the flags, the subdued marketplaces, and the gossiping crowds.

Mother's ship will be at sea now.

She could not see any ships. Only a storm of troubles, and whenever she sought to make sense of one, another threatened to disrupt her focus.

Some of our subjects are lost with the ale boy. Cal-raven's alive, but where? Jordam's off again, convinced that Auralia has returned. Me—why, I have a beastchild in my care. A beastchild. I've put her in a sealed chamber in the infirmary. Deuneroi, how do I do this?

She looked north and east over the Cragavar horizon toward Fraughtenwood.

And Tabor Jan is moving farther and farther away.

A rock sailed past her head, so close to her cheek that she felt the air of its passage. Before she realized what it was, an angry shriek sounded from a mob below: "Jaralaine!"

And then the crowd took up the cry. "Jaralaine! Jaralaine! Just another Jaralaine!"

Cyndere ducked and crawled within the scant protection that the bridge's parapet offered while rocks clattered around her. Beside her, the dogs barked at the missiles as if they might scare the stones away.

Within a few more rapid heartbeats, guards surrounded her, their arrowcasters aimed down at the mob. She stood, dusted off her clothes, and finished crossing the bridge, straight and proud, her temples burning and her breath short.

Back in her tower, she crawled onto a corner of her couch and folded herself up tight, hugging a pillow to her breast. She stared at the floor with its scattering of chalk drawings. "Jaralaine," she whispered. "Why would they call me Jaralaine?"

"Queen Jaralaine stole House Abascar's colors." Her brother Partayn stood in the other doorway. "She called it The Wintering of Abascar."

"The Seers' potions. We've taken away what our people loved. Is that it?"

Partayn stepped into the room, carrying his twelve-stringed tharpe. "You dodged the stones. Now dodge the words. They're small-minded hind-heads."

"They'll find all manner of justifications for violence now." Bitterness soured her voice. "They'll cheer at any accusation hurled against the throne. Rage feels good. It's easier than thinking."

Partayn struck a cheerful chord, defiant hope resonating in the tharpe's wooden frame. "How was beachcombing with the beastman this morning?"

"I showed Jordam where I found the oceandragon's skeleton. We fed pieces of fish to the beastchild. You wouldn't have believed it. I don't think we should call Jordam a beastman anymore."

She rose and walked to the wall where a mirror had once hung, took a cloth, and began to erase some of the details on Jordam's chalk-drawn likeness—the rough edge of his mane, the large fang that bulged from his upper lip, and then she lightened the scar on his forehead where a horn had once protruded. "It's like watching a fever break. I'm beginning to see it—the man he might have been without the Curse."

"That's your mission now, isn't it? Breaking fevers."

"It's a beginning."

"Where is Jordam now?"

"Gone. I told him I need his help to bring in any Cent Regus who will accept our care. But first, I said, we must cure our own problems. We must expose and abolish the lies here at home. When I said that, he became troubled. He said he needed to go and find Cal-raven. He said..." She drew a furrow in the beastman's brow. "He said he'd told a terrible lie."

Partayn arched an eyebrow. "Jordam's feeling guilty? He's gone to confess?"

Cyndere sat down and drew a chalk tattoo on the palm of her hand.

"You wish you'd gone with him."

"You'd never allow it. And you're master of Bel Amica."

"Cyndere...the Deathweed."

"I know. But Jordam's out there."

"Jordam might survive a Deathweed attack. But you..." He turned a tab on the tharpe's wooden neck and a spring broke with a loud, sour *sproing!* "Krammed out-of-tune piece of butterfly dung!"

"I'm in just as much danger here."

Partayn sat beside her and touched her forehead, her nose, and her chin as he had when they had played as children. "What're you going to do, little sister? You can't live with Jordam in the wild. You can't keep him here. But you're unhappy when he's gone."

"He's my closest tie to my husband. When I'm with him, I feel like Deuneroi is close."

Partayn rose and went to the window. "What if I were to find the source of the Deathweed, Cyndere?"

"Partayn, I don't want to talk about this."

"Just pretend. Like when we were kids dreaming up adventures. What if I led a force down into the Core?"

"You're not leaving me here."

"The beastmen are weakening, Cyn. They have no chieftain. I spent enough time in slavery there to know my way around. What if I were to find the source of the Curse and destroy it? Imagine."

"We've just sent mother off. I won't be left alone. Not with things in such a state."

"Free the forest of Deathweed, and Tilianpurth could be a station where we work to cure the beastmen. Jordam could help you. You could live there. I know how you love the place."

"The well's gone, Partayn. We'd need to find another source of the enchanted waters. And Deathweed isn't our only problem."

"Ah, yes. Ryllion and Cesylle. That brings me to my news."

She looked up.

Partayn leaned against the window frame. "Cesylle's dead."

Cyndere slid from the edge of her seat to kneel on the floor. Her initial response—a surge of relief—was quickly erased by a wave of questions. "Emeriene. She must be devastated," she said. *But she'll be free,* she thought. "What happened?"

Partayn related Myrton's account of the Seers' deadly secret, the fire, and Cesylle's demise.

"The forest," Cyndere whispered. "What if Myrton's right? We'll have to seal up the city like a tomb and surround it with fire."

"I must go back to the Core, Cyndere. It may be our only chance. We have to find the source and set it ablaze. Stop the Curse at its root."

"Emeriene." She climbed back to the couch. "Little Cesyr and Channy must be sick with all they witnessed. I should go to her."

"Emeriene's asked to be left alone with the boys. Even by you, Cyndere."

"Even me?"

"She's a wreck. She's as upset about King Cal-raven as she is about losing Cesylle."

"Cal-raven? Why is she upset about..." Then she gasped. "He's out there. In the forest."

"I've sent a company north. On vawns. They'll catch up with Tabor Jan. They're carrying torches and seabull sacks full of torch oil. We'll hope they don't need it."

"Who? Who did you send?"

"Eight defenders, two healers from the infirmary, and that one-eyed glassworker."

Cyndere joined him at the window. "Are you sure Emeriene said I couldn't visit her?"

He shrugged. "You don't have to obey her."

Cyndere walked out of the chamber.

She chose the stairs—she wanted to keep moving, without having to wait for the lift.

A couple of sisterlies passed her on the stairway, startled at her fierce demeanor.

Emeriene's free of Cesylle. But it won't give her any peace. And her boys... To see their father burned up before their eyes... They were already angry and reckless. What will she do?

She turned the corner and strode swiftly to Emeriene's chamber. The answer to her own question hovered within reach, but she was too terrified to reach for it.

A rope dangled from the handle to Emeriene's door—a cord of towels knotted together.

"What is this?" She pushed the door open. "Emeriene?"

The room was quiet. The window's curtains seemed restless in the chill. Everything was just as it had always been, except for the broken mirror and the arrow that lay among glass shards spattered with dark, dry blood.

Emeriene's sisterly uniform was tossed across the table, cast aside like a cocoon.

Cyndere returned to the entryway and took the rope of towels in her hands. Her eyes stung with unshed tears.

And as she ached for yet another loss, the tower shook. A sound like a thousand shattering mirrors daggered the quiet. The air filled with dust. The Seers' Keep had come crashing down, and nothing was left but chalk white clouds wisping away on the wind.

16

The River Guardians

A shadow among shadows, Aronakt clung batlike to the wall high above the gathered underground travelers. With the crisscrossing strands of elaborate ivy as his ladder, he ascended with his eyes on one of the narrow, daylit breaks in the cavern ceiling.

As others watched him, murmuring about his chances, the ale boy looked at the mouth of the river where the outgoing wind met the incoming water and stirred it into froth. The air sang a soft, whirring note, and he remembered blowing lightly into empty ale bottles in the Underkeep.

The river's mouth was wide enough for five rafts side by side, and the passage upriver glittered green. "We should keep going," he said to himself. "It's too soon to climb back to the surface."

Petch scowled at the ale boy. "We have no choice. That passage might become too narrow, or the ceiling might drop too low. And then where would we be?"

There was a sound like a ripping canvas. Aronakt scrabbled at the wall, the ivy tearing loose under his weight. As others backed away from the rain of dust, debris, and insects, Aronakt plummeted, his ragged overcoat fluttering like a brascle's wings. "Aronakt, my love!" screamed two Bel Amican women, and then they looked at each other in disgruntled surprise.

Batey jumped forward, reached out, and caught the gangly climber.

Aronakt seemed unfazed. He stared intently at a tremendous ivy leaf he had torn from the wall. He tried to bite off a shred, but his teeth left only a dent, and he spat out red juice as he cast it down. He walked away, the two anxious women rushing to his sides, each eager to express greater concern than the other.

The travelers began to sit down, bowing under the rush of the wind. Even the Abascar survivors were looking defeated. The hungrier they became, the more their dreamlike delirium faded and their attention became affixed to the urgent, practical work of staying alive.

Batey stood rubbing his mustache with his knuckles and looking down at the ivy leaf. "Some of these leaves are big as bedsheets. They'd make good tents. Or..." He walked down to the shore, then flung the leaf out like a flag over the water. Wind whipped it violently, sucking the length of it toward the tunnel.

He pulled it back, grinning. "Let's put a raft in the water."

Three of the Bel Amicans pushed the foremost float out and then climbed aboard while two others held it fast to keep it from floating back across the space they'd covered. Batey climbed onto the raft and gave an edge of the leaf to another passenger. "Hold it tight. Lift it upright. I've built enough boats in Bel Amica to know—all you need for a sailboat is water, wind, a raft, and a canvas. Now..." He turned to the waders who held the edge of the raft. "Climb on."

When the raft began to move against the current, the wind filling the leaf-sail, Batey looked back, eyes flashing bright white and wild. "And that is today's lesson," he shouted.

Petch, who had watched all of this with arms crossed, suddenly dropped his skeptical pose, snatched up a glowstone, splashed anxiously into the water, and climbed on the raft with Batey and his five helpers.

The raft picked up speed, and a few moments later it was gone, Petch's glowstone fading like a spark.

After a stunned silence, the other travelers rushed to the wall to tear at the large ivy leaves.

The ale boy was the last to climb aboard one of the sail-borne rafts. In the tunnel as he lost sight of the gold-lit cavern, he thought he saw something splashing against the current—something like a large hand, its fingers striking the water and paddling hard in pursuit.

The tunnel roared with wind, with the spray of water against the rafts' leading edges, and with the excited cries of the passengers.

But after the initial thrill of swift progress, there came the fear of what might happen next. Occasionally the ceiling dipped so low that it ripped at their sails.

They sailed for what seemed like several hours, right on through what they assumed was a night. In time they found themselves scudding between banks of terraced earth, where shining eyes watched them, thick as fields of stars.

Irimus Rain saw Kar-balter reach for an arrow. "I wouldn't do that. If you hit one, the others might be angry. And we don't know what they'll do."

The boy scooped up a handful of water, examining it in his glowstone's light. "Water's clearer here. Still too gritty to drink, but better."

"Look." Kar-balter folded the sail and handed it to Em-emyt, so the float slowed. "The rafts ahead are moving in to shore."

Among the crowd on the bank, they faced a sobering realization. "We've hit a spot that's too tight," said Alysa, a Bel Amican woman who had proven so resilient with an oar that she'd taken turns steering several rafts. "We can't sail on. The ceiling's low ahead, and the river's narrow. But it's shallow. We can walk."

"We're not all here," said Irimus. "Where are the first and second rafts?"

"They've gone on," said Alysa.

And so the procession moved on, most of them striding forward against the slow and tepid flow. But the weariness proved too much for some, and they lay on the rafts that the line pushed upstream.

The ale boy, too small to walk upright in the current, lay on the foremost raft with all their collected glowstones so he could illuminate their path.

In this stifling vein, they labored on, the sounds of their gasps and groans echoing all around them, loud and close. In time it seemed they were imprisoned in an everlasting travail, and one by one they would stumble, catch one another, and carry each other along. But the Abascar survivors, feeble as they were, began to sing the songs of the night hours. Their harmonies seemed to strengthen them, propelling them like a march-chant for a troop of soldiers.

The songs faded twice at a sound like distant thunder. Dust wafted from the trembling ceiling.

"What was that?" asked Nella Bye. "Earthquake?"

No one had an answer. But each time the flow of the river changed—the first time it quickened and the level rose slightly, and the second it slowed and grew shallower, as if somewhere a great wheel had turned.

"Eat," whispered Nella Bye.

The ale boy woke to something bitter on his tongue and a circle of blurred faces around his raft, looking at him.

"It's just some bits of a fish that Cormyk caught."

"No," he breathed, closing his eyes. He felt waves of heat wafting through his head and shoulders. "Not yet. Wait." He tried to call up a face for the name Cormyk. How far had they traveled together without even knowing one another's names?

"Ale boy." Irimus Rain's silver beard wagged over him. "We admire your discernment. And if there were good fish from clean water in front of you, you would be a fool to eat this tasteless meat. But this is what we have. Cormyk was a fisherman in Bel Amica, so he should know if it's likely to make you sick."

The fisherman. The ale boy remembered him now. An aging, quiet man whose face still wore the horror he'd suffered in captivity.

"Are there fish for everybody?"

"No," said Irimus. "We're passing around the two he caught. Feeding the weakest first."

The ale boy tried to refuse, but his body worked against him, taking the piece that Nella Bye pushed into his mouth with her thumb. He chewed it, then swallowed and choked. She lifted her cupped hand to his lips. "I strained this through a clean stretch of cloth on my cloak. You need it."

He swallowed. The water tasted like grass tea at first and then the ferment of an orange peel. He gagged and coughed.

As he came to his senses, he saw that they were moving into a more spacious passage. The exhausted walkers clambered back onto the rafts and argued over who would take up the rowing. But the debates quieted as they looked up in amazement.

Torchlight revealed that the ceiling was thickly webbed, and there was movement in the silvery mesh.

An enormous cavespider slipped out through the milky weave and hung suspended in the space behind the last raft. Its slender, glassy legs twitched as if it were counting the bodies. Then it sprang away out of sight.

When Irimus whispered the news to Nella Bye, her unseeing eyes widened. "Please don't say any more," she whispered.

The spider reappeared, scuttling across the water's surface on the fibrous pincers of its feet. As it did, it drew a thin, almost invisible taut line, just above the water.

"What is it doing?" whispered Irimus. "It almost looks like it's setting a trap for us."

"But it's behind us," said the boy.

Nella Bye shrieked, and they turned.

A smaller spider, this one about the size of a rain canopy, had alighted on the front of their raft. Its body was as big as the ale bottle that the boy had stashed in the travelers' cargo and just as green and glassy. The glowstones' light filled its form, highlighting delicate organs that pulsed and twitched. Its eyes were like clusters of purple fish eggs, and its teeth were like little knives that sharpened one another.

Three of its feet were fastened on Nella Bye's head.

"Don't move," the ale boy told her.

Irimus drew out a dagger.

Nella Bye clenched her eyes shut, baring her teeth, and emitted a faint squeal as the spider stroked her brow with the edge of a fibrous foot.

"Is it hurting you?" Irimus asked.

"No," she squeaked. "It's...prickly like a thistle."

The spider made no aggressive moves. It just kept its foot against Nella Bye's forehead, then prodded lightly at the ragged fabric over her left shoulder.

Suddenly it released her and skittered around to perch on the back of the raft.

"They're...they're not after us," said the ale boy. "They're after something else."

No sooner had he said it than something came swimming aggressively upstream behind them, running right into the low-slung line. It looked like a living tree branch, but it thrashed like a bearcat caught in a trap.

"Another big bug?" asked Kar-balter.

"I don't think so," said Irimus.

The travelers watched, horror-stricken, as the captured pursuer became tangled in the line. Its limbs twitched fitfully, and it kicked and fought the web. The more it struggled, the more of its wooden, nine-legged body became glued. Meanwhile, the spiders went to work. Standing on the surface of the water, they spun their thrashing prey, wrapping it in a thick cocoon.

Other cavespiders descended from the ceiling, casting lines across the water behind the rafts.

"More sensible spiders I never have seen," said Irimus.

"That thing," said the ale boy, "it's not welcome on their river."

"And they're expecting more," whispered Irimus. "Let's go. I'd rather meet more of these spiders than any more of...that."

Behind them, the spiders left their catch suspended like a trophy.

Weary as he was, the ale boy could not sleep. The spiders and the wooden claw had reminded them all that they were vulnerable and that they had no idea what to expect ahead.

They did not wait long for the next surprise.

"That's...ice," gasped Aronakt, pointing to the stream ahead.

"How can there be ice on the river?" asked Irimus Rain. "It isn't cold enough."

"It certainly is ice," said Kar-balter. "An island of ice floating downstream."
The ale boy wanted to rise, but he could not.

He heard a sharp crunch. "I've got it with the oar," Kar-balter shouted.

"Look," said someone else. "Snow flowers!"

"Those only grow on mountain ice," said Irimus. "Must have come from far away."

A moment later Nella Bye held a cupped hand to the ale boy again. "Here you are. Try this."

He touched his tongue to an ice crystal. The fierce clarity of it shocked him. He took in a mouthful and held it there. His teeth ached, and then his head ached. But the melt that trickled down his throat was immediately invigorating. It was as though wires pulled taut throughout his body relaxed.

"That's good," he said. "That's very good." He closed his eyes, recognizing a faint scent from Nella Bye's frosted hands. "We have to keep going."

17

Homeless Dreamers

"Good thing your patrols never found my highwatches." Cal-raven's voice came from the darkling branches above. Then he landed hard, his boots stamping deep impressions in soft, loose soil. "Without them, we'd go hungry."

Ryllion woke, jittery, the evening around him a blur. "Food?"

Cal-raven tossed him a leather pouch. He sat up and leaned against a boulder, dizzy with hunger and punished for lack of something that only the Seers could give him—but what? He feared that he knew the answer.

He loosened the sack's drawstring, and with a claw he teased out some green nuts and shelled seeds. "How'd you keep pests out of the stash?"

"Made the pouches from gorrel hide." Cal-raven laughed as Ryllion choked.

While Cal-raven arranged kindling, whispering as if to give the fire an invitation, Ryllion watched him, bewildered. Cal-raven looked more like a merchant fallen on hard times than a king. His red hair had grown long and ragged. His beard was long too, but uneven, revealing deep scars on his face.

What is this man made of? he wondered. *He laughs so easily with one who recently plotted to kill him.*

He caught a few words, and he knew that Cal-raven was building that new house in his imagination. The thought made him anxious. What chances would he have among stragglers he had mocked and abused? Would they respect their king's orders? Would Cal-raven keep his promise and give him a chance to make amends? What would happen when House Bel Amica found out?

They won't shrug and say, 'Oh, when Ryllion killed Deuneroi, it was just the Seers' influence.' They'll demand justice.

Cal-raven struck a sparkstone, and a yellow flame slithered through the kindling, revealing the low, mossy trunks of the trees.

A brascle called from above. Both men tensed. Any other bird call would have been welcome in this lifeless forest. But brascles meant beastmen. This one was close.

"Where are we?" asked Ryllion. Sick as he was, their days of slow travel in search of the Abascar company's trail were blurring in his memory.

"Edge of Fraughtenwood, a journey west of the Throanscall." Cal-raven shook his head. "The last time I was this far north, I was driving beastmen from the site of my father's folly. He tried to dig a channel from the Throanscall."

"Why?"

"He wanted streams to flow through Abascar, water to bless my mother's gardens. But then she ran away. He was humiliated. The dig became something else. A demonstration of control."

"Is that why your father rejected the Seers' help? Fear of losing control?"

"He wanted Abascar to provide for itself—food, water, everything—so no one would have to go outside. He once loved the wild, just as he loved my mother. But then the wild took my mother. Losing them both, I think his heart broke twice."

Ryllion finished the last of the small, stale meal. "You speak as if you cared for them."

Cal-raven scowled, staring into the flames as moths fluttered about his head like troubling memories. "I think I understand my mother. I cannot put a wall between myself and the wild unless I wish to cut myself in half. I'm also my father's son. I want to build a house that will shelter my people from harm. I must not repeat their mistakes. I want my people to enjoy all the gifts the Expanse still has to offer, all the things my father and mother denied them for fear or jealousy."

"There were stories in Bel Amica. I heard your father cast out the teacher you loved."

"Scharr ben Fray told me tales of the Keeper. How it would crush Cent Regus hordes. How it would carry injured travelers across the Expanse to healing waters. How it would hide from those who sought it but take the most determined believers to a great city of many towers. Bell towers. I would dream of making that journey. I would wake hearing that music. Fourteen shining notes. I'd go out into the forest searching."

Cal-raven turned to face him, a silhouette against the fire, sparks rushing up behind his head. "You really don't remember the dreams?"

Ryllion doubled over, groaning with the sense that jaws were grinding up his guts. He seethed until the pain passed, then spoke through clenched teeth. "At the shipyard where my father worked, I fell from a boat's prow. I seized a piece of driftwood and stayed afloat. I carried it for days after that. It looked like a winged horse with a dragon's tail. It was only an accident of wood and weather, but it seemed so familiar." Ryllion felt as if he were setting down his armor in the presence of an enemy. "I gave it a name. Don't all children name their toys? Decided I would build a boat and place it on the prow. Like a protector. But the foreman of my father's ship saw it and mocked me. My father stepped between us. And that night he returned from the shipyard with cuts on his face. So he beat me."

"For that toy?"

"No. With that toy." A snarl slithered into his voice. "The foreman had punished him for failing to rid me of such childish dreams. The foreman was a man of certainties." He paused. "It's strange. The foreman knew my toy looked like the Keeper even though I never said anything."

"He recognized it."

"Men make right what's wrong through strength, my father said. So I pursued strength. And I caught the Seers' attention. They told me that they could help me become stronger and that my ambition was given to me by my moon-spirit. It was my responsibility to fulfill it. So as I grew, I followed their counsel."

Cal-raven stared intently into the dark. "It isn't easy to discover that faith has made you a fool. It's hard to know what to..." He stopped and stood up. "Did you hear something?" He snatched up a piece of kindling and carried its flame to the clearing's edge.

Ryllion listened. The forest was restless, as if a wind were rising. But there was no wind.

"On a few occasions," he said, "I've seen a shadow in my dreams. It's a terrible feeling. I wake sensing that the Keeper is angry. Angry that I cast it aside."

"Then let me quiet your fears." Cal-raven returned to the fire, drew a second burning brand from the flames, and brought it to Ryllion. "I've seen the Keeper. The beast that inspires these dreams and stories is an animal. A beast of bone and blood. It's magnificent. But it does not grant your wishes. It does not heal wounds. It's as likely to destroy what you love as it is to tear down what's in your way. And yet..."

The brascle cried out again, a shrill and angry call, and wheeled away southward.

"And yet the dreams go on," Cal-raven said softly. "I don't understand this. But perhaps I've been wrong to think that the Keeper is what I've been looking for. Perhaps the Keeper was just a lure. A guide. A piece of a greater mystery. Auralia said that the Keeper sent her to Abascar. But what did it send her to do? Show us colors we'd never seen. A glimpse of another world. When I saw them, I felt such longing. I knew I had to find their source. When I find it...that will be Abascar's new home."

The fire crackled, one of the wedges of cottonbeard crumbling into ash.

"You're a fool; it's true," whispered Ryllion. "You've gambled everything on a dream. And it's all fallen to pieces. You're like me. Except that you have something I do not. You have hope. I have none, but if you think you can find help for me...I will go with you."

Cal-raven nodded. "When we find Tabor Jan's company, you will have to hide yourself until I can persuade them to accept you."

Ryllion reached up to scratch at the remnants of his mask of bandages. Then he tore them away, and fresh lines of blood ran down his face. "I do not expect them to forgive what they—"

"Hush." Cal-raven raised the fiery branch. "Something's moving."

Ryllion's ears twitched, and his nostrils flared. "I smell torch oil. Someone else is traveling. And not very far away."

"I'm going back up to the highwatch," said Cal-raven. "Perhaps I can—"

With a calamitous noise, the highwatch crashed down from the treetop.

"This clearing," gasped Ryllion, backing toward the fire. "It's. . .larger."

"The trees," said Cal-raven. "Ryllion, they're moving. They're leaning away from the fire."

As Tabor Jan's company prepared for the last stretch of their venture through Fraughtenwood, Milora woke with the troubling sense that a hooded man had been standing beside her bed and staring intently down at her, wringing his hands. She had not feared him, sensed no sinister intent. He had been the frightened one.

She did not like feeling that she had the power to frighten anyone, especially while she slept.

She also disliked the feeling of being seen. She could answer so few questions about herself, she felt unsettled by the thought that someone else might see her first, might guess her story, might have power to reveal an origin, a truth, a purpose.

She rose quickly and slipped out, finding that once again she could tiptoe past watchmen without being seen.

Climbing a nearby hill, eager to rise above the trees, she felt like a drowning woman drawn up from the sea just in time. A few steps shy of the large coil tree at the top, she stopped, startled by a leaf of vivid colors that seemed to promise the full flush of autumn.

A false promise, she thought. *This forest is dead.*

She ascended slowly, staring at the leaf as if it were a map of a lost world. Then she turned westward and saw another cluster of hills, one of which bore a barn that looked like a beast propped up on its forelegs and fighting for life.

Turning north, she eyed the peaks of the Forbidding Wall with unease. She held the colorful leaf up against the dark cloud world that waited beyond the mountains.

I would set you like a flower in a vase, to let you burn as long as you are able.

She heard a singsong tone from the coil tree, and her heart pounded. *Someone else is sneaking about.*

It was Obrey.

Milora crossed her arms. "What do you think you're doing? Nobody's allowed to leave the camp."

"Then what do you think you're doing?" the girl snapped.

"I'm a grownup," said Milora.

"I wish you weren't," said Obrey. "I want somebody to play with."

"You're my responsibility," said Milora. "Your grandfather says so. And I say you shouldn't run out into the dangerous woods."

"And who do you think taught me how?" the girl replied. "You told me that we're wildflowers, that we grow best when we're free. And then you scold me for steppin' outside the camp just like you do when nobody's lookin'."

Milora sighed, slumping down and gazing out over the dire woods and the webs of dead undergrowth that had sought to spoil their journey. "This world's finished with wildflowers. I can't wait to get back to the glass mine. It's more a home to me than Bel Amica."

"I liked Bel Amica," said Obrey.

"I would have liked it better without all of those...*people.*" Milora tousled Obrey's hair. "But I do love you, Obrey. I love how you find play in everything."

"You made beautiful things in Bel Amica. Like the window full of colors. You should have told them it was yours."

"If they found out it was mine, they would start asking for things. Things to make them happy. They don't know why I like to make things."

"Why, then?"

"I just see things, and they seem like pieces of other things, and so I try putting them together to see what happens. To see part of the world I haven't seen yet. Like when you ask me questions, and more questions, and more questions. I should stop talking now. You're still a child. You should get to play as long as you can without having to worry about the why."

Obrey thought about this, carving eyes next to the knob of a root. "It's like playing 'What's Your Face?'"

"How do you play that?"

"Well, my mama would hide her face from me behind her hands or a plate or a blanket and make me lean forward. I knew what her face was like. But I wanted to see it again. All of a sudden. Ha! I liked the surprise. And it would be new and familiar at the same time. And we'd laugh. And I'd say, 'Do it again.' Then she. . .then she died. And sometimes I feel like I'm still playing that game. But she doesn't jump out anymore."

"Yes, it's like that. The things I make are like the blanket that hides the face. Once I've woven a veil, I can search for the mystery that it wants to reveal. I hear it whispering through. . .something new every time."

"I understand that," said Obrey, trying hard to sound like a thoughtful adult. "I'm trying to figure things out too."

"And what are you trying to figure out, Obrey?"

"These things." She lifted a plain sack of interwoven reeds and spilled a pile of trinkets—small stone figures, some painted, some plain, with intricate costumes of colors so vivid they shone. There were sticks of colored wax. There were brushes and little cups of paint sealed with corks. There was a thing made of leather and feathers like a winged horse with a long tail. And here was a puppet—a plain stocking with buttons for eyes and long silverbrown hair, like a doll waiting to have the details sewn on.

Milora took the puppet and slowly slipped her hand into it, pulling it up to her elbow. She worked its mouth uncomfortably, for her hand was too large for it. "Obrey, where did you get these things?"

"Krawg gave 'em to me. He said he found 'em in Bel Amica. They were thrown out in the trash, somewhere in an alley below the marketplace." Then she stopped and sighed. "I lied," she said.

"You lied?"

"Krawg told me not to tell. But he stole them."

"He stole them."

"He stole 'em from a bad Bel Amican who was tricking folks into giving 'em up."

"I see." Milora looked at the figures with a strange, prickling feeling of dread, as if they were living things with sharp teeth. But then she reached forward, took two small, crooked figures, and stood them side by side. "These go together," she said, and then she paused, noticing that they had tiny gemstones for eyes. One figure was missing a gemstone. "Yes," she said again. "I'm sure of it."

"Why?"

Milora set them by the blue line of tall grass. "And this..." She lifted the animal of leather and feathers and set it in the depression. "It lives here, beneath the lake."

"Why?" asked Obrey. She seemed alarmed by Milora's announcements. Then she took the bag and set it behind her as if she were protecting something.

A large autumn leaf floated down and settled at Milora's feet, resembling a bird that fans its feathers to warm its wings in the sunlight.

"This one here..." Milora took the figure of a man on horseback. "He's the prince of the realm. He rides to high places so he can see the whole world around him. He's looking for something."

Obrey began to dress the tiny figures, fitting them into capes and costumes. With each attempt she glanced sidelong at Milora, who nodded almost imperceptibly or scowled. "You sound so sure," Obrey said skeptically. "Why is it that way? And who made it so?"

"There's somebody missing," said Milora in a funny voice, moving the mouth of the sock puppet.

Obrey sighed. "I think I'd tell a different story."

"You probably would," said Milora.

"And it would mean different things than yours."

"Something's missing." Milora reached out to poke Obrey with the puppet. "And I think it's hiding behind you." She laughed, but it was a forced laugh. Why was she behaving this way, provoking poor Obrey? Why was she so eager to see the last piece in the bag? "The play cannot begin until all the people are in place."

Obrey pushed the puppet away. "There isn't anybody else. And if there was, it wouldn't be part of this play. It would be mine. Something special. I'd call her queen of the stars."

"No," said Milora. "Her name's Auralia."

They both sat in silence. Milora was terrified, holding her breath, wishing time would stop and save her from whatever came next.

"You don't know that." Obrey crossed her arms. "You can't know that. It's not yours to decide."

"I'm not deciding," Milora whispered. "I'm remembering."

Obrey slowly came to her feet, her face reddening. "Why is it that way? And who made it so?"

The question hung in the air like the chime from a bell.

"Who's that?" Obrey's gaze had shifted, puzzling over something at the base of the hill. "See? That hooded man looks so small from here. He looks like..." She pointed to one of the two figures that Milora had set by the line of blue weeds.

"Go see what he wants," said Milora.

"I think it's Krawg." Obrey brushed off her grass-stained leggings and went running in stumbling strides down the slope.

Milora looked at the cloth bag that lay in the flattened grass where Obrey had been. She slipped the puppet from her hand, took the bag, and turned it inside out. A figure fell into her lap with a small pinging sound.

She glanced down the hill. Obrey was approaching Krawg, but he was still looking up at the scene beneath the tree as if he were waiting for something to happen.

Milora scowled and flicked her fingers at the air as if she could snip him away like a fly. Then she turned her back and held the tiny, chiming figure in her lap.

It was the image of a young woman dressed in a cloak so billowy and flowing that the figure within it looked like someone rising from a rippling pond. Milora turned her over and found the delicate shape of the young body taking shelter within the cloak canopy, a snail within a shell, her legs posed as if she were running. The body shifted within the cloak.

"You're a bell."

She pinched the figure's shoulders and shook her lightly, striking a perfect shimmer of sound. As she continued, the sound intensified and the bell began to warm in her hands, flowering into color. She trembled. It was as if the colors flowed from her fingertips, bringing the figurine to life.

And not just any life. The young woman's face was bruised, her silverbrown hair flecked with dust and scraps from the forest. Her cloak bloomed with luminescent hues. And those tiny, fragile hands clutched the cloak tightly, raising it slightly in her flight.

Milora was frightened. Frightened as she always was by what her play revealed, what appeared without her intention, as if she were not making but discovering secrets someone had prepared for her. With such a revelation would come a sense of responsibility to share it. And that would bring more trouble than she could bear.

On one of the figurine's fingers, Milora found a fleck of green no larger than a grain of sand.

She touched her own emerjade ring. The curtain fell, and the light came in. She knew her name.

The two old Gatherers, their eyes—all three—bright as gemstones, teaching her about the strange and limiting ways of House Abascar.

Stealing sweet rolls from their kitchens and hurrying off into the woods to prepare feasts of berries and bread.

The huts. The alarms when beastmen were near.

Prince Cal-raven on his horse, fierce inquiry in his eyes.

The injured beastman crawling into the lakeside caves, healing as he rested on her blankets, watching her labor deep into the night to braid all colors together into one bright cloak.

Deep Lake. Its secrets. Its ripples and disturbances. Its wings.

The boy who had been knocked from his raft and then crawled up on the shore before her cave. The friend. The questions they had asked each other. The questions they had asked of color and flame.

The zeal to share glory with people who had closed their curtains, who wanted to be flattered, who wanted what they had seen before. Their fearful king.

But Cal-raven had come to visit her. Cal-raven had asked her questions. He had been frightened and mystified. He had promised to help her. *Auralia,* he had whispered. *Auralia.*

"Poor Cal-raven," she said, choking. "This world's bound to fail us. We'll never find each other here. I've lost my play. You've lost your dream. What would it cost to find another chance? Too much."

The ground rumbled. The bell toppled and fell from her knee, tumbling into the interlacing roots. More leaves came showering down, their green fading to grey, edges curling.

The ground around her began to crackle like a shell breaking open.

She reached for the bell among the roots. It was stuck between them. She dug at it furiously, prying it loose.

Dissonant tones—like bows drawn across stringed instruments out of tune—surrounded her. She looked down and saw some of the trees below were cowering like old men in great travail.

Krawg stood there, lifting Obrey up and looking around in dismay.

Among the trees the green tents were collapsing. The company was packing in haste. A horn—an alarm—sounded from the camp.

Auralia looked at what remained of Fraughtenwood. The sea of dead and gnarled trees leaned against the mountains like the ocean against a rocky shore. Her gaze rose up the low mountains to the higher mountains to the intimidating, snowbound heights and then to the swirling world of cloud, like a tidal wave waiting for permission to crash.

She took a step forward, but her other foot was fixed in the grip of a coiling root. She sprawled in the dirt, sobbing as she kicked against its clutches. The root tore free of the base of the tree. Its grip tightened.

The bell fell from Auralia's hand, chiming a note of sugar on the air. The root released her, shocked.

Then the tree turned, an invisible hand twisting it around. The bark split and peeled. And as if they were suddenly too heavy, the boughs groaned, broke loose, and shattered into wriggling twigs.

Auralia snatched up the bell and pressed it to her breast as she ran down the hill. When she looked back, the roots were following her, having torn themselves loose from the tree, slithering and twitching along like worms.

18

The First Feast of New Abascar

Silver cave crickets flitted between blades of tall grasses in this whispering marsh tunnel. Puffs of grasswisp seemed to sleepwalk on the breeze, and when they drifted into torches on the travelers' rafts, they dissolved in bright flares.

"I wish you could see this, 'Ralia," murmured the ale boy, for in his exhaustion the details of his environment were illusory and deceptive. Faces blurred, time sped up and slowed down.

For a moment he remembered that it was not Auralia who cradled his head in her lap. Nella Bye stroked his forehead with her fingertips as if he were her child. And even though she could not see, she replied, "It's beautiful."

"It's difficult," answered Kar-balter, straining against the oar-stick, his torso running with sweat.

"It's getting louder." Em-emyt, poling on the next raft, cocked his head as a sound like soft drumbeats crescendoed into a cacophony.

"We're sinking!" said Kar-balter.

The rafts dragged on grit and silt, slowing to a stop as the noise faded. Water rushed past as if in a hurry to escape. It disappeared, leaving the tunnel a muddy slick of silt and grass, stranding the raft parade.

"Since when do rivers just stop flowing?" Kar-balter stabbed at the silt as if he could shock the river into starting again. "Wait. What's this?"

Slick, silver shapes writhed and flopped in the muck all around them.

"Ha-ha!" Kar-balter dropped the oar and jumped off the raft, groping for them. He knelt among a tumble of massive golden boulders, closing his hands around an eyeless eel with black-and-white stripes. Then he stood, eyes widening. "Umm..."

All around him the golden boulders were rising from the muck—*smuck, smack, slosh!* Sturdy feet lifted their flat undersides from the river's floor.

Kar-balter climbed back on the raft.

The shapes were all similar—rugged domes, each barbed with a single white horn that angled forward. They were shells, and from breaks in the edges emerged blunt-beaked heads to probe the air.

"Golden hermits," said Em-emyt. "Some of the best eatin' that rivers have ever served up."

Kar-balter dropped the eel. "Let's cook one."

"Not yet," said Irimus. "If the river stopped, it can start again, right?"

With their sharp horns aimed upriver, the turtles marched together as if to battle.

"Follow them," rasped the ale boy, listening intently to the echoes. "There's more water ahead. And a big open space."

"It's all our dreams come true," Kar-balter groaned. "Another cave." He began to cry.

They towed the rafts through the marsh until they came to a stone barrier and stared at it, astonished. It stood as high as Kar-balter's shoulders, damming a vast lake from the tunnel.

"Did this just spring up like a gate?" Kar-balter peered over its edge. "By Calmarcus's booze. Not sure what we've found...but we've found it."

Crystal stalactites hung from the ceiling as densely as brush-bristles. Glowing in subtle gradients of peacock blue, peach-skin gold, soft lavender, and the silverblue of Deep Lake's twilight, they were the earth's grandest chandelier, their lights mirrored in the lake. The river poured in from the north and flowed out through various shadowy exits where the voices of many streams sang and sighed.

"It's like a crossing," said the ale boy as Irimus lifted him to the view.

Em-emyt grunted, climbing over the barrier, then splashed into the lake. The ale boy laughed when the old soldier surfaced, for he looked like nothing more than a disembodied head bobbing along.

"Have we found the others? Do you see Batey?" The tallest in the company, Raechyl looked over the barrier for the man she loved. "Where could they be?"

Em-emyt paddled his way to the left along the edge of the bowl toward a place where the bank had been exposed. The ground was rumpled like disrupted blankets, thick with the roots of underground trees that grew in a small, silvery grove. The ale boy counted seventeen slender trunks with outspread boughs like shrug trees. When the breeze gusted, leaves like silver coils streamed out over the lake and spiraled down to glitter on its surface. Around the crooked bowl, more trees were submerged, branches straining to keep fruit-heavy foliage above the surface.

The turtles were rearing up, pawing the barrier with the stout stumps of their legs. So the passengers, three to a turtle, lifted them. The turtles' legs flailed, but their craggy faces remained expressionless, accepting whatever was unfolding. When the turtles were released on the other side of the barrier, they splashed heavily and sank. Then their golden domes surfaced again to drift like barges with tarps thrown over their cargo.

"There goes a delicacy," said Em-emyt as one paddled past his fat head.

Next they lifted the rafts over the barrier and climbed onto them to float across the lake. Currents swirled around them, winding toward the exits. Kar-balter suggested that they row after the turtles to the tree-grove shore, while the lake's current tried to pull them aside and into another tunnel.

"Batey might have taken any of these passages," said Raechyl. "How can it be that the river flowed through one gate and now it flows through another?"

"Rivers don't move like Bel Amican trains, switching tracks and taking different routes," mused Kar-balter.

"They do here," said Irimus. "And I suspect that some of the sources are clearer than others." He scanned the array of trickles, rushes, and streams spilling into the bowl from different heights, and then pointed to the central source—the wide incoming river. Bright wings danced in the arch of its mouth. "Cavebirds."

"Food," said Kar-balter. "See why they're excited? Fish are jumping."

"Can you see the colors?" the ale boy asked Nella Bye, touching her chin so she faced the ceiling's blue and pink array.

"A little. Looks like a child's painting."

The ale boy remembered thinking the same thing in Auralia's caves.

"Like the Northchildren say," murmured Mulla Gee, "the world's full of canvases."

As the rafts coasted to the smooth bank, the passengers climbed off and lay down, famished and exhausted. Kar-balter pressed on toward the flowing source, eyes on the leaping fish. Some Bel Amicans followed with a net.

"It's like we're inside a body," said the ale boy.

"And this is the heart," said Irimus Rain.

"Look!" called Alysa. The tireless Bel Amican had moved through the trees and a field of jagged stone teeth to touch the smooth stone wall. "Someone was here. They've painted a story."

Faint sketches illustrated a familiar sequence—a crowd of children following a giant who led them away from a rising line of mountains.

"And so our great ancestor Tammos Raak fled over the Forbidding Wall," murmured Irimus, tracing the lines. "He set up the city of Inius Throan, but his children fought for power...here. They turned against him...here. He fled. Here he's climbing the tallest starcrown tree. I've never seen this version. He's sending a signal with a mirror or a glowstone. As if he's calling for help from the northern mountains."

"What's this circle?" asked Alysa.

"I'm not sure. But it seems to be like a boat in the sky. A boat carrying ghosts."

"Moon-spirits?" asked Raechyl.

"The boat." Irimus stared at the picture, incredulous at this variation of a story he'd known since childhood. "The boat crashes into the starcrown trees. Tammos Raak falls. His tower topples. The earth breaks open."

"I know where we are," said Aronakt, gesturing to further reaches of the walls. They were lined with tremendous pillars, smooth columns crisscrossing, some as stout as marrowwood trees, others as slender as snakes. "Starcrown roots," he said. "This story took place above us."

"Mawrnash," said Irimus.

"The water!" came Kar-balter's voice from the mouth of the incoming river. "It's clean here! And look!" All around him enormous otters swam, dove, wrestled, and blinked at him curiously.

"They're well-fed," laughed Em-emyt. "The birds seem healthy too. I'd say this current's clean. We can eat these fish."

"The birds," mused Aronakt. "There are so many. There must be a way out and not far off."

"Glory!" shouted Kar-balter. He had caught a heavy tree branch that had sailed into the lake. "Look at this!" He took the oar and began paddling toward shore, towing the branch.

As they drew it ashore, they marveled. Its leaves were green, and a shrillow's nest rested in a clutch of twigs. As Kar-balter pried apart strands of the nest, eggs tumbled out. Alysa's quick hands caught them and gathered them into a pile. "This grew above ground," she said.

"Who will help me build a fire?" shouted Irimus. "We have what we need for a meal."

Kar-balter burst into tears again, this time for joy.

As the Bel Amicans spread the net and cast the spear, gathering fish on the rafts, the Abascars moved about on the shoreline, gathering driftwood from the exposed banks and stacking it for kindling.

Leaning back against Nella Bye, who sat against one of the trees, the ale boy watched a fire bloom on the bank and passengers crowd around it. Ark-restor held one of the old Abascar shields upside down like a frying pan over the fire, and Alysa carefully cracked a shell. The crackle and spatter as the egg spilled across the hot metal was a pleasing sound, as was the scent of seared fish. The crowd groaned with longing and then laughed.

"I thought I'd brought everyone from slavery to starvation," said the ale boy, his throat tightening with emotion.

"But we'll eat tonight," said Nella Bye. "You've fulfilled your promise, dear boy."

"Not quite yet," he said. "We're still underground. But the air is fresher. I think we're close."

"Closer than you think," said Nella Bye softly.

"What do you mean?"

"There's a break in the wall here behind us. It goes up. All the way to the surface. I can smell it."

"How do you know? What makes you—" The ale boy's question caught in his throat as a cool breeze that smelled of needled trees brushed his face.

"Keep quiet for now," said Nella Bye. "Don't interrupt them. If they discover this path, they'll all rush up through the wall."

The boy stood and crept up the steep slope, slipping through the stone teeth as if trying not to wake a monster. He leaned into a break in the wall, where he saw muddy footprints that had dried upon the natural stair.

I've found them. Batey, Petch, and the others.

Then he heard the sound—a man's voice crying out, answered by the sound of a harsh, bitter shout. He leaned wearily against the edge of the break, closing his eyes.

And then, as the fireside crowd was entranced by the scents and sounds of their project, he quietly ventured up into the dark.

For Batey, Petch, and the five other Bel Amicans, leaf-sailing had been a thrill at first. Batey had surrendered himself to the rush, confident the others were not far behind.

But when they'd struck the narrow place, their sail slapping across the passageway and stifling the wind, his excitement had quickly collapsed. He was hungry and exhausted.

When Petch argued that they should fold up the sails and press on, Batey tried to challenge him, saying they should wait for the others. But no one had found the strength to fight Petch's passion to take charge.

Entering the large lake where streams flowed in and out, Petch had seen a cave-bird escape through a break. He persuaded the others to follow him up the narrow crevasse.

Moments later Batey found himself fighting for consciousness. Face down in the dirt, he struggled to free his wrists from their bonds. His captor pulled off his boots and tied his ankles.

Four filthy, bare-chested mercenaries in vawn-leather trousers stalked around their victims, who were stacked like firewood. A metal rack struck a stark, ugly silhouette before the bonfire, and a man's rib cage hung there, an array of blackened bones.

Shredders. Well, that undoes the claims that they've been eradicated.

He turned his head the other way and saw weapons and oars heaped in a corner, next to several Abascar hunting spears and a few of the best Bel Amican beast-man wire traps. Out of habit he began to calculate their value, but he caught himself. *Focus, Batey.* He blinked through a trickle of blood. *Ah, yes. I've been struck in the head.*

But unlike the three Bel Amican soldiers—Gibhart, Crowcus, and Stallobo—Batey remained awake enough to notice the other prisoner. As the mercenaries prowled about, emptying pockets, stripping away garments, and casting them onto another pile of pillage, they stopped to prod a young woman with a mop of bright red hair who was begging for mercy.

Before he could see anything else, Batey felt the heel of a boot on the top of his head, and his chin was pressed into the dirt. From the white dust spilling off that boot, he could make a guess they were near Mawrnash.

The shredders conveyed that they wanted to know how the travelers had found their cave and passed their guard. They had obviously been too busy to discover the break that led down a zigzagging path to an underground river.

Shredders were known for their swift, silent slaughter of travelers and for their appetite for human flesh. They did not take prisoners or keep slaves. What did these barbarians want?

"Torch oil," spat one voice. "Pitch. Anything that burns."

Deathweed, Batey thought. *They're desperate for fuel to protect themselves.* He fought to keep his wits, to consider how he might distract them, to keep them from finding the river and endangering Raechyl.

The pressure on his head ceased. The one with the boots leaned forward, his black braids, decorated with bits of animal bones, spilling down from a pale, scarred head. "Give us burn stuff." He pointed to a barrel against the wall. "Barrel for give more. Hurt you not so much."

"We've got nothing," squealed Petch. "But down below. Where we came from. A river. There's a stream of flame oil fouling it. I swear by Thesera the queen."

That earned Petch a kick in the jaw.

"Kramming Deathweed," said the black-braided shredder. "Six it took. By night. Six."

Down at the end of the line, the unfamiliar woman was gasping and protesting.

"We could join you," Batey said. "Eight more to fight the Deathweed."

A boot to his jaw snapped it out of joint. *I hate that,* he thought, spitting out a tooth.

Hulking about like a pack of Cragavar monkeys, the shredders conferred.

Did no one tell them stories when they were children? Batey wondered as the room began to spin.

Something changed. Another figure had appeared. Batey's senses sharpened.

In the spinning room, the ale boy moved across the cave in a cloak so filthy and tattered that it seemed rather useless. He carried a dead torch, went straight to the bonfire, and stuck it into the flame's blue center.

The mercenaries stopped talking. They watched the boy as if he were sleepwalking, glancing at one another to confirm that they all saw the same thing. Then they spread into a half circle and stalked toward him.

The boy lifted the torch in anything but a threatening manner. "I've an invitation," he said, unsteady on his feet. "You're hungry. You're thirsty. Let these travelers go. Come down and join us. We're catching a lot of good fish down there. And..." He paused, catching Batey's eye. "We could help each other."

Stupid boy, Batey wanted to say. *You've volunteered to be the shredders' first course.*

The boy backed to the wall of the cave, keeping the torch in front of him.

"Boy, get out." Petch had been turned over onto his back, and his beard was smoking where they had singed it with torches. "Don't lie to them," he roared. "You'll make everything worse."

"I'm not lying," said the boy. "We're cooking a meal down there." When a shredder sneered some incomprehensible question, he answered, "I serve Cal-raven of New Abascar. I'm taking these folks to him."

"Cal-raven?" gasped the woman with the fiery red hair. "I...I know him! I'm his friend! Please, take us with you!"

The boy stepped slowly along the wall. The shredders matched his steps like a pack of drooling dogs readying to pounce. He reached the corner and leaned back against the pitch barrel. The shredders closed in, laughing, unsheathing small razors for which they were famous.

The boy climbed into the barrel, aimed the torch downward, and plunged it into the oil. The shredders' laughter turned to screams, and they dove at him.

The barrel exploded outward. A wave of heat blasted across the floor, singeing Batey's mustache and scorching his face.

One shredder flew backward, impaled by a wooden lance from the shattering barrel. Another turned in circles, his chest on fire. One clasped a hand to his face and ran to the rope ladder. The fourth man fell with something attached to him—a boylike figure made of fire.

Batey fell asleep.

When Batey woke, the cave was almost empty.

He lay on his side, his jaw hanging slack. Next to him Petch lay chest down and crying softly. The ale boy stood over them, naked, black with soot and ash. Smoke spiraled out from him in thin lines.

"Think you're a hero?" Petch sobbed. "Well, forget it. You were lucky. I found the way out."

"That runaway shredder sealed the cave," the boy answered. "He'll bring back others, I suspect."

The stories were true, thought Batey. *The boy's a firewalker.*

"Listen," said the boy, "do you want to come down to our feast? Or will you stay and wait for the shredders to come back?"

"We'll come," said the redhead.

"Unbind me, you insect," Petch spat. "What's wrong with you? You can't invite a slaver to join us."

"Mousey may be a slaver," said the ale boy. "But if she's telling the truth and she helped King Cal-raven, it's his decision what should happen to her."

The redhead—the boy had called her "Mousey"—was rummaging through the piles of pillage. She turned, lifting up a large white tunic. "Here you go, fire-boy. This should fit you just fine."

"Helk," rasped Batey. It was difficult to speak properly with an unhinged jaw.

Mousey knelt beside him. "Nasty bruises. Here." She clamped her hard little hand under his jaw. He screamed as the bones went *clok!* and then he flexed his jaw and thanked her. Finding that his bindings had been burned through, he rose up and looked around for his boots.

"I've still got my vawn's saddlebag," said Mousey. "Shredders didn't search it yet. I've got bird strips. Cheese traded from a merchant and these." She brandished two bottles of goldenwine.

"You're in," said Batey.

As they began to leave, Petch wept.

Batey smiled at the boy. "I think he's made his choice."

The boy paused. Then he returned to the spluttering captive. "If I set you free, you must promise to forget about that ladder. If our company learns about it, they'll give up the journey and try to get out. Shredders and worse might be waiting out there. And we've come so far. We're so close to something better."

Raising his voice in what sounded like a final assault against an invincible fortress, Petch roared, "You don't even know where you're going."

"No," the boy replied quietly. "I don't. But I do know that this is the way."

Batey shouldered the bundle of the shredders' pillage—all that he could carry—and said, "Make him promise that he'll keep quiet for the rest of the journey."

Petch's head slumped against the ground. "I promise," he wheezed in defeat.

The return of the missing Bel Amicans to the camp transformed the survivors' meal into a celebratory feast.

Raechyl and Batey were inseparable, and while Petch staggered down to the water to sulk and wash his wounds, the ale boy was welcomed like a hero. Everyone wanted to embrace him, but no one did. His skin tingled and stung, as it always did after the strange magic of firebearing protected him. They unfolded one of the broad ivy leaves they had used for sails, and he lay down upon it. Smoke wisped from his edges, and he looked like a sacrifice set upon an altar.

He watched Batey pick through the shredders' plunder. "This rope they used to bind us," said the Bel Amican, "it's the leather they use for reins on vawns and horses. Good, strong cord. Could come in handy."

Kar-balter rafted out to the incoming river, filled the boy's water flask, then brought it back and anointed him, trying to cool his smoldering skin. Nella Bye clothed him in the white tunic and blue trousers that Mousey had found. They presented him with ripe, white fruit from boughs of the silver-leaf trees.

"Do you think it's time?" Kar-balter asked him quietly. "Time to open the bottle? We don't have to share it. It's Abascar ale, after all."

"We share it with our companions," said the boy. "There are no Bel Amicans, no people of Abascar, no Gatherers or slavers here. That's what Cal-raven would say."

Listening at a distance, Irimus Rain smiled.

A few moments later they gathered in a circle. The sail leaves made purple tablecloths, and each person looked down at a bite of seared fish, slices of silver-leaf apples, strips of fried egg, one ripe riverbulb, and then—from Mousey's saddlebags—a dash of nuts and seeds and crumbs of Bel Amican cheese. The uneasy glances at the red-haired woman dissolved at the sight of such treasure.

The fire burned low, and the thick forest of stalactites above illuminated everything in shifting rays of color.

The boy sat, his legs folded beneath him, shakily holding the bottle of ale. All eyes were on him. He pressed his palm to the top of the bottle, then lifted his hand with a flourish, and—*pok!*—the cork appeared between his thumb and forefinger as easily as if he'd snapped the cap from an acorn. There were murmurs around the circle. How had he opened it without a corkscrew or a knife? Suddenly the tricks of an ale boy's trade seemed a matter of mystery.

He walked around the circle, beginning with their most unlikely guest. Kneeling, he poured a splash of fizzy ale into Mousey's half-shell cup. He continued to Petch, who began to explain why Bel Amican ale-craft was superior to Abascar's until Batey's scowl shut him up. The boy served Batey and Raechyl, Alysa and Wilkyn, then Crowcus, Gibhart, and Stallobo. He poured for Mandacath, Brink, Nukirk, Joustra, and the other Bel Amicans. The Abascars waited, smiling at one another as if this reminded them of something.

"Our company," said Mulla Gee, "is larger than you think."

Somehow there was just enough ale for the boy to serve all his companions.

"You should make a speech," said Nella Bye.

The boy looked down at his strange new costume and at his purple, fidgeting feet. Then he raised the bottle. "This ale was brewed by Obsidia Dram. Nobody knew her story. Nobody even remembers which king appointed her to work in the breweries. But everyone loved what she gave them. Every day and night she worked to fill bottles with surprises. She'd say, 'We want them to feel new things are possible. We want to wash away their fears and disappointments.' She wanted us to savor this. She wanted to turn strangers into family. Let's drink in honor of Obsidia Dram."

And together, they did just that.

The ale was sharp and clear, like a note from a struck copper bell. Then it fizzed, and fireflies filled the drinkers' heads, notes of honey and orange on their tongues. Nella Bye giggled, giddy, as she placed her shell back down.

They ate. And they savored the meal as if they had forgotten about the threat of the shredders. But Petch kept glancing toward the break in the wall, anxious as he cleaned his leaf-plate.

As they passed around the water flask, Batey filled his shell and stood. "I propose we drink to this—the strangest treasure I've ever seen—a remarkable boy we call Rescue. We knew he was peculiar. But we had no idea."

They drank. And the ale boy discovered that the water was as extraordinary as the Abascar ale. As it cleansed his tongue and throat, it also washed away a glaze of sadness and helped him taste the sweet, brisk air.

Some Bel Amicans who had been drinking the river water long before they reached this cave only shrugged, saying they tasted nothing special about the water from the source. But as they spoke, the boy could see dark green stains on their tongues from the sludge they had swallowed before.

"This," said Nella Bye, "is what water was meant to be." Then she smiled. "I can see you," she whispered. "It's all coming back."

"What will you do in New Abascar, Nella Bye?"

"I'll tend to the children and the old," she said. And then she fell silent rather than darken this gathering with memories of the daughter she had lost in Abascar's collapse. "What about you? What will you do when there's no one left to rescue?"

He sighed. "It feels like that day will never come."

"Let's say it will," she said, poking his knee. "What will you be?"

He shrugged. "An ale boy, I suppose. People will always be thirsty."

Out on the lake, otters played with their food. When that strange, resounding thunder sounded again, shaking the ground, the golden hermits began swimming upstream, surging toward the source.

Some of the travelers got to their feet. Others spread their hands upon the ground and looked warily at the ceiling, at the spires of shining glowstone, which suddenly seemed like an array of spears ready to be thrown. Dust rained down from the stalactites. The trees shook loose clouds of leaves.

"Look," shouted Kar-balter, pointing at one of the out-flowing streams.

A ridge was rising to close that tunnel, just as ridges were closing other exits nearby. But across the cave, other gateways were opening as barriers descended. The water flowing into the lake began to rush out into those passages as well.

"That's what caused the thunder," said Em-emyt.

"That's why our river stopped flowing," said Kar-balter, and he hurried down to his raft.

"That's why Cyndere's well went dry," muttered the ale boy to himself.

"Someone's engineered this," said Irimus, "to share this water with the world."

"So, ale boy," said Nella Bye, "what did you think of the Abascar ale?"

The boy smiled. "I liked seeing everyone drink it the way it was meant to be tasted."

"You didn't taste it?"

"There was just enough for the eighty-nine shells. But don't worry. I enjoyed pouring. And seeing everyone smile." Then he bowed his head. He seemed smaller, as if he had lost something in the fire. "My last sip of ale was with Auralia. I'll celebrate when I see her again."

He slid sideways so he could lean against her, resting while the people picked crumbs from their leaf-plates and Mousey began pouring cups of goldenwine. He began to tremble, and a tear spilled down his face. "I killed them," he said brokenly. "Those men up in the cave. I tried to make them stop. But they wouldn't. I killed...I..."

She gathered him into her arms.

Batey eyed the incoming river, where birds went on dancing and the turtles were bumping against one another, making steady progress against the stream. "I've got an idea," he said, winding a length of cord around his hand.

When the ale boy woke, he knew he'd slept for hours. He also knew that he no longer felt any pain from his fiery ordeal in the shredders' cave.

The water will heal us all.

His head rested in Nella Bye's lap. But they were not on the bank of the river. They were moving again along the misty river, and the vapor that he breathed was invigorating and cool. Nella Bye smiled down at him, and the bruises on her face were gone. Her eyes were bright and sharp.

"We're moving upriver," she said. "The turtles, they seem happy to pull us."

Then another figure leaned over him. It was Mousey the slaver. She leaned in close to him as if she'd kiss his brow—and he would not have minded that much.

"Fireboy," she whispered in his ear urgently, "I'm still here. I didn't run away."

"I'm glad," he sighed. "Wait, did somebody else run away?"

Nella Bye told him the tale.

Soon after they had bound their rafts to the turtles like carriages to horses, they had turned to find that the rafts at the back of the company were gone, having cut their bonds to their turtles. Aronakt, Petch, and seven Bel Amicans had abandoned them, taking the best spears and the rest of the food with them.

19

The Glassworker Homecoming

"It's like Barnashum," murmured Brevolo to Tabor Jan. "Except that it's beautiful." Winding through waves of rocky hills north of Fraughtenwood, Tabor Jan had led the anxious company to a lush valley where the air whispered with breezes from dancefanner ferns that spilled down to the base of a towering mountainside cliff.

It was a view that struck all of them silent. Down in that depression a tall, toughstalk fence protected a fort that was built against the cliff wall. The fort was made of several stout, black-brick structures with tall, swooping rooftops that glittered with green glass tiles. Cobbled walkways connected the buildings, each path sheltered by red canvas.

Dull brown tents surrounded a central courtyard, their circle broken by a broad avenue that ran to a dark tunnel in the cliff's face. People were pushing empty wagons inside the tunnel and hauling burdened wagons out.

Frits voiced his surprise at the tents. The old glassmaker had never seen them before. He held a hushed, anxious conference with the miners' scout who had come to determine the business of this unexpected company.

Tabor Jan watched Frits quietly instruct the scout, who then took his vawn back down to the mine to report the travelers' purpose.

"He came to say they've no room for guests," said Frits. "He was surprised to see me. There's trouble down there. Deathweed has driven merchants from across the Fearblind North to seek refuge, and many have come to our fort. But merchants aren't easy company. Looks like I've come home just in time."

They made their way down to a hastily organized welcome party. Horns rang out, the sound bright and clear as a sunlit mountainside. One would blast from a balcony high on the cliff wall, and another would answer from the canyons between nearby hills as if it were an echo. Then a chorus of similarly crystalline calls would come from all directions, catching notes that had fallen and casting them back into the air.

"What are they?" asked Tabor Jan.

"Glass trumpets!" shouted Obrey, breaking free of the company to hop and skip down the path. "Milora, look! There's Dynise! There's Lindsy! And Amilynd and all the rest of my friends!"

Milora whispered in Frits's ear and then followed the girl, carrying a heavy saddlebag over her shoulder.

"Milora's a strange one," said Tabor Jan. "Lost in her own head."

"It's a wonder Cal-raven didn't fall for her," Brevolo laughed. "He always likes them half-crazy."

"That's not fair," said Tabor Jan.

Brevolo looped her arm through his. "I think we should change our plan," she said. "What can it hurt if we stay awhile? Have some good meals. Get some sleep. Maybe pick a fight with some merchants."

Tabor Jan frowned. "The longer our people live in Bel Amica, the more difficult it will be to draw them out of there."

"One night," she whispered, tugging on his arm. "Haven't we earned that? Wouldn't we travel faster and feel stronger if we had a good meal and some rest?"

The miner clan was a small but muscular company, strangers to the sun, their pale skin smudged and stained with mine dust.

Nearly three hundred in number, they were boisterous, social people who clearly lived for their celebratory evenings, supping together on blankets around the open courtyard, with rain canopies ready to be raised if weather required it.

On this night they shared a meal of simple grains and herbs with more than a hundred merchants who clustered in small groups and other rough-looking strangers who muttered suspiciously to one another. And yet, all visitors enjoyed generous helpings from the miners' provisions. They accepted cups of tea from leaves grown in modest gardens and greenhouses. Later, as they cupped their hands around bowls of warm rice wine, a woman with a voice of tremendous power sang from a stone balcony on the mountain's cliff, and the song carried all about the region in sustained echoes while the sun went down.

Frits, when he stood and addressed those gathered, seemed years younger. His voice rang out with renewed vigor as he commended those who had overseen the mine in his absence and praised his people for their generosity to needy visitors. His speech quietly assured the newcomers that this was a temporary arrangement, a clever way to remind them to have some respect. If they would help the miners resist the new threat that had troubled his company in Fraughtenwood, they would be welcome guests indeed.

He earned a ripple of affectionate laughter when he described how House Bel Amica had fallen in love with young Obrey. Some of the tension dissolved. He also spoke of his relief that Milora had come back free of the Seers' poisons. The hesitant applause suggested that even the miners were not entirely sure what to make of the despondent young woman.

Then he asked everyone to consider the plight of House Abascar's missing king. After describing Cal-raven's courage in striving to rescue prisoners from beastmen, he asked for a long moment of silence that they might all meditate on his selflessness and his vision for an honorable house.

Frits is thinking of the future, thought Tabor Jan. *He is thinking of how he wants to see Abascar rise. It would be good for his clan.*

One of the glassworkers, clad in a vivid green wrap, walked up to Frits carrying a package wrapped in white strips. Frits called Tabor Jan forward.

"A gift for King Cal-raven," he said. "Only he can open it. If the darkness never releases him, let this package remain closed until a ceremony in his memory."

Tabor Jan bowed in gratitude, embracing the gift.

"And there is one more blessing we would bestow…" Frits broke off, tears spilling like splinters of glass.

"Is there a problem?"

Frits raised his countenance, struggling to collect himself. "It is with a heavy heart that I make this offer to your house. For I am loath to suffer this loss."

"We're already friends," said Tabor Jan softly. "We'll share any blessings with you, however valuable. Cal-raven would not have it any other way."

"But this…this is difficult." Frits turned. "Milora, will you come forward?"

Milora, looking scared and awkward, rose. She approached, and Tabor Jan noticed that she was empty-handed.

Obrey broke away from her friends and dashed to stand at Milora's side. Grabbing her hand, she looked up quizzically.

"What do you offer us?" Tabor Jan asked.

"Myself," said Milora. "Myself and any ability I might have with glass or other arts. To New Abascar's glorification. To help ready it for King Cal-raven's return."

Tabor Jan's eyes widened.

Obrey let go of Milora's hand, a storm breaking across her face. Then she seized it again with both of hers. "And me too!" Obrey announced to Tabor Jan. "I'll come too!" Frits reached for Obrey's hand, but she turned her back, scowling. "Cal-raven needs a queen!" she exclaimed.

Laughter spread as Frits knelt before Obrey. "Granddaughter, I need you here with me. Who will take care of me if you go? If Milora makes this journey, you'll get to go with me whenever I visit King Cal-raven. We can bring them gifts of your own making. You're old enough now to have your own glassworking mitts and begin teaching others as Milora has taught you."

Tabor Jan welcomed Milora in a clumsy embrace, for it seemed that this unusual ceremony called for it. But as he did, he glanced fearfully at Brevolo, who put on a mock scowl and wagged her finger at him.

Wynn made his way toward the stables. Tabor Jan had asked him to brush the vawns and horses and make sure they were fit for tomorrow's journey up through rocky ground, and he had obeyed, if only to be alone. Once again he found himself surrounded by strangers who made him feel invisible.

The Abascar visitors were given a line of tents along the courtyard's edge. Most travelers sat out in front of the tents to watch constellations decorate the dusk and to marvel as the courtyard came alive with hundreds of candles. Frits sent miners with second helpings of the sweet rice wine.

As Wynn wound through this scene, past musicians who played lullabies on glass flutes, he knew that nothing would help him sleep. The sheltered walkways and the courtyard were quiet enough. But the feeling in the courtyard had changed. The fort's guards, who regularly patrolled against bearcat attacks, were out in numbers, pacing the walkways and alert in the watchtowers. The various factions of visitors remained close together, murmuring. A palpable tension intensified. Some merchant clans surrounded themselves with arrays of torches, looking as if they were plotting a fiery revolt.

"What's happening?" he asked a guard.

"One of our watchmen is missing," the guard replied. "His blood was found at Fraughtenwood's edge. We suspect Deathweed."

"Give me a bow and some arrows, and I can help," said Wynn.

"Why don't you go to the tent for the Abascar children? Leave the arrows to those trained to use them," the guard answered.

"Do you know who I am?" Wynn growled.

The guard walked away.

Wynn marched across an avenue and into the stablehouse, flexing his hands into fists. He was already in a sour mood. He hated farewells. He hated ceremonies where others were honored while he was forgotten.

He was even more distressed to think that Obrey would stay here when the company departed. She was pretty, she liked to make trouble, and she was always up for an adventure. He'd dreamed of luring her out of the camp and telling her stories about life on the merchant roads. He might even give her a kiss on the cheek, if she wanted. Maybe she'd run away with him. Maybe he and Obrey could be like a father and mother to Cortie—merchants in the wild, with no commitment to anybody but themselves.

We could leave. Make a life of our own. Why not? To them, we're just a story that makes them feel good about themselves.

As he moved past stacks of grass bales, a breeze brushed his ear. Luci sat above him on a hay bale, swinging her feet as if to show off her painted bark-fold shoes.

"We made it, Wynn," she said. "No more forests. Tomorrow we'll find New Abascar, and you and me can explore it together."

Wynn was dismayed. The triplets had made him feel uncomfortable from the moment he met them among Abascar's survivors. It had been strange enough to see them compete for his attentions, all three with the same freckled face.

"Madi says hello," said Luci.

And that was the other problem. When Madi had fallen into a well and never returned, Margi and Luci had started saying that they heard her voice in their heads.

He reached for a harsh retort, but then Obrey peered over the same stack of grass and swung her feet down, wearing the same colorful shoes. She elbowed Luci knowingly.

Why is it Luci who asks to hold my hand? Why not Obrey? Those triplets are stonemasters. Their hands scare me.

He walked past the girls, trying to adopt the look of grim determination that Captain Tabor Jan always wore. But Luci's sister Margi came running through the stablehouse, looking grim herself. When she saw her sister and Obrey sitting on the shelf and Wynn standing at their feet, she scowled and reached up to her sister. "Help me up."

"Brevolo asked me to cheer Obrey up," Luci replied proudly while Obrey reached down to help Margi up.

"You're not the third sister," Margi muttered, deciding to climb up on her own.

"I'll come back to visit you, Obrey," said Luci. "I rather like the light here."

"Yes," said Obrey. "It tastes like snow." She handed Margi a pair of bark-fold shoes to match their own. "We made these for you."

Margi put them on and smiled, all jealousy forgotten, and soon all three girls were swinging their feet.

"Madi tells me we're getting closer all the time," said Margi. "And she says we're being watched over."

"Shut up with all the pretending," Wynn snapped. "You're such children. Madi's not talking to you, Margi. My mum and papa are dead, and they don't talk to me. And there's nobody watching over us. If we aren't ready to fight, we'll end up dead as your sister. I'm done with all that pretending. I'm ready to fight the Deathweed. I stopped the Seers and the beastmen in Bel Amica."

"You didn't do that all by yourself," said Obrey in the tone of a condescending adult. "Luci and Margi helped. And Cyndere shot an arrow. And it was Tabor Jan who found the trouble in the first place. You can't be a soldier yet. We're not even old enough to be parents."

"Someday Wynn and I will be parents," said Luci flirtatiously.

"You should be in the children's tent with Cortie," he barked. "We should have left you in Bel Amica."

"Captain said we had to come," said Luci. "He needs stonemasters 'til the king comes back."

"Well. . .he needs me too." Wynn cringed even as he spoke, each word making him feel more ridiculous. *I'll show them,* he thought.

He marched down the path between the many stable stalls. When he reached the vawns of the Abascar company, he began to brush them slowly, keeping himself inconspicuous while Jes-hawk, Brevolo, and Tabor Jan were having a hushed conversation nearby.

As silvery scales fell around his feet, he heard Jes-hawk say, "I don't like this. We're already welcoming people into Abascar who haven't earned our trust. People who haven't fought for survival beside us."

"Take another look at her, Jes-hawk," mumbled Brevolo. "If Milora tried to do us any harm, she'd probably hurt herself."

"House Bel Amica robs people of their loyalty. I never imagined my sister could give us trouble. But Lynna betrayed us to Ryllion." He drew an *X* in the dust on the stable floor as if imagining a target on Ryllion's forehead. "Now he and my sister are out there somewhere laughing at how she humiliated me."

"Ryllion's not laughing," said Brevolo. "He's running for his life."

"We can't punish Milora for something your sister did," said Tabor Jan. "We'll accept her pledge of service because we need a strong bond with these miners. They know these mountains much better than we do. Jes-hawk, you have to bury this grudge."

Wynn moved from the line of vawns to the horses, brushing the mane of a sturdy black colt as he listened.

"Besides," Tabor Jan was saying, "Milora seems sincere in her desire to support Cal-raven. He'll need those who respect him. Some of our own people have lost faith."

"But should we bring the glassworker with us now?" asked the archer. "Maybe someday when New Abascar is ready. But right now she'll be just another mouth to feed."

Brevolo scowled, nodding. "Now that's true. And when we find New Abascar, we'll need muscle, not pretty windows."

Tabor Jan did not answer, but he looked suddenly tired.

"I'm sorry," said Brevolo softly. "That was harsh. I know Cal-raven wants to make room for everybody. He'll think it's wonderful to welcome a quiet, muddle-headed glassworker just the way he's been sweet to those poor orphans."

Jes-hawk elbowed her sharply, and she turned, readying an angry retort, only to see Wynn standing there, frozen.

She laughed, raising a hand to her mouth. "Wynn! Oh, child, I didn't see you there!"

He did not answer. He just tightened his grip on the brush as if it were a weapon drawn in a challenge.

20

Fire in Fraughtenwood

The glass whistle that knifed the silence brought Jes-hawk leaping from sleep toward the flap of his tent, where his forehead met Tabor Jan's formidable chin.

"I need an archer," said Tabor Jan, now on his knees and clutching his bearded jaw.

"I was dreaming," said Jes-hawk blearily, lying on his back and waiting for his vision to return. "My sister...she attacked us with a shard of glass."

"Forget Lynna. We've a real nightmare."

Jes-hawk struggled to his feet, pulled on his riding jacket, and shouldered his quiver. "Have the miners turned against us?"

"No. A Bel Amican distress flare. South of here. In Fraughtenwood."

"Did we leave someone behind?" He moved toward the door.

"Behind?" Tabor Jan snorted. "Jes-hawk, aren't you forgetting something?"

Cursing, Jes-hawk turned back for his trousers. When he was fully dressed, Tabor Jan took him by the arm and pulled him out into the dim early morning. "You think it's the king, don't you, Captain?"

"I don't know."

"Who's riding? You, me...Brevolo?"

"She's already gone."

"Ahead of us?"

"Couldn't stop her," Tabor Jan growled.

"Nobody should ride into Fraughtenwood without—"

"Don't tell me what I already know." The captain was running now, and there was Krawg, holding a torch and leading the horses. "I've sent Shanyn to catch her."

"But why did Brevolo leave?"

Tabor Jan thanked Krawg and mounted the horse. "Wynn, that impossible child. He was listening when the watchman told me they'd sighted a flare. I told the boy to prepare our three best animals. A few moments later he charged out of the stablehouse on that colt he stole from Bel Amica. Frits's watchmen let him go. He's off to play hero. Again." Tabor Jan's clenched teeth were bright through his beard. "Brevolo found out. I told her to let him go."

"Why didn't she?" Jes-hawk was on his horse, and they moved through the settlement, which was coming to life.

"She thinks Wynn wants to prove himself. You'll remember that she said something last night that kicked him in the arrogance, so she blames herself for this...this foolishness."

At the torchlit gate, the watchmen waved them through. Tabor Jan reprimanded them for letting the boy pass.

"Where are we going?" Jes-hawk's forehead throbbed.

"We answer the distress call. And hope we all come back alive."

They rode up from the valley of fern trees, southwest across the gloom-dark hills, and descended back into Fraughtenwood.

Under dawn's first flush, Brevolo's vawn slowed, then skidded in the chalky dust beneath the trees, and stopped beside a tangle of brambles. The light of her torch revealed that something was moving beneath the thorns. It was the colt, collapsed, half-covered as if someone had tried to conceal it.

Keeping one hand on the reins, Brevolo jumped from the saddle and knelt before the colt, then stood up, sticky with blood that was spreading across the ground. The animal was wheezing and twitching, nearly dead.

Shanyn arrived and rode a circle around the scene. "Tabor Jan is..."

"Furious. I know." She looked again at the scrap of bramble that lay over the horse's haunches. "Strange." She surveyed the clearing, then took cautious steps into the trees. "Did the boy kill the horse and try to cover the evidence before he ran off? I don't understand."

Something hot splashed her head. She turned. Two bare feet dangled right before her eyes. Blood poured down on the dust. She looked up.

Wynn was hanging from a tree limb.

At first she thought the colt had slammed him directly into a low-hanging, spear-sharp branch. But then she saw that the boy's back was to the tree and that the branch had struck him from behind. Even stranger, the limb was raising him slowly into a bundle of sharp branches that were clutching at the air like the legs of some gigantic insect. Wynn stared forward, open-mouthed, hands raised as if he'd been clawing at the back of his head. Then his arms fell limp, and he kicked Brevolo sharply in the mouth. She crouched, blood spilling from her lips, moaning in shock.

Wynn made no sound. There was only the creak of the branches as they lifted him and then the snap of bones breaking.

Shanyn screamed and looked away.

Brevolo leaned forward and lost everything that was in her stomach. Then anger caught fire within her. She roared in a fury, drew an arrow, sparked its tip with her torch, and fired it into the trunk of the tree.

Something curled around her foot. She put another arrow to the string, lit it, and fired it into the slithering root. It recoiled, the tree pulling it back like a whip.

Then all the tree's roots burst from the ground, tearing themselves off the tree to thrash toward her.

"Get out of here, Brev!" shouted Shanyn. "Go back. I'll follow you."

Brevolo turned to answer her, and she saw the brambles that lay over the dead colt slide off like a blanket and begin to crawl in spasms toward her.

Shanyn's vawn, terrified, threw the rider free and bolted. Shanyn landed, tumbling, and Brevolo caught her by the arm and pulled her away from the advancing branches. "We'll take my vawn. We have to answer that alarm."

In the distance Shanyn's vawn shrieked as if it were fighting something.

"What's happening?" Shanyn gasped.

"The woods are cursed." Brevolo caught the reins of her frightened vawn, and she and Shanyn rode together.

Trees began to move as if in a windstorm. She tried not to look at the canopy of branches over and around her, for she thought she saw the shapes of long-legged, skeletal creatures stalking them through the boughs.

Shanyn pointed to a flickering red hue on a hilltop ahead. In the increasing light they could see a dark pillar billowing skyward and bending west across Fraughtenwood.

"We've found them," said Brevolo.

On the hilltop they found small fires scattered all around an ancient barn that appeared to have caught itself in midcollapse. Archers and torchbearers were striking at predators—creatures like bizarre beetles and crickets made of branches and bark.

Brevolo rode the vawn in a circle around the scene, calling out that help had come.

"These kramming monsters," said Shanyn. "What's in the barn that they want?"

"Life, I suppose," said Brevolo, reining the vawn to a halt. "We're going in there."

She spurred the vawn forward, and as they reached the door, they met an old man on his way out to blow an alarm horn. He saw them and stumbled aside.

"Warney!" Brevolo was astonished.

"Brevolo! Shanyn!" Warney pulled at his wisps of hair. "Help us! The Seers have cursed the forest!" He pointed to the leaning barn. "Bel Amicans! Children!"

Inside, between the animal stalls where horses were rearing and shrieking, they found four wagons loaded with large sacks made of seabull hide and covered with heavy tarps.

Someone stepped out from one of the stalls—a woman with her arms around two small boys.

"Sisterly Emeriene?" Brevolo gasped. "What are you doing here?"

Emeriene limped toward them. Something about her had changed. Her eyes were red, her face haunted, and she clung to her sons as if they would keep her afloat on stormy waters. "These wagons," she was shouting like a deranged patient in the Bel Amican infirmary. "They're filled with torch oil."

Brevolo blinked.

"Partayn sent them. He knew you'd need fire to save yourselves from viscorclaws."

"From what?"

Emeriene pointed out toward the violence. "Viscorclaws. Deathweed's corrupting the trees. It's the Seers' revenge. And fire's our only defense. But we can't let the fire touch our cargo..."

Brevolo looked up into the rafters, where smoke was coiling as if readying to strike. "Blazing Tower of Tammos Raak...if the fire reaches the cargo, this hilltop and everything on it will turn to ash in a heartbeat. Let's get you out of here."

"You need this cargo," Emeriene insisted. "And we need these wagons. There aren't enough horses and vawns for all of us. The whole forest is turning to viscorclaws."

Brevolo looked back to the entrance. "We're taking all of it north through Fraughtenwood. As fast as we can."

The four horse-drawn wagons—the first crowded with passengers, the others heavy with oil sacks—were brought out of the barn into beams of the eastern sunrise.

Archers lined up alongside the wagons, armed with flaming arrows and shooting whenever another tangle of vicious branches came crawling forward.

From her vawn Brevolo issued the command. Shanyn echoed the cry from behind her.

The horses charged forward, as terrified of the flames around them as they were of the viscorclaws beyond. More of the monsters were waiting, clearly visible, some the size of thorn bushes, some the size of trees.

Leaving the smoking hilltop behind, the wagons thundered down the stony slope. The first, carrying Warney, Emeriene, her sons, and several other Bel Amicans, pulled away fast. The heavier cargo wagons were slow, and archers inside them held torches as far from the flammable cargo as they could.

Viscorclaws scrambled and tumbled down the stony hillside on both sides as the frantic parade lumbered along. Those on the right prowled intently, but those on the left seemed to slow as if the ground had gone sticky.

"What's happening?" Brevolo called to Shanyn, gesturing to the slope.

Mounds of stone were melting and sliding, drowning the crawlers in liquefied rock.

They heard an explosion behind them. The barn had collapsed.

Below them, Fraughtenwood was restless, branches shaking like the limbs of animals caught in traps. *We'll never get through.*

"There's a rip in this oil bag!" an archer shouted from the hindmost wagon. "We're spilling fuel."

"Patch it," said Brevolo. "Patch it or drop it."

Brevolo looked back again. The whole hillside had changed. What had been a field of scattered boulders now looked like a sculpted shell. Except for a few clusters of jerking wooden limbs, the viscorclaw swarm was paralyzed, caught in a gluey tide.

Stonemastery, she thought, looking about.

"Look out!" called an archer from the second wagon.

A tree, its roots ripping free of the ground, plunged down between the second and third wagons.

The horses pulling the third wagon reared. The drivers steered them around the treetop. A crackle of splintering wood seared the air as blackening branches tore themselves free of the trunk and clutched at the earth for a hold.

"Get the wagons away from the tree so we can burn it!" Brevolo roared.

Already clusters of twigs were dragging themselves toward the wagons like scraps of metal drawn by a magnet. Shanyn shouted for arrows.

Three wagons had escaped the scene. The fourth was motionless behind the tree.

Brevolo's heart sank. She leapt off the vawn and let it run ahead with the procession. Then she hurried back around the tree.

One of the wagon's drivers was already dead, a cluster of crawlers flinging pieces of him around the trail. She ran at them, picking up his fallen torch and swiping at his attackers. The predators scattered, limbs aflame. Then she turned her attention to the wagon. Inside, another fallen man thrashed about, screaming, arms wrapped around what appeared to be a tangle of vines.

She threw the torch away from the wagon. Then she reached with both hands into the man's bloody embrace and seized the hard backbone of the many-legged monster that had torn into his chest. She raised its wriggling bundle, shouting with the effort. It bent its flailing limbs backward to aim sharpened claws at her. One of its talons punctured her left wrist, numbing it at once.

As the wounded man slumped, silent and still, between the cargo and the wagon side, Brevolo stumbled to her knees in the puddle of his blood.

A dark figure with a torch leapt aboard. He seized the viscorclaw with a massive hand and dragged it away from her, uprooting the claw from her arm. She drew her arm in close against her and blinked into hazy sunlight.

Her rescuer, growling like a beastman, pressed the torch's flame to the frantic viscorclaw. Then he flung the fiery predator away and thrust out a hand to Brevolo.

She recognized his face with its terrible scars and gigantic, toothy grin.

With her good arm she reached around behind her and unsheathed a dagger. "You lying, murderous, traitorous fiend!"

Ryllion jumped from the wagon, the dagger sailing past his ear.

Brevolo righted herself, found a loose arrow lying in the wagon, and leapt after him. "You don't get to help us, you Seer-serving coward!" As she stalked toward him, someone sprang to her side and seized her arm.

"Let him go, Brevolo."

She dropped the arrow.

This soot-blackened newcomer picked up the dead driver's sword. "Ryllion's here to help. Settle things with him later." He laughed. "Don't you know me?"

"Master!" It was Shanyn's cry. She dropped from her saddle. With one hand grasping the reins of the frightened steed, she reached out with the other to clasp the king's open hand. "You're alive!" She did not even see Ryllion.

Brevolo scowled. All she could think about was how Ryllion had lured her away from Bel Amica and sought to seduce her. She had not told Tabor Jan, although she knew he might suspect it. Worst of all, she had almost given in, enthralled with Ryllion's strength and promises.

Beside her, Shanyn was saying, "You're making a habit of dramatic returns."

"Not on purpose," said the king. "Get this wagon rolling."

There was a commotion behind them. The path was blackening with viscorclaws. Brevolo spat at Ryllion. "If my king would let me, I'd knock out your teeth for a necklace." Then she clambered onto the blood-stained driver's bench and slapped the reins. "Move!"

The animals could not have been more eager, as they pulled the wooden cart around the disintegrating tree.

Advancing crawlers made a sound like a stream of snakes. Cal-raven and Ryllion raised torches and swords and strode to meet them. They became a frenzy of motion, scattering black branches across the ground around them.

Brevolo urged the horses on, then glanced back to see a small twist of smoke rising from the wagon's tarp. She abandoned the reins and climbed on top of it. There she found a viscorclaw's dead, burning husk. She swept it off with her hand before the flames could burn through the tarp, and it fell into the dirt on the path behind, flowering into a blaze.

Then she saw the spray of oil from the cargo bag, showering the ground behind the wagon. She slid back down to the rider's bench. The horses were running hard now, without anyone steering them, and the rugged ground set the wagon to bucking as if it were trying to break free.

Lying against her numb left arm, she reached to one of the rods that bound the wagon to the horses' harness. "Gonna let…this one…go." With her knife she sawed through it. It snapped. The wagon veered sharply to the right, bound to the horses now with only one harness strap. She shifted and cut at the last tether.

The horses stumbled forward as they suddenly lost the weight of the wagon. They sprawled in the dirt, then kicked themselves back upright and leaned forward into a desperate run.

The wagon, stopping suddenly, threw Brevolo into the dirt and cast its cargo forward as well. She felt the weight of the oil bag fall on her, a splash of warm fuel seeping through her hair and running in syrupy lines down her back. She crawled out from beneath the bag, spitting out dirt and debris.

Several crawlers dropped from beneath the wagon and advanced.

With her teeth Brevolo pulled off her riding glove and looked at the fresh, blue marriage tattoo on her left hand.

She could still feel the burn of it.

Tabor Jan had tenderly sketched it the night before while she lay stretched across him, the breeze cooling their warm, exhausted bodies in the chamber that Frits had given them as a gesture of privilege. She had brushed tears from her husband's face—her own tears. That had made him laugh. For the first time since the days before Abascar's fall, a deep line in his brow had smoothed over as if it had never existed.

"I understand that you live for Cal-raven," she had whispered.

"Not anymore," Tabor Jan had said, and she had felt his voice reverberate in his ribs.

"No, you mustn't say that," she said. "These people must think that you are New Abascar itself. That they can depend on you. That you will act always and only in its best interest."

"Even if Cal-raven returns? Even if he charts a course that drives you mad?"

"I am pledging myself to you, Tabor Jan. And you are a man who keeps his promises. I may not always trust those you trust. But while the people of Abascar depend on you, you can depend on me. I'll keep you safe."

"You'll be my foundation?" he murmured, touching her eyelashes with his fingertips. "If that's so, shouldn't we trade places?"

And then she had laughed, resting her brow on his shoulder.

Remembering this, Brevolo raised her hand and kissed the rune of Tabor Jan's name.

Then she reached down for her sputtering torch and growled at the viscorclaws as if she were a fangbear protecting her den from predators.

As Cal-raven swept away the last of the viscorclaws from the path behind the wagons, he heard horses shriek, and he turned.

He saw the horses charging off without the fourth wagon. He saw the cargo lying on the ground before the halted cart. A cluster of viscorclaws dropped from their hold beneath the wagon and stalked a torch-bearing figure.

"Brevolo?"

One of the viscorclaws sprang at her. She fought with it, falling back. The attacker sprang away, its back ablaze. Others came scrambling down to keep her from rising. The torch fell from her hand and touched a trail of seeping oil. It looked like a snake of flame was born, and it slithered from the torch toward the cargo.

Cal-raven drew in a breath, but his shout was erased by a noise like a thunderclap.

The ground shook. A fireball engulfed the whole scene, leaping into the sky, red and gold on a pillar of luminous blue, bursting with tumors of smoke. A ring of dust and heat spread outward, slamming Cal-raven to the dirt.

"Get up!" Ryllion dragged him to his feet. Now they were running past the mountain of smoldering debris as blazing shreds drifted down upon the dead forest underneath a spreading continent of smoke. "This fire's just beginning."

"Brevolo," the king groaned.

"It's too late," Ryllion roared. "Go after the others. They need you. I'll keep my distance."

Cal-raven nodded, numb with shock. Leaving Ryllion behind, he ran.

A short distance ahead he found Shanyn riding her vawn in a circle to slow the two liberated horses. Cal-raven stepped toward the rearing, foam-spewing animals, speaking softly and holding out his hands. Then he stepped between them, grabbed the reins of one, and sprang onto the saddle of the other. "I've got them," he shouted. "Go."

And so Cal-raven rode after Shanyn's vawn in pursuit of the other wagons, north through Fraughtenwood. The horses needed no urging; they ran as if wolves snapped at their heels.

He saw Tabor Jan just ahead, and a burden heavier than the thought of the threat surrounding him almost dragged him to the ground.

21

Battle in the Fearblind Ravine

As rubble spilled into the canyon and poured down toward Auralia, she stepped into a heavy boulder's lee. The world seemed to be going to pieces. Behind her, Fraughtenwood was in flames, the smoke a swift tide breaking against these rising hills. The air still crackled as trees twisted and separated. And every few moments an unseen hammer smote the ground.

Her ankles bled from scuffs and falls. But she knew she could not rest. The Abascar company, which had set out from the glass mine close-knit and ordered, had scattered in haste as a fiery rain and advancing viscorclaws besieged their caravan. Auralia did not want to be outside the circle of King Cal-raven's protection come nightfall.

When Cal-raven had arrived at the glass mine bloodied and severe, Auralia had wanted nothing more than to run to him, to hold out her hand with its emerjade ring, to awaken his memory of her. But as Krawg and Warney's meeting became a riot of embraces, curses, and accusations, the king declared there would be no rest, no meal, no reunion celebration. He announced that the foothills of the Forbidding Wall were in the path of a rushing storm made of fire and predators. The Fraughtenwood flames were spreading fast, devouring viscorclaws and trees without distinction. It would not grant travelers any grace. Some from the Abascar company that had gone out from the glass mine to answer the hilltop distress call had lost their lives in the first surge of that storm.

She could see in the king's ravaged expression that he had witnessed horrible things. But he did not detail the dire tidings during his urgent appeal at the glass mine gates. Still, rumors did their damage, disheartening the company. At the sight of Tabor Jan, stumbling and colorless, her heart sank.

The king wanted Tabor Jan's company to assemble and depart at once, follow him north and east through the foothills, and seek refuge in the destination he had chosen. He wanted them ready, packed, and moving without the burden of broken hearts. Auralia was ready.

He invited Frits to close the mine and bring his people along in search of higher ground, greater safety. Bowing in gratitude, Frits declined. He would seal his workers into their tunnels and meet viscorclaws with fire. So without any more ceremony than a promise of collaboration once the crisis passed, House Abascar and the miners parted ways.

They did not leave without new companions. A host of the merchants camped in Frits's settlement quickly pledged themselves to strengthen the exodus. Abascar's company was larger now, armed with fire and a wealth of torch oil, trekking eastward through the barren hill country along Fraughtenwood's northern border, toward a pass Cal-raven had found in old Bel Amican trade maps—a dry riverbed that wound its way up the sloping country toward the Forbidding Wall.

A figure pushed through the dustclouds and seized Auralia's wrist. Krawg.

"If I tried to tell this blasted story," Krawg shouted, kicking away the debris that had piled up around Auralia, "they'd say it was impossible. Too much badness crashing down on too many folks too fast. Fire, crawlers, now a quake? What've we done wrong?"

"Wrong?" Auralia stepped out from the boulder's protection. "With all this badness crashing down, I'd be more inclined to say we must be doing something right. And that wasn't an earthquake. It was something heavy hitting the ground. I've felt it in these parts before."

"I'd say it was Old Wenjee falling down," Krawg said with half a laugh. "But then, she's dead, so I shouldn't."

"Wenjee." Auralia winced. "That name's familiar."

Krawg fixed her with a startled gaze. "You know that name?"

Auralia nodded softly. "I think so." She could see the question in his bloodshot eyes again. He had recognized her before she recognized herself, and she knew that he was afraid to ask.

"For the love of mashed beets, we can't stop. Come on." They pressed on through the desolate gullies and ravines. The hills here swelled like waves on a turbulent ocean, and all about them jags of crimson rock protruded like the prows of sinking ships.

They picked their way cautiously through the maze, wary of landslides. Needlebushes defied the bitter soil, and it seemed all the snakes, rats, and gorrels fleeing the Expanse had gathered in their sparse shade.

As Auralia ran on, following Krawg's awkward stumbling stride, her eyes were drawn to the pluming clouds above snowbound peaks. "Just. . .just look at that," she exclaimed. "An endless white sheet strung on a line as long as the horizon."

"Or a dam pressed to breaking," said Krawg, "and we're all about to drown."

Auralia laughed in spite of the trouble. It was coming back to her, the way she and Krawg used to exchange wild descriptions.

"It's like. . .like the land itself is a ship and that's the sail," she said.

"Come on, Milora." Krawg scowled at the front line of the smoke's dark tide as it advanced upon the Forbidding Wall.

Auralia looked back. "Where is everyone?"

"They can't be far."

But all they heard was the burning, which moaned and whistled like some sinister choir. A ferocious noise turned Auralia around to find flames pursuing like a ravenous tiger, blackening one patch of scrappy green after another.

"Keep going," said Krawg. They moved in where the ground grew stonier, and the ravine became a deep canyon.

She heard the crackle again. The knuckled limbs of a massive viscorclaw fingered the precipice of the rising ridge to her left. It appeared to be seeking refuge from the flames. It hissed, and she knew it sensed them now.

She crouched down among the bushes, whispering a warning. Several steps ahead, Krawg saw the viscorclaw and stood very still.

The crawler, about the size of a bear, tumbled down into the ravine, landing between them. It sprang up onto its spearlike feet, poised and tense. But then it slowly lifted two of its seven legs as if choosing Auralia as better prey.

Backing toward the brush fires, she squinted through the smoke. Heat from the advancing flames engulfed her. She choked and collapsed, pressing her sleeve over her face. The needles of a bush beside her blackened and blazed.

She thought she saw Stricia, Ark-robin's daughter, a ghost from long ago, through the fierce red inferno, shards of lantern glass brilliant on the floor in front of her. "Wretched girl," Auralia muttered, dizzy. "You don't love Cal-raven at all. But I do."

The viscorclaw stalked toward her like a massive centipede, its oily sheen flickering in the firelight. Then she leapt and pressed her hands against the hot stone of the escarpment, crying out.

"Auralia!" Krawg shouted, running to her.

"Krawg, stop!" she answered.

The rock liquefied under her hands, stone spilling down like a mudslide. The melt caught and engulfed the viscorclaw, and it fought like a giant insect trapped in honey, rolling in the slow wave. As the stone solidified, it became a new ridge that blocked the ravine, and the crawler's muddied spikes jutted up through the surface like points of a dark crown. Auralia gulped in air, then spun to face the old Gatherer.

"What did you call me?" Her voice wavered.

Krawg blinked, realizing the name he had shouted. Then he looked down and stammered, "I mean… I'm sorry… I…" He waved his hands in the air as if groping for a sure defense. "I knew a stonemaster once. An artist. She had that name. Your name is Milora, and I…"

She rose, sparks glittering on her cloak, and stepped forward to wrap her arms around her old friend. She felt him tremble, and when he tried to speak, he could only cough. Then he pressed his hands to the sides of her head and touched her small nose with his, which was substantial.

"You can't tell Cal-raven," she said. "You hear me? You can't tell anybody. I'm not. . .I'm not ready."

"Well, ballyworms, Auralia," he laughed through his tears. "I don't understand this. But I'm never lettin' you get out of my reach again. Good thing Warney caught up with me, because you got lots of explainin' to do. . .to both of us."

Looking over her shoulder, he groaned, "We gotta move."

They climbed over the buried crawler, Krawg taking Auralia's left hand in his right and drawing her along.

"You're famous, you know," he said. "They tell stories about you in Bel Amica. The stories are all wrong, but I guess that happens."

"I don't want stories," she said. "I didn't do anything much."

"Fire!" he said. "Run."

Smoke thickened, rolling over them like a stampede of frightened animals. Krawg was ahead of her again as walls of fire brightened alongside them, and his voice was lost in the inferno's roar.

And then there was a horse and a rider crashing through the barriers of memory and dream. The rider looked down through the smoke. He reached out for Auralia, clasped her hand, and lifted her up easily before him.

"Cal-raven." She leaned back against his smoky garments, turned, and felt his beard against her cheek.

"Come, Milora. I think you're the last one on my list."

"But Krawg—"

"Jes-hawk's got him. Jes-hawk tells me you have a bad habit of wandering off into danger. Don't make me chase after you again."

They plunged through flame and darkness together.

Much higher up the slope, Cal-raven rode the horse into a canyon wide enough for three horses abreast, and they slowed as they caught up to the company.

"Seventy-seven," he said. "The fire's stalled back there, and there's not much for it to burn here. This is our chance to—" He was interrupted as two men on vawns pushed through the company to face him.

"We're stuck, Cal-raven," wheezed Tabor Jan, sliding from his vawn, his face hollowed by grief and rage. "We were wrong. I've gone up this ravine. It forks, and all its branches head back down."

Jes-hawk explained that, on closer inspection, what had seemed an open run ahead ended at a sheer reflective wall that had given the illusion of an ongoing corridor.

It sounds, he thought, *as if a stonemaster has raised a barrier to stop us.* As he listened, Cal-raven looked up and saw a figure crouched on the rim of the canyon.

Ryllion, he thought. *I told you to stay hidden.*

Jes-hawk whirled, notching an arrow. "Shall I shoot?"

"Save your arrows for viscorclaws." What little resolve Cal-raven had left began to crumble. The people were exhausted, if not injured, and the losses of Wynn, Brevolo, and two Bel Amican drivers were weighing them down. "We've no other enemies here."

As the exhausted company moved in closer to hear him speak, the ground trembled with another mysterious shock. A wide patch of slate broke free of the wall just behind them, sliding and shattering against the opposite wall.

"What is shaking the world?" Warney cried.

"They're coming!" Tabor Jan roared, pointing to the path behind them.

Spinning around, Cal-raven saw viscorclaws crawling up the ravine, scrambling like a swarm of insects newly hatched, moving with the single-minded purpose written in the poison of the Cent Regus Curse—to consume without a thought.

Tabor Jan dismounted his vawn, snatched torches from a merchant and a Bel Amican, then marched past Cal-raven toward the river of predators, expressionless.

"Help him!" Cal-raven cried, although he knew not who might answer.

As if competing for the kill, viscorclaws climbed over one another. And the captain met them, swinging the torches, dodging their sharpened thrusts. The creatures' aggression overwhelmed him. He became a figure clad in writhing branches, their claws striking like scorpion tails. He turned the torches back against himself, falling to his knees. Viscorclaws leapt free, burning and crumbling.

Cal-raven sprang from his horse and raced empty-handed toward the blazing man.

"Watch out!" Jes-hawk cried behind him.

Cal-raven glanced up to the canyon wall's edge to see a man hoisting an enormous tree over his head. It flung sheets of flame into the sky. Then he cast it down into the swarm advancing on Tabor Jan. The blazing tree exploded into sparks, embers, and smoke. Viscorclaws scattered, leaping to the walls. Tabor Jan rolled into the smolder, bellowing, crushing the attackers into the embers.

Cal-raven and Jes-hawk seized the captain and dragged him from the fiery debris. The ruined tree was burning itself out, and the viscorclaws were shedding their charred limbs and tensing for another surge.

The figure then leapt from his high vantage point and dropped through the haze.

Cal-raven gasped. It wasn't Ryllion at all. "Jordam!"

"rrRun," Jordam barked, his shoulders hunched. His massive hands opened and closed like the mouths of hungry predators. "rrRun fast! Strongbreed!"

"What?"

"rrRun!" The beastman picked up the torches Tabor Jan had dropped, and he turned to face the viscorclaws.

Tabor Jan, painted head to toe in blood, reached up and grasped Cal-raven's arm weakly. "I can walk," he said through bloodied teeth.

As the crowd collected, Milora urged Cal-raven's horse toward the king, her eyes on the beastman beyond him.

"Get back, Milora!" Cal-raven ordered.

"Master!" The combined cry from the sisters, Margi and Luci, seized his attention.

Jes-hawk was aiming an arrow at the top of the ridge ahead.

Time seemed to slow down. He felt his plans dissolving, his voice breaking. The people began to move like a herd of sheep, panic-stricken, rushing to one side of the canyon, then the other, then toward him.

Two lines of red-armored figures lined the edges of the canyon there, wielding enormous bows and thick wooden missiles.

The Seers have sent the Strongbreed. Again I've led my people to slaughter.

Cal-raven's horse shrieked and fell, taking Milora with it.

The Bel Amican guards knelt down in a line, some aiming left, some aiming right, and launched volleys of arrows that clattered off the assailants' armor.

The captain stepped in front of Cal-raven, and he tried to push him aside. "No, Tabor Jan."

"I will not let them strike you," he roared.

Cal-raven looked back. Jordam was in a frenzy, lashing at the viscorclaws with two heavy whips he had set ablaze. The crawlers seemed intent on getting past him, as if he did not interest them at all.

Jes-hawk staggered sideways into the king. The bristling shaft of a beastman's arrow protruded from an eruption at his left shoulder. Cal-raven felt the wind of an arrow brush his face. Another ripped through the slack of his tunic sleeve.

A shock rocked the ravine.

Strongbreed, unleashing a unanimous snarl, dropped to a crouch in confusion.

Rocks and rubble rained over Cal-raven. Battered, he knelt, took hold of a stone, and unleashed a surge of stonemastery. The stone fanned out like a rain canopy, smoothing into a broad, curved shield, which he cast to Tabor Jan's feet.

Blinking in surprise, the guardsman lifted it just in time to deflect a heavy arrow. "Cal-raven!" He pointed to the wall just ahead.

A cave was opening.

Margi and Luci, pressing their hands to the canyon wall, were boring a depression into the stone. Luci yelled, "There's a break in the wall here! There are... echoes, master! Open space!"

Cal-raven spread another rock into a shield and dashed to the girls. With his free hand he leaned against the wall, groaning as he pressed what shreds of strength remained out through his fingertips. Stone melted away from him as if he were spraying flames into a snowbank.

It's not enough, he thought.

An arrow embedded itself between his fingers in the softening stone.

Then Milora was beside him, her palms beside his. He was surprised at this but had no chance to make sense of it. Pressing with all her might against the wall, she uttered an impassioned cry. Cal-raven felt a shudder of power unlike any he had known in his training with Scharr ben Fray. The wall burst open, revealing a burrow that reached a large, echoing space beyond.

Milora stepped back.

"More," Cal-raven shouted as his faithful defender Bowlder stepped between him and the attack. Together the stonemasters broadened the opening. As travelers began to crowd around them, archers formed a perimeter, raising shields and firing arrows outward and upward.

"It's not enough!" Cal-raven said, for the passage was still too narrow for anyone to slip through.

An arrow struck Bowlder's side, and he fell hard as a stone statue, growling like a wolf in a snare.

Another shock rocked the earth, and an avalanche of rubble cascaded down, catching an arrow midflight, skewing its trajectory. Cal-raven glimpsed Jes-hawk, his left arm hanging useless, trying to crawl toward Bowlder to draw him out of the arrows' reach. He heard Hagah barking madly in the distance, and the sound brought a sob to his throat.

The Strongbreed howled, distracted from their purpose by something only they could see.

As Jes-hawk pulled Bowlder to the wall, Cal-raven pressed his hands to the stone and bellowed, blasting energy against it. The break opened enough for Margi and Luci. Shaking and crying, they climbed up through the burrow into safety. Working the stone from inside, they opened the tunnel further.

"Say-ressa." The healer slipped in, carrying little Cortie in her arms, her hands already bloody from tending to the fallen.

Cal-raven would not even remember how he roared then, compelling everyone into the cave as heavy arrows clattered against their shields.

They crawled. They staggered. Abascar survivors, Bel Amican soldiers, and merchant strangers. They pressed themselves into the waiting cave as a storm of large, blind-eyed reptiles took wing and rushed into the air, awkward and frightened as moths driven from a cupboard.

Defending the travelers until the last was through the door, Tabor Jan spun around with a cry, falling hard beneath his shield, an arrow in his neck. Cal-raven cried out as if he'd taken the blow himself and dragged the captain back into the cave, tears blurring his vision. As he did, Luci, Margi, and Milora brought down a curtain of liquefied stone to seal off the cave.

"Wait." He lifted the shield and dared to stick his head back out.

Jordam was deep inside a storm of flames, smoke, and scattering viscorclaws. There would be no helping him.

Feeling as though he was sawing off an arm, Cal-raven sealed the door.

In the torchlight they listened. Arrows thudded against the solidifying stone.

"Jordam!" Milora threw herself against the closed door. "We have to open it again."

"No," said Cal-raven, pulling her back, perplexed by the glassworker's fury. "We stay here now. We save these lives. While we can. Until the Strongbreed are—"

The cave shuddered. Dust, stones, and shreds of root crumbled from the ceiling. Then a sound like a hundred trumpets resonated through the stone seal, followed by a deep reverberation. Those earthshaking drums rolled on and on.

"What in the name of Tammos Raak?"

And then there was silence.

"Are we doomed to hide in caves and cower through earthquakes?" someone cried.

They waited.

Milora, her face streaked with tears, walked back into the shadows. Cal-raven, Margi, and Luci quietly layered more stone over the door.

The company clustered in the dark, weeping and gathering around the wounded, where Say-ressa was already putting her hands on them and whispering.

Margi and Luci had collapsed against each other. Milora spread her arms around them like wings, and Krawg—old Krawg, still standing, unharmed—stood over them, his hands on Milora's shoulders. "I'm glad now," said Luci, "that Obrey didn't come with us."

Tabor Jan was choking as Say-ressa tried to stop the bleeding from his wound. Cal-raven knelt beside the captain and clasped his hand. Tabor Jan squeezed back, faintly. Blinking through the gore, he sighed. "Tell me." His voice was just a thin rush of air. "Tell me we'll be there soon." And then he closed his eyes.

Cal-raven tensed, but Say-ressa nodded her head. "He'll live. In what condition I cannot say." She turned to Jes-hawk who lay unconscious, his chest in spasms, his shoulder shelled in blood. Beside him lay Bowlder, his body unmoved by breath, a cloth already covering his face.

Outside, thunder rolled on.

"What is it?" fretted Krawg. "What's happening out there?"

Cal-raven walked to the barrier and pressed his ear against it. He heard nothing. No viscorclaws. No striking arrows. He melted away a patch the size of his fist.

As tendrils of smoke drifted in, he heard a frantic barking. Incredulous, he began clawing at the stone to open a wider gap.

"Is he crazy?" said one of the merchants, standing up as if to stop him.

"Hagah!" Cal-raven shouted. "My dog is out there."

He opened a hole the size of his torso, just enough to see a pile of Strongbreed bodies outside, their armor melted around smoking carcasses, sprawled across the floor of the ravine.

And his hound came leaping through, nearly knocking him to the ground in his joy. Cal-raven embraced the dog. "How did you survive out there?" Then he peered back out into the smoke-darkened day.

"Sing praises to the name of Tammos Raak!" came a cheerful voice. "His gifts have saved you again!"

Cal-raven crawled out into the open, stood, and fell back against the wall.

"That can't be a dragon," said a Bel Amican from the tunnel. "There are no dragons."

A creature green as spring grass, with legs as thick as marrowwood trees and a body the shape of a long-tailed grasshopper, perched on the canyon wall, lashing its tail proudly. Shining, armored segments of its body swelled and scraped against one another as it inhaled and then sprayed an exultant geyser of flames into the sky. It peered down with eyes like glass globes. Then it thrust its head toward Cal-raven.

Clinging to a fringe of bristles behind the dragon's twitching ears, Scharr ben Fray barked a command and then grinned at Cal-raven. "This is Reveler," he said. "The first Fearblind Dragon to breathe fire in the Expanse since the dragons departed for the Eastern Heatlands."

"You know its name?"

"*She* told me," said the mage as if the answer must be obvious. "She also made me promise to deliver a feast the size of a cattle herd for all the favors she's done for me." He nodded to the woodsnout that was barking up at the monster. "And that includes snatching a very familiar dog from the middle of a viscorclaw swarm."

The mage slid from the dragon's neck, then made his way down to Cal-raven and embraced him.

"Teacher."

"You're going to get there, Cal-raven. Reveler and I had to burn half of Fraughtenwood to rid the region of Deathweed predators, and then we roasted what remained of the Cent Regus Strongbreed. But now the road is clear to Inius Throan. I can show you to the gate. And I've brought maps of the city and of more than that, Cal-raven. Maps to pastures. Maps to gardens. Treasures from the casket of Tammos Raak. Everything we need. New Abascar will rise."

22

A Fleeting Glimpse of Daylight

With Batey's strong cord leashes looped over their shiny white horns, the golden hermits paddled upriver, two or three to a raft. They moved with the solemn determination of sailors who, after dossing on the docks for days, finally return to the sea. Their bright orange eyes glinted as they strained the high stems of their necks, surveying the path ahead. Though their beaks were fixed in permanent scowls, they seemed happy to have company, their tails slapping the water.

Strengthened by the feast, hints of goldenwine sweet on their tongues, the travelers left their complaints behind. While thoughts of the deserters haunted their silences, when they spoke at all, they voiced all they longed to regain. They murmured the names of their loved ones. They talked about the salt sting of Bel Amica's morning mist, the patterns of Abascar's hourly songs. Autumn leaves. Snowfall. Children. Horses. Cake.

One man lay along a raft's edge, reaching down and combing the silt along the bottom, scooping it up, letting it trail in silver lines through his fingers until his hand was filled with translucent gems.

"Imagine," the Bel Amican whispered to one of his kinsmen. "Imagine what price these gemstones will bring in the market."

Soon several Bel Amicans lay on the sides of their rafts, combing river sand for jewels.

The ale boy, intrigued, cupped a handful of water to his lips. "Yes," he told Nella Bye, "this is the water Jordam would bring to help the beastmen. It's the water that brought you back. The source must be close."

The Abascar travelers were content to observe. When one sang the Midnight Verse, the rest wove new harmonies. The song, once a simple promise of dawn's approach, was now infused with an aching dissonance that spoke of weariness and loss, which only made the chords of its hopeful refrain stronger, opening up deep reservoirs of longing.

The songs offered beauty back to all that the travelers saw until the boy wondered if the colors that surrounded them might be a response to their singing, just as the song itself was born of seeing daybreak.

What kind of house will these dreamers become? What will it be like to live among people who don't fidget in fear of what's around the next bend? What kind of melodies will they compose?

He guessed that they would make strange company. Mysterious. Aggressively curious. Scary. Ignoring urgent concerns, distracted by insects and clouds and children. Each would live with one foot planted in another world. No more worry about their reputation. No more sugarcoated persuasion. No more flourishes designed to solicit a shower of coins. Only riddles and play and prophecy.

He guessed that they would hear no more songs about a Keeper who granted wishes. Instead, they'd sing of magnificent creatures that lured people out of the dark, away from all they thought they owned, and showed them something grander.

As the song rose and fell, he noticed Mousey sitting alone on the back edge of the last raft, trailing her feet in the water. Her shoulders shook, and her head was bowed so that the mop of red hair concealed her eyes.

He rose and climbed gingerly from one raft to another to join her. She looked like a rag doll salvaged from the toy box of a violent child. Her arms were scarred with tattoos and crisscrossing scabs from fights and abuses. Her face was a patchwork of bruises, and her breathing was uneven.

He placed a hand lightly on her shoulder. She looked at him and laughed in embarrassment. "Sorry, there. I just...I just don't know if I should be here. I don't deserve to live in your new house. I've done things. I've...I've sold people."

"King Cal-raven likes to give folks chances to change," the boy replied. "He has friends who are beastmen, friends who are thieves. You won't be unusual. Tell me what happened. How'd you get caught by shredders?"

She shrugged. "I found my partner's secret stash of coins. Ya see, we'd been stashin' away what folks paid us for...for our trade. We were gonna buy a place all our own on the islands. Get free of work. Free of danger. But then I found she'd been takin' some and hidin' it elsewhere. I didn't say nothin' until the day she pulled a charade, sayin' we'd been robbed. I told her I knew where she'd put it. I left, carryin' my half of it all. I just couldn't believe she'd lie to me."

Mousey rubbed her hands fitfully. "But we were slavers. Sellin' travelers and wanderers for money. I was tired all the time for foolin' myself that it didn't matter. Kept blamin' others, sayin' that if I didn't do this, somebody else would, so I might as well earn a living. Why should I blame Brown for what she done? Anyway, I went off on my own. And I think she got mad. Set the shredders on my trail."

She glanced at him out of the corner of her eye. "We'd have made a fortune on you if we'd nabbed you. Firewalkers are rare."

The ale boy didn't know what to say to that. So he put his feet in the water beside hers and watched the passing lights paint them different hues.

"Brown's free of me now, anyways."

"And you've got us now," the boy said. "You chose a better way. Changin' things for better is hard work. Like rowin' upstream. I watched Jordam do it. He got stronger. So he could walk away from the Core." He shrugged. "Maybe Brown's free. But she's alone."

As they floated along in quiet, his attention drifted from the glowstones that fit together like puzzle pieces along the ceiling, to the arbors of ever-more-extravagant trees along the banks, and then at last to the raft on which he rested.

Mostly, the raft was a wide wooden door with a few gaps punched through it. Someone had patched a break with a wooden shield flecked with fading paint—an illustration of impossibly muscled warriors. The striped background suggested an unfamiliar flag. Perhaps this piece of pillage had come from House Cent Regus itself before the fall. Another gap was nailed over with a wooden plank—a game board marked with a path of squares that spiraled inward to a bright, star-shaped center.

Bound to the front of the raft, an angular piece of buoyant wood helped the float cut faster through the flow. It may have once hung on the wall of a school, for runes scrawled across it spelled out platitudes describing an honorable citizen.

He felt as if he floated on the wreckage of the history of the world.

"Do these colors exist only here?" he heard Irimus ask. "Or have they always been out there, and we haven't noticed?"

"All I know is this," said Nella Bye. "I can see clearly again."

Later, as the boy drifted through memories of Auralia, Nella Bye drew him back to the immediate circumstance. "Are you seeing this?"

Trees crowded the river, their trunks of braided strands flexing with the currents.

"Yes," he said dreamily.

"What if our kingdom has trees with roots that reach these waters? What kind of fruit will they bear?"

As they floated around a bend, he noticed a painted figure on the wall. Across the purple curve someone had rendered a white creature that reminded him of the Keeper. But this creature seemed to have fins rather than legs. It was sleeker, with a snaking tail and ears like kites. Someone had plastered brightly colored petals into the stone so they seemed to flower from the creature's mouth. He started to say something, then fell silent.

"Is that rain?" asked Irimus. "Or snow?"

The golden hermits pulled them into a corridor lined with trees, grateful giants that held out their boughs to one another high above. Flowers caught in their canopy shone with a ghostly blue aura, shedding a steady shower of petals that drifted down, fizzed when they met the water, and spun as they dissolved, causing small shimmering whirlpools in the river.

The passengers watched, hypnotized and quiet.

We're reversing Tammos Raak's journey. We're drawing closer to the Wall. If the Great Ancestor's escape into the Expanse was such a glorious thing, why is the world more beautiful the closer we come to the Wall?

The boy caught a petal on his hand. He had seen these blue flowers somewhere before, but not in a tree and never so large. He carefully tucked it onto his tongue, felt it melt like a sugar wafer.

"Everything that lives here has all it needs," said Raechyl. "I could almost live here."

"It won't last," said the boy.

"Why not?"

"We've found it," said the boy. "It's bound to change."

"Rescue, look." Nella Bye smiled. "Look at your hands."

He opened them and saw that the dark red color that had emerged from the flames was peeling away like sunburn. His new skin was almost the color it had been before his fall in the Cent Regus Core.

He felt a sting in his eyes and rubbed them with his knuckles. When he drew his hands away, they were wet with an oily darkness. He realized that he felt warm with fever. His throat began to ache.

And yet somehow he knew this was necessary.

He caught a few more petals and tucked them into the pocket of his loose white shirt.

The turtles tired and crawled up onto fallen trees, dripping and humming deep sounds of happy exhaustion. The passengers decided to sleep awhile as well.

In this hush Batey visited the ale boy. "I'd form an army to defend this place," he said. "But that doesn't mean I'm giving up on Bel Amica. Rescue, we've got to go home. People are in trouble up there. And the more we lie here looking at pretty lights, the easier it is for me to forget my duty."

The ale boy nodded. "We're fed. We're not thirsty. I think we're safer than before. Maybe it's a good time to find a way out."

So while the others slept, Batey and the ale boy swam through the fence of trees, climbed up on the rocky shore beyond it, and began to examine the shell-strewn banks. Clearly, this was an otters' feasting ground. They explored in opposite directions. The boy moved up the tunnel, where birds flitted this way and that, and toads splatted along down to the water.

Reaching the shore's end, he waded into the shallows and stepped cautiously into a crevasse in the wall. He found himself waist-deep in a narrow stream bathed in a flood of white sunshine. The water was surprisingly clear; he could see his bare, scarred feet along the smooth river floor. Fish chased each other around his ankles. A striped, eyeless eel with a toothless mouth nibbled at his legs, its scratchy tongue scraping for moss or water bugs.

As he refilled his water flask, he smelled smoke mingling with the perfumes of abundant cave lilies. Then he moved on toward a commotion. A deep ache flared, a feeling he had come to know. Something was in trouble nearby. Something needed his help.

As he straightened, he saw a spill of rugged earth on the left where part of a wall had collapsed, opening a window to bright, turbulent daylight above. Outside, ribbons of smoke twisted past an array of contorted, blackened trees. Flames lashed at the tree trunks.

Those aren't Cragavar trees. That's Fraughtenwood. And it's on fire.

Deep impressions—hoofprints—punctured the rubble incline. They led into the stream and then emerged again on the soft soil to the right.

He heard trouble frightfully close. Something stirred behind ivy curtains that draped the wall. Drawn by invisible strings, he walked up and gingerly pulled back an edge of the ivy.

A tremendous display of antlers burst forward. The antlers thrashed, striking the hard wall with sharp cracks, dragging strands of ivy. Crawling away on all fours, the boy saw the blood-streaked face of the animal—a stag of magnificent size, lying crumpled behind the curtain.

His ears pricked toward the boy, the stag bared his teeth and seethed. His eyes were clouded, and his hide was purple and red, burned hairless. He held one front hoof suspended.

"You can't see me clearly, can you?" the boy asked. "You're burned too badly."

The stag's nostrils sucked noisily at the air, and he shook his antlers as if to assert that he was in complete control.

"You're mighty. You're glorious. I can help. But you'll have to put down your pride."

The daylight flickered, and waves of twisting flame crashed past the opening. The grasses around the cave-in cowered, blackened, and disappeared in smoke. Heat wafted into the tunnel. The stag pawed at the ground and wheezed what would have been a bellow before smoke scorched his lungs.

The boy uncorked the flask.

The stag sniffed the air again. His ears swiveled back as a great tree, somewhere unseen in the conflagration outside, groaned and exploded. A spray of sparks and smoke billowed up into the sky.

"I won't hurt you," whispered the boy. "You're thirsty. And your wounds need washing."

The stag's nostrils opened, the flesh of the muzzle around it scarred with heat.

"You are such a beautiful king," said the boy. He cupped his hand, poured a splash of water into it.

The stag lifted his head, listened intently to the world all around, then slowly lowered his muzzle, extending a cracked, purple tongue.

As the stag drank, the boy's eyes glazed with tears. For a moment he felt that all these things had happened so that he might be here, in this moment, offering a sip of water to a desperate king—a touch of comfort, a rumor of a place where water was pure and enlivening, where help came when you needed it.

The stag licked the boy's hand dry. Then his muzzle swung around and nudged the flask.

"There's more," said the boy. "A whole river of it."

"Boy!" That was Batey's voice somewhere in the distance.

The stag bit his hand lightly with thick, square teeth, and the boy poured him another handful. He winced, trying to keep his gaze from the magnificent ruin of the creature's scorched flesh. "You have to let go of this place," said the boy. "Go north. This water spills from somewhere."

The stag kicked at the ground, lurched to his feet, and then struck the ale boy with a hard thrust of a hoof. The boy sprawled into the dirt. He heard a thud and a splash, and he saw a shadow pass into the sunlight.

Holding his chest, he fought for breath. The stag was now a proud silhouette stark against the wall of fire, and then it was gone into the conflagration.

"Get back here!" Batey called. "Trouble!"

Batey lifted the boy and carried him, running along the shore and diving back out to swim through the tree line. "They're coming!" he panted as he approached the others.

"Who?" asked Irimus, sharper than he had been since years before Abascar's fall. "Shredders?"

"The runaways. They're armed and look like trouble. Get back on the water."

"All of them?"

"Five. And...and they're not right."

The golden hermits were asleep and refused to rouse, offering deep groans of discomfort when they were jostled.

"We'll row," said Batey.

A venomous hiss sounded in the corridor behind them.

"Was that one of...them?" Kar-balter whispered.

The ale boy saw Batey cast a fearful glance to Raechyl. And now he, too, was afraid.

At the end of the tree-lined corridor, they passed beneath a red arch into a high-ceilinged space lit by patches of blue flowers. A thick pillar—perhaps a tree trunk—dressed in a coat of trailing white moss stretched up to press against the ceiling, which was studded with strange growths like large, folded flower buds. Beyond the pillar they heard a continuous thunder.

"A falls," said the boy.

"Will we go over?" Kar-balter yelped.

"No," said Batey. "We're going upstream."

"Then we may be trapped," said Nella Bye.

Daylight painted the far end of the cavern, which was terraced in great swells of stone draped in pink sheets of minerals. Through breaks in the clouds that stormed and steamed from the falls' concussion, they caught glimpses of a vast pool.

"There's our way out!" said Batey.

A crooked stair rose from the shoreline just to the right of the falls and ascended into a shaft in the earth.

"Batey!" Nella Bye grabbed his arm and dragged him down.

A spear sailed over the Bel Amican.

What looked like Aronakt stood at the front of the first pursuing raft. He wavered awkwardly in his tattered cloak, like a Cent Regus merging of man and bat. His jaw hung open as if it was broken, and fresh scars raked his face. His eyelids were drawn back, and his eyes swiveled loosely.

Hunched low behind him on the raft, the others were also familiar, also distorted, their flesh in shreds, their gazes fixed on the travelers with something like hunger, something like rage.

"He looks like..."

"I know," said Batey.

"What's that in the water around them?" Irimus squinted, then answered himself. "More of those crawlers the cavespiders caught."

Feelers, thought the ale boy. *Feelers uprooted. There are so many.*

"To shore!" Batey cried. "Into the tunnel, where we can block them with fire!"

The water was troubled, shaken into a roiling turbulence. Debris fell from the ceiling, splashing the river and battering the rafts. The field of hanging buds exploded, each one unfolding leathery wings. The bats cycloned around the cave's white pillar, then rushed downstream in a chattering storm.

The ale boy thought of the sign he had seen painted on the passage wall like a warning.

The rafts closed in around the pillar, and the passengers clung to each other. Some spread cloaks as if to shield themselves. Others brandished torches, readying for the attack. Some clutched at the pillar's white moss for a hold to keep the rafts from slipping away.

But then the pillar turned. Its outer crust split open, broke loose, and peeled away. At the top, two spheres brightened, crackling with energy. A low rumble spread out from the pillar, and it began to bend in half, its heights descending toward the pursuers.

The travelers shouted to each other, rowing their rafts away as the pillar broke apart.

From each side suddenly unfurled massive wings that, spanning the breadth of the cavern, exposed a slender body of glittering silver scales. The creature swelled with breath and a reverberating voice. The eyes, infused with light, illuminated a blunt, ferocious visage and vast jaws dripping with flame.

The creature raised a mighty tail and smashed the river, shocking waves into a rush. Thrusting its horns at the pursuers' raft, it caught the assailants in the white light of its eyes. Its snout, rather like a bat's but large enough for swarms of bats to nest in its nostrils, twitched as if it were reading the air.

Beneath its wings some travelers rowed their rafts to shore, while others leapt off and swam. They splashed from the shallows and huddled together. The wings blocked out the daylight and any access to the stair.

The ale boy tried to follow but stumbled. He was caught. He looked down and saw one of the strong leash cords looped around his foot. He fought to untangle it.

The man who had once been Petch hissed at the creature, shaking a sharpened oar as if to spear a seabull. The spidery crawlers clawed at the air.

The creature waited.

The five assailants unleashed a wave of curses in unfamiliar voices, raised what weapons they had left, and flung them. The creature's jaws opened, and it coughed a flicker of light. The spears were engulfed, incinerated.

One of the assailants uttered a command, and crawlers sprang in clusters toward the beast. Again those great jaws opened. This time flames poured out, paving the river in fire, immersing the crawlers and the assailants' rafts.

Not a scream escaped the blaze. When the gusting fire abated, scraps of smoking, blackened bodies floated downstream among the charred splinters of the crawlers.

Five ghostly figures remained, hovering in the haze, bell shaped and trailing barbed tentacles, like jellyfish.

The creature growled, snapping its jaws at the phantoms, which swayed but could not be caught.

Turning its head, it brought those glassy globes of white light in close to the shore so that the ale boy lay under its bristled chin, like a mouse hiding under a furnace. The scene before him on the shore wavered, illusory in the heat. Dumbstruck with fear, none of the travelers dared move.

"Please, have mercy," Raechyl whispered.

The creature sniffed the air. The Bel Amicans trembled, but the Abascar survivors spread to form a circle around them. Together they began to sing the Early Morning Verse.

The creature blinked its eyes. In the center of those bright globes, dark pupils solidified—it was examining them. Then it emanated something like a purr from a mountain-sized cat.

From the cloud of blue ghosts, another lash of dissonant screams cut through the song. The creature reared up, pawing the air with its black-clawed forelegs. The horns splaying from its head spread into a wide crown, and it crowed like a rooster. It folded in its wings, exposing the stairway.

The crowd walked with excruciating caution to the foot of the stairs. But Nella Bye stopped and looked back. "Rescue?"

The creature's eyes narrowed as if it were listening to some far-off command. The ale boy got to his feet, still tightly knotted in the tether.

The ghosts, shrieking over the water, caught a current of air and streamed toward the stairway.

The creature sniffed at the ale boy and then exclaimed a bell-like cry. It cocked its head as if in disbelief, and then it unfolded its wings again, sealing off the boy's view of his companions and blocking the ghosts from reaching the stairway.

"Please," he said. "I'll do whatever you wish. But may I go and see Auralia soon?" He tightened his grip around the strap of the water flask and closed his eyes.

A wave of water swept over him, lifting him off the ground. He felt a hard tug at his ankle, and he fell. His raft washed back into the river and pulled him from the shore. He felt the water close over his head. A mighty hand lifted him out, then set him down on the raft, and he saw the creature rushing downstream, bearing the raft before it, the blue ghosts streaming along behind, screaming.

23

THRESHOLD

Eyes like ovens sealed in glass. Dark eyelashes fanning a face encased in intricate, fireproof shields. Scales green as new clover and, growing like a lacework of beetle-black mortar between them, shiny new shields that would someday guard the creature's whole body.

Entranced by the Fearblind Dragon's strange, alien nature, her unfamiliar textures and jagged lines, Auralia wanted to sculpt a model or paint a picture. At times Reveler seemed more plant than animal or something halfway between—the way she sprouted barbs where no other animal was barbed and the way her head seemed a giant seedcone that had grown in segments. As Reveler stretched and groomed and crawled impatiently over the canyons, sniffing the rocky crevasses and sneezing smoke, her sinuous grasshopper legs started rock slides. She commanded attention from the shaken and even the wounded, as if she were a dancer on a stage.

Auralia had seen a great deal of the life the world had to offer. But she had never seen a dragon until Scharr ben Fray arrived, steering Reveler as if she were a vawn, to save this company from those viscorclaws and bow-wielding beastmen.

And yet, there was someone more fascinating than the dragon in Auralia's view. Krawg and Warney had helped Bel Amican soldiers carry the wounded into the smoky daylight where Say-ressa could examine them better, and King Cal-raven moved among them. He bowed over each patient as if it were his duty to heal every scratch. He would wear himself out with apologies and vows, unnecessary as they were. "Auralia, you greedy wretch," she muttered to herself. She felt foolish, for she coveted his attention, wanted him to truly see her and recall her real name. But he carried so many burdens now. How would he ever find time for curiosity?

She fitfully fingered the ring he had failed to see on her hand.

He spoke quietly not only with the Abascars but with the others who had helped them, ministering to the merchants and the Bel Amican guards. He also knelt before Sisterly Emeriene, putting his hands on the shoulders of her young children and speaking quiet words of comfort. Emeriene seemed like a woman suffocating, and Cal-raven's attention seemed to be the air she wanted to breathe. Her gaze followed him everywhere.

Say-ressa whispered to him over the fallen, and he knelt to question Jes-hawk about the journey and all they had endured. He even held the archer's right hand as Say-ressa's sharp instruments probed the bones in his left shoulder, stitching together torn edges. But nothing was harder to endure than the thudding of Tabor Jan's boots against the ground as he endured Say-ressa's needles while she teased out shards of the Strongbreed arrow. He had no voice to scream, but his whole body fought as if a predator were upon him.

Say-ressa would have no way to repair the captain's deepest wound. Word had spread quickly of the marriage tattoo.

Bodies heal faster than hearts.

She thought of Jordam the beastman and looked up a spill of boulders where the dragon had buried some struggling Strongbreed. Sitting on a high, flat stone, Jordam watched the king. Arm's length to his left sat a stranger draped and hooded by a heavy canvas. The two glanced at each other like dogs that take a dislike to each other.

Auralia climbed up on the rock, feeling like a thrush alighting between two wolves. The stranger had large, bruised, fidgeting hands, and his breathing was feeble and ragged.

Jordam picked at the wounds the viscorclaws had torn. When she had seen these hands before, they had been gloved in hair. Now but for their size and their brittle black nails, they seemed almost the hands of an ordinary man.

He glanced at her, anxious. "You...hurt?"

"No," she said. But then she looked at her own hands and rubbed them together. "Yes, my hands. I don't...I don't do that very often."

"rrMake stone change?" He shook his head and puffed air through his teeth. "rrStrange. Show me?"

Misunderstanding, she held out her open hand. "My wrists hurt mostly."

He gingerly took her wrist and stared intently at her fingers. "How?" he asked again.

"Oh. I see. Well, only some people can do it. Some say it means I'm descended from Tammos." She said the name again slowly—"Tammos"—as if it reminded her of something.

Jordam shrugged, surrendering his question, and released her hand. She began to etch faint figures on the stone. "I prefer to do this."

"rrShouldn't have come."

"Why did you come?"

"rrHurt." Jordam pressed his hand to his chest.

"You need healing? You should tell Say-ressa."

"rrNo. Must...give words to the king. They hurt to keep inside."

On the stone before her, she drew the man she had once sculpted—a simple figure with arms spread wide. In the space above him, she outlined the figure that she saw on her ring.

"rrKing should...punish me," Jordam grumbled. "Send me away."

"No. You saved us. The viscorclaws could have killed you."

"I am...rrCent Regus. They are not made to hurt such as me."

These words aggravated the stranger; he twitched as if he too were feeling Say-ressa's needles.

"You were brave to fight them," she said.

"I bring more trouble than I stop," he answered.

She felt an impulse to tell him what to do. To comfort him. To urge him into a good decision. But she knew it was not what he needed right now. He needed to hurt, as she was hurting. "We're all trouble," she said. "Sometimes we do our best, and it only makes things worse."

In the awkward pause that followed, she mustered the courage to say, "Forgive me. Do I know you?"

The shrouded figure sat still and did not turn to meet her eyes.

"rrTravels with the king," said Jordam. "King's helper."

"Is he sick?"

"Yes," came the miserable sigh from the hood. "I'm sick." She could not see his eyes, but he seemed to be watching the crowd intently as if he feared them.

"Did the viscorclaws hurt you?"

The stranger's hands wrestled as if molding an answer. "No," he sighed at last.

Jordam's stare told Auralia that she was inspiring his curiosity. Startled, she turned away. She watched the king, weighed the risks, and knew that the time was not yet right. "I came to help the king too," she said. "But he is very busy. So I'm waiting."

Jordam nodded. "rrHard. Waiting."

"Yes," she agreed, surprised at the force of her reply. *I should leave,* she thought. *I got his attention before, and look at all it's cost him. All that I made is lost. Scattered. Buried. Misunderstood.*

The dragon's disgruntled groan from higher up the slope drew their attention. The mage had climbed onto Reveler's head and was now spurring her across the mountainside on some urgent mission.

"I should go." Auralia reached out and brushed Jordam's forearm with her hand. "It is good to see you. To see how you've grown."

At those words he turned to her sharply.

She pulled her hand back as if it burned, slipped from the boulder, and made her way down to the path.

No one noticed or tried to stop her.

A short while later, when the sounds of the camp had diminished behind her and she had turned up another north-running path, her journey was interrupted by a herd of bleating, disgruntled rock goats. Large as horses, they clattered and trotted anxiously down the dry streambed, eyes wild in fear, some gnawing on mouthfuls of wild grass they'd uprooted earlier.

Her feet gripping both edges of the canyon, the drooling dragon stalked behind them, whimpering with desire. The mage upon her head held her back from devouring the terrified animals.

As the gargantuan creature moved past, the mage glanced down at Auralia curiously. "This company's going to need help from all available hands," he said. "And it's still a long journey to the gate. You might not want to go on foot."

"Maybe I've chosen a different journey," she replied.

"Young woman, we're going to open the gates of Inius Throan. This is a story that generations will tell. Your name can be part of the legend."

"I've become a legend," she murmured. "It's awful."

The mage did not hear her for Reveler's breathing. "And Cal-raven's people will be the safest in the Expanse. You can trust him." He spurred the creature on, moving over Auralia.

She stopped, fingering her ring. Cal-raven's ring.

With hard and jolting steps, the goats complained about their passengers. Their bleating sounded so much like grown men moaning that even the wounded could not help but laugh.

They made steady progress. These paths would not permit wagons, but with Scharr ben Fray's help, the survivors strapped pallets for the injured across the dragon's back, and the mage instructed her to crawl low to the ground at the front of the procession.

In this way Tabor Jan, Jes-hawk, three Bel Amican guards, and two merchants were borne on a winding passage through the ascending foothills toward high mountain cliffs. The exhausted travelers eyed the path that the mage had cleared, uncomfortable to think of what might fall on them from the heights or what might follow them in and trap them there.

Through the night their torches lit the way, as did drifting clouds of lantern-bees that emerged from hives inside the walls. What might have been a starry strip of sky above was dimmed by smoke. Ash fell like snowflakes.

Auralia stayed with them, sullen and silent, except to whisper comforts into her anxious rock goat's ear. "You'll be rewarded," she said. "Ehh," moaned the goat.

At times she glanced over her shoulder. Jordam and the shrouded stranger kept their distance, perhaps listening to ensure no one followed.

Somewhere, a bearcat roared. That set the goats into a riot of noise, but the dragon uttered an ultimatum, and the canyon was silent for another long stretch. Auralia could hear the mage murmur in a strange, guttural pattern, and Reveler dragged her tail, stirring up dust for the procession to cough its way through.

When at last they came to a fork in the path before a massive wedge of stone, the mage dismounted the dragon, and she quickly scaled the rock to perch there like an eagle on a ship's high prow.

As the travelers released the goats, the animals turned and brought their muzzles in close around Auralia. This strange behavior bewildered the company, and Auralia looked to Cal-raven. But he seemed not to notice, hurrying with Say-ressa to attend again to the wounded.

Krawg approached, bringing Warney along with him.

Auralia, overcome with affection for the dumbfounded Gatherer, slid from her goat's back and hurried to embrace him.

"See?" said Krawg quietly. "She's older, but she's...her!"

Warney choked, his bony body shaking. Clearing his throat he said, "Gotta 'gree with you there." He wrapped his feeble arms around her. "Why do ya look..."

"Older?" She wiped her sleeve across her eyes. "Not sure. Not yet, anyway."

"Where've you been? We thought we lost you. In Abascar's fire."

"I remember the fire. But not much else. Maugam. The dungeon." Her whisper faded to a trace. "Radegan," she said, wincing. "Poor Radegan. And then there were flames. A young woman with a lantern. Northchildren. Then...then I was elsewhere. But I was restless. Something...something seemed unfinished. I woke beside a river, and I...I was different. I must have asked to be different."

"Asked? Who could you ask that could make such a thing come true?"

"Let's not talk about this," she whispered, and then she insisted again that they keep secret all she had revealed.

"But think of their amazement, 'Ralia! The celebration!"

"The king must keep his mind on his mission. Until we're safe inside."

"Well," said Krawg, "when the time comes..."

"When the time comes," she agreed.

Meanwhile, Hagah barked at the front of the stone ship, tail wagging with wild anticipation.

The sun rose.

As the great wedge of stone, a small mountain in itself, began to reveal rich red colors in the sunrise, Cal-raven sat beside Tabor Jan and clasped his hand. The captain's breath was shaky, but his eyes were open. Except for a window around his face, his shoulders, neck, and head were ensconced in a clay cast that Cal-raven had molded with stonemastery.

"Brevolo's name will be carved by the gate," Cal-raven said. "And I'll sculpt her image just inside, where she'll raise a torch in welcome."

"Be cautious," Scharr ben Fray said to him a few moments later. "You will make a host of promises in these early days if you are not careful. Honor the lost by attending to the living. Remember that these first days will become a story passed on for generations. They will be, in themselves, a foundation that shapes the future."

"When we bring our people from Bel Amica," Cal-raven murmured, "we'll raise the colors that carried us through dark days in Barnashum. We wouldn't be here without Auralia."

"Or the Keeper who sent her."

Cal-raven turned away. He did not want his teacher to see the tremors set off by that name.

Scharr ben Fray gripped the young king's shoulder. "Let me show you something. A treasure kept hidden in Tammos Raak's Casket since he was driven from this place so many centuries ago." He gave Cal-raven an ancient, yellowed cloth cloaking a heavy object.

Cal-raven unfolded the cloth. A ring with three keys fell into his hand.

The mage smiled.

Cal-raven examined the ridges in the wall, finding nothing symmetrical, nothing crafted to make this spot seem anything more than a rocky corner. But then his fingertips lingered over a smudge of grey stone that looked like mortar. "Stonemastery. Hastily done. Somebody's been here before us. Not many years ago."

"Alas," said Scharr ben Fray, "another stonemaster walked in Inius Throan before us. He wanted to be the last."

Cal-raven closed his eyes, trying to calm himself.

"It wasn't me, Cal-raven."

The king began to clear the smudge of stone with a swipe of his raw, aching hand. What he revealed was, indeed, a black plate that opened into a deep keyhole.

The mage's smile faded. "That...that's not right." He placed his hand to the wall, his thumb and forefinger framing the broad slot. "It's far too large for any of these keys. It's a decoy. Or..." Then he flinched, visibly angry.

"Warney!" shouted the king.

The Gatherer was at his elbow in an instant.

"I need your sharp eye. Find me another keyhole. None of these keys will fit what we see here."

Warney looked at the keys. He looked at the keyhole. "Beg to argue," he said. "Specially with men so learned. You're right—those keys're too small for this lock. But Krawg's taught me all about breakin' in, beg your pardon. He knows every kind of lock, every kind of key. I've never seen puzzle keys before. But if you'll give me just a few heartbeats..." He held up the keys and then, with a few quick twists, he tangled them so that they latched together, teeth flaring in different directions at the end of the interlocking rods. They fit the keyhole perfectly, and Warney turned them slowly, his eye widening in surprise.

"That," sighed Scharr ben Fray, "was to be the king's honor."

Warney turned whiter than usual, but Cal-raven ignored the mage's growl, pressing his hand to the plate and listening.

A few moments passed. Warney scratched his chin. He scratched his elbow. He scratched his hindquarters.

A distant *boom* echoed in the wall. The goats began screaming like men, then turned and rammed their horns against the canyon wall as if to bore themselves a cave. The wedge-shaped column of stone—the entire towering prow of the ship—began to rise, shaking rubble from the wall.

The travelers quickly retreated as a door the height of two men and the breadth of ten was revealed darkly before them.

Echoes reverberated beyond.

"What else did you find in that casket?" Cal-raven whispered.

Scharr ben Fray beamed as if he had longed to savor this moment. "Welcome to Inius Throan."

Cal-raven turned to Say-ressa. "Can Tabor Jan stand? I want my guardsman to be the first through this gate."

Say-ressa nodded uncertainly.

Then Cal-raven called for Jordam.

The beastman hesitated. Then, keeping a hand on Ryllion's sleeve, he marched forward like a soldier with a captive. Ryllion kept his masked face downturned, deep in the shadows of his hood.

Scharr ben Fray leaned in close. "How long must I wait before you tell me about your...special guest?"

The mob was as silent as the stone of the canyon while the beastman and the stranger waited for the king's instructions. Cal-raven scanned the audience. He saw Milora—that strange, secretive glassworker—and noticed tears on her face. Krawg stood beside her, wringing his hands. And there—Emeriene, clasping her sons' hoods to keep them from running forward. She seemed especially curious about Ryllion, which is what he'd hoped to avoid.

I must get him safely locked away. We can't have any revenge killings within these walls.

"Jordam, you're an honored guest in my house. In gratitude for all you've done to save House Abascar, I invite you to be the second through this gate. And you." He spoke quietly into Ryllion's hood. "You've yet to earn any honors. Take this as a gesture of trust."

Ryllion nodded, seeming properly terrified.

"Teacher, follow them. Margi, Luci, and dear Cortie...you will be next. I will proceed behind with Krawg, House Abascar's storyteller, on my right and sharp-eyed Warney on my left."

Scharr ben Fray laughed, shaking his head. "As thoughtful as I remember. A man who would make signs of all things."

"The rest can follow. The merchants and our guests from Bel Amica, you also are welcome. We will be a house with an open gate."

"The viscorclaws will be so pleased," said the mage, amused.

Tabor Jan approached crookedly, every step a test. The brace around his head was sturdy. He paused and clasped Cal-raven's hand with his own. A tear slid down his face, but he would not meet the king's eyes. Then he moved into the dark like a man carrying a burden far heavier than the brace.

Auralia covered her mouth to stifle a nervous laugh, delighted by the sounds beyond the gate. Every footfall echoed so that the company seemed to be welcomed with applause.

Then as her eyes adjusted to the dark space, she shuddered at the spectacle. Somber giants lined the walls of the long, narrow entry hall—armored men and women with their hands raised over their heads to grip the hilts of stone swords. Runes were faintly legible in the stone blocks that protruded beneath their feet.

"The children of Tammos Raak." Scharr ben Fray dusted one of the blocks.

Roaches scuttled over the rubble-strewn, dropping-crusted floor. "Not my idea of a royal carpet," grumbled Krawg, trying to stand on tiptoe.

Auralia was most delighted by the small, slender, redbrown climbers slinking up and down the edges of the figures. "Zooey-cats," she said. They peered down at the newcomers with eyes that mirrored orange torchlight, and they fitfully licked at their forearms in agitation before blurring into their burrows behind the statues' shoulders. Far above the figures and their cat colonies, birds anxiously beat at the dusty, sky-lit heights as if trying to scare intruders away.

"Cwauba birds," she whispered. "So this is where they come from."

The stretch ended at the foot of a long, curving stair that ascended to heavy wooden doors, which were parted just enough for a man to slip through.

"This is good," said the king. "Any invaders will be forced to move in a narrow parade." He pointed to the burrows beyond the giants' shoulders. "Archer points. Easy to pick off trouble from above."

"What's more," said Scharr ben Fray. "We'll find a trigger somewhere. These giants are not fooling. They'll bring those heavy swords down and dash the skulls of unsuspecting intruders."

In the rain of dust and feathers, Warney found another keyhole just inside the entrance. "Strange," he said, "to have such an important gate controlled by keys."

"Indeed," said Scharr ben Fray. "In a secure house the raising and closing of the main gate is the work of many in concert, to keep too much power from falling into the wrong man's hands. That's just the first of many mysteries I mean to solve in the upcoming days." He strode urgently to the foot of the stair. Cal-raven started after him, but the mage held up his hand. "Wait."

A flicker of lanternlight appeared in the gap of the second gateway high above.

"Archers," called Scharr ben Fray in a sharp whisper.

The company behind him drew together.

A figure appeared through the gate, raising the amber lantern high.

"Who are you?" Scharr ben Fray's harsh question repeated and diminished. "And how did you get in?"

The figure, barefoot and dressed in a slight gown, descended with nimble steps, the golden light illuminating a soft, feminine smile.

Someone whispered, "Northchild!"

Auralia recognized her at once. "Nella Bye."

"Oh!" Jordam stepped away from the hooded stranger and strode forward swiftly, moving past the king. Auralia saw Jes-hawk try to rise from his pallet, his hand groping for a weapon.

Jordam, moving up the stairs, opened his arms. The woman set down the lantern and disappeared into his enormous embrace.

Scharr ben Fray's mouth opened and closed, and he seemed distraught, as if some privilege had been stolen from him, some plan disrupted.

Cal-raven looked back at Auralia, incredulous. "How do you—"

He never finished his question.

After stepping down from the last stair, Nella Bye had come to kneel at his feet. "Welcome, King of Abascar. We've been waiting for you."

"Nella Bye," the king whispered. "You...you were in the Cent Regus Core. I heard that you..."

She looked up, sharp eyed. "We were attacked. There was trouble. But the ale boy and Jordam, they came back. They rescued us. The ale boy brought us on an underground river. We found a stair. And it led us...here." She spread her arms.

"I won't believe it until I see it," Scharr ben Fray said quietly.

"I believe it," said Cal-raven.

"You've nothing to fear," she laughed. "Well, except that this city is something of a zoo. But as long as its furry, feathered, and scaly inhabitants cooperate, I believe it is ours for the taking. We've even begun to sweep it for you. Although..." Something splatted on the floor near the king's feet, and Nella Bye looked up toward the distant wingbeats. "Clearly we have a great deal yet to do."

"They've even begun to sweep it," Cal-raven laughed, incredulous. He turned to his teacher. Scharr ben Fray shrugged. "Rescue brought you here? On an underground river?"

"rrRescue," Jordam confirmed, his voice resonant with the tone of a doting father. "O-raya's boy brought them."

"The ale boy?" Auralia grabbed Warney's sleeve to keep from staggering.

Cal-raven took another step toward Nella Bye. "All of you? Is the queen..."

Nella Bye bowed her head. "I am sorry, master."

The king looked at the beastman. Jordam took a step back and choked.

"And where is my ale boy?" asked the king.

Nella Bye was silent for a long while. Then she looked at Jordam, a note of solemn apology in her voice. "In the last moments of our journey, as we ascended the stair to this house, the creature..."

"rrMust...must not say..." Jordam was shuddering, retreating further into the shadows. "No."

"We think it might have been the Keeper," she said. "It took the boy down the river."

Auralia, her whole body quaking, took Krawg and Warney by the hands and sank to her knees.

Cal-raven shook his head. "The boy has something powerful watching over..." His voice trailed off. Then he turned to face his people and raised his voice. "Abascar has suffered so much. But here...here is a blessing. Let us remember this when our story is told. They will say it was just some mad entertainer's fantasy. But here stands Nella Bye."

Then he turned and asked softly, "Do the doors at the top of these stairs seal tightly?"

"They do. A trustworthy second barrier. A keyhole is also there that, I can only assume, serves as another way to open and close the front gate."

Cal-raven turned and walked back through the crowd as if moving through a dream. He stopped directly before Auralia, who climbed awkwardly to her feet. But Cal-raven's gaze passed over her, shifting from Krawg to Warney. "Will you two take the first watch? If anything or anybody comes to our open door, you are to let them through the first gate. But not the second."

"Master, I... What if the gate... Now, not fast enough... I... Surely..."

"Krawg," said the king, "if you see any kind of danger coming, get up the stairs and close the second barrier. That should give any viscorclaws time to enter and stand on this threshold. Then seal the front gate from behind the second barrier, locking them inside." He looked up to the statues' shoulders. "And we'll prepare a fiery surprise for them."

"Honor, well. Something I... We could never... Yes!" That is what Krawg said. And then he added. "My pleasure."

"Now to rather urgent matters," said the king. "Nella Bye, is there water?"

She laughed. "There is plenty of that, master."

"Anything to eat?"

"Wait until you see the orchards. They're a mess, the trees climbing all over one another and heavy with fruit."

"Please don't say that the trees are climbing anywhere," muttered the mage.

"I want to see everything," said Cal-raven. "But first lead me to the others. House Abascar is made of people more than walls or towers. After all those prisoners have suffered, it's time to welcome them home."

24

The Foundation

When wild roosters began to crow their claims to sovereignty, Cal-raven was already awake, savoring what remained of the night's calm.

On this, the morning of his fourth day in Inius Throan, he sat on the floor in the wavering shadow of his breeze-blown hammock. This had once been Tammos Raak's royal bedchamber, but Cal-raven preferred a hammock, and so he had suspended himself in a canvas between two of the three pillars that supported the ceiling. He could lie in the dark and imagine his way back to afternoon naps in the Cragavar trees, in the days before Abascar's future had been set upon his shoulders.

The pillars' three murals, lit by dawn's first rays through the glassless, east-facing windows of Inius Throan's royal citadel, enthralled him again.

On a path between Forbidding Wall peaks, Tammos Raak led children in a parade around the north pillar's girth. With an enormous shield, the Great Ancestor deflected the fiery arrows that followed them while the frightened brood rushed southward into the Expanse.

On the central pillar's scene, children nestled like baby birds around Raak's feet while he sheltered them with two shields raised like wings, hiding them from the searching gaze of eyes above the mountains.

On the third pillar, their fragile camp had been replaced by a great city encased in shields thick as a tortoiseshell. The city flourished in its concealment—the children danced and smiled.

That was Tammos Raak's story. For a while. He established a house for them. And then it broke into pieces from within. Cal-raven touched the scars where gemstones had been pried from the mural. *Thieves. I suppose they're part of the fourth chapter, the one Tammos Raak never had the chance to tell.*

Cal-raven's sleep had been fitful and feverish. His imagination was overwhelmed by all he had seen in three days of exploration, while his body ached from the recent ordeals. In childhood he had dreamed of Inius Throan. Yet the thrill he should have felt in seeing it emerge from myth and time was lost in the realization of how much toil lay ahead and the unshakeable ache of all that the journey had cost him and his people.

My teacher is eager for me to name this New Abascar. I cannot. Not while most of my people are still far away in Bel Amica. Not while viscorclaws prowl in the space between us and crawl to besiege us. How can it have come to this? Where are your colors, Auralia?

He dreaded opening the door. He knew he would find a decanter of apple juice and new wildflowers for the vase on his windowsill. That offering had greeted him each of the three mornings since their arrival.

He had no doubt who had brought them.

Through Emeriene's eyes Inius Throan was less like a city and more like a cluttered attic with the roof torn off.

A world of restless imagination, stranded for centuries in the lap of seemingly impenetrable mountains, the ancient ruins were disintegrating, yet full of marvels. She had followed a short distance behind the company that shared Cal-raven's tour of the wall, straining to hear the hushed observations.

"Looks like a house dreamt up by a crazed child desperate for attention," the king observed. "It's a world of unfinished ideas."

His words turned her around, and, yes, her boys were still following, shouting about which of Inius Throan's fourteen towers they would take as their home.

Irimus Rain glanced back at the children, then leaned to whisper at Cal-raven's shoulder, and the king turned suddenly and strode back to face Emeriene. "Sisterly," he said, "I didn't know you'd followed us."

"I...I was just... I was brooming for a look," she stammered. "I mean, a broom. Looking for a broom. To sweep the threshold stairs."

"I'm sure," said Cal-raven, repressing a smile, "that there is invention enough in this company to make a broom." He then asked if she might be willing to direct the teams that would clear the streets and assess the condition of Inius Throan's primary structures. "How different can it be from commanding sisterlies in Bel Amica?"

While she felt the weight of this request, it pleased her. The sight of the city had set her to twitching, awakening her lifelong inclination to organize chaos and restore missing pieces. "It would be an honor," she said. *And it will help me take my mind off you,* she told herself.

"Come with us," he said. "Irimus will map what we find, and you can make your plan from there."

She understood his careful, formal manner. What else could he do in front of so many witnesses? But she worried about how things would be different when they were alone together—and she wondered if such an occasion would ever come. *For all I know, he's sculpted a statue of Lesyl inside his chamber,* she thought.

Fourteen ivy-gowned watchtowers were set at even intervals on the walls. All but one wore an antlered crown around a pointed cap. And all but one had belfries enclosing massive, rust-gold bells. The bells sheltered worlds of their own—webbed nests for birds, bats, and spiders.

But one belfry—the westernmost—had collapsed. She wondered what song the bells might have played together and whether anyone would guess the missing note.

As they moved along the impressive city wall—sweeping spans of seamless stonemastery that joined the fourteen towers—Irimus Rain was already sketching all that he saw, from streets to wildlife, to make maps and guides as he had in House Abascar. He even stopped to sketch a hairy forty-legger, cleverly camouflaged and scuttling along the mottled stone until it found a sun spot where a knotted bundle of its kind were soaking up the warmth.

From this height Inius Throan looked like nothing more than a trash yard of broken crockery. There were cracks in everything. Birds streamed from a scar in the grandest sanctuary—some kind of ceremonial assembly hall—so that it looked like a half-lidded stewpot emitting bursts of steam.

Beyond that sanctuary, avenues spread out without symmetry or reason, alleys branching off like strands of a crazy spider's web. They zigzagged through neighborhoods, spectacular piles of slumping huts whose sunken roofs and flattened layers made them appear as stacks of broken tiles in a crowded masonry yard. Bleating rock goats with corkscrew antlers climbed over them as if they were mountains, and every time they bleated their manlike complaints, the children would howl with laughter and bleat back at them. Flocks of clucking flurries skittered underfoot, rushing across the alleys, reminding her of marbles from an overturned toy box rolling beneath the furniture.

Below, a bearcat—broad and glistening, dark as dried blood—slunk around a corner. The children converged on Emeriene as if she could defend them. But when the cat looked up and saw the newcomers on the wall, she lashed her flat tail and stood up, spreading herself to the full breadth of her body, wide and thin as a bed quilt. Then she turned and floated over the ground like the fan-rays Emeriene had seen in the shallows of the Rushtide Inlet.

In a haphazard crossroads, monkeys napped lazily in the bowls of multilevel fountains. Occasionally one climbed atop a fountain, beat his chest like a drum, and bellowed his defiance. "We have our work cut out for us when it comes to winning the hearts of the locals," laughed the mage at Cal-raven's side.

But Cal-raven seemed uninterested in the animals. Emeriene could see that his gaze was drawn to stone, to structure, to statues. Some courtyards were arranged around gigantic figures that had lost definition with the passing years and weather, though flaunts of sculpted muscle, proud brows, clenched jaws, and corrugated chests were still apparent. *They might have been based on actual men,* she thought. *If so, then history has been, for men, a steady decline.*

As they descended from the wall, the guards flexed their bowstrings, anxious. Cal-raven, listening to Irimus and Batey relate what they had discovered, led them toward the grand hall, and she felt as if this were a royal procession—the king marching to his throne room.

Just outside its ivy-curtained gate, Milora, Luci, and Margi surrounded a raised block that no longer supported a statue. They spoke in urgent whispers, then moved along a shattered line of stone that was probably a fallen statue's remains and started pushing one of those pieces back toward the block.

Already the dreamers are dreaming, she thought.

"Do you boys want to help them with the statue?" she asked. But Cesyr and Channy snorted and puffed, strutting as if they were soldiers. "Where's the city's fight ring?" asked Channy.

Inside they moved through a low-ceilinged room that had turned into a forest of shallow-rooted toughstalks. A herd of miniature deer huddled among the slender trees, led by a buck the size of a dog, who shook his antlers in defiance, then retreated, leading the herd in a swift and silent departure through a hole in the wall. A cloud of deer-flies hung in the air, surprised, buzzing indignantly, then funneled out through the same exit.

Moving through an archway, they found the vast sanctuary they had anticipated. In the light of the broken dome, the floor rose in crescent-shaped tiers to a dais that was missing its throne. A stairway stretched up the center, and others ran along the sides. The company was quiet in awe, and the truth of what they saw made Emeriene feel watched, as if a monarch of extravagant powers might pronounce a judgment from an invisible throne.

Wind rushed in through the dome's break, carrying snow-finches in clouds that exploded and imploded, then streamed out through windows around the remaining span of the dome.

Cal-raven remained silent while the others talked and made plans. He scowled up through the hall. *He doesn't like it,* she thought. *He doesn't like dividing people into levels and categories.*

Irimus Rain quickly volunteered to design a new throne. Cal-raven reminded him that there were far more urgent matters needing attention—like a rigorous examination of Inius Throan's boundaries, a search for gaps that might let in a viscorclaw. The less the people feared a Deathweed siege, the more freedom they would feel to chase out the ancient shadows and make it their home.

Hearing this, Emeriene began at once to organize those inspections. She approached Sparolyne, a soldier sent by Partayn who had for years made a circuit of Bel Amica's bastions to ensure their strength and integrity. "We'll reinforce any failing pillar," he vowed, "and seal up any break."

Cal-raven did not stay long in the royal sanctuary. He led them back out through a busy sprawl of structures. They moved through spiral-walled mazes—possibly galleries. The corners of some bunkhouses and the empty frames of greenhouses seemed to have been crushed, perhaps by a prowling Fearblind Dragon.

"Where is Reveler now?" Cal-raven asked his teacher.

"She's gone home into the Eastern Heatlands to rest and restore the shields she lost in Jenta's furnace."

"You must have made quite a promise to win her help."

"Even now," said the smiling mage, "my ravens are luring muskgrazers from their burrows and driving them across the sands in a herd so large they could drink Deep Lake down. They'll go right to Reveler's doorstep so she can fill her belly for days. She would never go hungry as it was, but the event will attract the attention of the males. She's a lonely dragon. Thus the temper."

As the explorers proceeded, plump grey birds that sheened when they caught the light—the people had taken to calling them "merchants," all except the merchants, of course—waddled complacently under their feet, oblivious, stalling the explorers. But a passing cloud-hawk or the shadow of a lurking zooey-cat startled them and they hiked up their feather skirts and fled on long legs that were surprisingly sturdy, surprisingly blue. A pack of yipping, rabbit-eared lurkdashers chased their tails and ran down a litter of gorrels that had sprawled lazily and stupidly in a sun-dazzled yard.

The wind played upon the ruins as if they were an orchestra out of tune, and howlermice gathered on piles of rubble, thrusting their long snouts skyward as if inspired to sing their lonesome dissonance. "Make a note," said Emeriene to Irimus. "We'll want to be sure those rodents are soon a part of Inius Throan's lost history."

Jes-hawk, one arm in a sling, still carried his arrowcaster. And as the king's party left the sanctuary to move through an overgrown orchard, the archer shot a large stag as it leapt between curtains of berryvines. Bel Amicans quickly carried it to the kitchens.

Entering a formidable library that had lost its south-facing facade, they found many levels lined with rows of shelves that had been overrun by a pride of viscorcats who bathed themselves, hissed and swiped, and watched the newcomers from the shadows. As the company watched them, they vanished one by one, tufts of fur from their hurried departure drifting in the air like clouds of moths. Some wooden shelves had rotted, leaving only metal brackets from which vines swayed like the king's own hammock.

They ran their hands along trickle-sculpted walls rough as tree bark. Cal-raven handled doorknobs that snarled or leered or laughed with animal faces. Some were inviting to the touch, molded to resemble a small pumpkin, a thrush, or a beetle with an iridescent veneer. Others he would not touch, thrusting the shutters or doors open with a boot. They opened moth-shredded draperies, sometimes to windows, sometimes to stone, sometimes to shocked cliff-chickens sitting on egg-crowded nests. Emeriene quickly collected those eggs for Adryen and Stasi in the kitchens.

Walking in a single-file line around the library's upper echelons, in trepidatious steps, Cal-raven drew back a curtain that concealed a high window. Wild red chickens scattered from the sill in a panic, revealing a view of the courtyard below, where Milora, Luci, and Margi had somehow raised a boulder onto the statue's foundation. They were hard at work, sculpting.

"Will you sculpt another gallery in honor of the lost?" asked Irimus.

"No," said the king after a moment. "Our minds have been too long on death."

At once he interrupted the tour and announced he would pay a visit to Sayressa and the wounded.

The healer was busy as ever, shooing a Bel Amican guard out the door and strictly instructing him to rest and to drink only the invigorating waters from the river beneath Inius Throan. She told the king that Jes-hawk had not yet returned to have his dressing changed. And Tabor Jan was struggling, his breathing ragged, his coughs still bloody. He went into a spasm with every absent-minded swallow. Cal-raven knelt beside him, but the captain still would not meet his gaze. Meanwhile Say-ressa was bending busily over every patient, every pallet, the drape of her silver hair trailing softly over those who slept and suffered.

Departing this temporary infirmary, their solemn silence was interrupted as Kar-balter, who had marched boldly into the ground-level entrance of a low, stout mill tower, ran back out screaming as if his cloak were on fire. The tower shuddered with a muffled cacophony. A stream of fork-tongues flew from the windows that pocked the tower's sides to reel shrieking away over the city walls and into the mist.

"Apparently," Kar-balter said when they could calm him, "I've found the king of this blasted zoo. He's a fangbear. And so well-fed by volunteers who have crawled or flown into his den that he's grown too large to leave it."

An archer, glad to be useful, marched forward with a ready arrow, but the king raised his hand. "We'll consider a way to release the poor creature. Let's build a cage to hold him and wheel it to the threshold, where we can send him out into the canyon."

Cesyr and Channy stood open-mouthed, disappointment quickly warping into anger.

"Boys," whispered Emeriene, her arms around them, "tell me this. Who is stronger—the man who attacks what looks dangerous, or the man who dares to control his fear and find a better way?"

A strange unease curdled her awe as they wandered web-strewn halls. Fading murals still displayed simple, idyllic village scenes—comfortable cottages and castles filled with light in a world devoid of decay or destruction, intolerant of imperfection. Each mural was being invaded by the tentacles of mold and moss.

Surely these portrayed a world that this city's residents had longed to know. But they were such selfish dreams. The pictures offered no sense of history and no sense of future, no awareness of suffering or brokenness—no vision. And no sense of story. They reminded her of a traumatized woman she had found among Abascar's survivors in the Bel Amican infirmary. This woman had sung sweet little songs to herself, rocking back and forth, her mind fixed upon forgetting what had happened, determined to ignore her present difficulty, unable to move or acknowledge her wounds, much less accept help for them.

As they moved on, Emeriene began losing her sense of direction, dizzied by the mazelike arrangement that led them in circles and to frequent dead ends. But it was as if the designs were only intricate indulgences of line and motion. Inius Throan was a wonderment, and yet there was a wrongness, as if each street had little to do with the next, had half turned its back to the other, declaring its boundary.

So she was relieved when she heard Cal-raven murmuring to Scharr ben Fray, "It's like one of Yawny's mealtime mistakes—a bite into a sweetberry cobbler souring against a knot of salted grazer jerky."

As they moved quietly back out into dusk, the aggressive, angular textures of the streets seemed to shout for a passerby's attention, to keep her from lifting her gaze to the emerging stars as she walked.

"It was the first city," said Scharr ben Fray. "Raak's people were eager to give shape to everything they could imagine."

"Artists learn by imitation," said Cal-raven. "Teacher, surely you cannot think that this was the world's first city. What we've seen here—it's full of advanced invention and craft."

"It was the first generation of Tammos Raak's descendants," said the mage. "They had gifts we cannot imagine."

"But they didn't work together well, did they?" Cal-raven countered. "There's no guiding sense here reconciling this city into a whole."

Scharr ben Fray nodded, but his slight scowl suggested impatience. "If any cities existed before this one, Tammos Raak left them behind. No doubt for a reason."

"And why," Cal-raven continued, "do we never hear tales of Tammos Raak's origins? Who were these children he made the residents of Inius Throan?"

"Perhaps we will find answers here, beneath the ivy and rubble. I've always marveled that there seems to be no story about the mother of these children. There are no stories of a queen within these walls." Then the mage glanced back over his shoulder at Emeriene. "Not yet, anyway," he laughed.

Emeriene stopped in her tracks, terrified as others glanced curiously in her direction. Cal-raven did not turn around, but his pace seemed to quicken as if he were eager to outrun the suggestion. Feeling the blood rush to her face, she knelt down and pretended to fix a tear in Cesyr's shoe.

"Give them a goal, Cal-raven," Scharr ben Fray continued. "Wonder and hope will quickly burn out. Exhaustion is coming. Then impatience. And anger. They need to see their king's vision."

"An event," said Cal-raven. "To mark the end of one journey, the beginning of another."

As Cal-raven looked out his citadel window and watched dawn's long arm paint the mountaintops, he wanted nothing more than to forget it all and go to Emeriene. She was like a deep well of clear water in this filthy, crumbling house. And he was so very thirsty.

Why did you risk your life, and your sons, to come here?

He knew the answer. It terrified him. It was one of two secrets he carried. And both were dangerous.

The other secret was waiting in one of the wall's fourteen towers, in a chamber below its belfry. He watched its window, then looked down. Jordam slumped wearily against the ground-level gate, faithfully guarding it while he picked at a bowl of seeds and berries.

Jes-hawk walked slowly past Jordam. The archer, his left arm still bound up in its thick sling, his right hand propping his arrowcaster against his shoulder, paused and looked up toward the dark window.

Ryllion can't remain a secret forever. I promised him help. But I've made him a prisoner. Perhaps I was rash to make such a promise. My people have lost so much; their mercy will have its limits.

Jes-hawk walked on, clearly muttering to himself.

Hasn't Jordam killed more innocents than Ryllion? And there he stands guard. But he saved House Abascar from a slaughter. Abascar owes him some gratitude.

Cal-raven pounded his fist on the windowsill. "That must be the heart of my appeal to Partayn and Cyndere. Ryllion is no different than a beastman. He can be cured. Jordam might join me in pleading for his pardon."

Scharr ben Fray appeared, walking the same circuit as Jes-hawk. The mage paused too, regarding the beastman as if he were just another curious creature inhabiting this wilderness. Then his gaze drifted up the tower to the high window. Cal-raven caught sight of a gloved hand at the curtain.

The mage then walked on down the avenue, and Cal-raven saw that he was approaching the yard where Milora, Luci, and Margi were hard at work on their project. Mousey, the red-headed crook, had joined them. She was not a stonemaster, but she was merrily wheeling a cart back and forth from the scatter of crumbled statue. The stone block now supported a large and handsome pair of feet.

At once Cal-raven reached for his cloak, suddenly inspired to meet the day's challenge.

Approaching, he asked, "Whose feet are these?"

"New Abascar needs a statue of its king," declared Luci.

"To think I almost killed you once," laughed Mousey, a sharp whistle escaping through the gap in her teeth. "Now I'm helping to make you immortal."

Cal-raven held out his hands. "Please, wait!"

The sculptors paused and met his gaze, except for Milora, who bowed her head as if expecting a reprimand.

"I...I am grateful. You honor me. But we've more urgent tasks for stonemasters."

"Like what?" Mousey wore a flirtatious smirk.

"We must begin another way," he said, "and I have an idea that should please you. I will not tolerate any statue of myself—not during these early days when I have yet to earn such an honor. But I would raise a monument at the center of this city—not one, but two statues."

When he had spelled out his instructions, Luci and Margi went right to work. But Milora had fallen into a familiar solemn silence, as if she were waiting for something.

Scharr ben Fray stepped up to Cal-raven. "Master," he said quietly, "I want to show you something."

The mage took Cal-raven up to one of the belfries where he had swept out a bell with a broom, casting nests and webbing to the wind.

The bell was enormous, but intact, its sheen a merging of copper, rust, and silver.

Scharr ben Fray raised a large rod from the floor where it was bound by a chain to a ring in the corner. "See the emblem on this hammer?"

With a slight nod, Cal-raven acknowledged the familiar shape of the Keeper.

"Go ahead," said the mage.

The king waved him off. "I doubt these bells were ever meant for celebration. When they rang out across the valleys and streams, I suspect they rang for alarm. Let's wait for...for an occasion."

Scharr ben Fray's smile seemed forced, and he cast the hammer into the sludge of bird waste.

He's dreamed of this for hundreds of years. And now that he is here, I am in his way.

"I taught you to respect stories of the Keeper. They gave you hope. They inspired your leadership. And now, here, we can see that the people of Inius Throan dreamed of the Keeper as well. So forgive me, King of Abascar, but I must ask for an explanation. Since I found you in the canyon, any mention of the Keeper has made you scowl. When you do, you look like your father."

Cal-raven fought to control his expression. "I found courage in those stories—it is true. I searched for the Keeper my whole life. When I found it on Barnashum's doorstep, I was overjoyed. And then...then I learned something more."

"You saw them," the mage whispered.

"Thirteen," Cal-raven growled. "Thirteen Keepers in cages. Captured. Tortured. Helpless. And one empty cage remained, for one either hunted or already dead." He took the bell-hammer from the ground and raised up its emblem. "Any one of them might have been the one I saw in dreams. I don't know which one left the tracks I sought as a child. But none of them, not one, is immune to Cent Regus claws or the Seers' conspiracies. I had believed I was tracking the answer, the sovereign, the invincible authority. Something I could trust. But now," he said bitterly, "I am at the end of my belief."

"In Jenta we call them the Imityri."

"What?" Cal-raven asked, incredulous. "They have a name? And you knew it?"

"The Aerial have studied signs of their passage for generations, Cal-raven. Sometimes we thought there were many, sometimes one. It was a mystery to me why people everywhere would dream of the Keeper yet their dreams would differ so greatly."

"You told me the stories were true!" Cal-raven's voice echoed in the tower.

"The story of the Keeper is true. But it is a simple first step toward real understanding."

"Don't speak riddles with me, Teacher. You told me the stories as if they were history. I believed they were leading me."

"And why regret that when such belief inspired courage and vision? You were never wrong to believe in the Keeper, Cal-raven. There comes a time when all myths and superstitions crumble. But they inspire us to investigate mysteries. They strengthen us in ways that help us survive. They give us hope. These little illusions that kindle our questions go away when we arrive at the answers to which they were leading us all along."

"But I don't want this answer!" Cal-raven exploded. He turned and struck the bell.

The sound hit them both like lightning and threw them against the walls. It surged across the ruins and stopped the people in their tasks. Dust rose over Inius Throan as the wave shook every stone.

His ears ringing, Cal-raven climbed to his feet and looked out into the haze. He looked right at the tower where Jordam stood guard. The beastman was on his feet, staring in their direction. A hooded figure watched from the tower's high window.

"I want to know there is a greater, sovereign intelligence in this blasted, crumbling world," he said, uncertain if the mage could hear him. "Just as I want to find the destination that Auralia's colors promised."

"We all want those things," said the mage, coming close to Cal-raven. "That desire drives us toward becoming the sovereignty we hoped to find in the world. It leads us to solve every mystery until we live in the perfect house and have nothing left to fear."

"To strive. And strive. Are we any closer than our ancestors? I'm not convinced. That's why I followed the Keeper. We are broken. And when we seek to save ourselves, we fail. But if I could follow those tracks to their maker and show the Keeper my devotion, then it would lead me to where broken things are repaired, where what is torn can be mended, a place without fear or suffering. That was the promise in my dream. That is what I tasted when Auralia revealed all the world's missing colors. A better, uncursed world. The end of all fears. That's the story you told me. I let my dreams get the better of me. And I was wrong."

Scharr ben Fray raised his hands, closing them as if lifting silent puppets, just as he had when he had taught a much younger Cal-raven. "Hush. I told you the story of the Keeper because it is the most powerful story I've ever known. Look at where this story has led us." He moved to the sill and gestured to the city spread out beneath them. "Now we can amend that story and shape the future."

Cal-raven was thunderstruck.

"King of Inius Throan, King of New Abascar, hold on to your story. It is the ladder you have climbed to this height. Be grateful. Enjoy the view." He turned and put his hand on the bell as if to quiet it. "In a world such as ours, you can despair over its emptiness, like my brother, and let death's certainty rob you of all joy. Or you can make life what you wish, building on a story that pleases you. For the sake of your people, sustain the myth, as I sustained it for you. It will unite and inspire them and make your name great."

Cal-raven looked down at the bell-hammer.

"If they see your faith falter now, Cal-raven, you'll lose them. They'll stray. And the world will fragment into contending stories and dreams, as it did here long ago.

Tammos Raak set the children free, but he failed to captivate them with a vision. So they came up with four flawed visions of their own. Abascar, Bel Amica, Cent Regus, Jenta. I saw in you, from the very beginning, an imagination that could grasp whole worlds of vision. That is what makes a king, Cal-raven. You are already greater than your father. You surpassed him years ago."

Cal-raven slumped to the ground and put the bell-hammer across his knee. "You're asking me to rule upon a lie. To build upon denial."

"Lies? Denial? Those are my brother's words. Vision. Imagination. The road to understanding is a path of increasing pain, Cal-raven. Everything fails. We need a big, beautiful dream to help us forget so we burn right through to the end. Don't go quietly. Let what you've seen inspire you. You'll become like Auralia, giving the world something to remember you by. Look at what she achieved in her sublime delusions."

Cal-raven propped his elbows on his knees so he could rest his brow against his palms. "Give me an hour alone," he said.

"Of course, master." And yet the mage hesitated. Cal-raven could hear his teacher's unspoken question. But Scharr ben Fray surrendered and disappeared down the stairs.

"No," said Cal-raven quietly. "I'll keep my secrets awhile longer. I cannot bear what will come if I reveal them now."

He rose and staggered to the sill. The world below seemed illusory, unsteady, as if the tower were leaning.

Steam seeped from vents in the cobbled avenue, carrying rumors of activity in the underground kitchens.

The dreamers will go on dreaming.

When Cal-raven finally came out of the tower, Batey passed him, pushing a cart loaded with apples from the overgrown orchard. The Bel Amican stopped, giddy, and scooped up an array. "King of Abascar, look at the bounty we've discovered."

Reluctant, Cal-raven stared blankly at the apples' extravagant colors.

"There must be twelve varieties," said Batey. "Some I've never seen before. Not even from the islands."

"Master?"

Hearing Emeriene's voice, Cal-raven could not move. She limped forward into his view. She was draped in the same stormcloak she had worn on the road, but she had washed her hair so that it gleamed like raven feathers, and her gaze was bright with hope.

"King of Abascar," she said carefully, "your chamber is cleaner now than when Tammos Raak himself slept there. You shall find it is finally fit for a king."

"I'm sure," he said softly. "I'm sure I will."

She bowed awkwardly and waited. The silence became uncomfortable.

Her boys ignored them, inventing a game with fragments of colored tile among lines they'd chalked on the paved ground. "These," said one, "are the beastmen pieces. And these are us. And this is where they fight."

"Take an apple," said Batey, holding out three for Cal-raven to choose from. "I'll help you. Otherwise you might spend all day deciding."

Without looking, the king took one and nodded, unsmiling. "This will do."

"The pieces are falling into place for you, aren't they, Master of Abascar?" said Batey with a grin, his eye on Emeriene.

Cal-raven turned to leave, paused, and said, "Thank you, Sisterly. For your patience. Bear with me. I have...too much in my head today."

And then he walked away, feeling like an older man than the one who had climbed into the belfry. "If I am to amend the story," he said, "then I'll make a madness they'll never forget."

It was the cloud rising from the kitchen that gave Cal-raven the idea.

In it he caught a scent of wild cherries. He walked back to his tower, but instead of returning to his bedchamber—Emeriene's announcement had made him somewhat wary of seeing her work—he stepped into the room below it.

This room with a tall, carved fireplace reminded him of the hearth he'd loved best in childhood. He was twice the size he had been when he last played with sculpted figurines between his father's fireplace and his father's stockings. But this fireplace was twice the size of that one, so he felt strangely comforted by the familiar proportion.

Sometimes when the world was crumbling around him, all he needed was an idea.

What if? he thought. *What if?*

His idea continued to unfold.

"Master," said Scharr ben Fray, startling him. The mage was standing at the window with Hagah napping in the sunlight at his feet.

"I would set my chair here," Cal-raven said absently, holding his hands out as if to grasp the back of an invisible throne.

"In memory of your father," said the mage.

"And here, a great round table." He gestured to the center of the room.

"For proclamations?"

"Perhaps." He did not look toward the mage. "Only if they are more thoughtful proclamations than any my father ever made."

"Or your mother."

Cal-raven turned his back.

"What would be your first proclamation?" the mage asked quietly.

Cal-raven stared into the imaginary fire, hesitating. His eyes narrowed. Was that the white scar returning? He had not seen it in days. He could hear footsteps on the stair behind him. And then Jes-hawk's voice at the door. "Master?"

He did not turn.

"It is with a heavy heart that I trouble you, master."

"It cannot be heavier than mine."

"Shall I come back?"

Cal-raven shrugged and said to Scharr ben Fray, "A feast, Teacher. I shall proclaim a feast for all who have gathered here. It would be a shame to let such bounty go another day without preparing a proper feast."

Scharr ben Fray stepped to the imaginary proclamation table, straightening his robes as if eager to take part in some manner of play. "May I be your witness?"

"Be my witness, Scharr ben Fray. I propose a royal feast for all members of my house and all guests within these walls." He turned sharply. "Well? What is it?"

Jes-hawk was baffled by the king's manner. He took a step back and scratched at the cast on his shoulder. "You asked me to report suspicious behavior from our guests."

"Who is it?"

"One of the Bel Amican guards, sir. Joneroi. After Say-ressa dismissed him from her quarters, he went straight to his chamber, lit prayer lamps, and began appealing to moon-spirits."

Scharr ben Fray scowled. "That ruinous religion has no place within these walls. It turns us against each other, and the house will not last a season."

"Right. Only true faith here." Cal-raven could not repress a sneer. "How did he achieve this? We've given out no bowls for lanterns."

"Took one from the kitchens, I suppose," said Jes-hawk, stammering.

"Simple problem, simple solution. Make it clear to him that I forbid the Seers' ceremonies here, just as their own queen has forbidden them. Now may we continue with something of actual importance?"

"A feast," said the mage, "in honor of your achievement."

"No." Cal-raven threw his apple core into the fireplace. "What have we found here? A fortress built with boasts instead of beauty. Inius Throan is a closed fist of power. Every corridor designed to seal people in and content them. This place reeks of choices made in fear."

Jes-hawk had stepped back into the doorway, his gaze shifting from Scharr ben Fray to the king and back.

Hagah, raising his head, barked at the mountains.

"You're still here, Jes-hawk," said Cal-raven. "Are you serving as a second witness? Or is there more?"

Jes-hawk swallowed hard. "Forgive me, master. There is more. One of our defenders lost his arrows. We found they'd been taken by Gaithey, one of the merchant guests."

"Fantastic."

"It's worse than that," said Jes-hawk. "We found him lining up a shot at Jordam."

"What?"

"We interrupted him in time. He ranted about ridding the world of Cent Regus mongrels."

"I've sworn to protect Jordam." Cal-raven stepped through his invisible table, and though he was not much taller than Jes-hawk, he loomed. "No guest in my house can overspeak my word. Lock that merchant up."

"In the…in the dungeon, master?"

"The dungeon?" Cal-raven looked at Scharr ben Fray. "Do we have a dungeon?"

"Oh yes," said the teacher. "A corridor of simple cells. We need all three of your keys to open and shut them."

"Here are the keys, Jes-hawk," said the king. "But return them directly to me."

Jes-hawk looked at the keys, terrified.

Cal-raven grabbed the archer's hand and pressed the keys into them. "Now, where was I?"

"Proclaiming a feast," said the mage.

"Ah, yes." Cal-raven began to pace. "A feast in honor of Rescue, who followed the tracks of the Keeper and saved so many of us from fire and trouble." He half shouted his decision into the cold fireplace. "I will ask Krawg to tell tales of the ale boy's courage. And we will raise our glasses in hope that he is well." Then he added quietly, "Wherever he may be."

He turned and made a gesture of removing an invisible ring and holding it in the space above the invisible table.

And he held it there, closing his eyes. "What more, Jes-hawk?"

"You know how I feel about having guests within these walls, master. We've been abused by certain Bel Amicans. We've been betrayed by my own sister because of the Bel Amicans' influence. And we have plenty of Bel Amicans in this house, not to mention merchants, strangers, and a beastman."

"Get to the point," said the king. Had Jes-hawk guessed it was Ryllion in the tower?

Jes-hawk spoke quickly, as if pleading his case before a judge. "Partayn instructed the guards that he sent after us to search for a missing item. The queen's cup. He thought one of us might have taken it."

"Partayn ordered them to look through our belongings? They have no right to search without my permission unless they would dare suggest that I stole it myself."

"They found it, master."

Cal-raven opened his eyes. "It was Warney, wasn't it? The glassworks inspired the One-Eyed Bandit."

"The truth is more troubling, master. It was Milora."

Cal-raven lowered the imaginary ring and turned to stare at Jes-hawk for a long time. "She confessed?"

"With furious excuses, yes."

"What does she say?"

"That the goblet was crafted for a different table than Thesera's."

The king shook his head. "She's a glassworker but not a Bel Amican. And she had a difficult time in that house. Perhaps she made the goblet herself."

"She's compromised our bond with House Bel Amica," Jes-hawk shot back. "The queen's hunting a criminal we've welcomed into these walls."

Cal-raven looked into the cold fireplace.

"May I offer some counsel, master?" Jes-hawk pressed on.

"Oh, be so kind."

"You are thinking that they're more than mere crooks," said Jes-hawk. "That without them we might not have survived the ambush in the ravine. That's true. But they were fighting for their lives back there. Soon we'll face contention over territory within these walls. It is time to be clear that Abascar is a house of law."

"Throw Milora in the hole, then?" Cal-raven muttered. He stood like a statue during a long, grave silence, until Hagah, sensing the discomfort, whined anxiously and trudged across the room to lean his head against Cal-raven's hip. At last the king turned to his teacher. "How would you have advised my father?"

"The goblet belongs to Queen Thesera," said the mage. "This was a crime against her. She must determine the consequences. It is only for you to deliver the offender back to Bel Amica. But one needn't be Maugam and flog the offenders. I'd suggest you deprive them of the ale boy's feast. Lock them up for the night and give them time to ponder their offenses. Refrain from your father's cruelty, but show your people that feasts are for those who deserve them. Build your reputation as the good sovereign."

Cal-raven reached down to scratch Hagah's head. The dog's tail thumped the floor.

"Master?" asked Jes-hawk. "What are your instructions?"

Cal-raven walked to the window and leaned on the sill, looking down as if he were thinking of jumping. "Let it be as my teacher has said."

"Then I take my leave, master."

"I give it to you gladly."

Jes-hawk departed in a rush.

"I am going to the kitchens," said the king. "I am suddenly very thirsty."

25

The Futures of House Bel Amica

The ocean teased the netterbeaks, withdrawing the surf's grey blanket to reveal tide pools teeming with sun-timid life. The birds celebrated, screeching and leaping about, fighting over rabbit-slugs, scamperpinches, pincushions, starfish, and schools of bright orange zippers, until their throats sagged with cargo.

On the morning's foggy shore, Cyndere sat just out of the beastchild's reach, calmly watching the creature pace back and forth. Careful not to show fear, she stroked the long back of the black viscorcat, Dukas, who had reluctantly come along on the stroll.

The beastchild took bold, proud steps at first, already walking on her small, sturdy, red-haired hind legs, trailing the cord that Cyndere had bound to a jagged fang of stone. Her feet were as nimble as her fingers, and she picked up shells and stones and sniffed them one by one. Sometimes she cracked them with the sharp teeth of her froglike mouth. Sometimes she held them up to the side of her head, to the small earflap, which was shaped like a dinner roll.

Cyndere waved to the four guards, who kept their distance to avoid distracting the beastchild. Vigilant, the two farther down the sandy strand waved in return, as did the two who waited back the way they had come.

"May I draw you a picture?" Cyndere approached the black, glassy rock and unpocketed a piece of chalk.

Dukas remained where he was, tail twitching, glaring in judgment at the beastchild.

In the rock's reflective surface, Cyndere could see herself—her yellow hair, short as a boy's, ruffling in the breeze; and the black stormcloak that had been Deuneroi's, draped around her shoulders. She tightened the cloak's cord at her throat. It was good to have something of Deuneroi's with her.

"I'll draw someone you might recognize."

The beastchild grumbled, standing at the length of the cord, picking at the slits of her nostrils. But as Cyndere drew the first bold strokes, she saw in the reflection that she had the creature's attention.

She had already grown fond of the large, whiteless eyes staring with such fierce interest from a face furry like a raccoon's but lumpy and toadlike in shape. And the sound—the beastchild's body seemed a hive of chirping crickets. "What's human inside you?" she murmured. "How much of the Curse can we tame?"

She drew the outline of Jordam's head and shoulders—a very different drawing than she had first made of the beastman. Almost twice the size of any Bel Amican soldier, he was still an impressive figure, his arms long in proportion to his torso, his hands hanging to his knees. His head was a crooked, pock-marked monument of scars, hairless now except for a half-crown of black, bristly hair circling from one ear to the other. His eyes had changed—they were blue and piercing as a wolf's. His long sloping nose was still noble as a lion's, his jaw still frightfully bold. No Bel Amican boots yet fit his feet, but he wore garments now, sewn by sisterlies, and he'd made his own belt out of two soldiers' sword-belts.

As Cyndere filled in these details, the beastchild began to purr, drawing closer, transfixed.

Cyndere paused, then lifted a giant sea-snail's shell to the beastchild's ear. "Hear that?" she said. "That's our very own far-off country. I'll take you there someday. We'll walk on ground no one has seen before."

The beastchild took the chalk from Cyndere's hand and sniffed it. Then she stepped up to the rock and began to draw small, intricate crease lines along Jordam's fingers.

Cyndere stepped away. "I'm not the only one who misses him."

Dukas, impatient, ambled around her legs, whimpering for attention. Absently, she stroked the ridge of his spine.

A guard shouted for Cyndere's attention. A man on horseback rode south along the beach toward her. She swallowed her surprise, folding her hands behind her back.

Partayn arrived with his typical bluster, riding a full circle around the rock. The beastchild crouched to growl, but Cyndere set an example by calmly resting on a piece of driftwood.

Partayn jumped down, patted the horse's shoulder, and then sat down on the sand. Dukas butted his whiskered brow against Partayn's shoulder. The bearded man wrapped his arms around the giant cat, and they wrestled in the sand. This, like most human behavior, bewildered the beastchild.

After the tussle, Partayn leaned back against his sister's knees and watched the Cent Regus orphan. "Do you know how hard this is? For years I dreamed of plots to kill the Cent Regus."

"This is how we change what you knew, brother. We're making it known that the Curse can be broken. That monsters are made from lack, but they can learn to tame their urges." She knotted her hands around the sharp shells. "We've got to find another well, Partayn. I've been reading grandmother's journals. She heard stories when she was a child. Stories that say the Cent Regus came to Bel Amica for help when the Curse first took hold. But we were happy to see the Cent Regus weaken, thinking it would give us an advantage. We told them that they deserved the consequences of their actions. What might have happened if we'd helped them?"

Then she turned sharply. "What are you doing here, Partayn? You ignored my counsel. You rode south to find the Curse and destroy it. I've been waiting for reports of your death."

He brushed sand from his beard. "You told me it was a fool's errand."

"And you told me that we had no choice, that the forest is filling up with viscorclaws. You said we have to kill this problem at the root. But here you are."

Partayn stared out at the grey, where the sky blurred into ocean. "We made camp at some bear caves behind Juliweir Hill. And I finally opened my water flask."

"And?"

"Blazing crolca, Cyndere! I drank, and the slumberseed oil knocked me out for two whole days."

Cyndere blinked. "Slumberseed oil? In your flask?"

"You know what happened."

She thought about this while Dukas offered Partayn his belly for scratching. Then she laughed. "Wasn't me! If you insist on riding into danger like that, I want you wide awake!"

He frowned. "That leaves...one obvious culprit."

"A culprit who loves you. What did you think would happen, singing with her, collaborating?"

"I guess she'd rather I didn't ride off into battle."

"She doesn't want to compose a lament over your death."

"When I woke, I wasn't right in the head. Worst nightmare. My troop was replaced by beastmen. Weird beastmen too. Reptiles. Bird men. I tried to wake myself up."

"And?"

They paused as the beastchild leapt on Dukas to wrestle him. The cat, furious, broke away and loped to a safe distance, then groomed his front paws to pretend nothing unseemly had happened. And as soon as the disappointed beastchild turned to go back to the drawing, Dukas went after her for a tackle. They tumbled about in the sand.

"One of my men, Rohrich, said that beastmen had come out of the cave. He'd tried to wake me, but I was under the spell of the slumberseed oil. The beastmen had not hurt them. They'd offered water to my men."

"What?"

"Rohrich led me back into the caves, and I saw them. Seven beastmen. Malnourished, feeble. But they'd found a well."

Cyndere put a hand to her heart. "Were there...blue flowers?"

"Shining blue." He drew a few petals from his pocket.

Cyndere covered her mouth to repress a shout.

"But that's not why I came back." He smiled, looking at the beastchild. "Quite an artist you've got there. Look at that. It's Jordam. Right in front of us."

Cyndere's rush of questions was disrupted by the sight. The drawing was now more detailed than anything Cyndere had ever drawn. The beastchild had given Jordam a long, ragged kilt and put a torch in his hand. She'd sketched long red lines across his arms—open wounds from a struggle—and given his toes broken claws.

"I'm waiting, Cyndere," said Partayn, amused. "But all I see from your new pet is suspicion."

"Waiting for what?"

"I got your message."

"What message?"

"A messenger arrived at our camp. He said you needed me. And that the creature needed me too."

"I sent no message."

Partayn stood and shook himself off like a hound. "No reason to deny it, sister. I couldn't ride any farther. I couldn't bear the thought that you might be in some kind of trouble. And besides, now that I've found these beastmen, I want to go back. Quickly. With Jordam, if you can summon him. These Cent Regus might be a great help to us. If they can help me kill the Curse at its root, we'll make the forest safe again, and you can go back to live in Tilianpurth. You, Jordam, and anyone who will help. We'll make it a place where beastmen can heal. We'll give House Cent Regus the help we should have offered in the first place."

The beastchild uttered a stream of cricketlike chirps, offering Partayn the piece of chalk.

Cyndere's voice was low and solemn. "I swear, Partayn. I did not send you such a message."

"I'll find that messenger," he growled. "And I'll give him a thrashing."

"What did he say. . .exactly?"

Partayn opened his mouth. Then he stopped. He stared past her toward the sea, stricken by some dawning realization. The wind brushed back his wild hair, and his eyes filled with tears.

He turned and walked to his horse. Dukas, disappointed, draped his tail around himself in a stately pose and watched him ride away.

The beastchild began another drawing. Another outline. A boy. A boy with large worried eyes, a cloth wrapped around his head, and a water flask in his hand.

Cyndere walked down to the edge of the tide pool bed, stepping into a maze of the blackstone teeth. She paused. In the corner of her eye, she saw it again—the glimmering shape of a figure standing beside her.

"I don't know how much longer I can do this," she said, her voice breaking. "Now that Emeriene's gone, I cannot deny it. I can never replace you, Deun. But if I'm going to make this voyage without hurting somebody, I need help. Help with this beastchild. And this house. I can hear the horns of the harbor, but the fog is too heavy out here."

In her mind's eyes she drew the tentative lines of another likeness. But she had no practice drawing this face. Not yet.

With a sharp snap the chalk in the beastchild's grip broke and crumbled into dust. The creature looked at the powder spilling from her hand. Then she looked at the unfinished drawing. She began to pant in frustration, kneeling to try to press the crumbs back together. Unsuccessful, she threw back her head and unleashed a long and mournful howl, unable to repair what was broken, unable to fully realize the image that burned so vividly in her mind.

Partayn pushed his way through the crowded marketplace, followed by frantic guards and surrounded by people who stopped and cheered for him.

He knew that they were happy to have him in charge, even though they were still complaining over their new limitations. He could always win them over with a song.

He reached a guarded door and was welcomed into a grand cavern where an orchestra was rehearsing an anthem.

Lesyl, who directed them, glanced back over her shoulder and let her arms fall to her sides. The music stopped.

The choir looked at Partayn. Partayn looked at Lesyl. Lesyl slowly smiled, then wiped tears from her cheeks and stepped down from the stage. She walked to Partayn with her gaze fixed on the floor. He cleared his throat and glanced from side to side, anxious as if she were the sovereign and he a cornered subject.

"I don't know this song," he said.

"It's. . .it's for King Cal-raven."

"Oh," he said. "Oh. I see."

"No, it's not like that at all," she said softly. "It's a song about his vision. His dreams have always inspired me. You know that. For a while I confused that inspiration with. . .something else. It was a way to survive. But when we arrived here, I knew that my part of that vision could only come to fruition here. And that my role was bound up with yours." She took his hand. "Come. Listen."

She drew him up the stairs. He raised his hand to the musicians. They beamed back at him as if they knew some kind of secret.

"You sent a messenger for me."

"Did I?" She smiled.

"Your message. . .your message. . ."

She drew him behind a curtained door into a closet of shelves crowded with instruments. She took his hand and pressed his palm to her belly. "I said that I need you, and so does the child."

Dizzy, he reached out to catch himself and grasped the edge of a shelf, which collapsed. Bright copper horns and a huge round drum crashed down and spilled out under the curtain. They heard the drum keep rolling, and then it thundered down the stairs to crash somewhere below.

Partayn tried to comprehend the joy in her face, the gleam in her eyes. His own vision blurred.

"We've been...hasty," she whispered. "Haven't we?"

"Yes," he whispered. "Forgive me. Since the Cent Regus prisons, I've found it difficult to control myself around...around beauty such as yours."

She wrapped her arms around him, knotting her hands together at the small of his back. "I'm going to make it very easy for you—for us—to do the right thing."

"I hope you will." He cleared his throat and felt a smile finally find his face. "Maybe...maybe a few clumsy opening notes can still become a song."

"You're being hasty again, my love." He heard fear in her voice. "Do you realize the consequences if you choose this? You're inviting a woman from Abascar to be queen of Bel Amica."

"I can't think of a future more beautiful than that. I think the remnant of Abascar may be the best thing that's ever happened to Bel Amica."

26

Setting the Table

Kar-balter lay inside a dry, empty cave, looking up at a window lined by long bars.

Imprisoned again. What'd I do this time?

A hand appeared beyond the bars, casting a five-fingered shadow. The hand was as large as the white-haired fire-breather he'd seen on the underground river. Kar-balter whinnied in fear as he realized that this was not a prison at all. This was the hollow belly of a massive stringed instrument—the world's largest perys, he supposed—and its giant string-plucker was about to perform.

A finger lightly touched a string. Its sonorous *plung!* rang out in waves.

A sharp, wet shock washed across him. He woke to find himself seated on the high guard-walk that surrounded the Royal Sanctuary of Inius Throan. Hagah had come bounding around the curve, a splash for every loping stride, barking at the distant bell tower.

"You blasted hound, you soaked me!" Kar-balter yelled, but his cry was drowned out by another ringing bell, another note reverberating. Then rang the third, and so on, with Hagah barking at each tower in turn as if to say, "Again! Again!"

The feast, thought the guard, rising. Afternoon sunlight illuminated the gleaming clutter of Inius Throan. It seemed the ancient city might forget the passing storm by nightfall.

By the tenth chime, Kar-balter had circled the Sanctuary's outer guard-walk. He saw a figure in the tenth tower's window—a pupil in a candlelit eye.

The king's big secret. And the beastman's still standing guard. What a strange crew we are.

The thirteenth bell sounded, and the tone lingered. The progression felt incomplete, and he tensed, waiting for a fourteenth note to resolve the melody. But there was no fourteenth note. And the suspense burned like an insect bite he couldn't scratch.

"Viscorclaws," he muttered, returning to his assignment of surveying streets around the Sanctuary. "What's the world come to? I guarded King Cal-marcus from grudgers and assassins. Now I'm looking to shoot at twigs and branches."

Captain Tabor Jan wasn't taking any chances. He had sent instructions that bowls of the Bel Amican torch oil should be set around the city wall, where archers could use them to light arrows if any viscorclaws appeared.

A lump of stone on the city wall was waving, just between the third and fourth tower. Kar-balter waved tentatively, then laughed and waved more certainly. It was Em-emyt at that post, barely tall enough to see over the battlement to the rocky gullies of the canyon beyond.

"Just like old times," he laughed. "Except different. You were dead for a bit. I think it helped. You were grouchy and mean. Now you're happy as a geezer with a lapful of grandkids."

To think that there's a river down there that pumps life into a carcass, he thought. *In a few years no one will believe it. They'll have cooked up a hundred explanations. They'll say you were only knocked out.* "Nothin's scarier than a fellow crawling out from under death's heavy curtain," he sighed.

Satisfied for now, he stepped through a door in the Sanctuary wall and emerged on a balcony overlooking the assembly space inside.

The lowest tiers of the descending floor sparkled with water while a young Bel Amican guard swept rain puddles from the floors. Lacking tables, people had spread canvases, blankets, and leaves in long stretches across each crescent span. They would dine upon the Sanctuary floor, dream of the tables they'd construct, and relish whatever simple bites the cooks had made from the bounty of this overgrown, forgotten kingdom.

"They'd better serve me up a heaping plate," he muttered. "I don't want to go back to the days of looking down at what others have got."

"Do we have any more of the water?"

Say-ressa hurried into the kitchen and stopped as the heat stunned her. She might as well have stepped into an oven.

Pushing through clouds of steam, the healer surveyed the long, stone counters. Emeriene, Luci, Margi, and Raechyl were listening to two streams of instructions from Adryen, who darted about intently and unpredictably, like a dragonfly, and Stasi, who stirred a pot of thick batter like an oarsman rowing upstream. Before each of their helpers, a stone pot shaped by one of the stonemastering sisters was filled with some kind of concoction. Beside them, piles of berries sparkled, wedges of honeycomb glistened, and flat fry cakes were stacked fifty high.

Fires crackled in a broad, low stove, and Batey stood prodding shreds of bird meat around a sizzling pan that spat splashes of grease.

Stirring sauce in a bowl, Adryen marched up to Say-ressa with all the authority of a queen. "A custard of cream from the rock goats' milk." The button-nosed cook, no taller than the young sisters, had to lean back to meet the gaze of the willowy healer. "We whip up the cream with wild blue garlic and a dash of ground hajka peppers. Then we mix oil and peppers into a sauce to pour over the custard, and we serve it with wedges of fried bread. Make sure the bread's made with blue grain. The colors are important."

"Water?" Say-ressa repeated. "The decanter of water you brought up from the river below the house, it's empty. And I've got nothing else to ease our wounded through their pain."

"The king wants that water for the feast," said Adryen, gesturing to three crude stone pitchers sitting in the corner away from the heat and the spattering grease.

"And he asked me to try to make sure that everyone attends the feast. That's going to take some healing magic that my hands have never delivered." Say-ressa stepped aside as two small boys came running through the kitchen, wielding sticks and shouting.

Emeriene flung herself into her sons' path, grabbed their arms, and dragged them aside. "What did I tell you about running through here while we're cooking? Go back to the corner and play with the toys that Luci and Margi made for you."

"But we're hunting a beastman!" shouted Cesyr.

"No, a Seer!" shouted Channy.

"There are no dangerous beastmen here," she snapped. "And the Seers are far away. Go back to your corner." She grabbed Cesyr's chin. "Look at me when I'm talking to you."

"That stove looks like the one Papa jumped in," he said.

Emeriene let go and stepped back. Then she grabbed him by the shirt. "Don't you bring that up within these walls. You hear me? We've left that all behind."

"So if we can't hunt beastmen and Seers, who can we hunt?" asked the younger one.

"Tomorrow you can play outside and pretend those sticks are viscorclaws." The sisterly looked up at the healer with an exasperated apology. "They're upset. An unfamiliar place. And they've seen...they've seen terrible things."

"I wish I could help," said Say-ressa. "Some wounds are hard to reach." She walked to Batey by the stove. "Would you take me down to the river?"

Batey sprinkled seeds across the sizzling meat and a spicy fragrance thickened the air. "Soon as Adryen says that this bird is cooked enough."

"I can manage," sighed Adryen. "Go ahead."

Batey took a torch and led the healer out through the back of the kitchens, down a steep crooked stair, through winding corridors, muttering as he sought to remember the way.

They walked a long distance, and Say-ressa had time to observe that this passage was not adorned with statues or any other signs that it had been part of Tammos Raak's kingdom.

"It's amazing," Batey mused. "Those sisters. They're making something for the feast, and they say they're following directions from their lost sister, Madi. A recipe from another world."

They moved down another stairway, and she could hear it now. The hair on her arms stood. *Dear Robin, if only you could see what I'm seeing. A waterfall under the world.*

They stopped abruptly. Cal-raven was climbing the stair.

"Why are you down here? And alone?" asked Batey.

"I hoped to glimpse this white creature...this thing that defended you on the river."

"It was magnificent," said Batey. "You've never seen anything like it."

"I have," said the king. "As my mother fled from its destruction, she fell into my arms, and the creature watched her die."

Say-ressa felt as if she'd been struck. Batey uttered a fisherman's curse.

The rush of the falls filled an awkward quiet.

"How fare the wounded?" the king asked.

"They suffer, but I am hopeful. The smoke and ash from the dragon's forest fire has given some a horrible cough. Several needed new bandages for injuries. The captain may be able to join the feast if I give him something to muffle the pain. He can't eat yet, but he can swallow this water. He'll be showing off quite a scar after the brace comes off."

"I should get back," said the king. "The bells—when we hear them again, we assemble."

"We'll gather some water and go back with you," she said. "The water will help with the healing. You should drink some."

He bowed his head and moved past her, ascending.

Margi and Luci, singing the Late Afternoon Verse, entered the royal hall through the two entrances at the back, one on the northeast corner, one on the northwest.

They smiled and waved, for the vast hall was empty. Then they looked at the raised platform between them.

Where choirs will sing, thought Margi.

Where actors will perform, and reports will be given to the king and his council, thought Luci.

They descended the five tiers.

Cal-raven had insisted that the hall be arranged in reverse, with the king's table set at the lowest, rain-darkened level instead of on the heights.

At each spread of mats, they arranged plates for the diners, so every company could see one another and look down over the descending tiers to a view of the king and his company.

Seventeen plates were arranged around the king's spread. The girls smoothed the mats, then straightened a special span of cloth prepared for the king himself—a patchwork made from scraps. The travelers had agreed to cut strips from the cloaks they had worn through Fraughtenwood, and Nella Bye had sewn them together so the king would see before him a sign of their gratitude, their bond, their story.

A window above the mantel opened. Irimus leaned forward and hung an ornamental drape above the fire. Then he reached through with a flagpole and set it in a slot that had been carved there. The flag itself was bound up, yet to be revealed.

The king will not believe it when the trays are brought from the kitchen, said Margi.

Nor will he believe what he tastes, came the answer.

Luci shrugged. That thought had not come from her.

The sisters felt a thrill, a charge, another affirmation that their sister, Madi, was nearby, reading their thoughts and responding.

You're here? they asked together.

Yes. Tonight a great deal will happen. And I'll be watching.

A feast! thought Luci. *I wish you could taste it.*

I speak of much more than a feast, came Madi's quiet thoughts. *I'm told great things will happen. But I don't yet know this chapter of the story. I've come to be a witness. Be careful, sisters.*

There are many other Northchildren in this house tonight. They say that everything changes. Be gracious to everyone.

"Why?" Margi shouted. "Why must we be gracious? What's going to happen?"

When there was no answer, she scowled and counted the plates. Luci, narrowing her eyes, removed candles from the crate she carried and set them out in a line.

"It's too quiet in here," said Margi. "I miss Lesyl. She'd give us some music. It's a shame the king lost his true love."

He hasn't, came Madi's answer. *Not yet. But if he's not careful, he will.*

27

The Ale Boy's Feast

At the second sounding of the bell, Cal-raven rose from the bed that Emeriene had made from the pelt of a bearcat.

It was time for him to put on the ceremonial garments that Mousey had provided. The former slaver, eager to please, said she had found them among prizes in the shredders' cave and had kept anyone else from discovering them. She'd known she wanted to present him with this gift. *As an apology,* he thought.

He undressed and unfolded the white shirt, the green trousers, and the brown vawnskin cape, but as he laid them out across the pelt, he hesitated.

These are a king's garments. But I am not ready.

The thought of Mousey's stolen kiss—a lifetime ago, in that slaver's wagon—turned his mind in a different direction. Cal-raven wanted understanding. He wanted to fall into the arms of someone who would accept what was left of him, and demand nothing more.

But Tabor Jan's example cautioned him. To open himself to the possibility of another loss, another wound, seemed foolish.

Every time I meet Emeriene, she meets a different man in a different world. She should learn what I've become. And so should I.

He felt a breeze brush his ankle, like someone teasing him with a feather, and he knelt down.

Air was rushing from a crack in one of the pillars.

Looking at the mural depicting Tammos Raak's escape over the Forbidding Wall, he noticed, for the first time, in this particular angle of light, that the stone on which it was carved was not centuries old like the rest.

He put his hand upon the picture and let the restless magic stir.

The mural melted away.

A keyhole.

As he fetched the keys, Cal-raven felt that familiar pulse of curiosity that had led him out from Abascar's walls.

A bird with a tail of red ribbons soared high above the dining hall, followed by two frantic chicks. She landed on a balcony rail, and as her two followers alighted beside her, her breast expanded, red feathers flaring out, and she performed a trilling melody that made Warney think of sunlit fountains in springtime.

He watched the bird, studying the exquisite textures of its vibrating feathers. He smiled to see that all the diners around him were staring with similar delight. Only Krawg, seated just two plates to Warney's left, seemed despondent. So he seized the clay goblet from the mat before him and raised it in a silent toast. Krawg, seeing the gesture, reluctantly did the same.

"The king made these cups, you know," said Warney. "Shaped them with his own hands. Just for this." He sipped the water. He could swear that the drink was improving his vision. And judging from the whispers of the guests, it affected them the same way. For that bird was far above them, and yet they praised her smallest details.

"Lookit us, Krawg," said Warney. "This is the king's table. And we're at it."

"The Midnight Swindler and the One-Eyed Bandit."

"The royal storyteller and the Seers' destroyer! You know who I wish could see us? Those blasted duty officers who used to thrash Gatherers with their riding whips."

"So where's the king, anyway?" asked Krawg, glancing anxiously about. "I'm hungry."

Warney's eye scanned the crescent of candlelit faces. In the center, before the fireplace blaze, two spaces sat empty. To their right, Tabor Jan sat rigid, his neck bound up in a brace, closed fists resting on his knees. He could not turn his head, so he turned his torso left and right, surveying the scene intently. His bearded face was purple, but at least Say-ressa had washed away the mask of old blood. He looked like himself again.

Krawg sat beside Tabor Jan, shifting uncomfortably on the stone floor. Then there was an empty place, and Warney at the end.

On the other side of the two empty spaces were Jes-hawk, arm still in a sling; Say-ressa, dabbing at her eyes with a napkin; and Jordam the beastman, dwarfing everyone in the crescent. He hunched, anxious beneath a heavy cloak that was far too small for him. Shanyn sat beyond Jordam, glancing at him worriedly and often staring at his massive hands.

Facing Krawg and Warney, Emeriene sat between her boys, holding their wrists as she hissed at them to stop glaring at the beastman. Beyond these three, Irimus Rain and Nella Bye sat beside another empty space.

With no warning the window above the fireplace slid open, and Scharr ben Fray appeared over the mantelpiece. Warney saw a sparkle, clear as flecks of glass, on the mage's cheeks.

"This," he declared, raising a glittering instrument, "is the gift that Frits gave to our King Cal-raven." It was a glass trumpet, like those heard at the glass mine, and when the mage put his lips to the mouthpiece, he sounded a note so perfect and piercing that everyone in the royal hall straightened in surprise.

Then the mage spoke.

"May we all show such honor to our king. Generations ago, a man of extravagant powers established Inius Throan. He meant it to be the new world's heart, a home for his persecuted children. But the children in their ambition turned against one another and their master. They scattered and fought until only four remained. Those four established the four houses. And they would torment their master until, fleeing from this refuge, he fell."

"This is going to be a long story," groaned Warney.

"I'm hungry," muttered Krawg.

"We know the rest," said Scharr ben Fray.

The old men breathed sighs of relief, lifted their goblets together, and drank. The water stunned their senses, burned its way down their throats, and set them to trembling.

"The four houses became blinded by their own faults and foolishness. But a few sought understanding. They paid heed to their dreams. And to the Keeper."

The hall was more silent than it had been when it was empty.

"One man in particular sought the Keeper from the time of his boyhood. Led by dreams and colors, he promised his people a safe place, where dissonance would be turned into harmony. A house without tyranny. Where all voices are heard. Where wisdom speaks louder than might. That dream has been costly. And you have all paid part of that price. That very heavy price."

The mage let those words hang in the air for a few moments, then continued.

"I have heard that after the fall of the house of King Cal-marcus, Tabor Jan made a promise to the Abascar survivors."

Tabor Jan was still trying to turn around to see the mage as he spoke.

"Tabor Jan told you to strive with all of your strength and that your king would match you step for step, loss for loss, labor for labor. He was right. Your king has done that, and more. So for the glory of his vision, I give you the new flag of this house."

He drew the gold tie that bound the flag. From the mast a sky-blue banner unfurled, bearing fourteen representations of the dream creature.

Fourteen Keepers? Warney wondered. *Is the water playing tricks on my mind?*

The creatures were arrayed in a great arc over a diamond-shaped patch of colors that Warney recognized. It was a small kite that Auralia herself had painted and flown, a kite that had hung on the gallery wall in the Blackstone Caves.

As the audience stared in silence—baffled, perhaps, by the design—Scharr ben Fray continued. "Lady Say-ressa, Abascar's healer, would you raise up your gifted hands and lead us in welcoming our king?"

Say-ressa stood, her long hair spilling down around her knees, and looked up to the back of the hall in expectation. A question marked her brow, and she glanced at Scharr ben Fray worriedly.

The hall was quiet.

"Find him," said the mage, lowering his voice.

Say-ressa shook her head. "The king asked me to stay beside Jordam."

Tabor Jan tried to stand, but Emeriene jumped to her feet. "Allow me. I know where to find him." She pointed a commanding finger at Cesyr and Channy, her unspoken instruction clear, then departed up the central stair and out through the back.

Out of breath, her weaker leg aching, Emeriene stepped into Cal-raven's chamber.

"We've got to construct a Bel Amican lift," she muttered. "I'm just not a climber anymore."

She looked around. Cal-raven's garments lay strewn on the floor, and his new kingly costume lay spread across the bearcat pelt.

"Where are you?"

Scattered beside his pillow, she discovered small stone pieces and bent to pick one up. It was unfinished but had two slender legs, one wrapped in a cast.

I'm in his mind. Here. In his new house.

She lifted a silver platter. He had finished the bread and water she'd left for him. Catching her reflection there, she ran her fingers through her short, black hair and practiced a few expressions of surprise. "There you are!" she whispered. "Well, where have you been hiding?" Then she lifted his pillow to her face and breathed in deeply.

Behind her she heard a hinge creak. In one of the room's pillars, an open door echoed with distant noise.

Beyond that door she saw the stairway spiraling down.

"Cal-raven?"

Absently hugging his pillow, she quietly took a step, letting her unbending leg down first, then following it with the other. Down one step, then another, into shadow and faint torchlight.

She came at last to a short corridor. It was dark, cold, and lined with barred cells—a small, secret dungeon. Almost all the cells were closed and dark, but one was open and glowing with torchlight.

Cal-raven stepped out, holding the light.

Emeriene screamed.

The king, naked, screamed even louder.

Then Emeriene laughed and turned away from him. After an awkward moment, she tossed the pillow over her shoulder, and he caught it.

When she glanced over her shoulder, the king looked disgruntled, covering himself with the pillow.

"You're late for dinner."

"Oh. I suppose I am."

"I'll…I'll wait in the… Shall I wait upstairs?" She was almost certain she could hear his thunderous heartbeat. "What are you doing down here? What is this?"

"I don't know. I just discovered it."

"Your feast is ready and waiting." She began to ascend the stairs, trying not to picture him behind her. But then, unable to restrain herself, she said, "I must say, Master of Inius Throan, it is good to…good to see you again."

He laughed, but the laughter sounded strained. He seemed distracted.

Back in his bedroom, she peered out into the hall. "Your garments are ready."

"I can't wear those. We dine to honor the ale boy, not me."

A moment later she turned. Cal-raven wore a dull grey servant's cloak.

"I think you are a troublemaker." She dared to reach and straighten his collar. "As you were when I met you."

He met her gaze in surprise.

"I expect nothing from you. Nothing at all. And if you sent me back to Bel Amica, I would accept it and understand it. But when the feast is over, should you ever desire my company…I will come."

Surprising her, he took her left hand at once and kissed it. Then he pressed her small, cold knuckles to his forehead. "You came after me, even after I disappointed you... I've worn out this world, Emeriene. I have come to the end of a journey, but I feel no joy, no comfort, no glimmer of gladness, save that you are here. All surprises in this place thus far have laid burden upon burden on my heart—all except your appearance. And had you not come, in time I would have summoned you myself. I—"

"Shh. I know. If this were the last night of the world or the first of a new one...for all of our losses and disappointments, for all we have endured, that would be enough for me." She reached up and put her right hand alongside his face.

"Master?"

Scharr ben Fray stood in the doorway. "What a relief to find you...in such good hands."

As King Cal-raven descended the stairs, passing tier after tier crowded with quiet, hungry people, Say-ressa's voice broke in the midst of her welcome.

Everyone rose, so fiercely aware in their strange intoxication that they struggled to keep their balance.

To their astonishment their plain-dressed king walked around the lowest crescent of diners, asked for them to be seated, and then placed his hand on Jordam's shoulder.

"Tonight we welcome the first man of a new House Cent Regus. He has learned to oppose the Curse within him. We'd have perished if he had not warned us of danger at Barnashum. Some of us are here because he brought us out of Cent Regus prisons. Jordam is a friend of this house."

Young Cesyr growled, disgusted, and looked away from the king. Channy watched his brother, then bared his teeth at the beastman.

Ignoring them, Cal-raven met Jordam's gaze, and even though Jordam was seated, he was still eye level with the king standing beside him. "I failed you, Jordam. I abandoned you at the gate of the Core. I lost hope and wandered away. That was a mistake. I ask for your forgiveness."

Jordam stood. He was shaking. "rrMaster," he mumbled. "I..." He scratched at his ear and murmured something that only Cal-raven could hear.

Cal-raven heard Jordam confess that he had lied. The Cent Regus chieftain had not killed Jaralaine in the Cent Regus Core. Jordam, in a killing frenzy against the Strongbreed, had not seen Cal-raven's mother in their midst. He had found her dying among the beastmen he slew, impaled upon one of their weapons.

Cal-raven heard all of this and closed his eyes.

"rrMine, the blame," said the beastman. "Me. Not chieftain. Not...not the Keeper."

Cal-raven knelt and touched the scar he had given Jordam's foot at their first meeting. "We've made our mistakes, even as we sought to do what was best. Never think of it again."

Then he stood and faced the assembly. "We've made our mistakes. I've made more than anyone. And yet, here we have a chance to start again. Because of one young man."

He then walked past the two empty place settings, taking the seat between Krawg and Warney instead.

"Master?" Krawg exclaimed, pointing to the empty space in the center.

The king did not reply. He gazed up at the assembled followers and friends, the people he loved. Each face reminded him of others, some waiting in Bel Amica, some lost in Barnashum or Abascar's ruins.

"You have waited for my vision of our house. I shall give you two. For we honor generous hearts tonight. And generous hands. For as long as we live here, two empty thrones will remind us, inspire us to follow their example, and sustain our hopes that they might yet return."

He broke off for a moment, wondering where this strength was coming from.

"The ale boy, the one we call Rescue—many of us owe him our lives. All of us owe him our gratitude. His head, his heart, his hands—they are a vision for our house. And Rescue was inspired by Auralia. All of us know what she offered. She invited us to a world of forgotten colors, a fulfillment of our longings. Everything she made, from candles to kites...and all she touched, from stockings to stones... began to speak to us of what is possible. She said she was sent by the Keeper. And I, in spite of all I've seen, still believe her."

As he said that, he knew he believed it.

He heard a sniffle to his left. Krawg was weeping.

"Her head, her heart, her hands—they are another vision for our house. We will not exalt ourselves as better than other houses. I will value your life as my own, and in leading you, I mean to serve you, as I ask you to serve each other. In this way Auralia and Rescue have shown us something so lovely that I long to know the source of it. So they will remain before us. And I proclaim a new name for this house."

At that moment Warney too burst into tears.

The house came alive with voices as the people stood and repeated it after Cal-raven.

House Auralia. House Auralia. House Auralia.

Krawg stood and embraced the king.

Jes-hawk half lunged at the Gatherer, but Tabor Jan grabbed his arm.

Krawg sank back to his place on the floor, unspeakable things dripping from his nose, and accepted the cloth that Emeriene offered him. Then he blew his nose, a noise every bit as loud as the glass trumpet's report and yet quite the opposite in quality.

Everyone there would have a different recollection about which was most surprising of the dishes carried from the kitchen.

For Ann-moryn, there was the garlic custard, made from rock goats' milk and drizzled with a spicy hajka sauce. For Irimus Rain, there was the baked sweetroot mash. For Loyselis and Lar-yallen, there were mugs of spicy smoke-bush tea. For Pol-morys and Elysruth, there was summer-bird pie. For Jaysin who would ring the bells, a roasted fish drawn from the secret river (and he would have the strangest dreams that night). For Manda and Tonny, expecting a child, there were sweetglory rolls. For Jenn and Gabe, who tended to the animals, a stew of boar and grandvine. For Cus-velyr and Yeltse, a bowl of cold, candied cream.

So engrossed were they in their meals that they barely noticed a series of small disturbances at the king's crescent.

The first came when Say-ressa said to Cal-raven, "Master, the beastman is ready to deliver the plate we've prepared for...for your guest."

"Of course," said Cal-raven.

Even as he replied, Kar-balter approached and waited for attention. Cal-raven motioned him forward, and he heard a word he'd dreaded hearing. "Viscorclaws, sir. Em-emyt spotted one on the slope beyond the southeastern wall."

The king called Jes-hawk over, gave him the glass trumpet, and sent him off, saying, "It may be the best alarm we have. But Jes-hawk...don't break it."

His distress was interrupted as Scharr ben Fray appeared at his side, kneeling ceremoniously, offering a long, wrapped bundle. As Cal-raven drew the cloth away, he found himself speechless.

"I fashioned this sword," said the mage, "with Reveler's fire."

I've seen this before, thought Cal-raven. *In a dream. I stood on a precipice. I saw the Keeper fall from the sky. I heard someone rush up behind me...* He took the sword by the hilt and raised it, and though he found it a pleasing weight and balance, it seemed a tremendous burden. "Forgive me, Teacher," he whispered. "I am...overwhelmed."

A Bel Amican survivor called Jephanas, a self-proclaimed scribe of unproven gifts, stood and recited a poem, hastily composed and far too ambitious, describing Cal-raven's journey. And as he did, Adryen entered with the dessert—a large bowl of cloud pudding.

It was only when Cal-raven turned to offer the pudding to Krawg that he noticed the old man was gone. Warney shrugged, gladly accepting the bowl and smacking his lips.

Then old Mulla Gee, standing on the highest tier, began to sing the Early Evening Verse with a voice that trembled like a ribbon in the wind. A few moments later everyone had paused to sing along, and the sanctuary was filled with their voices.

In that resonant music, for a moment, Cal-raven could almost imagine a future.

28

Breaking Threads

Auralia fingered the stone on her cell's back wall, looking for lodes of color. Ignoring the taunts of the two prisoners caged across from her, she softened blue stone into clay and drew a winding river.

"Your old friend's been gone a long time with that token you gave him," sneered Joneroi. "Wonder what he'll sell it for."

She tried to ignore him. Krawg was a thief, yes. But he also loved her. He would take risks for her.

With her fingertips she whisked green along the blue river's edge, leaning in and considering each detail. Trying to remember.

If I can get back there, to the beginning. If I can smell the grass and remember the view of the sky. Maybe I'll find it again. The lightness. The desire to play.

But the river seemed too ideal. It flowed the way she wanted it to, not on its own. And the grass was too perfect; not ragged and webbed and rooted among worms and beetle swarms, like she remembered.

She smeared a violent rift through the river. "I can't do this anymore."

Just then she realized that her tormentors had chosen a new target for their insults. She turned to see Emeriene's sons. They had chased each other down into the corridor, throwing stones and laughing, but stopped when they realized they'd drawn the attention of their caged kinsmen.

"Boys," rasped Joneroi, "if you were men, you'd go out there and lift the keys from King Cal-raven. But you're not men, are you? You're the spawn of a traitor."

"Why'd the guard let them down here?" That was Gaithey, sulking in the corner of his cell. "He should lock them up. Just in case they've got any of their father in 'em."

The boys quickly changed their game, pelting Joneroi and Gaithey with stones. When Auralia told them to stop, they turned against her.

"You're a thief," the boys cried. "You can't steal from our queen."

Auralia blocked one stone with her forearm. She missed the next one, and it struck her chin. The boys went back to throwing at the men, spewing curses and threats. "Crooks! Traitors! Seers' pets!" This time she kept silent.

As the men cowered in their corners, battered and bloody, Cesyr and Channy grew more vicious. Stones rang loudly off Auralia's bars.

Then the boys stumbled, crying out.

Auralia looked through the fingers of her upraised hands and watched the floor begin to ripple. She ran to the bars and saw Luci and Margi kneeling at the end of the corridor.

"Girls, let them go," she laughed.

The sisters brushed off their hands. The boys, frightened, ran off, their shoes clattering with clods of hardening clay. They disappeared deeper into the next chamber, whimpering with hurt pride.

Margi and Luci gripped the bars of Auralia's cell. "Looks like you're hurt."

"Bruises," she said. "And a cut." She dabbed blood from her chin with her sleeve. "Go and fetch Say-ressa. Those two are hurt worse than me."

"What's all the noise here?" Jes-hawk appeared in the corridor. In one hand he held his arrowcaster. In the arm that emerged from the sling, he cradled Cal-raven's trumpet. "Prisoners stoning prisoners?"

"Emeriene's boys," said Margi. "They did it."

"The boys? Cesyr and Channy are here?"

The girls pointed down the corridor. "Troublemakers," said Luci.

"They've lost their heroes," said Auralia. "They know Ryllion and their father were full of lies, and they're humiliated and angry. They'll grow out of it. If we're good to them."

Jes-hawk frowned at the rocks littering the floor. "Boys!" He waited, but there was no answer. "Channy. Cesyr." He set the trumpet on the floor and marched farther into the dark. "You're wasting my time. I'm supposed to be up on the wall."

Then came a curse and a commotion. "I think," came Jes-hawk's voice, "the boys may...have found...a way out..." His voiced sounded strained, and it echoed.

"Good thing this dungeon's so secure," laughed Gaithey, blotting a cut.

"The king has to let you go, Milora," Margi said, impatient. "We've gotta show you something."

"The statue's almost finished," Luci whispered.

A cry like a bird's distressed chirp cut the air. Then a sound like someone pounding on drums.

"Jes-hawk?" Auralia called.

Margi and Luci hurried down the corridor into the next room. A moment later Margi shouted back, "There's a vent here. In the wall. He's gone through!"

"It goes up," Luci called. "I feel wind."

"That'd be from outside the wall," said Gaithey. "Outside the city."

"Probably a vent to air out the stench of whatever died here," muttered Joneroi.

"How big is it?" asked Auralia.

"The boys could have fit through," said Margi.

"But not Jes-hawk?"

The girls did not answer.

"If he didn't go through," growled Joneroi, "where is he?"

"Nowhere," said Margi. "There's nowhere else."

Luci scoffed. "That's impossible. It's too..." She paused, then screamed.

"Blood!" Margi shouted. "Spilling out!"

"Run!" shouted Auralia.

The girls scampered back into the corridor, terror in their eyes.

"Shut the door!" whimpered Gaithey.

"There is no door," said Joneroi, sounding frightened and nervous.

"Girls," said Auralia. "Up."

Luci and Margi ran to her, climbed up the cell bars, and perched on the top like frightened birds.

A ten-legged viscorclaw—a full-grown, serpentine branch from a coil tee—came stalking low to the ground like a feline. Its black legs were dripping, but it had no head, no mouth. *They seize and shred,* thought Auralia. *Poor Jes-hawk.*

When it reached Auralia's cell, it paused, turned.

"Now!" shouted Luci.

The sisters leapt down, landing on either side of the crawler. They pressed their hands to the floor in the same moment as Auralia and, with a unified shout, sent a rush of stonemastery into it.

The crawler tensed to spring but, as the floor softened, found it could not launch. It fought, legs dragging up strands of molten stone. Then it tipped and sank.

The girls jerked back their fingers and stepped away.

The crawler's legs suddenly reappeared, thrashing. But its spine remained trapped as the clay became stone.

"Go," said Auralia softly. "Call the guards. There may be more."

"But—"

"Go. They need a warning. I'll do my best to stop the next one."

Joneroi and Gaithey remained crumpled in the backs of their cells, mumbling prayers and counting all the things they'd done right to earn a rescue.

Auralia watched the crawler's extended fingertips. They jerked and twitched, then slowly weakened. She began to breathe deeply again but only to ready herself for the next stage of the growing trouble.

Standing at the base of the tower where Cal-raven had ordered his secret guest to stay hidden, Jordam looked past the tower to the stars, yellow and orange through the smoke-hazy sky.

Awestruck, he forgot his errand—to give Ryllion a portion of the feast. He forgot himself. Stars had rarely been visible in Cent Regus territory. He had first noticed them on the shore of Auralia's lake. But here in the northern highlands, they seemed closer somehow.

I've done what I came to do.

He felt lighter, almost giddy. Cal-raven's forgiveness—and more, the king's own apology—had affected him deeply. He felt as if a fever had broken, cool sweat tingling on his newly hairless brow and neck. The night was alive with possibility.

Ryllion should know this feeling.

He stepped into the tower and ascended the stairs. Cal-raven had asked him to guard the Essence-poisoned soldier in the canyon after the dragon's rampage. It had been a tense, difficult meeting. Ryllion, who had been following the company and hiding in the rocks, showed no signs of making trouble; he seemed humbled, even embarrassed, to stand before Jordam.

"Ryllion's trying to change his life," the king had said. "As Cyndere helped you change yours, help me protect him. If they find out who he is, Bel Amicans will kill him. I want him to live."

The tower was silent as Jordam ascended, and he worried that Ryllion had run. But there he was, leaning feebly on the sill of the high chamber window, draped in his heavy robe.

"rrBrought you food." He offered Ryllion a plate wrapped in a ragged cloth. Ryllion took it with trembling hands and unfolded the cloth to find bread, strips of meat, and a cup with a small measure of the secret water.

Ryllion thanked him. "I've known no stranger moment than this. To be fed and protected by a...a man of House Cent Regus. One that Cyndere herself befriended. You are Deuneroi's dream come true, Jordam."

"I know," said Jordam. Then he paused. "rrTrue? You there...under Abascar? You..."

"I killed Deuneroi," said Ryllion. "I was afraid. And I wanted strength."

Jordam nodded, silent.

Ryllion set the plate down. "Are you allowed to take me outside? I want to see the stars."

"rrYes," said Jordam. "Stars are very good."

They made their way out of the tower and up a long stair to an unguarded stretch of wall. They stargazed in silence for a while, until Ryllion turned and leaned against the parapet and looked up at the moon.

"For many years I believed the moon was the source of all good things. But Myrton told me he's studied it. It's just dust. A ball of dust. The sun is shining somewhere, and the dust catches the light and casts it down to us. A reminder. Some hope in the dark."

Jordam stared at the moon, amazed. Such an idea had never occurred to him before. *It's like...O-raya's boy. Bringing help into the dark.*

Ryllion looked down into the dark gully beyond the wall. "I laughed at him. Thought I knew everything. I said, 'It's more than dust.' But he agreed. He said, 'Oh, yes, dust is just what it's made of. But it has a purpose. Like everything. It's all some vast conspiracy to keep us from pride. And despair.' And then he moved off through his greenhouse. And I realized, the place was full of mirrors. Not mirrors like those the Seers made, to show us ourselves. But mirrors reflecting light, helping all those green things grow."

Jordam closed his eyes. *There will be two moons at O-raya's caves tonight. One in the sky. One on the water.* His throat clenched, and his eyes filled with water. *I must go there. Soon. To see if she's come back.*

"When the Seers turned against me," Ryllion went on, "I thought I'd start to hate the moon. But I don't." He gripped the wall as if worried he might fall. "You give me hope, Jordam. If you can find a new life, maybe I can too. What was it?"

Jordam grunted, baffled by the question.

"What...what brought you out of the Curse?" Before Jordam could answer, Ryllion held up his hand. "Emeriene mentioned that girl from the stories. Auralia."

"O-raya," said Jordam, "made me know...I was thirsty." He pressed his hand to his heart. "For...something I didn't have. A good...strength. Then, Bel...*Sin*-der...

she came. And she had good strength too. She shared it. And then...O-raya's boy needed help. I could be strength. Strength for him."

Ryllion nodded. "Strength for him."

"Now." Jordam shrugged. "He is gone. Needs help, somewhere. And Bel. She needs help. Help with the little one."

"The beastchild."

Jordam was surprised that Ryllion knew. "Yes. rrWant to help her grow. So small."

"That will be difficult."

Jordam nodded. "Like...climbing a mountain."

Moonlight gilded the rocks below. A disturbance, a small pattering of stones, drew Jordam's attention, and he saw Ryllion tense.

"Something's down there," Ryllion hissed.

"rrCrawlers?" asked Jordam. "Feelers?"

They listened.

Ryllion pointed down at the gulley. Two small figures moved about on the rocks. Jordam was impressed. Ryllion's eyes were as good or better than his own.

"Emeriene's boys?" Ryllion asked, incredulous.

"rrHow?" Jordam rumbled. "Outside the walls? Did they fall?"

A burst of fire. The boys had found a sparkstone and lit a branch, which crackled and spat.

"Are they burning a viscorclaw?" asked Ryllion.

"No," said Jordam. "Those branches don't move."

"Just playing then." Ryllion leaned forward sharply. "But what's that? Something's moving. Toward them. Creeping up the gully."

And then Ryllion was gone, leaping over the parapet, clutching at faint ridges and ledges with his claws, scrabbling his way down.

Jordam barked after him. Unarmed save for the torch, he ran along the wall until he was right above the boys.

Ryllion dropped to the gully and sprang into the space between the boys and the advancing viscorclaw. *He has no weapon,* Jordam thought. He barked again, then tossed the torch out into the air. It fell, sparking, trailing a ribbon of flame. Ryllion caught it easily.

Torchlit, the boys stared at Ryllion's back as he lunged toward the advancing viscorclaw. Burnt, smoking, the crawler retreated.

As it did, Ryllion cried out and fell. His robe was on fire. The boys were attacking him from behind, beating him with burning branches.

"rrStop!" Jordam roared.

Ryllion rolled across the rocks screaming. One of the boys pulled something from his pocket—a gleaming blade—and struck.

"No!"

Jordam vaulted over the edge and fell, dragging his nails along the wall. But he did not have the claws that had once helped him climb like a bearcat. He slowed his fall but still crashed into the rocks.

He leapt to Ryllion and beat on him, trying to pound out the flames. Ryllion was groaning, the fight going out of him. Jordam's hands were sticky with blood. "rrNo!"

The boys lit new branches, readying to come for Jordam. "rrHow you get out?" he growled. His fearsome voice drove the children back.

They pointed forward, directly into the shadows where the burnt viscorclaw was coming back.

"You!" came a shout from the wall. Jordam looked up and saw two guards staring down, holding up torches. "What's happening down there?"

"rrCrawlers!" Jordam roared. "Tell the king!"

The guards did not move, lifting torches higher as if that would help them see.

"Don't help them," shouted one of the boys to the guards. "We don't want them here. A beastman and a traitor!"

Ryllion clutched at the embers of his chest, the source of the pulsing bloodstream. Jordam pulled out the knife. Ryllion wheezed suddenly, kicked against the rocks, and went still.

The viscorclaw advanced.

Jordam lifted a flaming branch that the boys had dropped and leapt at the predator. Moments later it was scuttling away, fire spreading up its spine until it crumbled. Now Jordam noticed the vent and saw signs in the dust that confirmed this as the boys' way out. He stuck his head in the shaft and sniffed.

A mess of carnage reeked in the passage. Something, or someone, had been ripped to pieces there.

As the boys approached him slowly, wielding lit branches, an arrow struck the stones at his feet. He looked up. One of the guards was clumsily firing into the dark. Jordam shouted for the king, but the guard did not understand.

So Jordam ran at the boys. Frightened, they dropped their torches. He raised his arm in anger, then paused.

Stop, Jordam.

He drew a deep breath.

Stop. No killing.

Restraining himself, he struck the older child down with a measured blow. Then he lifted that unconscious boy and stuffed him under his arm. The smaller child began to cry, and Jordam seized him by the back of his cloak. "Don't fight," he growled.

Then he turned to the wall, puffing a sigh, and began the perilous climb. His cargo wailed and struggled while moonlit arrows streaked past him like stars across the sky over Deep Lake.

An arrow pierced him just above his collarbone, and he lost his grip, slid, and caught himself. Wheezing and snarling, terrifying the boy, he climbed further until he heard one of the guards say, "That's Jordam. He's got Cesyr and Channy. Stop shooting!"

A few moments later Jordam was sitting down on the wall, leaning back, pressing his hand against his wound to try to stop the bleeding. One of the boys raged, telling the guards to kill Jordam, while the other still lay unconscious.

One of the guards ran off, and in hardly any time at all, Emeriene was there, shrieking and running to gather her children into her arms. She looked at Jordam with fury.

"Ryllion's dead," Jordam said flatly.

"Ryllion?" asked Kar-balter. "Who's Ryllion?"

"Where?" Emeriene demanded. "Where is he?"

"rrCal-raven. . .tried to help him. Told me to guard him."

Emeriene's eyes widened in amazement. "The stranger in the tower?"

Jordam gestured to the boys and explained how they had climbed out into the wild. He described how Ryllion had jumped down to save them. Emeriene's expression was a fit of bewilderment.

"rrRescued them," he said. "Fought the crawlers."

"Viscorclaws?" exclaimed Kar-balter. "Where?"

"The crawlers. . .they killed Ryllion?"

Jordam could not speak. If he told Emeriene the truth, what would happen to the boys? But he knew the trouble that would come from lying about a death. He remained silent. And as the guards scanned the darkness and Emeriene comforted her boys, Jordam took advantage of their distraction and staggered away.

He was thinking of that vent the boys had crawled through and the smell of blood. He would seal it, then go hunting for viscorclaws.

Lanterns flickered in the dungeonhouse, but Jordam found no guard on duty and no one inside.

Two men charged up from the dungeon and past him, fleeing as if they were hunted. He could smell the blood of their scrapes and gashes, in spite of his own blood soaking his arms and chest.

He leaned weakly against the doorframe. A man's voice was raised in distress below.

A flicker of light caught his eye. He descended. Figures draped in gold shrouds vanished, stair by stair, before him. A wave of dizziness spun him around, and he grabbed at the wall, then tumbled down the stairs.

He landed in the dungeon corridor. He could see rocks scattered along the path, indicating a struggle, and distorted stone that suggested stonemastery.

All the cells were open. Krawg stood beside one of them. The old man's eyes were wet with tears, and in his hand he held a ring with three keys. "Did...did the king send you to arrest me?"

Jordam shook his head, bewildered. He glanced into the cell.

"Jordam," said Milora, standing up. "You're just in time."

He blinked, his vision blurring. He saw a strange mess of colors on the wall behind Milora's small, slender figure. But the scent, the voice...

"O-raya," he said.

Auralia flung herself into his arms. He choked, lifting her off her feet and pressing her cheek against his. An unfamiliar feeling seized and shook the breath from him.

"My beastman," she whispered. "You know me."

The shaking would not stop. He held on to her while the world spun around. "rrLooked for you," he gasped. "Couldn't find you."

"You've found me. And I know your name this time. You never told me." She leaned against him. "May I still call you Hairy? You're not so hairy anymore." She leaned back from him, looking down at his shoulders and her arms, which were now stained with blood. "You're hurt! Put me down!"

"Yes," said Jordam, ignoring her alarm. "rrCall me Hairy." He let her down and scowled. "Why?" he wheezed, reaching out to shake the cell's open door. "Why lock you up?"

"I was a fool and a thief," she said. "I took from Queen Thesera the goblet I'd made for Cal-raven. I meant no harm—just wanted him to notice me. But the queen had the right to claim it. It was her furnace, her glass. Now I've made all kinds of trouble. So I'm leaving."

"Leaving? rrCan't get out," Jordam growled.

"Krawg has the king's keys," said Auralia. "He...he borrowed 'em to get me out."

"We've sealed the vent," came a girl's voice from deeper in the dungeon. "Nothing's gonna crawl through here now."

"rrNo!" said Jordam, his large hand fastening around Auralia's arm. "No leaving, O-raya. Take me too."

"You can't leave us!" Krawg gasped. "You just got here!"

"Krawg, a long time ago King Cal-raven gave me his Ring of Trust," said Auralia. "He promised me he'd keep me safe. But he's forgotten. And now he's got all kinds of trouble to worry about. I can't fix it for him. Best thing I can do is get out of here. Before I get angry and cause any more trouble." Her voice was sharp with bitterness. "And I could cause a lot of trouble."

"Just show them who you are," Krawg said. "Show 'em tricks and inventions and things! Play like you used to!"

"Krawg, I can't play on command," she laughed sadly. "When I remembered who I was before, I wanted to be that girl again. But now I'm older. I've changed. I feel different. The world's heavier. I can't…I can't make the colors work together. And it wouldn't make a difference if I did. Nobody's paying attention."

"rrGo back to caves," said Jordam. "Where O-raya belongs."

"Don't tell me what to be." Anger flared in her voice. "Don't tell me where I belong."

"No…no leaving. The boy…the boy…" Jordam slumped forward.

"Hairy!" she said, squeezing his thumb in her small hand. "Krawg, we've got to help him down to the river. We'll take him there. That's a way out…isn't it?"

Krawg nodded, picking up the glass trumpet that Jes-hawk had left in the corridor. "I'm takin' this horn," he muttered, "in case we need an alarm."

"Take me with you," said an unfamiliar voice.

Ryllion stepped out of the stairwell shadows.

Seeking to conceal himself in a cloud of swirling fireflies, Pretor Xa drifted north toward Inius Throan.

The blue, bell-like membrane of his mind cast itself open, then contracted, pulsing its progress, trailing those long, serrated strands of memory, thousands of years old, along behind. Memories. Of bodies he'd put on for disguises. Of beauty he'd distorted, then dismantled, to demonstrate his power. Of rivers he'd poisoned. Conspiracies. Flattery he'd flung into the endless appetites of human hearts.

Potions he'd mixed. The exhilaration of watching Deathweed take root in the world.

Happening upon a crow's dead carcass, the Seer's blue ghost dove into the open beak. The bird suddenly coughed, fluttered, and leapt awkwardly into the sky, flinging itself toward the mountains' stony feet. No calls answered its raucous cry. Nothing remained alive in the smoking ruins of the Fearblind North below.

It soared over the Forbidding Wall's foothills, reptiles and rockspiders scuttling away before it. The dead crow's talons tensed and struck, snatching a coiled bloodsnake from beneath a boulder. Landing on a rain-wet ledge that knifed the night air, it pecked the neck of the snake until its body stopped thrashing.

The bird collapsed, its wings splayed across the rock. Pretor Xa, disembodied, wriggled from the bird's form into the snake's lifeless cord.

The snake's body shuddered, slithering secretively between the mountainside's jutting bones. Urgently, the miserable Seer strove for miles until he rode the reptile into view of Inius Throan.

The yellow moonlight comforted him. That sphere of mawrn, the Seers' watchtower, remained suspended even though all other endeavors were on the verge of failing.

The moon was all that remained of the Seers' original bodies—the shapes they had cast off. He could only vaguely remember what it had felt like to be fully embodied, flying through vast fields of stars like a whale in the ocean, to war against the others. They had hated the mystery, because it was greater than they were. That hatred fueled their flight from its presence, and their bodies had begun to break down. Rather than endure such humiliation, they'd scraped off their flesh. It was better than begging for healing, for restoration. They would go on and inhabit the shells of their choosing and rip apart those unions of heart, mind, and body that had come from the mystery.

Dwelling within the cloud of their own self-destruction, Pretor Xa and his allies had sought to ruin the mystery's children. But the mystery's fortress was shielded, and they could not enter through aggression.

We meant to erase all the beauty. But by the mystery's designs, torn threads weave themselves together again. It's maddening. Every act of destruction revealing, in time, our ignorance. We've made nothing that stands on its own. We've only the pleasures of making suffer all that mystery loves.

The other Seers were away, searching for new bodies to wear back to the Cent Regus Core before their favorite secret was discovered. Their most enduring work of distortion. A boast greater than the Cent Regus chieftain's grandest prize.

Pretor Xa hated the other Seers. They hated him. But their collaboration had been necessary in order to conspire against the one who claimed authority. Who dared suggest they could not stand alone as masters of themselves.

But Pretor Xa was less concerned about their collective secret than his own. His best work. Ryllion, whom he had shaped from boyhood. Seeking Ryllion's body on the shores of Deep Lake, he had found signs that the man was alive. Following those signs, he'd come here. To the threshold of Inius Throan.

Ryllion drew him like a magnet. He could not say why. Perhaps it was the strength that he had cultivated in the man. Perhaps it was the way Ryllion listened with such trust, the way he took risks to achieve great things. His dutiful secrecy. His ambition.

I need mawrn, thought the snake-bodied Seer, gazing at the moon through the milky beads of the snake's eyes. *I have so little power, so little comfort, no strength.*

The Seer found a nest in the rocks. It slithered in, surprised a cliff monkey, and sank venomous teeth into its neck. The monkey flailed, shrieking, and went limp.

I used to enjoy this.

Pretor Xa swam through the venom, filling the monkey's body. He raised it to its feet. It stumbled as he learned its bends and balance, but he forced it to the base of the towering wall.

The Seers had watched from their sky-bound fortress as the one rebel among mystery's inventions became frightened of all he'd abandoned. Tammos Raak's fear had led to division, and division to violence. He fled his house, climbed the tallest starcrown, and called for aid from the mystery. The Seers had flown down into the Expanse to smash the starcrowns, dragging Tammos Raak from the stage.

Had mystery come to make puppets of its inventions and drag them back over the wall? No, it would never force its workmanship to comply. That would betray weakness. Fear. And it would make mystery tyrannical.

Controlling the monkey's body as if it were a spindly puppet, Pretor Xa staggered wearily along the base of the city's sky-reaching wall.

Ahead, in the rocks, he saw a crowd of shimmering figures gathered around a body on the ground. Swelling with hatred, he drove himself at the huddled company and they scattered, fading. What remained was a crooked carcass, an open crater smoking where its chest had been. The dead man's face was contorted in anguish, and it was familiar.

This isn't my beloved Ryllion. He's unstitched and gone.

Pretor Xa lost control of his animal shell. He flung himself against the hard ground beside Ryllion's body. Then he raised himself and dashed the monkey's skull against a boulder. He bled into the air, illuminating Ryllion's shell in a soft blue glow.

He'll live beyond my reach and sight, while I must start again. The very best I can accomplish out here. . . the mystery suffers and absorbs it. Transforms it.

He looked at the broken shell at his feet.

He looked at the wall of Inius Throan.

29

THE RING OF TRUST

With silent steps King Cal-raven kept to the shadows and followed Scharr ben Fray through the alleys. The old man had said nothing more during the feast, barely touching the bounty offered to him. He moved now like a man who wakes to the smell of smoke and who hastens to fill a bucket with water to save his house, fearing it may be too late.

I've disappointed you, Cal-raven thought. *You want me to prepare a place where you can chase your questions, declare your discoveries, and be the revealer of wonders. You'll remain unbound and solitary. I'll be your student and carry the weight of commitment.*

But I've seen something you haven't. And my vision for this house no longer corresponds with your plans.

Scharr ben Fray ascended a stair set against the side of a bulky stone structure crowned with spikes. As the mage disappeared through the door at the top, the king paused. For a moment he remembered following Old Soro into the Mawrnash hut, knowing that what he found inside could change everything.

When Cal-raven stepped through into the lantern-lit room, he did not see his teacher. Beneath a suspended lantern, a scroll, glimmering with runes, was spread across a long, leaning table with only three legs standing strong. Beside it waited a large blackstone casket gilded with gold.

The scroll provided a map, and its ancient lines seemed to waver like vines on a breeze as he approached. *Inius Throan. And here, he's marked the path down to the enchanted river. He's looking for a way north, through the Forbidding Wall.*

He sensed a rush of stonemastery behind him. Scharr ben Fray was sealing the door.

"You needn't have been secretive," said the mage. "I meant for you to come. I've much to show you."

"So I'm a captive audience." Cal-raven shook his head. "You mean to reveal your plans for my house. You're accustomed to having that power over me, knowing I live in a world shaped by your self-serving revelations."

The mage laughed quietly. "Well, if there was any question about who holds power here, you settled that at the feast. House Auralia, eh? I should have known."

Cal-raven turned his back and pointed to the map. "This river...it's a vulnerability. Viscorclaws are prowling outside the walls, and the river is unguarded."

"It is a problem," sighed Scharr ben Fray. "It should be guarded. But not sealed off."

Cal-raven closed his eyes. "Tell me what you found in Raak's Casket."

"I will show you those things. But let me study them first. They may be a trick of my brother's devising. And you have better things to—"

"You're worried, aren't you? Worried your brother solved a big mystery before you did. You want to be the voice of revelation." He opened his eyes. "Show me what you found in the casket."

Scharr ben Fray narrowed his eyes to golden splinters in the lamplight. "Scroll upon scroll. And they contradict one another. You're asking for confusion at a time when House Auralia needs a decisive, confident king."

"I am confident in this—that all I counted certain might have been a lie, and I am truly skeptical of all I've ever said." He pointed to the casket. "The scrolls. They say Tammos Raak was a liar. Don't they?"

Ah, he thought, watching the struggle in the mage's face. *I've surprised you at last.*

"I haven't had time to study them closely."

"Now you're a liar too."

Scharr ben Fray looked down at the casket, ran his hand slowly across its golden lid. "Reveler retrieved Raak's casket for me. It has been protected by the Jentan furnace since Tammos Raak sent it to the School for safekeeping. They're his treasures. Why would he keep testimonies that call him a liar?"

"Because they were written by his brothers and sisters," said Cal-raven. "He couldn't bring himself to burn their histories after he slaughtered them."

Cal-raven's words struck the mage hard. He slumped forward, spreading his arms across the casket, huffing like a wolf guarding its den. "You read these scrolls. When I wasn't looking."

"No. But I did find something else your brother meant to hide."

"What?"

"A secret dungeon. Beneath my...beneath Tammos Raak's chamber. It was sealed for centuries, I think. Until your brother found it. He tried to hide the keyhole by crafting a stone mural over it. But I recognized the recent work. I opened that small dungeon, and when I explored those few cells, I found pictures. Pictures drawn by prisoners that Tammos Raak couldn't bring himself to kill right away. They probably starved in their cells after he fled. But the walls tell their story."

Scharr ben Fray's eyes widened. "You...saw this?"

"It's a different story than I've ever heard. Tammos Raak led brothers and sisters—not children—from beyond the mountains, down into the Expanse. He lured them from the safety of their homes with promises of wealth and power. They expected pursuit. They expected a fight. Thus, the design of Inius Throan. But only the Keepers followed them. Peaceful guardians, sent to invite them back home with reminders of all they'd left behind. Raak's brothers and sisters were haunted. The Keepers drifted into their dreams and the dreams of their children."

He pointed to the map, tracing the walls of Inius Throan. "These towers, they're for archers. Fourteen of them. Tammos Raak's defiant message that he would shoot down the fourteen Keepers sent to bring him back."

Scharr ben Fray sat still, eyes pressed shut, brow furrowed as if he were trying to wake from a nightmare.

"But life beyond the Wall was hard. The runaways' senses suffered. They saw fewer colors. It was hard to make things grow. They were miserable. Tammos Raak's plan was failing. He was afraid. He was angry. So to preserve his kingdom, he slaughtered those brothers and sisters who opposed him and locked up those he could not bear to lose. Those prisoners would write this story on their walls."

Scharr ben Fray sighed. The strength went out of him. He rose and limped weakly to the solitary window.

"Their children were too young to know what Tammos Raak had done. They were too young to speak or read. Too young to think of opposing him. So he invented a story to tell them about how he had saved them. They grew up ignorant of his crimes."

"There is a letter of appeal in this casket," sighed the mage. "From one of Raak's sisters who followed him to this city. She begged him to let her go home. She said that she was afraid. She had nightmares. The moon was full of faces—leering, jeering phantoms. She said that deceivers had lured them down into the Expanse to destroy them in order to hurt the one who had made them."

"Now you're telling Krawg's story," said Cal-raven quietly. "Isn't it amazing? Krawg swears he made the six tricksters up. But I think it's true. I think that story's hiding here." He tapped the back of his head. "The Seers are tricksters, and they're trying to poison everything good so we don't remember our true home and go searching for it. Their aim is to rule us by making us think we rule ourselves. That way we'll never go home."

"It's a lie," spat the mage. "It has to be. How could Seers have kept us from the truth?"

"They didn't," said Cal-raven. "We've all dreamed of the Keepers. We've all sensed the call. But our pride has made us fearful. And we've resisted."

"Tammos Raak's master must have been a tyrant."

"Remember how we made statues together? You taught me the joy of collaboration. And what about the joy of being a good captain or a good father? Is that tyranny? To serve someone who serves you, for the joy of it?" As he stepped toward the mage, Cal-raven's eyes fell to a canvas contraption folded in the corner. "Is that a kite?"

"It's not a kite," the mage laughed, clearly happy to have kept a secret. "Do you see any strings? I've finished what my brother started. I'll be gliding from mountaintops soon. Escaping the pull of the earth and seeing what nobody has ever seen." He met Cal-raven's gaze. "It could be yours, Cal-raven. You could cast yourself from this tower and soar over the city. The first flying king."

"Don't change the subject," said the king. "Tammos Raak tricked a generation into thinking he had saved them from a curse. In fact, he kept them from their true home and covered up his murder of their parents. He made himself out as their savior when he was just a jealous runaway. A traitor. An interesting trick, don't you think? Seem familiar?"

"It's the strategy that the Seers whispered in Ryllion's ear," said the mage, "as they prepared to conquer Bel Amica. Kill the royals offstage, but onstage present yourself as the kingdom's savior."

"The oldest trick in their library." Cal-raven continued around the table. The mage flinched, but the king only placed a hand on his shoulder. "You've seen how this house is decorated with pictures of cozy places no one would ever need to leave. A world without trouble. Without decay. Without a shadow. Such a world does not inspire people to risk anything or seek out truth. Nor does it acknowledge what we see every day. Our own failures and lies."

Scharr ben Fray pulled away and rounded the table to keep them apart.

"But Auralia's colors...they reconciled all of the world's broken things into beauty." Cal-raven looked at the folded glider in the corner. "Inius Throan isn't Abascar's true home, my old friend. It's the Seers' last, best trap to prevent us from finding it."

"A good story, Cal-raven," said the mage. "But you know you'll find the lie of it. You'll lose your faith in this just as you lost your faith in the Keeper."

"Oh, I still believe in the Keeper, Teacher," said Cal-raven. "I've just begun to see it—and those like it—as messengers sent to help us. They're works of art and nature, meant to remind us of home. They declare the glory of mysteries we've forgotten. They lure us to new places. Encountering them, we ask questions and venture beyond our self-made borders. They comfort us in the dark. But now I believe that my Keeper was sent, Teacher. Sent by one who waits for us to come home."

"You've the finest imagination I've ever seen," Scharr ben Fray roared. "All of us learn to see shapes among the stars, to connect the dots with lines and name them. It is how our minds work, to impose stories over the chaos so we can live with it. And we always will. Best to choose a good story. Otherwise you end up despairing." The mage suddenly looked older and lost. "Like Ryp," he said.

Cal-raven was silent.

"Ruffleskreigh's returned from Jenta with news. My brother saw Deathweed reach the School. He cast himself from his window. He took flight, for a few moments. Deathweed snatched him from the air." He opened his hands. "Your people may despair if you drive them on to some imagined destination. Tabor Jan's halfway to despair already. Wouldn't it be better to stay? To wrap your people around a new story? You just might save the world from the Deathweed if you do and rescue it from Ryp's surrender."

"It's too late. The master of the Keepers is leading me. I've come this far, and I'm not giving up now. Beauty is leading us home."

"You may find nothing at all. Or else a tyrant who takes away your freedom."

"And I may find the freedom to choose what is best and go on choosing it. All the time. Free of disappointment. Like kites that fly for their master for the joy of it. Without strings."

"It saddens me that you cannot imagine a life without someone to serve."

"It saddens me," said Cal-raven, "that you think joy comes any other way."

Scharr ben Fray held out his hand. "Lend me your keys. I'll follow the river to its source. I'll come back to tell you if you're right." His voice was low. "You have to stay. You promised House Auralia's people that they could depend on you."

"I promised," said Cal-raven slowly, "that I would lead them."

There was a commotion beyond the wall where the door had been. The mage touched the wall and opened a window.

Tabor Jan's face appeared, and his voice, a rasping whisper, cut through it. "Master, there's been a killing."

"Let him in!" Cal-raven shouted.

The mage opened a door in the wall, and Tabor Jan stepped through.

"It's Jes-hawk, Cal-raven. Emeriene's boys found a break in the dungeon wall and went through. He went out to save them and a viscorclaw cut him to pieces."

"Oh, no." Cal-raven sank down against the casket. "No."

"It's worse. Your...your guest. He also tried to save the boys. But apparently viscorclaws got him too."

"Ryllion."

Tabor Jan and Scharr ben Fray exchanged a look that made Cal-raven feel suddenly sick.

"Ryllion? The Bel Amican traitor?" Scharr ben Fray snorted in disbelief. "That was your big secret?"

"And there is something else," rasped Tabor Jan. "A dark cloud is rising in the south."

"The forest fire is burning again?" asked the mage.

"No," said the soldier. "I don't think so. It's different. We'll know better as dawn spreads."

"Viscorclaws," said Cal-raven.

Scharr ben Fray went pale. "The forests. The Cragavar. Fraughtenwood. They're disintegrating, Cal-raven. They're coming." His face flushed, and he growled through clenched teeth. "You see? You've enraged the Seers. They're unleashing their worst to keep you from moving on."

"Moving on?" Tabor Jan looked at Cal-raven, shaken by the words.

Cal-raven shook his head. "Tabor Jan, find Luci and Margi. And Milora. No, I'll go. We need all the stonemasters we have to help us seal up the house. I want anyone who can shoot to stand on the wall with arrows and fire."

He marched to the door, then paused and gripped Tabor Jan's forearm. "My friend," he said softly, "I trust you. Do what you deem necessary. And tell your men—if they see anything breaking through a wall...don't wait to measure its danger."

"You know me, Cal-raven. There's a reason I always win the hunt. You're the kind who hesitates. I'm the one who shoots."

With that, the king descended into the night.

Hand on the hilt of his new sword unsheathed, Cal-raven entered the main dungeon's guardhouse for the first time.

Down the stairs he found the corridor empty and the cells on either side quiet.

He stared into an empty cell, astonished. "How?" Absently, he reached into the pocket at his side for the keys.

My keys are gone.

He slumped against the doorway. *I had them at the feast. Who could have taken them? No one has touched me.*

He closed his eyes. *Someone embraced me.*

"Krawg!" he choked. Then in utter disbelief that the old man would betray him, he reached into the pocket again.

He drew out an emerjade ring.

He stared at it in the faint lantern light. The green circle gleamed, sculpted in a figure he recognized because he had crafted it. It was the shape of the Keeper. It was the Ring of Trust that he had placed on Auralia's finger.

"Krawg," he whispered, "where did you find this?"

He moved to the next cell, and his breath caught in his throat. The colors swirling across the back wall reminded him vividly of another cell he'd seen that surprised him—a cell in Maugam's dungeons.

The truth of the matter began to shine like a spark behind his eyes. He did not understand it at first. But as it brightened, everything else began to make sense.

"Auralia," whispered Cal-raven. "I've been blind." And then, "I've broken my promise. I've failed you."

"They're gone," said a voice. Warney stepped out of the shadows.

Cal-raven began to shake with anger. "It's her, isn't it?" he cried. "She's come back. Why didn't anyone tell me?"

"She made us swear." Warney's voice quavered in fear. "She wanted to be recognized."

He lunged forward, driving Warney back against the wall. "Where is she?"

"Krawg told me to tell you he's sorry. He had to help her. She wants to leave."

Cal-raven staggered away, incredulous. Then he stopped, drew in long breaths, and closed his eyes. "They have my keys. Where would they go?"

"If it's any comfort, they'll move slowly," said Warney. "Jordam's a bloody mess."

Cal-raven thought of the map on the mage's table. *Where does the river come from?*

Then he dashed up the stairs. Shouts rang up and down the avenues in the dark. A wind moved through the house, disturbing those who had fallen into intoxicated sleep. He hastened to the kitchens.

Adryen was there cleaning up, and as he hurried in, she stepped in front of him and grabbed his sleeve.

"What is it now?" he shouted in a rage.

She drew back, cocked her head, then offered him a goblet. "You never drank a sip at the feast."

Impatiently he seized it and drank deep. An unexpected wave of gratitude welled up within him. He paused, catching his breath, the fever of anger cooling. He looked around at the piles of dishes, the scatter of crumbs, the splashes of sauce and batter, and Stasi who had paused in her dish scrubbing to acknowledge him.

"Thank you," he said. "Thank you both for feeding us through the winter in Barnashum. And for this feast. It was...revelatory."

Taken aback, Stasi laughed and shrugged, while Adryen made a dramatic bow like an actress on a stage.

Cal-raven took the goblet from the kitchen and descended through the tunnels, the water burning in his throat, opening the eyes of his eyes, the ears of his ears. At the bottom of the long, crooked stairs, he arrived at the riverbed.

The river was gone. The ground was dry. The tunnel was quiet.

Cal-raven dropped to his knees beside one of the rafts that the travelers had abandoned, set the goblet upon it, and prodded at the silt of the riverbed with the point of his sword. "How is this possible?" he asked.

"I don't know," said Krawg.

The king rose.

Krawg stood at the base of the smooth, sculpted swells of stone that had been a rippling falls. "It's just like Irimus Rain explained. The river changes. Can't make your plans around it."

In the stone the king saw a gate of black glass that had been concealed by the falls. He walked slowly up to it and touched it. It was cold, and he could sense that it would be utterly unresponsive to stonemastery.

This is the way back, he thought. *Tammos Raak kept it locked.*

"Krawg," he said softly, "where are my keys?"

The thief held them out. "I..." Tears dripped from the frazzle of whiskers under his nose. "I promised I wouldn't tell," he said. "But I can't bear it. She's gone through."

"Auralia? Through this gate? All by herself?"

"No," said Krawg. "She's got Jordam and Ryllion with her. She invited them along but told me I must stay. For you. I gave her your trumpet. For an alarm."

Cal-raven blinked. "Ryllion? But he's..." He lifted the keys. "I'm going after them."

"Master!" whispered Krawg. "Someone's coming."

Cal-raven tensed. Then he stuffed the keys in his pocket. "You didn't see me."

He stepped to the left side of the gate and opened a depression in the stone. By the time Scharr ben Fray descended the stair, Cal-raven was encased in the wall, peering through a narrow crack, straining to hear the voices over his thundering heartbeat.

The mage stopped halfway down the stairs when he saw that the river was gone.

Then he looked at Krawg. He looked at him for a long, tense moment. Krawg began to pace awkwardly in front of the black gate like a nervous, flightless bird. When the mage continued his descent, he moved slowly. Cal-raven could almost hear the pending ultimatum in the mage's mind, boiling. Krawg stopped pacing and performed a strange dance of anxiety involving elbows and tiptoes.

Then the mage, in the soothing voice of a father coaxing an irresponsible child into a confession, said, "Krawg, storyteller of House Auralia, I have a few simple questions for you. Calm yourself. Have you seen the missing prisoners?"

"Yes," said Krawg.

"Did they pass through this gate?" He lifted his fist, and Krawg flinched, but the mage struck the door, knocking slowly, waiting.

"Afraid they did."

"And how did they do that without the king's keys?"

"They had the keys. Somehow."

"Do you have the keys now?"

"No, Master Scharr ben Fray."

"We're locked out?" The mage stepped to the wall and pressed his hand against it, melting away a slide of stone that spilled out across the floor. This only revealed that the tunnel itself was encased in the dark glass of the gate, and the mage's powers would not change that. Glowering, he walked a circle around Krawg. "Who went through?"

"Auralia."

"You're lying."

"You call her Milora."

Scharr ben Fray stopped. He laughed a joyless laugh. "What an interesting story. Let me guess. One of your imaginary tricksters went with her."

"No. But Jordam did. And Ryllion."

"Ryllion! Amazing. There are reports everywhere that Ryllion was killed tonight by viscorclaws."

"Killed?" Krawg was surprised. "Well, that might explain why he didn't look so well."

"Do you realize the danger they're in? That's the way back to the Curse!"

"Auralia says there isn't one," said Krawg. "And she's never told me a lie."

"Milora's a thief," said Scharr ben Fray. "That makes her a liar. She just told you something you wanted to hear. Now, I'm going to hope that Cal-raven thought to make a stone replica of those keys. If he hasn't, then we had better start hoping that those crooks don't come back with an army to destroy us. Because if they have the keys, we can't keep them out. Now go get Cal-raven."

"I'm waiting here," said Krawg, utterly failing to sound resolute. "I take orders from the king."

"Cal-raven may be the king," said Scharr ben Fray. "But he follows my counsel. I've been planning New Abascar for ages. I'm the only one who..." He stopped, seething. "Those keys should be mine."

"Teacher."

Tabor Jan stood halfway down the stair, leaning against the wall, exhausted. His face was purple from the effort and his breathing ragged. In his left hand he held his arrowcaster, and a batch of arrows was clenched in his right. In his brace he looked like a man whose head had been bandaged back onto his shoulders.

Scharr ben Fray went to the foot of the stairs and described the situation. "I'll find Cal-raven," said the captain. "But not...anytime...soon. I've done about all the walking I can take. I need to lie down."

"I'll go," said the mage. "But, Captain, guard that gate. We've no idea what kind of destruction might come back through. We must preserve this house. I've come too far, worked too hard, since long before you were born, and I'm not going to let it all crumble now."

"And I," said Tabor Jan, "have lost too much. This is where the journey ends."

As the mage disappeared back up the stairway, Cal-raven felt a thread inside him snap before he could catch it.

My last true friend in Abascar.

He felt a sob escape him. The frail stone shell around him cracked. Tabor Jan whirled, staring at the stone. Another crack, and a bit of the wall fell away.

I won't deceive him like this, even so.

Cal-raven shrugged the shell off in a rush of sand and staggered out of the wall.

Tabor Jan's bowstring sang. An arrow buried itself between two ribs on Cal-raven's left side, emerging beneath his left shoulder. He clutched at it, coughing out dust, and fell.

"My king!" Tabor Jan reeled and fell, crying out. He threw the arrowcaster aside and crawled to Cal-raven.

Krawg was hysterical, tearing at the wisps of hair behind his ears and then turning to pound on the gate and call for Auralia.

Tabor Jan drew the knife he'd used for clearing the path in Fraughtenwood and sliced quickly through the arrow at the base of its feathered shaft. "Forgive me," he was saying. "I thought it was Deathweed. I...oh, forgive me, forgive me."

"For following my orders?" Cal-raven rasped. "Told you...not to hesitate. You see now...how worthless I am...as a king."

The captain reached around to Cal-raven's back and jerked the arrow through. The king choked and blood spewed from his wounds.

"I'm sorry for what I said." Tabor Jan's face was a river of tears. "You're my friend. My king."

"King? No. That's what the world expected me to be. I was born to be something...else. Forgive me. For all I've cost you."

"Go for Say-ressa!" Tabor Jan shouted at Krawg.

"Will she put all that blood back in him?" Krawg replied in a squeak, and then he collapsed, unconscious.

"I can't leave you," the captain moaned.

"I can leave you," said the king. "And I will if you don't bring Say-ressa."

Trembling, Tabor Jan stood. "I wish I'd missed."

"You never do," said Cal-raven. "It's why I trust you." He smiled, resting his cheek on the bloody ground. "Probably...why Cyndere...wanted you to stay. Now go."

Tabor Jan obeyed.

Cal-raven, snarling like a wolf full of arrows, crawled toward the black gate. It almost looked like he was swimming. "Krawg," he hissed, shaking the old man.

Krawg, blinking as he awoke, saw the king point toward the goblet that still rested on the abandoned raft. So he rushed to retrieve it. Cal-raven drank it down, then poured some over his wound. "Probably…too late." He pulled himself to his feet.

"Master," said Krawg, "you won't get far."

"Far…as I can."

"Command me to go with you."

"Something…more important," said the king. "If I don't return, do this." With a bloodied hand, he drew a small circle from his pocket. "For Margi and Luci. They'll know what to do." He pressed the Ring of Trust into Krawg's hand. "And this…this is a gift for Scharr ben Fray." He pulled from his pocket a small grey stone etched with the outline of a footprint.

"What is it?"

"It was sculpted by a child. Long ago, down on the banks of the Throanscall. The beginning…of a journey."

The king drew the puzzle keys from his pocket, fit them together, and shoved them into the lock.

"Shall I keep the keys?" Krawg asked. "Shall I shut the gate behind you?"

"No. So long as Auralia is on the other side of this gate…it stays open."

He turned the keys. The gate opened.

30

The Great Ancestor

Persistent as a bad memory, a beastman leapt from one stone outcropping to another, then dove into the current and paddled along in pursuit of the ale boy's raft.

The creature's roar had startled the boy out of half sleep to find that his white, winged guardian had left him. All he had was his water flask and his green glowstone, which was wedged between two panels of the raft.

The current carried him swiftly, slamming his float against turns he recognized, and eventually pushing him back into the great bowl, the crossing, where they had enjoyed the meal.

He leaned over the edge to visit his reflection. The water was so turbulent, the figure's edges blurred as if forces were streaming through him. It seemed as true a reflection as any.

With no way to steer the raft shoreward and no strength to swim, he watched the stalactites' colorful glow fade as the flow poured him into a different tunnel than he'd traveled through before.

The chase began to feel like a dream outside of time. He clung to the raft's edge with one hand and to the water flask with the other, listening for the wet slap of his pursuer's progress.

He sang to calm himself, to fill himself with breath and release his fears. The voice that echoed back was strange, changed by the journey. The quiet tones he'd sung into the Underkeep's dark were replaced by something bolder, more determined, and tinged with desperation.

How he wished he could surrender his upstream striving through time, float back to those days with Auralia on Deep Lake's pebbled shore. To whisper with her underneath the stars. His loneliness ached more noticeably than any bodily pains, which were constant now.

He let himself drift back even farther to Obsidia Dram, his guardian in the Abascar breweries and the closest thing to a mother he'd known. He'd practice pouring a perfect glass of Har-baron's dark brew and then watch her pour another. As the thick head of foam at the top of the glass thinned, Obsidia held the glass with both hands, her eyes sparkling.

Such strange eyes, Obsidia's. Quick to delight. Slow to darken in anger. And they peered out of a face that was almost masklike, darkly marked, like wood grain.

"Remember," he murmured now, "when you taught me the best routes for rolling barrels out to the harvesters? I liked those days. I liked it when you'd roll me slowly in the barrel. I'd tumble about, knowing you were there outside the barrel and laughing, keeping me from rolling off a cliff. Steering me around a tree. When I laughed, it echoed, laughs like bright leaves tumbling around inside the barrel with me."

There was no reply, of course.

"I thought of that when Jordam hid me inside that old, cold stove. I wished I could hear you through the wall. And I sure wish I could hear you now. I've been underground too long. You told me it wasn't healthy. I need to see the sky." He closed his eyes and tried to imagine it.

He heard the splat of his pursuer landing awkwardly nearby.

"Jordam might help this hungry creature." The raft rocked as the river grew agitated. The water flask sloshed. "Half-full," he said. Battered, scarred, it had not yet broken. "I'd give it to him if I thought he could restrain himself. But I'd best keep it with me. You told me not to give away good stuff to folks who would just gulp it down."

Nevertheless, it hurt to withhold healing from this wretch with its wide, milky eyes and its sagging jaws.

The water surged fast enough to keep him ahead of his pursuer. "If only it were flowing in the opposite direction." The distance he and the others had gained over days of hard rowing he now covered in very little time at all. "Don't suppose I'll ever see them again. I'll be moving through the Core soon. If you can hear me, would you send someone to help me, like you sent that duty officer when I got lost and stuck in the berries?"

A sound rose over the rush of the stream. He had heard it before. A moan from the Cent Regus abyss. An inexplicable misery.

He knew, then, that he was close. Close to the dark lake that had broken his fall.

The long, unspooling groan diminished. The boy lay still. Something had changed. He no longer heard someone following him. He sat up, looked back, and saw the beastman watching him, unwilling to follow him farther.

The raft struck rock. He heard a crack. A piece of it broke loose and spun away, while the old door remained caught on something beneath the surface.

He lay flat, holding on. Then in the green light of the glowstone, he saw a strand of black, muddy shore and a stairway running up through a break in the wall. The stairs were chaotic, as if the ground beneath them had sought to shake them off, bending each stair to a different slant.

He heard a splash and saw the flask begin to sink. He lunged and caught the strap with one finger before the raft dumped him off. He crawled and kicked until his hands and feet felt loose ground and he could drag himself to the shore.

He forced himself onto the stairs. "Climb out of sight. Just a few steps. Then, rest." He could swear that the stairs beneath him shifted, the earth underneath them writhing in discomfort. "That will give you more time to send help."

The stairs were cold, the air oppressive, and the glowstone seemed reluctant to highlight details of the walls. He found himself longing for fire, for the voices he sometimes heard in the flames—his father and mother calling his name, reminding him of their love.

There were no flames. But there were voices. They sounded stale, like age-old cries that had fallen unheard, seeping through the ground, slipping into the earth's own throat where they went on and on and on. Voices in the grotesque Cent Regus speech, distorted and spiteful. Cries of people calling for help until their voices weakened and turned to gasps.

The walls fell away, and he stumbled forward. As he did, the voices were cut short as if a dagger had severed the earth's throat. He had disrupted something. He felt suddenly visible, as if he'd stepped into the circle of a silent vigil.

Slowly he raised the glowstone.

He knew a seat of power when he saw it.

This was a chair made of blackstone, outlined in spikes, and set in a circle of cauldrons like the ornament of a ring. A staff rested against it, and the silver ferrule at its tip glinted in the crystal's glow.

A Seer's been here.

The gurgling cauldrons smoked and steamed. Ladles large as boat oars rested inside them. Bones were strewn all about—large as the ribs of seabulls, small as the frames of hummingbirds, and familiar as those of men and women. Intricate hands. Empty skulls. And the crumpled spirals of children too small to have been born.

A massive stalactite of clay, clad in a nest of intricate fibers, hung from the distant ceiling into the center of the cauldron circle. A pulse like the earth's own heartbeat thrummed from within.

One of the cauldrons erupted, a wave of ooze curling over the lip and splashing on the floor, and a foul stench singed the boy's nostrils. He knew at once that he had found what all the beastmen sought—the materials that mixed to make Essence. It was still a stew, not yet the distillation of pitch that beastmen craved.

He backed away from the circle, too troubled to look. His gaze was drawn to more familiar sights. The chamber was surrounded with gaudy boxes of bones and pillage from the world's richest kingdoms—armor, sculptures, relics, scrolls, game pieces, farglasses, saddles, racks of enormous antlers, chairs, a broken rain canopy. He could see that the debris overrunning the cart positioned to contain it had fallen from a chute that descended through the wall.

There, amid the treasure, he saw the long and pale fingers of an adult's open hand, reaching up through rubble.

He could not move at first. Then he leapt toward the cart and began to pull the treasures away. It was Jaralaine.

"I have the secret water," he whispered. "I can bring you back."

As he studied her, he felt something break open within him, and what resolve he had left began to spill away like sand from a broken hourglass. He began to shake and to weep. They had labored so long together to free the prisoners, to help the beastmen, to keep each other hopeful in the dark.

He took her cold, stiff hand in both of his own, forcing himself past the fear. "I will be your son," he said. "Just like you asked me. Remember? Before you started calling me Raven, you said you'd make me your own, make me heir to Abascar. I don't want to be a prince. But you. . .you'd make a good mother. I won't complain."

As he scrabbled at the flask's crumbling cork, Jaralaine moved. At first he thought she might be waking. But no, a Deathweed tendril was coiled about her leg, pulling her away.

A groan shocked him as if the chamber were a drum that had been struck. He looked up at the strange pillar of tangled cords and misshapen clay that hung from the ceiling. What he saw this time brought him to his feet.

Sculpted in the clay he saw a face. A face once human. Distorted, swollen, stretched—two dark cavities where the eyes had been, nostrils like deep cuts, and then the cave of an open mouth.

He looked again, interpreting what he had seen before a different way. This column, this descending mass was not made of stone at all. It was a pulsing, living thing imprisoned in a bundle of Deathweed. No, it was the source of Deathweed. This man, suspended upside down, had evolved beyond the boundaries of human definition, his legs becoming roots thick as tree trunks that ascended, divided, and spread across the ceiling.

And those two feeble roots that reached down to almost touch the floor, those were the limp, elongated remnants of the man's arms, ending in tiny stubs that had once been fingers.

The creature was gasping long, deep lungfuls of air.

"Strength," it said.

"What…," the boy whispered. "Who are you?"

The creature closed and opened his lips like a fish.

The boy's eyes traced the suspended creature's body up to where it frayed into a multitude of limbs that spread and disappeared into the earth. Mosses hanging from those limbs bled the black rain that pooled and sank into cracks in the floor.

"The Curse. It's from you. The feelers, your limbs. The Essence, your blood."

The creature did not respond. It faced him, eyeless.

"The Seers…they fed you, didn't they? For a long, long time." He looked about at the carts along the wall, loaded with carcasses, bones, faces.

Then he said boldly, with the certainty of solving the riddle, "You're Tammos Raak."

The name echoed in empty space.

The creature's lips closed and opened. Closed and opened.

The ale boy looked at Jaralaine's broken body. "I want you to let her go," he said weakly. "Give her back to me. Please."

The creature's tongue emerged from between its lips, a stump, pale as a piece of ancient firewood.

"You're thirsty. The Seers have been gone for a while."

The boy felt something within him fail. His hope, perhaps. For what he now must do seemed inevitable, as if it had been written down and he could only fulfill it.

And so he made the most laborious journey of his short and troubled life, putting one foot before the other across the poison floor, passing between two cauldrons. He stumbled and nearly dropped the flask.

The creature's lips closed, then unglued from one another again.

The boy reached up.

Tammos Raak's nostrils flared. A wheeze of air rushed up into that wretched body. Then the creature unleashed a storm of sound—a lament, a longing, a thirst.

The boy cowered, ears ringing. He clutched the flask to his chest as if it were the last scrap of his raft floating on a turbulent river. *He smells the water. He recognizes it.* When silence returned, he stood, reaching up to set the mouth of the flask on the creature's upper lip.

Tammos Raak convulsed and turned, and the flask fell aside.

The room brightened. The boy watched, bewildered, as five blue phantoms swam through the air, curling around the suspended prisoner as if to protect him.

A thick tendril of Deathweed from the shadows above lashed out like a whip, flinging the boy across the chamber. He hit the wall and fell in a heap. The flask dropped, spilling water across the ground.

The boy crawled forward, tipped it upright. "Go ahead," he shouted at the imprisoned giant. "You don't deserve it anyway." Then he crawled back to Jaralaine. Her right arm was still cast out, her left folded across a bundle against her body. He lifted the flask and put the spout to her lips.

Accompanied by a wrathful roar, the Deathweed tendril lashed out again, snatching the flask from the ale boy and casting it like a stone toward the prisoner's own head. It flew deep into Tammos Raak's throat. His lips sealed shut, and his misshapen face crumpled in discomfort as he fought to swallow the flask.

The lips opened and closed. It was gone.

The ale boy collapsed against the treasure pile, his head resting against Jaralaine's cold breast. "That's it then," he whispered. "Served my last drink, and I've got nothing left." His hands gripped the folds of cloth beneath Jaralaine's arm. Something inside him felt broken, sharp-edged, crooked.

He did not know how much time went by. He dreamed awhile, images drifting through his mind.

He was sitting with Obsidia Dram, and she was hunched over a stream, catching water in a basin while he sifted grain in a bowl. She was clumsy, moving as if everything she wore were several sizes too large. And that hunch between her shoulders—had she been born like that, or was it an injury?

"Do you like kites, my boy?" she asked. "I don't suppose anyone's ever taught you to make one."

"Auralia," he had answered. "I saw some kites in her caves. You should see the ribbons she ties to the tails."

"I'd like that," said Obsidia. "I'd so like to go and meet her sometime. She sounds. . .she sounds like family."

"Oh," said a whisper.

The dream shattered, and the ale boy woke, his teeth chattering.

The suspended man was staring at him. With eyes. Eyes that had emerged from the dark depths of vacant cavities. Small, human eyes.

"Ohh," the creature sighed.

He sees.

So cold he couldn't move without shaking, the boy reached for the bundle caught in Jaralaine's embrace. "I'm sorry," he whispered. "But I'm going to need to borrow this."

Intending only to draw it around him for warmth, he shook it out, and it unfurled. As the cave filled with light and color, a slight red ribbon was cast into the air. The ale boy caught the string and unthinkingly threaded it through the loops to bind it at his throat.

He felt a spark. The cloak brightened. The darkness vanished, vanquished by the full spectrum of Auralia's colors.

In this way Tammos Raak beheld again the glory of all he'd abandoned.

The light of all colors flooded his cell—whiter than white, infused with every hue the Expanse had ever known and worlds more than those.

The light burned deep into the great ancestor's gaze. Colors penetrated his mind and body like rivers saturating a desert. They resonated like the meeting of strings and a bow. They sang in a language that his heart—frail and buried deep within the many-chambered engine that had encompassed and overpowered it—had forgotten.

Received, these colors were not discovered but recognized. Memories broke the dam that he had set up against them, and they quenched his fearful, wasteful desire to be separate and solitary, to be disconnected from the whole. For he knew that these colors had been sent by his sister as a declaration of love, love in spite of all his offenses.

He saw the whole Expanse from a high place, through a lens of crystalline cloud. The stark white and black of winter; the rough, seething green of spring; the ripeness of summer; and autumn's smoldering fire. This was the view he had once known from the home he had abandoned.

Like a stone cast to shatter a vast and frozen sea within him, the light shocked his broken heart to beating once again.

He was caught by surprise. Before he could open up the deep reservoir of lies he had gathered to shield himself, he felt a powerful emotion welling up from deep inside.

Gratitude.

I abandoned my family. I rejected the gift of who and how I was invited to be. I left my sister and my source behind. And yet here is an invitation. I can be sewn again into their dance, join their music. I can live.

This burst of life drove the water from the flask that Tammos Raak had swallowed coursing through his body, out into his limbs.

The root of the disease, which fed upon the stony deadness in Tammos Raak's heart, had nothing left to eat, for his heart was alive again. The shock of that deprival shot out through the roots of Deathweed, out through the limbs, the fingers, the filaments that lurked in the ground of the Expanse, that wormed their way into the trees of the forests, that distorted the nature of all things green and growing.

The trees of the world shuddered in a distress felt by the crawling branches they had cast off to fulfill the Curse's appetite.

The poisonous pump providing Essence to those who craved its deforming influence slowed to a stop. The Curse of the Cent Regus was broken, and all that had gone out from him began to wither and crumble, unable to poison anything further. It became nothing at all.

Stunned, the Deathweed shivered. For it had always been eating, never satisfied, ever pursuing an ongoing emptiness. But now it had been tricked into absorbing something that satisfied, and all its needs dried up. It tasted relief. Its wretched web of distortion was cleansed, becoming a net of white threads spreading throughout the fabric of the Expanse—bones around which new forms of life would grow.

This quake cast a cloud of dust into the skies all across the Expanse.

The Seers' grand designs had failed. They could craft nothing themselves but more opportunities for their rival to redeem and reconcile, increasing mystery's mastery and sharpening their shame.

All that remained now was a surrender to joy.

Tammos Raak saw the five blue suspended ghosts flaring with rage at their humiliation.

Relief spread out from his tiny heart, warming him to the furthest reaches of his distorted form. He drove the last wisp of his strength into a word of gratitude, hoarse and hollow, spoken into that chamber filled with colors.

His heart, unprepared to sustain a life, beat a few times more, and then collapsed. His sight faded slowly, its last vision a wild dance of colors, as he waited for the Northchildren to come and unstitch him from this exhausted body and carry him home.

Hearing the last word of Tammos Raak, the ale boy sensed the relief in it.

He tried to move, each breath a shock like the blow of an ax. He reached again for Jaralaine's outstretched hand, and as he did, he saw the wicked grasp of the Deathweed surrender her body and shrivel.

Jaralaine tumbled to the floor beside him. He got to his knees and tried to lift her, but a searing pain ran jagged through his chest.

So he crawled. He crawled, dragging Jaralaine with him, his way lit by the colors he wore, as if he were pouring a river of fire down the stairs. Then the last spark of strength went out of him, and he fell down the stairs toward the river.

He saw a vast creature descend from the ceiling, spreading its wings. He felt the wind from their unfolding, and then he felt a soft embrace.

"Please," he whispered. "Take us to Auralia."

31

The Falls

T*his is where I stood in the dream.*

Cal-raven did not understand it. He had stepped through a door on the south side of the mountain range, walked a strange, resonating path, a pulse like the earth's own heartbeat thrumming around him. And when he stepped out onto a stony ledge, he was on the other side.

There, he had staggered down a rugged slope until the strength went out of him. Faint with loss of blood, he lay on the ledge and looked down at his sword, saw his reflection in the blade. His straight red hair. His long brown cloak. His scarred face and ragged patches of beard.

They'll say that I failed.

Colliding oceans of clouds engulfed the country that spilled down from the base of these mountains, the echelons of soaring birds before him, and the heavens above. It rolled like waves of foam about his feet. When the seams parted, he glimpsed still more clouds rising in pillars, curling outward.

They came from the light upon the snowy peaks around and behind him. They billowed from a lake that spread as far to the east and west as he could see. And they came from something—some tremendous, silent presence suspended in the air.

In the center of his view, a silver curtain spread, wide as House Abascar's walls. It spilled from the sky's realm of cloud like linen from a loom, crashing into the great, shining lake before him. Water sprayed up as mist, rushed at the shore in surges, foamed up in a wall of froth upon a radiant beach of bright gemstones.

"No one in Abascar, Bel Amica, Jenta, Cent Regus...or even House Auralia should be the guardian or gatekeeper for this."

Shadows slipped through the clouds above him, the angular outlines of creatures in graceful flight.

Scharr ben Fray would have kept this world to himself. He would have told me only what he thought would keep House Auralia in order.

"No."

Cal-raven struggled to his feet, and the wind enveloped him, whipping his brown cloak back over his shoulders. He took the ring of keys in his left hand and cast them from the ledge. They fell so far into the crevasses below that he never heard them strike a stone.

But he did hear, as in his dream, footsteps in pursuit. He gripped his sword hilt firmly and turned.

Old Soro, his kites trailing behind him, was skidding down the rocky incline above him, dragging the sails down with mighty tugs and murmuring to himself as though this were a very busy day.

"You! How did you... Why are you here?"

The old man pointed to the sword. "Do you intend to use that?"

Cal-raven quietly sheathed it.

"Will you let me carry you?"

Cal-raven turned his back and spread his white-sleeved arms as if to embrace the clouds.

Soro cast something into the bushes, and he heard a sound like sails catching the wind. Half turning, Cal-raven saw Soro's cape discarded, and the old man seized and lifted him.

The hunch beneath Soro's cape had unfolded, spreading into wings.

Soro soared into the clouds, his wings guiding them with greater grace than any kite.

"What are you?" Cal-raven shouted. "And why do you use kites if you have. . .if you have these?"

"Do you think wings can last in a world full of arrows?" he answered. "You think they'd let me do my work?"

They moved through clouds, where landscapes, forests, fields, and cities suggested themselves and then vanished as if drawn in the sky with chalk and erased.

Cal-raven blinked as water beaded on his eyelashes. They tilted into a sweeping dive, the world below greening into a field of softly rippling grasses. Not far away, gemstones glittered on the pebbled shoreline.

As they drifted to a stop and Soro released him, Cal-raven realized that he felt stronger, and the pain from his wound was muffled. *Perhaps I can go back. If only I can find her.*

Then he caught sight of two figures standing on the grass ahead of him, looking down toward the shore. A giant and a girl. The girl held a glass trumpet.

Jordam. And. . .Auralia.

Down at the water's edge lay a body. As he stared, a bundle of tumbling fog moved away, revealing the very creature that had caught him up in its claws on Barnashum's threshold. Unfolding layer upon layer of wings, the Keeper cupped its tremendous claws, grasping a mysterious blue cloud that trailed long and jagged strings.

"What's it carrying?"

Old Soro did not answer, but the wind snatched tears from his eyes. Then he spread his wings again, and lifting swiftly, he wheeled away into the clouds. As Soro vanished, the creature rose up on its hind legs, presenting its treasure of translucent blue and barking a sonorous sound like a salute to him.

Using his sword as a crutch, Cal-raven forced himself along through the grass, groaning at the ache in his chest and the burning down his left arm.

He called out Auralia's name, and she turned. She seized Jordam's hand tightly, as if she were afraid. Jordam said something to her, putting his other hand against his heart. Then he let her go.

She walked toward Cal-raven. And then she ran.

He stumbled, fell to his knees in a patch of tiny blue flowers that bloomed at the ends of coiling green stems. He took her hands, which were wet, and he knew that she had been wiping away tears.

He recognized the silverbrown hair, the inquisitive eyes, her small bare feet.

"You have to go back," she said. "This is the place where the Keepers bear us away."

"Auralia. You have to come back with me. Please. I've searched for you since I saw you in Abascar's dungeon. I searched for you even before that. Forgive me. You were right in front of me, and I didn't see you."

"You only thought you were searching for me," she said, and she pulled her hands away. "But I'm not what you need. You're following the colors I revealed to you."

The creature behind her bent its knees and then lifted skyward, pebbles falling from its feet. Auralia looked over her shoulder, and Cal-raven's gaze followed hers, up the span of the waterfall's curtain into the cloud world.

"Someone's going home," she said.

Canopies of soft light pulsed in the heavens—like lakes of shimmering glass beneath a veiled, suspended continent.

A flying mountain.

"Do you see it?" Auralia whispered.

The magnificent Imityri, wings outspread, were drifting in a slow circuit along the ragged edges of that sky-bound country. From the fringe of the hovering mountain, this waterfall poured, and others like it, silver threads of melt from the mountain's snowy gown—waters infused with all the colors of the world, purged of all corruption by invisible engines of wind.

"I see it," he said. "I've seen it before. Through a glass, from far away. It scarred me. And then again, in a painting. A painting I thought was unfinished. But I was wrong."

"And now you know," she said, "that there is no curse beyond the wall, save those we've made for ourselves. Take that to your people. Here, curses lose their power in the mystery, and all is reconciled."

Cal-raven looked past her to the pebbled shore, to the body lying before the creature's footprints. "Is that...was that Ryllion?"

"I'm not sure," said Auralia. "I thought so. But when they unstitched him, he seemed to be someone else." She clutched at her side as if the memory pained her.

Jordam knelt, touching the edge of the creature's footprint as it slowly pooled with shore water.

"Is Jordam... Will the Keeper come for him too?"

Auralia did not reply.

Jordam stared into the sky toward the mountain, and clouds roiled around him as if undecided. Out of the white heavens, one of the Imityri descended on its great array of wings, and lightning flared from its wing tips. From the fog rolling in from the water, a crowd of shining figures closed in around the beastman, who struggled to rise.

"No," she whispered. "Please. Jordam's story has only begun. It's not time."

"O-raya?" Jordam roared, eyes widening in surprise. Lurching forward, he fell, and his arms pounded the pebbles as if he were caught by an invisible tide. Then he shouted out a question, but over the falls' roar, his words were lost.

"We must help him."

"No, Cal-raven. The Northchildren are kind, and the Keepers can be trusted here."

"The Keepers."

"It's a good name. There are others. Out there, when they've been tending to mystery's design in the dark, they sometimes get tired and confused. Poisoned. Trapped. Impatient with each other. Keeps them from their work. But they remember more than we do. And the closer they come to the mountain, the clearer it all becomes."

"Their work?"

"Revelation."

Jordam was still, sprawled upon the shore, and the Northchildren moved in closer, reaching out. Their hands moved over his body busily, as if testing every seam and thread.

"What's happening?"

"Beyond the Wall's protection, Northchildren wear gowns to shield them from the Seers' corruption. Their deaths are behind them, the poisons drawn out." She sighed. "If mystery commands, they'll unstitch Jordam and bear him away." She shuddered and clutched again at her side. "As they did for me once. Someday you'll know. Sometimes the sky calls."

"If mystery commands."

"Yes."

This Keeper, settling in the waterfall's crash, spoke in a voice like an orchestra of horns, and the report echoed from the mountainsides. Then it lowered its great head to the shore, resting the bristles of its long gator smile against the pebbles, shells, and whiteshards that appeared to be bones. Its ears twitched and lay back as it slipped armored fingers beneath Jordam's form and lifted him up.

"They didn't unstitch him," Auralia gasped.

The Keeper raised its head, raised its forelegs, spread its tremendous wings, and was carried quietly from the ground as if by invisible strings. It hovered a moment, turning slowly as if to take in the view for sheer pleasure. When it saw Auralia, a burst of fire escaped its nostrils and then—there was no mistaking it—it purred a long and rolling song of delight. Driving back its wings, it shot up through the air, sleek and swift, carrying Jordam away, back over the Forbidding Wall.

"What curse?" Cal-raven found himself saying. The lake shone like fire, and exotic birds drifted on its surface like a fleet of ships. Enormous fish leapt from its depths in perfect arcs like dancers. And the lights blazing at the base of the mountain were fierce, burning mist from the lake.

"The lake does not flood its banks, but look at all the waterfalls."

"It drains into many rivers. Underground. To go out across the world." Auralia's breathing came short and quick as if she were forcing herself to bear some secret wound.

"No one who stands here goes back alive, do they?" Cal-raven whispered as Auralia gripped his arm.

"Some do," she said. "But they're changed. And likely to be tolerated as fools."

Cal-raven looked at Ryllion's shell.

"Don't be afraid. It's only the outermost, which grows from the thread of mystery within. That thread is ever more important than just the mind or heart, which are so easily poisoned. But the heart, the mind, the senses—any beauty they feel and remember is given to that innermost thread, which the Northchildren withdraw and the Keepers bear away for restoration."

"How do you know all of this?"

"I'm remembering. Here. In the mist."

"Auralia." He was dizzy, his strength bleeding out. "You're not leaving me. Not a second time."

She looked up. "The first time I went out, I refused the Northchildren's gown of protection. I wanted to do more than witness. I wanted to search for my brother, to remind him how to play. So I set aside my memories and put on the shell of a child. Children can play without the older folks thinking them mad. To play there, with deep memories of the mountain's colors, I thought I might recover some of those colors from the Seers' corruption and tease them to light in the dark. Maybe my brother would notice. And what better place to reveal the colors than a house that has lost them?" Auralia tried to laugh, but it became a choke. As Cal-raven kept her from falling, she whispered, "But when you cross over, you give up your memories. And I guess I never found him. Maybe the colors will."

"So why did you come back again?"

She smiled. "It was nothing quite so selfless, I'm afraid."

He held her, felt her warmth against him. "You were born this time for me. And we've found each other. We have everything we need, Auralia. To build your house."

"It's not for us to decide."

He looked back. Billowing clouds flung themselves against the harsh stone of the northern mountainsides. "Will it play out like this forever?"

"The old song says that when the story is told, all broken threads will be reconciled. The runaways will see what they have wrought—that a hand cannot be a body, and if it tries, it dies. They will remember the joys of good work, of making things with mystery. The Northchildren will go out through time, out through the worlds. We sit in circles and tell stories of all we behold. And so we exalt the mystery. For this was ever the end of all work—to witness, remember, and illuminate." Salt glistened on her cheeks.

A sudden clamor of birds drew their attention to a small, struggling form far away on the shore.

Cal-raven staggered toward the edge of the blazing lake's frothy tide. Auralia stayed behind, and with fear in her voice, she shouted, "Oh please! Oh no!"

A boy, his clothes in rags, flesh burnt to crimson and cracked in intricate lines, was trying to crawl away from the lake and back toward the mountains.

Cal-raven shouted in dismay. He raised his sword and, in a blaze of searing stonemastery, drove its blade deep into one of the boulders on the shore. The sword stood, hilt gleaming in the mountain's light, anchored in the stone and irremovable.

But Auralia ran past him and got to the ale boy first. Setting down the trumpet, she caught him up in an embrace, seeking to calm him, urging him to stop his striving.

But the boy, his eyes wide and unseeing, fought her. "Let me go," he said in a voice as forceful as a fallen soldier's. "Get away, Northchild. There's more to do. It's not right yet. I can make it better. It's what I'm for."

"Shhh," she said quietly. "I am not a Northchild. Not yet. Dear boy, the more you strive, the more broken threads you'll find. It is beyond our capacity to reconcile them all."

Clouds cast cool blankets over them that dissolved in swirls of vapor.

"But I know how to reach them. I must find Auralia, and together we can—"

"Ale boy," she said gently. "You've done enough. You brought the slaves out of captivity. You led them to Inius Throan. They will live on as artists and prophets."

"But she's out there, and I have to be with her."

"Ale boy," she whispered, her tears splashing against his face. "She is here."

"She is out there," he insisted. "I told them I wouldn't leave until I found her."

She put her hands on the sides of his face.

"Pin," she said.

He went still.

She kissed his cheeks, then cradled his head in her hands.

He relaxed. "Auralia," he sighed, exhausted.

She took the glass trumpet and folded his hands around it. "Do you feel this? It's perfect. It will make a perfect sound."

His fingers traced its lines. He lifted it, arms trembling, and aimed it at the sky, setting his lips against the mouthpiece, which was bright as a glowing coal.

"Go on. For all who are listening."

With a deep and shuddering breath, the ale boy released a high, piercing arrow of sound that flared from the trumpet's bright bell.

The sound—a cry of desire—brought Cal-raven to his knees beside them. As he put his hand to the boy's forehead, he saw a line of dark blood run down from Auralia's sleeve and fill her open hand. "You're hurt!" He reached for her robe and drew it off over her shoulders, leaving her draped in a fragile, silk nightgown. Through it he could see the wound—three deep gashes in her side.

"There was a viscorclaw by the river before we went through the gate," she whispered.

He shouted up at the clouds, but she seized his wrist. "Don't be afraid," she said. At her touch he began to tremble, for she was more beautiful than ever, her tenderness toward the child all the more affecting for the ugliness of the wound she'd suffered.

The trumpet blast still sang in the air, and the ale boy seemed to be listening to see just how long the clouds would sustain it.

Then came an answering note from the mountain above. The great darkness, framed by the green fringe of the hanging gardens, began to glow with the heat of a furnace. Sweeping arches of color were flung in all directions through the clouds, which were drifting down now in ever greater density.

"Listen." Auralia's gaze met Cal-raven's. "The Witnesses are singing. One of the Seers has given himself up. The Keeper has carried him home."

In that moment the clouds rolled and curled around them like waves, soft as feathers.

Together they watched a shadow appear, descending on a vast array of wings.

"It's time," said Auralia. "Look. One of the mystery's greatest dancers."

The ale boy closed his eyes, his hands still clasping the king's trumpet as if he were gathering the strength to sound another summons.

"So I wasn't fooling myself, following the Keeper's tracks."

Auralia touched Cal-raven's chest. "You've been faithful." She slid her fingers up into his hair, then leaned up into his kiss.

Cal-raven looked up again. "For one of us, this is farewell, then."

He saw with a measure of relief that it was familiar, bearing the shape he had sculpted a hundred times. And yet, there was something oddly indefinite about it as it passed between the shining light and the clouds, for it cast shadows in many directions, each one different, each one strange.

As the singing witnesses surrounded them with a song of sorrow and joy, the chorus full of voices that sounded strangely familiar, something changed.

The magnificent shadow above him divided.

Auralia and Cal-raven breathed dissonant gasps. For there was not one Keeper descending, but two.

Once again Cal-raven found that what he had perceived and said was not precisely true, and what unfolded was rather a wondrous surprise.

Epilogue

Many days later Kar-balter and Em-emyt took a shift guarding the black gate beneath House Auralia's kitchens.

Em-emyt disliked Tabor Jan's orders forbidding anyone to go through in search of King Cal-raven, Jordam, Ryllion, and Milora. Discussion of the matter had inspired myriad rumors and theories throughout House Auralia, and its ruler had promised to organize a second search effort, as the first had been a failure.

But Kar-balter was terrified of the black gate, so Em-emyt tried to allay his fears by changing the subject and reviewing all the recent good news, especially the absence of any viscorclaw sightings. As he did, Kar-balter opened the small jars of nuts and berries they'd brought along and were surprised by a pungent wave of slumberseed oil.

"This is unexpected," Em-emyt had time to announce before they were both asleep.

A shaft opened in the stone ceiling. A rope fell through. Knotted at intervals, it gave Luci and Margi, followed by Emeriene, Krawg, and Warney, an easy climb down.

"A few hours," said Emeriene holding her sleeve to her nose. "Thank you, girls. Now, seal up the ceiling, and come back for us when you hear the Late Afternoon Verse."

And that was how Emeriene and the two Gatherers managed to sneak through the gate in search of their friends.

They were astonished at the strange magic at work, that they could step through a door on one side of a mountain range and emerge on the other. Even more astonishing was the thick country of fog.

It was a quiet, still day, and the clouds appeared suspended, unmoving. The landscape ahead seemed only the first cautious outlines of a drawing, save for that clear and shining span of water.

They descended for a while, and then Emeriene, brushing tears from her cheeks, admitted that she could go no farther. She sat under a tree.

Krawg and Warney stared at the tree—a tall conifer, its branches spread and raised as if in praise. A bird with a tail of red ribbons stared down at them in amazement.

"Is that a kite stuck in the branches?" asked Warney.

"Certainly is," muttered Krawg.

"Who does it belong to, do you suppose?"

"What a mystery," said Emeriene.

"Puzzle, puzzle," said Warney, and that made Emeriene laugh through her tears, which pleased him more than he dared admit.

"What will you do while we're searching?" asked Krawg.

"I'll look through the farglass."

"For Cal-raven?"

"For understanding."

Far to the south at Tilianpurth, the aging guard Wilus Caroon awoke suddenly as a massive shadow passed over and eclipsed his sunshine.

He was sitting in his wagonchair on the wall, watching the woods around him—a vast graveyard of fallen trees, where new green shoots were sprouting up with surprising speed and fecundity.

"Wasn't so long ago this place was goin' to pieces," Caroon muttered. "I'll never understand it, but I'm glad it's over."

In the yard below, a new helper—a quiet old fellow who had walked out of the trees and volunteered for service—was lighting torches with sparksticks he kept in the tangles of his beard. Caroon was still uncertain about the stranger, but he worked hard and never complained.

"Say," Caroon shouted down. "What was that shadow just flew over? A big black thing, came straight toward me, and I shooed it away. Didn't get a good look at it."

The volunteer squinted up into the sky and shrugged.

Caroon snorted. "Probably just a bird. But there've been so many rumors of a sky-man that I'm startin' to see things that aren't there." He scowled and notched an arrow to his bow anyway, just in case.

The volunteer marched up the stairs, and reaching into his vest, he offered Caroon a dry bun of bread.

"What's this?" Caroon took the bread and sniffed it.

The man didn't answer. He drew a flask from his vest, poured red wine into a cup, and handed that over.

"I should report you, you know," said Caroon. But he drank the wine anyway. "Aw, never mind. I 'spose I rather pity you. Havin' to live with that and all." He gestured to the hunch between the old man's shoulders. "Must be a burden, carrying that around all the time."

Caroon watched him trudge down to join the Bel Amicans who were working steadily to replant the Tilianpurth gardens and bring the place back to busy life. Then he looked up at the tower.

Old Bauris was back in his chamber, looking out the window and smiling up at the clouds.

Today, Partayn would arrive with a large company. Caroon grumbled to think that they were going to fill this place with beastmen. Wretched, feeble, sickly beastmen at that. "They call 'em patients," he said. "I call them a herd." Here, Cyndere and Myrton would attend to the creatures' malnourished bodies and try to teach them self-discipline.

Cyndere's scouts were combing the newborn woods for another point of access to some kind of stream. Caroon had no idea what that was about. What was wrong with the water from the well inside the bastion?

It all seemed to him a fool's endeavor, especially those patrols Cyndere had sent in search of Jordam. "She needs him to help her speak with the beastmen," Myrton had explained. "And to help them learn to trust her."

"Sounds like askin' for trouble," Caroon had replied. "But if a beastman goes free here, I'm not sleepin' without this weapon at my side."

A cry rang out from the tower window. He pushed his wagonchair to the ramp and let himself rush down the incline to the ground. Truth be told, Caroon loved any excuse to plunge down that ramp.

Inside Tilianpurth, he took the lift up to Cyndere's chamber. Myrton stood by the open door.

"Puzzle, puzzle," the chemist whispered. "Cyndere walked in to find Jordam snoring like a happy hog in a mud bath. It's like something flew him in through the window."

They peered through the narrow span. Caroon scowled. What he saw did not look much like a beastman. A giant, yes—muscled and scarred. But not a monster. Cyndere, the beastchild anxiously clinging to her hand, knelt beside the murmuring sleeper, leaned down, and kissed him on the brow.

His eyes opened.

At last Krawg led Warney to the frothy edge of the lake in the cloud world beyond the Forbidding Wall.

"Do ya think they'll string us up in the hangers if they find out we came down here?" asked Warney.

"Yup," said Krawg. "So don't dally. Let's look for clues and be on our way."

"It's a good thing Tabor Jan's away," said Warney. "Otherwise, I'd be twice as worried."

"I suspect his journey will be longer than he told us," said Krawg. "He may be takin' all them goats and birds to Bel Amica for a gift, but you and I both know what's on his mind. Remember those last days in Bel Amica? Lots of hushed meetings with Partayn's sister. If you know what I mean."

"I caught sight of 'em one bright morning," said Warney. "Just a few days before you left Bel Amica. They were walking slowly along a stretch of wall, lookin' out to sea. I couldn't hear a word they said, but they looked mighty uncomfortable. In a good way."

"Time wasn't right."

"No. Not yet."

They moved on in silence.

"Is the time right now?" Warney cautiously asked.

Krawg shrugged. "House Auralia don't seem to need defending, for now. No sign of Deathweed anywhere. Everything seems to be settlin'. And yet, nothin's quite what we thought it would be." He laughed, shaking his head. "Strange day, that day."

"Which?"

"Day of the ceremony. Remember? All gathered in the Sanctuary, distraught. No sign of Cal-raven for five whole days. No sign of anybody. Nobody's come back through the black gate. Then Scharr ben Fray steps up. We're all silent. Tabor Jan's standin' there, lookin' nervous and upset. We're all sure it's an announcement that the old mage is our new king."

"Oh, that day." Warney puffed out his cheeks. "Strange day."

Krawg stepped up onto a rock and spread his arms, then boomed his voice as if to a great assembly. "People of House Auralia, for many generations, the line of Cal-raven, Cal-marcus, and Har-baron has ruled you. Now we're a whole new house. But we've lost our leader. And due to history's cruelty, we've got no child to sustain the line. So it falls to those Cal-raven favored. And among those, it must be one blessed with the gifts of Tammos Raak."

"Lucky for him, then," muttered Warney.

"I did not seek this privilege for myself," said Krawg, continuing the charade. "But I would strive to learn from the trials of your past kings. And I would strive to recover the glory we saw in Auralia's colors. Will you accept me as your king?"

"And then," said Warney.

"And then," said Krawg. "A shout."

"Not a shout. A great commotion."

"A trumpet of alarm from the Sanctuary gates."

"And those gates," whispered Warney, "they opened."

"And House Auralia's guardians ushered in she who had knocked."

"And she came right down the stair," said Warney, "like a living flame. All draped in 'Ralia's colors."

"That very same cloak," said Krawg. "Not seen among the people in many a season. And her name came rippling across the crowd in waves. Jaralaine. Jaralaine. Jaralaine. Our queen."

"And she strode up the stair to stand before the cowering mage. And she said, 'I declare—'"

"Let me tell it!" Krawg growled. Then he raised his hands as if to bless the birds that flew around them in the mist, birds flying strong, sure arcs like kites on hard winds. "I proclaim today the beginning of House Auralia's spring! A time for music and stories, for painting and sculpture, for discovery and new questions. A time to give shape to our gratitude."

"The people didn't know whether to laugh or cry."

"Then Queen Jaralaine proclaimed that unless her son were to return through the Black Gate, Tabor Jan would sit at her right hand for his faithfulness to her son and that should he marry, the throne would pass to his firstborn."

"And then the people were cheering again."

"And then she went out, and all the assembly followed her in fear and amazement. And she stopped before the stonemasters' statue."

"The beautiful statue," said Warney.

"Auralia wearing Cal-raven's ring and the ale boy pointing to the mountains."

"Yes. And there Jaralaine asked our forgiveness. One by one."

They walked on in silence, making their way down to the shore.

"Nobody'll believe that story," said Krawg.

"Truth never seems very true, does it?" said Warney.

Krawg kicked rocks into the water.

"Where do you suppose they are now, the three of them?" asked Warney.

"I don't plan to go back until I know."

"Ballyworms, Krawg. Look!"

Through a rift in the fog, a stone the shape of an altar emerged. From it rose a vertical line, bold as a binding promise against the water's shining span.

"Is that what I think?"

"The king's sword."

Krawg stood before it, thrilling in the storm of dread and hope that the sight inspired, troubled by all that it did not answer. "Not sure what this means," he muttered. "Haven't found what we came for. But we found somethin'."

"Look at that." Warney opened his arms to the spectacle before them. The turbulent lake that spun as a great whirlpool, disappearing into the earth. The waterfall crashing down from the blazing clouds. The blasting spray that rose to merge with the continent of vapor.

"Wish I was a painter," Krawg sighed. "I'd paint...this."

And at that moment, they heard a clear and searing note ring out through the fog.

"Someone is there!" Warney cried.

A figure was approaching along the misty shore of that bright lake, playing on a gleaming glass trumpet a song as bright and as vivid as Auralia's thread.

"I don't know that song," said Warney. "It's strange."

"But I know that face," said Krawg.

And Warney had to agree with him there.

A Guide to the Characters

House Abascar (AB-uh-skar)

Adryen (AY-dree-en)—A cook.

ale boy—A former errand-runner; a friend of Auralia; gifted as a firewalker who can pass through flames without burning; now a survivor beloved for rescuing hundreds from House Abascar's collapse and from Cent Regus slavery. Some call him "Rescue."

Ark-restor (ark-RES-tor)—A former cook; later captured and enslaved to the beastmen.

Auralia (o-RAY-lee-uh)—A young, artistic girl discovered by Krawg in the wilderness when she was an infant. Her artistry was an extraordinary revelation of colors with miraculous effects. But her artistry stirred up trouble in House Abascar, which culminated in the fiery destruction of the house. Only the ale boy witnessed what happened to Auralia in the calamity.

Bowlder (BOL-der)—A defender, distinct in his size and strength.

Brevolo (BREV-o-lo)—A soldier; daughter of Galarand, sister of Bryndei.

Cal-raven (cal-RAY-ven)—A stonemaster; king of House Abascar; son of Cal-marcus.

Cortie (KOR-tee)—Orphaned when her parents, the merchants Joss and Juney, were slain by beastmen, she and her brother, Wynn, were led by the ale boy into the care of the remnant of House Abascar.

Em-emyt (em-EM-ut)—A soldier; eventually captured and enslaved to the beastmen.

Irimus Rain (EER-i-mus RANE)—A strategist and advisor to kings of House Abascar; eventually captured and enslaved to the beastmen.

Jaralaine (JARE-uh-lane)—Former queen of House Abascar; wife to King Cal-marcus, mother of Cal-raven. She ran away from Abascar and disappeared when Cal-raven was young. Later she was discovered in captivity to the beastmen.

Jes-hawk (JES-hawk)—The finest archer among Abascar's defenders; brother of Lynna.

Kar-balter (kar-BAL-tur)—A soldier; eventually captured and enslaved to the beastmen.

Krawg (KROG)—Once a thief known as "the Midnight Swindler"; arrested and cast out to be a Gatherer; now a harvester. Famous for discovering Auralia.

Lesyl (LES-el)—A musician.

Luci (LOO-see)—One of the triplets who have the gifts of stonemastery and thoughtspeaking.

Lynna (LIN-uh)—Jes-hawk's sister, who worked at the Mawrnash revelhouse after Abascar's collapse; betrayed the Abascar remnant to Ryllion after their exodus from Barnashum.

Madi (MAD-ee)—One of the triplets who have the gifts of stonemastery and thoughtspeaking; lost when she fell down a well while trying to hide from Ryllion. Her voice still speaks to Margi and Luci from beyond.

Margi (MAR-gee)—One of the triplets who have the gifts of stonemastery and thoughtspeaking.

Mulla Gee (MUL-uh GEE)—Once a Gatherer; eventually captured and enslaved to the beastmen.

Nat-ryan (nat-RIE-un)—The "pillarman" of House Abascar, who inspected the columns that supported its foundation.

Nella Bye (NEL-uh bie)—Once a Gatherer; lost her daughter in Abascar's collapse; eventually captured and enslaved to the beastmen.

Say-ressa (say-RESS-uh)—House Abascar's beloved healer.

Shanyn (SHAN-un)—A soldier and House Abascar's swiftest rider.

Tabor Jan (TAY-bor JAN)—King Cal-raven's closest friend and captain of the guard for the remnant of Abascar.

Warney (WOR-nee)—Formerly a thief known as the "One-Eyed Bandit"; then a Gatherer; now a harvester in the remnant of Abascar.

Wynn (WIN)—Orphaned when his parents, the merchants Joss and Juney, were slain by beastmen, he and his sister, Cortie, were led by the ale boy into the care of the remnant of House Abascar.

House Jenta (JEN-ta)

Ryp ben Fray (RIP ben FRAY)—The eldest mage of the Jentan Aerial (the faculty of scholar-mages who teach in the Jentan School); a stone-master; elder brother of Scharr ben Fray.

Tenderly (TEN-der-lee)—An acolyte of the Jentan School.

Zhan ry Wren (ZHAN ree REN)—The eldest female mage of House Jenta, living on Wildflower Isle with the rest of House Jenta's society that has been tricked into confinement there.

House Bel Amica (bel AM-i-kuh)

Alysa (uh-LIS-uh)—A laborer enslaved by the beastmen; wife of Wilkyn.

Aronakt (AIR-un-akt)—An agile laborer enslaved to the beastmen.

Batey (BAY-tee)—A metalworker enslaved to the beastmen; husband of Raechyl.

Bauris (BOR-is)—A former soldier, once a guard appointed to young Cyndere; survived being thrown into a well by Ryllion; he seems mad to some, but others suspect he may see the world more clearly than anyone.

Cesylle (SES-il)—Emeriene's husband; a court representative; apprentice to Pretor Xa; a traitor.

Cesyr (SES-er)—Older son of Emeriene and Cesylle; given to the Seers as an apprentice until Cesylle's treachery was exposed.

Channy (CHAN-ee)—Younger son of Emeriene and Cesylle; given to the Seers as an apprentice until Cesylle's treachery was exposed.

Cormyk (KOR-mik)—A fisherman enslaved by the beastmen.

Cyndere (SIN-der)—The daughter of Queen Thesera and King Helpryn; widow of Deuneroi; sister of Partayn.

Emeriene (EM-er-een)—Cyndere's closest friend since childhood and highest ranking of her attendants, the sisterlies; wife of Cesylle.

Helpryn (HEL-prin)—Former king of House Bel Amica; husband to Thesera; father of Cyndere and Partayn; died in a shipwreck while exploring the islands of the Mystery Sea.

Henryk (HEN-rik)—A soldier serving as a guard at the harbor caves; father of Deuneroi.

Myrton (MER-tun)—Father of Emeriene; a chemist and gardener.

Partayn (par-TAYN)—Cyndere's older brother; heir to the throne of Bel Amica; a gifted musician; thought to be slain on the road to House Jenta, he was found by Jordam in Cent Regus slavery and rescued.

Petch (PECH)—A youth, captured and enslaved to the beastmen; preoccupied with gaining authority.

Raechyl (RAY-chil)—An artist; enslaved to the beastmen; wife of Batey.

Ryllion (RIL-ee-un)—Disgraced captain of the Bel Amican guard; apprentice to Pretor Xa.

Thesera (TES-er-uh)—Queen of House Bel Amica; widow of King Helpryn; mother of Cyndere and Partayn.

Wilus Caroon (WIL-us ka-ROON)—A guard at the Bel Amican outpost of Tilianpurth.

House Cent Regus (KENT REJ-us)

Jordam (JOR-dum)—First beastman to overcome the Cent Regus Curse through the influence of Auralia's colors and the encouragement of Cyndere.

The Seers

Malefyk Xa (MAL-uh-fik kZAH)—A master hunter and trapper and guardian of the Cent Regus Curse.

Palaskyn Xa (Pul-ASK-in kZAH)—Formerly a governor in Bel Amica.

Panner Xa (PAN-er kZAH)—The former overseer of the Mawrnash mine.

Pretor Xa (PRE-ter kZAH)—Formerly a military advisor to Queen Thesera and a mentor for Ryllion.

Skaribek Xa (SKAR-i-bek kZAH)—The fearmongering Moon Prophet.

Tyriban Xa (TEER-i-ban kZAH)—A surgeon and an alteration artist.

Other characters, human and otherwise

Dukas (DOOK-us)—A viscorcat, once a faithful companion of Auralia in the forest; eventually discovered in the wild, wounded, and adopted by Deuneroi.

Frits (FRITS)—Overseer of the glass mines north of Fraughtenwood; grandfather of Obrey.

Jayda Weese (JAY-duh WEES)—Manager of Mad Sun's bar north of House Jenta; a former Jentan Defender.

Imityri (im-i-TEER-ee)—Mysterious creatures sought by the Seers; studied by the scholars of the Jentan Aerial.

Milora (mil-O-ruh)—A woman who lost her memory and was discovered by Frits near his glass mine; given the name Milora by Frits in memory of Obrey's mother.

Mousey (MOUS-ee)—An independent slave-seller (or slaver).

Obrey (OB-ree)—Frits's granddaughter; her mother, Milora, died when she was very young.

Old Soro (SOR-o)—A secretive, resourceful healer and kite-master.

Reveler (REV-u-lur)—A female Fearblind Dragon.

Scharr ben Fray (SHAR ben FRAY)—A renowned mage who abandoned the Aerial (the scholar-mages of House Jenta); a wandering stonemaster and a wildspeaker; formerly an advisor to Abascar's King Cal-marcus and a mentor to Cal-raven.

Tammos Raak (TAM-os RAK)—Legendary ancestor of the four houses' royal families. Stories say he led the peoples of the Expanse in a daring escape from an oppressor, bringing them over the Forbidding Wall mountains to settle in the Expanse. Accounts disagree regarding the manner and cause of his disappearance.

The Keeper—A massive, mysterious creature who appears in the dreams of all children—and some say the adults as well. Children perceive it to be a benevolent guardian, but most determine that it is only a figment of dreams, probably imagined out of a need for comfort. Some believe it is real and moving about in the wild with vast powers of perception and influence.

Acknowledgments

Pass around the goblets, ale boy. It's time to offer toasts of gratitude to many who contributed to this—the final strand of The Auralia Thread.

To Lee Hough at Alive Communications, who showed as much care for my head and heart as he did for all four books in this series. What a blessing! I couldn't have asked for a better agent.

To Shannon Marchese, the senior editor of fiction for the WaterBrook Multnomah Publishing Group. She showed patience and discernment throughout, and her faith in my vision for this series has given me courage.

To Carol Bartley, the copyeditor, and the proofreaders, who made sense of an otherworldly encyclopedia, intertwining story lines, and convoluted time lines.

To Steve Parolini (noveldoctor.com), whose attention to characters, pacing, and plot greatly enhanced this series. And I'm grateful for his nearly instantaneous replies in correspondence.

To Kristopher K. Orr, for the fourth enchanting book cover in the series. What a beautiful underground river he discovered! And to Rachel Beatty, for yet another remarkable map of the Expanse.

To my friends at Seattle Pacific University and at Greenlake Presbyterian Church, who listened to me grumble when things got tough and who prayed for me.

To all who encouraged me every day via LookingCloser.org, Facebook, Twitter, Tumblr, artsandfaith.com, and beyond.

To Gregory Wolfe and his team, who inspire me through *Image* (imagejournal.org), and to the Glen Workshop community, especially Sara Zarr, Tara and Bryan Owens, and Bob and Laurie Denst. To my kindred spirits in the Thomas Parker Society and the Chrysostom Society. To my friends at the International Arts Movement, especially Kevin Gosa, Alissa Wilkinson, and Christy Tennant. To Steven Purcell and Marcus Goodyear at Laity Lodge, John Wilson at *Books and Culture,* and Dick Staub at The Kindlings Muse. And to Robert Joustra, Andrew Peterson, R. J. Anderson, Kathy Tyers, Robert Treskillard, Rachel Starr Thomson, Jenni Simmons, S. D. Smith, Esther Maria Swarty, Aaron White, and so many who blessed this series with thoughtful reviews.

To Linda Wagner, John and Margaret Edgell, Peyton Burkhart, and Beth Harris, in whose company *Auralia's Colors* first took root. To Adrienne Kerrigan and Anastasia Solano, who cooked up delicious support during busy evenings. To Luci Shaw and John Hoyte, godmother and godfather of this series, for their hospitality, generosity, and companionship. To the baristas of The Grinder, Richmond Beach Coffee Company, and Jewel Box Café, who kept me caffeinated.

To Linford Detweiler and Karin Bergquist, whose music fills our lives with beauty and insight and whose counsel and friendship are blessings. Thanks also to Sam Phillips and Joe Henry, whose lyrics gave me big ideas.

To Dad and Mom, for giving me a typewriter and an endless supply of paper when I was a kid. And for their daily prayers.

To Don Pape and Marsha Marks. I still have a hard time believing that they sought me out, showed interest in *Auralia's Colors,* and opened doors of opportunity. I'll be thanking them for the rest of my life.

To Anne, who made so many sacrifices so I would have time to write. She worked beside me every evening and "weekend" over the last few years as a good listener, a great editor, an inspiring coach, and a resourceful cat wrangler. On so many nights when I collapsed from exhaustion, she soothed my weary mind by reading beautiful new poems and journal entries. She's an extravagant blessing.

Above all, let's raise our glasses to the Almighty Imagination. These stories are my awkward attempts to capture and reflect some of the glory I see in the creation around me and to show gratitude for so many blessings I do not deserve. Be thou my vision, O Lord of my heart.

Drink up, dreamers!

About the Author

Jeffrey Overstreet was raised in Portland, Oregon, and now he lives with his wife, Anne, a poet and editor, in Shoreline, Washington. They write in coffee shops all over the Seattle area. He is the author of *Auralia's Colors, Cyndere's Midnight, Raven's Ladder,* and a "travelogue of dangerous moviegoing" called *Through a Screen Darkly.*

An award-winning film critic, Jeffrey writes frequently about art and culture for various Web sites and periodicals—including *ImageJournal.org, Paste,* and *Books and Culture*—and he is a frequent guest speaker on cinema, fantasy, and storytelling at conferences and universities around the United States. He is also a contributing editor for Seattle Pacific University's *Response* magazine.

You can find Jeffrey at LookingCloser.org and on Facebook.